About the Author

Andy Poulsom majored in creative writing at University of Chichester and has a career spanning the arts, education, media and the charity sector. *To Have and To Hold* is his first published novel. Andy lives in Godalming, Surrey and is married to Jessi. They have two boys, Noah and Aaron.

Andy Poulsom

TO HAVE AND TO HOLD

Dear Georgie,

At last - a first edition (sadly complete with typos) so have spent the summer ironing these out. You will notice that Aaron is featured on the front cover; Noah was very good at accepting that he would have been too old to fit in with the age of the boy in the novel. I would love to know what you think of it - and wishing you every blessing in all your educational and artistic pursuits.

AUSTIN MACAULEY™
PUBLISHERS LTD.

A CIP catalogue record for this title is available from the British Library.

ISBN 9781786932525 (Paperback)
ISBN 9781786932532 (E-Book)
www.austinmacauley.com

First Published (2017)
Austin Macauley Publishers Ltd.
25 Canada Square
Canary Wharf
London
E14 5LQ

Part 1

1
January 2012
Mark 43, Lizzie 34, Isaac nearly 2

A knock at the door

Silence had slowly settled upon the usually noisy household like a dust sheet over antique furniture. At first the sheer absence of noise was deafening. He was supposed to be marking a stack of A-Level Literature mocks, the unseen text, but was distracted by his unseen family, as he always was from the moment they left. Curious, he pondered aloud, as he meandered in and out of every room in the house, lukewarm mug of tea in hand, how someone could crave silence and solitude and yet feels bereft of the very cause of such chaos the moment they were no longer there. Would he ever be truly satisfied? Not that one again as he pushed that thought back amongst the waves of other impulses that crashed against the inside of his forehead, each vying for their own personal tutorial. Instead he focused on being present in the moment, a lifelong challenge for someone used to spending so much of his time either dwelling on the past or attempting to predict how his future would pan out. Procrastination would be his specialist subject if he ever made it on to Mastermind.

Marriage and fatherhood, like many other semblances of the conventional, had caught up with and overtaken him, receiving surprising little resistance. A career bachelor with an acute aversion to the mundane existence the majority seemed resigned to accepting, and a man devoid of any aspiration to work in the conventional way for a living, he now found himself in possession of a wife, child, cat, salary, health plan, pet insurance and even a sensible family car. Recently he'd begun paying into a pension plan. What had become of that melancholic, moody teenager renowned for sulking at parties and parents' evenings, the pasty undergraduate wallowing in existentialism and associated angst, the 'playwright' who'd

6

spent years gazing out of various windows in a multitude of rented cottages and apartments up and down the south coast but still without a published play to his name? Or even a completed one for that matter. A healthy sense of self-depreciation was his saving grace, without which he would be, by his own admission, unbearable to live with.

Leaving the kitchen in a state of semi-tidiness (all used breakfast cups, plates and bowls stacked neatly in the dishwasher, butter and spreads in the fridge and cupboards respectively, stray porridge oats swept from work surface into cupped hand and then into bin) he lingered momentarily at the door to the lounge, leaning on the door frame and taking in the now familiar sight of a play/war-zone left in a state of disarray as the source of such disruption is plucked from his range of brightly coloured tractors and diggers to be replanted into a car seat whilst holding on to the ear of his favourite soft toy (a bunny) and whisked compliantly off to the next destination, in this case a 'play date' with a mum and daughter who were on the same ward as Lizzie when Isaac was born. Despite a new found orientation towards tidiness (one of the many positive influences Lizzie had brought into his world), he and Lizzie were in agreement that the lounge would be a kiddie friendly environment during the day, with all related paraphernalia being gathered up in a wooden trunk that was then stuffed into the already heaving under-stairs cupboard each evening. Besides, they had a perfectly good dining room to reserve as adults only, free from the Tommee Tippee mug spillages, rice cake mush and regurgitated milk stains that marked Isaac's first year and the scratches and marks to the skirting boards, coffee table and walls that reflected his increasingly inquisitive nature and mobility as he approached two.

Tutting audibly (where once he probably would have salivated) as yet another garish glossy flyer for cholesterol busting pizza deals with free fizzy drinks had been shoved roughly through the letter box he ascended the stripped pine stairs to the first floor landing, unable to resist a peek into Isaac's nursery. A stripy hoody that was borderline wash/wear once more had been draped over the wicker basket that contained duplicate soft toys to those that inhabited his cot (in case of loss or damage and to prevent potential trauma) along with a pair of denim dungarees, a Christmas gift. A cliché I know, he thought, but just how dinky are they? The changing mat was lying at a jaunty angle (as the little fella had taken to struggling every time a nappy change was required) hence the toy elephant and story book lying upside down beside it; a newly discovered distraction technique. His Winnie-the-Pooh sleeping bag was in a dishevelled pile in the middle of the cot, the faithful fluffy Tigger scrunched up alongside it, his second

7

favourite soft toy to bunny (or Buddy as he was known to Isaac) that had accompanied him on his play date, as it did everywhere he went.

All had been left as it had been; a snapshot in time. It had surprised him how he had taken to fatherhood so naturally, especially during the nappy and teething months. He had seen himself being semi-engaged, rising above the 'ga-ga-ga' phase and waiting patiently until his lad was old enough to kick a football before fully immersing himself, as he had done with his nephew Harry. The depth of love he'd felt for Isaac even as a shadow on a 12 week scan had overwhelmed him and had grown steadily ever since. At times he had to check just how tightly he would hold him to his chest, as he would close his eyes and rest his chin on that head of silky golden hair, breathing him in and praying under his breath that the God his wife subscribed to would protect this little miracle they had been blessed with whilst also vowing to do everything he'd ever need to do to nurture his beloved son. His mates from Uni, all experienced dads by now, had, he felt, breathed a collective sigh of relief when (a) he'd announced he had joined their ranks and (b) to hear he'd finally got it; grasped what they'd been banging on about for all those years, stuff that he'd just written off as sentimental cliché, the stuff of shaving product ads and US made for TV dramas.

Ignoring their bedroom and the room that would be Isaac's when he was old enough (and when 'number two' was occupying the nursery) he made his way up a narrower flight of stairs to the rather grand and somewhat pretentiously named third floor guest suite and study. Like many Victorian villas typical of this part of Brighton, the third floor lent itself perfectly to self-contained guest accommodation comprising double bedroom, shower en suite and a small living room that also served as his study. He had always loved his little 'dens' ever since he was a boy; whether bunk bed, wood shed or under one of the many huge shrubs that grew in the garden of that large house in a picturesque village of Dorset, far from the madding crowd indeed. The top floor offered the type of refuge he yearned for, away from the chatter and clatter of visiting mums with their little bundles of joy, from well-meaning neighbours who would far outlive the warm welcome that Lizzie offered to everyone, even at times from Lizzie and Isaac themselves when the long wet Saturday afternoons led to a sense of claustrophobia, dissipated by half an hour on his own on the top floor with the radio murmuring updates on all the days' matches adding to this sense of rejuvenation.

Settling into his favourite battered leather armchair he'd picked up in a vintage furniture shop in the North Laines he lifted the walnut lid to the retro-style turntable that Lizzie had bought him for his birthday a couple of years ago. She'd bought him this partly because he requested it but also in recognition of him trading in his beloved BMW Z3 two-seater sports car for a second-hand silver VW Touran in anticipation of Isaac's imminent arrival; a sacrifice he still harped on about. He shifted uncomfortably, and, reaching into his back pocket found the source of this irritation; a six-inch green and red cloth very hungry caterpillar soft toy (that had come free with one of the many versions of the book they'd received as gifts for Isaac when he was born) that he must have absent-mindedly stuffed into his pocket as he'd done his earlier rounds of the house. Getting comfortable again he began the ritual that ushered in a morning or afternoon of being home alone. Opening the stained and cracked 7-inch plastic record case he rifled through classics from when he was a youth, starting with The Associates' 'Party Fears Too' followed by 'Blind Vision' by Blancmange, 'Love Song' by Simple Minds and the Tears For Fears hit 'Mad World'. There was a 10 year age gap between him and Lizzie so they each had a different soundtrack to their teens. She had grown up in a small rural village nestled in the South Downs near Chichester so neither could lay claim to being sophisticated urbanites but her anthems were, to his taste, too self-aware and polished, lacking the naïvety and carefree abandon of the early '80s. As was usually the case when he retreated into a nostalgic world of long fringes, long summers, suede pixie boots and cheap cider, he was saturated by a sense of loss, not of the lifestyle, nor even the freedom it afforded him but by the hope that reigned as he and his mates sat up on the cliff tops, swigging from a shared bottle of scrumpy, pretending to smoke and lying about 'how far they'd got' with various girls at the previous night's school disco. Theirs was a shared hope of a life less ordinary, one that lay far beyond the limiting boundaries of Dorset. It wasn't even as if his life had necessarily been an anti-climax, it just hadn't played out as he'd expected it to. This was a difficult emotion to share with Lizzie, who was far more down to earth than he was and possessed neither the time nor inclination for wistful glances over her shoulder to measure reality with life expectation. They were a happily married couple with a beautiful little one and another on the way. They had no financial pressures, a close group of supportive friends and family, either near to hand or within a few hours' drive and a nice house with a sea-ish view (that thing on the horizon between the sky and the land, madam) so what was there to be disappointed about? It was just that back then, lolling on the cliff tops, gazing up at the stars with the whole of their lives stretching before them it really did feel that the sky was the limit.

His New Romantic recollections were disturbed by the sound of the doorbell ringing two storeys below. He ignored it. He always did. Lizzie wasn't due back for hours and he utterly refused to entertain any unannounced visitors so he settled back into his armchair and smiled at the thought of how, having plucked up the courage all night to ask Jenny Ford to dance, he was making his way shakily across the sticky school hall floor to do so only to find that Phil McGladdery had beaten him to it. Conscious of being seen to be a cool customer, even at that young age, he'd pretended that he was heading to the canteen to buy yet another bottle of Panda Pop as Phil and Jenny swayed self-consciously hand in hand to 'Love Action' by the Human League. Bastard! The doorbell rang again, this time with more sustained pressure being applied by whoever was on the front step. Sod it, he thought and made his way clumpily down the two flights of stairs (with the words 'And I find it kind of funny and I find it kind of sad, the dreams I have of dying are the best I ever had' on repeat in his mind). He pulled open the inner glass panelled door with such force that it caused the inset panes to rattle, then the solid green wooden front door to find WPCSO Marshall standing on the second of the three whitewashed steps, her colleague, Sergeant Evans leaning on the side of a Ford Focus patrol car parked outside with one eye on her and one on the cockpit of the car from which emanated the steady static-punctuated stream of murmuring comms. He knew them both as they regularly paid visits to the VI Form College where he taught to talk to the students about the risks of drugs and alcohol, often with Lizzie alongside them in her capacity as a local youth and community worker. "Hi Emma," he said casually, his stomach already beginning to tighten in knots but he quickly convinced himself her unscheduled visit was to do with one of his tutor group being found smoking weed under the pier (again), or to arrange another college visit with Lizzie as the new term had started, ''Is everything okay?'' Her face looked pale and mouth pinched. "Can we come in Mark?"

2
October 2007
Mark, 39, Lizzie 30

First impressions last

He absolutely loathed training courses so was dragging his heels physically and metaphorically as he left his black Z3 amongst the assorted Honda Jazz' and Toyota Yaris' and made his way across the car park towards the long grey depressing looking community centre where the seminar was due to start. They had a deal in the tutor's common room, that they would draw lots as to who would attend the numerous non-core subject seminars and refresher days that were mandatory when working with today's youth, or young adults; he'd pulled out 'STAY CLEAN: STAY SAFE' and was still a little unsure as to whether he was to be inducted in a sexual awareness campaign or in food hygiene. Judging from the brightly coloured welcome pack, complete with street cool graffiti-tag artwork and bulging with a variety of luminous coloured condoms it was to be the former. As usual, all ability to make small talk deserted him and he completed his registration form in silence under the vacant gaze of a crusty dreadlocked thirty something with a name badge that read: Daz. Judging by his crumpled and slightly stained County Council branded polo shirt this clearly wasn't alluding to his washing powder of choice so he handed back the clipboard with a chirpy "All done Darren." He went through the swing doors to find exactly what he had expected. A long brown plastic-coated trestle table upon which was spread an array of literature, some fanned out, others in stacks, along with a box of free biros. Alongside this trestle table was another with the obligatory flask-like hot water dispenser, jars of fair-trade coffee and ordinary tea, sachets of sweeteners, semi-skimmed milk and, oh so Brighton, a selection of fruit and herbal teas to avail oneself of also. Rows of bright orange plastic chairs had been set out with military precision, facing a low stage upon which a small gaggle of facilitators were struggling to get their PowerPoint presentation to project onto a rickety looking screen. The hall was over half full/empty depending on how you viewed life and, judging by the fact that Dazza had wandered in, stack of registration forms in hand, the start was imminent.

He made a strong black coffee and, with an audible sigh, eased himself into a seat on the end of a row halfway down the hall, ideal for nipping out for a quick loo break, or just for nipping out and not coming back at all he thought. He was sure he'd be able to wing it with colleagues if it all became too much to bear. Sitting in the row in front of him were three women, all late twenties-early thirties, who had the whiff of the social worker about them. They were chatting animatedly, with the two on the outside having to lean across the one in the middle to make sure they all kept up and chipped in. He re-tuned his frequency to find them talking about different voluntary sector groups who were proposing forming hubs to deliver different community based programmes. The woman on the left who had bleached blonde cropped hair and hideous wooden giraffe earrings that even Pat Butcher would have turned her nose up stated, "I think we should be really wary of joining any of these consortiums." Before he had realised he was speaking aloud he'd replied, "I think you'll actually find its consort*ia* plural and consort*ium* singular, rather like stadium and stadia." The middle one, who it turned out, was breathtakingly, achingly, beautiful, swivelled round in her chair to fix him with her gorgeous deep brown eyes. Her gaze was followed by her two colleagues, with the more feisty looking one feigning a sweet smile and saying, "and what about penis then smartarse, would it be penii?" before returning to her colleagues who both looked taken aback by this acid response and then struggled to suppress their laughter. Although slightly stung at first, Mark could see the funny side and was preparing an equally witty riposte when the on-stage microphone suddenly screeched piercingly into life and an insipid looking middle-aged man with an unkempt beard dressed in a faded checked shirt and green woollen tie under a brown V-necked jumper and ill-fitting beige corduroy suit jacket began hesitantly to outline the schedule and format for the day. With a burst of enthusiasm he then introduced the keynote speaker, to widespread applause (no idea, thought Mark whilst clapping along and nodding his appreciation, hoping to catch the eye of the brunette who sat ahead and just to his right, to no avail, as she was focused on the stage). The prospect of next week's visit to the dentist for a six monthly check- up didn't seem so bad after all he thought, as he yawned, sat back, clicked on his free biro and prepared to graffiti the graffiti on the cover of his welcome pack.

Needless to say, he didn't last the course, as it were. As the first session concluded it became clear that he was not going to be let into the coven in front, who were talking animatedly about whatever nuggets had been dispersed from the stage, so he left abruptly, heading straight out of the main entrance and to the safety of his very own mini Batmobile, all grill and muscle amongst rows of bland hatchbacks. He was reminded of the scene in Alan Partridge when he'd attempted to convince his eastern European girlfriend that they were going to meet Bono at his mansion when they'd really turned up at a National Trust property. His girlfriend had asked him if all the cars in the car park belonged to Bono to which he'd replied, "Err, yes, Bono is known for having the largest collection of *hatch*backs in Europe." He'd bumped into Steve Coogan once or twice in restaurants and bars in Brighton, relieved that he'd never been drunk enough to yell 'AH-HA' as the poor bloke had probably had a gutful of that. Why poor bloke, he countered himself, as he was prone to doing, he (Coogan) had seemed to be acutely aware of his stature, he was rich and famous and holding court loudly whilst looking over the heads of those who were in his company, as if seeking a wider audience; Mark thought him to be a bit insecure. He might have been wrong though as, on both occasions he (Mark) had been terribly, terribly drunk. His all-time favourite celebrity encounter was out at Gatwick one half term a few years back when he was sitting in a coffee bar waiting for his flight to Barcelona to show on the departure board when Simon Day of The Fast Show fame went to sit in an empty seat at a booth next to where he was perched on a stool. "Someone's sitting there mate," he'd said, pointing at the empty booth without looking up from his Guardian. To be fair to the comic he'd responded with a wry smile to have his own catchphrase hurled at him and moved on to another seat, demonstrating a sense of goodwill by entering into the joke or it could have been simply a case of 'get me away from that prat before I deck 'im'.

Everything began to feel better as he settled into the tan leather seats and clicked on the Chemical Brothers' 'We are the Night' that was usually reserved for when he was driving somewhere outside a 30 mph limit. The mid-morning air still retained its sharpness but the early mist had given way to hazy sun so he decided to un-clip the hood and fold it neatly into place. He had justified the lack of electric hood to his colleagues in that it was prone only to human and not mechanical error and was nothing to do with a lack of finances or class. Donning his aviator sunglasses he fired up the 1.9 litre engine and steered the car serenely around and out of the car park, heading for home, via the South Downs where he would really open her up. He justified this quick adrenaline blast as he only taught in the mornings on Fridays so it hardly constituted skiving off. He loved the low growl of the German machine, the relentless surge of sound pounding out of the speakers and the looks he'd get from envious drivers trapped within their dull steel shells as he powered through the autumn air, all turbo injection, synth and bass. It was some years later, when *he'd* been driving a conventional hardtop car and had been overtaken by someone in dark glasses with the hood down and music up on a moderately bright winter day when he'd realised that the looks he'd been getting previously had been neither admiring nor envious.

Over the top

Friday nights were always down the pub with Pete nights. Pete was a history teacher at the college where Mark also taught and was a few years older than him. They both shared a love of the war poets, Black Adder, sports cars, footie and Stella. That's the lager not McCartney. They had been collaborating for years on a script for a play set in France during the First World War in which they'd cleverly woven in the lives of poets such as Owen and Sassoon. Deep down they both knew that it would never come to anything but Pete was married with a toddler and Mark knew how important this night out was to him before a weekend of Sainsbury's and soft play so it was a set in the stone arrangement that neither reneged on lightly. They had a title for their play, 'Over the Top' and a few rough drafts outlining character and plot, serving as justification for a few pints followed by a bag of chips on the way to their respective homes, a couple of streets apart. As last orders were called, this being a traditional boozer, he was struggling to get past the hard core locals who stubbornly insisted on spending the night on their usual midweek red topped bar stools despite the influx of Friday night drinkers rendering any form of conversation in the vicinity of the bar area impossible, when he vaguely recognised the figure of a pretty woman standing beside him. She was trying in vain to get the attention of the Aussie barman who in turn was busy flirting with a girl he recognised from the sixth form who shouldn't have been in there in the first place. Finally, he got the barman's attention by waving a tenner at him, a tactic that could always go either way and, just before the woman on his left managed to have a go at him for queue jumping, he pointed at her, yelling over the din, "She's next mate." The woman ordered, turned to thank him, paused, and, leaning in, said simply "Penis." After a bemused frown he then smiled back and replied knowingly, "Penii." They both laughed. "Sorry about earlier," he offered, "It wasn't really my thing."

"You don't say! Well it was mine. But I feel I must apologise for my colleague Jan, she has had a few issues with men lately and is still feeling a little bruised." He was just about to ask her why when Bruce came back with a lascivious grin and handed her three bottles of beer, taking her money and ogling her whilst asking him "What can I do you for mate?" In the time it had taken him to yell "Two pints of Stella" and compose his next witty line to the stunning brunette, her place in the scrum had been taken by a well-built tattooed young lady with multiple piercings and combat trousers, who, at a first glance, would not have appreciated penis or penii in any way shape or form. Surging back to the table with glasses held over head height to avoid spillages but still managing to slosh lager down the sleeves of his designer combat jacket he was met by the predictable digs from Pete of "Get a move on Casanova, I'm dying of thirst here," and "I think that's the longest you've been in a relationship since I've known you Mark, when's the big day?" He laughed it all off whilst at the same time scouring the bar for the source of such ribbing. She was *gorgeous*, he thought, and what's more, they'd even shared a joke. Clearly there was more to this girl than just a social conscience, the question is, how do I find out?

Highly strung

The weekend passed the same way that so many had before. Saturday morning designated to 'pottering about', especially after a night of indigestion caused by too much beer and late night fast food. Despite seeing the mysterious brunette being chatted up by the barman at closing time (she hadn't seemed that interested he'd thought) he was in high spirits as he and Pete ambled back from the pub, and he celebrated this new 'love interest' by adding a doner kebab with chilli sauce to his usual order of chips, leaving a trail of salad from the Preston Park Grill all the way back to the steps leading up to his place in Waldegrave Road. He'd been left the grand and slightly gloomy house by his godmother, a widow, ten years before and still felt guilty that he'd done so little to drag it up to twenty-first century standards, apart from installing a microwave oven and satellite TV. His pottering usually constituted leafing through the stack of mail that had built up during the week whilst eating a bacon buttie with brown sauce and mustard washed down with two or three cups of tea, the radio murmuring quietly in the kitchen and Sky Sports on a tad louder in the lounge. He listened to his answer-phone messages and, regular as clockwork, there was one from his older brother Johnnie, made from his hands-free the night before as he powered his Range Rover down from their mews house in Barnes to their country place in West Sussex. His brother, two years his senior in age but a lifetime older when it came to his attitude to careers ladders, property ladders and all things that generally headed in an upward direction was 'big' in channel marketing and promotions and spoke almost exclusively in corporate jargon. Every sentence seemed to be concluded with either grand or 'K' to denote monetary value, 'or solution in terms of moving forwards', (which other direction would you want to move in)? Mark wondered if Johnnie referred to his wife Sophie as a 'life partner solution' or an 'heir solution partner' and wouldn't be surprised if he had created a graph on his laptop to support her in achieving her maximum life goals potential in terms of capacity output per K of capital investment in terms of moving forwards.

Despite him speaking like a complete tosser and seemingly losing himself in a status driven world of targets and bonuses, dinner parties and 'quick half term breaks' to stay with friends at their villa in Corfu, Mark was begrudgingly fond of him, remembering how he always used to look out for him at junior school in a hair ruffling 'this is my snotty kid brother but he's alright' kind of way. Not much had changed in 30 or so years on reflection. Not bothering to call back he shuffled back up the stairs to dig out his other tracksuit bottoms, the ones without egg stains on, and a non-offensive T-shirt that he reserved for his one concession to physical exertion each week. Since meeting Vaz whilst both were taking a PGCE at Surrey University they still met up every Saturday morning at half eleven for a knock up on the free hard tennis courts in the nearby Preston Park, followed by a quick pint and a sarnie, paid for by the loser. Vaz' family were originally from Sri Lanka but he was brought up in the West Midlands so he could combine really cool jet black hair in a ponytail, striking features and a sparkling nose piercing with a mild Brummy accent that Mark would always accentuate in a vain attempt at putting him off his serve. As the ball would be in the air and Vaz' racket poised to connect he'd chime "Orrright skip?" or before match point, that he'd invariably be attempting to save, "Why catch the Slough train chum, don't you want to get there quickly?" It never worked. Mark checked his wallet and sure enough there was a crisp twenty pound note left over from his visit to the cash point the night before; he suspected that, as usual, lunch would be on him.

Aching, knackered, but not too smelly (he did a quick under-arm sniff whilst pretending to do some warming down exercises) he wrestled with the tuna mayonnaise baguette, unsure as to whether cutting it in half would constitute an admission of defeat or would merely draw attention to a slightly effeminate way to devour it (as it was accompanied by a pint of lager shandy). Vaz was having far more success with his beef and horseradish on granary and was basking in a more comprehensive thrashing of Mark than was usual during these semi-competitiveness matches, "6-3, 6-2, 6-1 mate, your heaviest defeat yet, so did you overdo it in here last night?" he asked, glancing round the all too familiar interior of the Park Tavern. "Not nearly as much as I'd have liked," Mark replied, quickly checking his toothy grin as he remembered once being on the receiving end of a tuna mayo grimace when chatting to another student teacher in the Uni canteen and it had scarred him for life, well, until then anyhow. "So, who was she?" Vaz asked, wearily. It was certainly not the first or the last time he'd ask this leading question. Mark shrugged and described his first meeting with the girl whose name still eluded him. She was wearing a name badge at the seminar, he recalled, but after their less than auspicious introduction he felt that a prolonged gaze at breast level may have made matters worse. Vaz shook his head sagely, "You do know what your problem is don't you?"

Mark mouthed the answer along, as if well-rehearsed, "You want perfection, and when you finally get it you'll decide it's not what you wanted after all, or that there's someone even more perfect just around the corner."

Two hours later, as he ran more hot water into the bath he'd been stewing in for the previous half an hour, he thought about his status as rapidly approaching forty, unmarried and single and that, on paper, this looked like he was some sort of sad, lonely loser but that just didn't tell the full story, or do his situation justice. There was, however, a difference between being a bachelor and a playboy. He clearly was not a 'player'

(Brighton's answer to George Clooney, achingly handsome and suave, still sexy with grey hair and with a queue of eligible nubile beauties all waiting with baited breath for the ultimate proposal) but it would have been harsh to have labelled him a loser also. He was an averagely built, averagely good looking bloke with streaks of grey appearing in his sideburns and stubble, with disproportionate expectations when it came to women and a love of his own routine. He'd had regular girlfriends throughout his adult life but that was the problem, they were just that; regular. The point Vaz had been trying to make earlier was that if Kate Moss had dropped herself into his lap he'd have probably enjoyed it for a while before pursuing Sienna Miller. He'd tried living with someone just the once, in a flat in a picturesque small town situated between Chichester and Brighton called Arundel and, despite loving the town and the swanky riverside flat he felt like he was being slowly asphyxiated. He wasn't sure that people had souls, but if they did then his was being crushed by the whole experience. It must be similar to what many people felt when they'd had an extramarital affair and got so carried away with the thrill of it all that they'd left their spouse and set up home with the subject of their fling. Imagine that sinking feeling to get just as hacked off as the used dental floss tossed in the general direction of the bathroom bin never quite made it, the cardboard loo roll tube remained in the holder on the wall next to the loo still unchanged, the tea stained mugs cluttered up the bedside table, the strained conversations over finances, who should take out the rubbish and whose family was to get a visit at Christmas. Wasn't this supposed to be different they'd lament? He'd heard someone comment on this scenario recently; "You still get the same bathroom smells." His was not a wild affair turned co-habitation, but the experience was as depressing all the same. The sense of liberation he felt when they went their separate ways was palpable, something he did manage to keep in check whilst he explained to his crestfallen, nest building girlfriend that it wasn't her, but it was him that was the problem and that it would be selfish of him to remain with her thus allowing her to pin all her hopes on a man who didn't seem wired to co-habit. He had come to the conclusion that he loved having women in his life but just not in his house. He never felt lonely or isolated either, as he was quite comfortable with his own company and never really got bored. Only the boring get bored was one of his infamous quips he'd repeat at staff drinks parties.

As was often the case during these Saturday afternoon soaks, he did wonder if it would always be this way and whether or not there was any truth in the theory that 'there's one out there for you' or whether this was just another urban myth. His thoughts turned to the girl he'd met in the pub the night before, how she'd looked up at him with those huge eye-liner framed brown eyes through a slightly jagged fringe and whispered her insult laden intro with a smirk. He'd never found the fact that someone was calling him a prick quite so sexy. Before long he'd imagined hurtling along the coast towards Lewes, the hood of the Z3 down, music blaring with her in the passenger seat, her head thrown back in laughter at one of his many witticisms caught above the sound of Faithless as they headed for afternoon tea, carrot cake and an arm in arm stroll through the quaint windy streets full of its charming little antique boutiques and second hand bookshops. He was snapped out of this pleasant daydream by the sound of the landline ringing and then another voice message from his brother booming from the lounge below, "Listen here you loser, don't think you can ignore my messages as usual. We're having lunch with some pals down in gay-town-on-sea tomorrow, so make sure you've dragged your sorry arse out of bed by 3pm as we're dropping into the hovel for a cup of Earl Grey before heading back to town. Oh, and do let Soph know if it's *too* much trouble to buy some fresh milk and some squash for the kids that didn't go out of date during the Crimean war. And you'd better make sure you've kicked your boyfriend out by the time we arrive; it'll only scare the children. Ciao." Well, he pondered, at least he had something to look forward to; a micro-waved lasagne, a couple of cold beers and an evening slouched in front of Sky Movies before afternoon tea with Richard Branson, Nigella Lawson and their perfect little offspring the following day. Life was certainly looking up.

The friends you would never have chosen

Despite not being a regular churchgoer he'd always taken great comfort from the sound of church bells pealing on a Sunday morning, in much the same way he loved to hear a train rattling along its tracks far off in the dead of night. He loved the solidity of their clanging and the consistency in the notion of people being called to worship in this way and romanticised about peasants laying down their sickles and walking through the partly reaped cornfields, drawn by the sound that had rung out at the same time for generations before them. Although not a practising Christian he had been brought up within a family that attended Sunday Communion services but stopped going as soon as his mum stopped forcing him to go. He did believe in God but felt self-sufficient enough to carry on stumbling through life without Him. But just as he hadn't fully embraced the God thing neither had he been taken in by the new-age pick and mix spiritualism that Brighton seemed to be awash with. In some parts of the town you couldn't turn a corner without tripping over an A-Board offering some type of 'wellness' either for you, your aura or your pet hamster, often with a promise of helping you find a healthy dose of inner Dosha. No sireee, he'd always preferred korma to karma. For him, a Sunday morning was an opportunity to take in some fresh air and clear his head ready for the inevitable afternoon and/or evening of marking or preparation that led to him resenting the fact that his working life had one foot firmly entrenched in his weekend (ignoring the fact that this was only the case due to his total lack of organisation the previous week). He'd always wander down towards the seafront that lacked the rugged cliff edged definition he was so used to as a boy, but such was his affinity with the sea that just to breathe in the salty air and crunch/slosh his way through the dry pebbles or sodden shingle, depending on the height of the tide, enabled his spirits to soar. If there is a God, he thought, then he's here with me on this beach and not in that brick built monolith up the road full of casual-slack wearing do-gooders. If he closed his eyes, took a deep breath, and tuned into the sound of the waves pounding or caressing the beaches he could find a state of awe that came somewhere close to his own form of Sunday worship.

"So they finally saw sense and re-instated Tiggy as the narrator, I mean, she's way ahead of any other pupil in her year at spoken English and her tap and ballet lessons has given her such, well, poise." He had glanced once more at the hideously outdated gold framed wall clock, now probably possessing a high kitsch value, to imply that this brief visit had been quite long enough but Sophie would never get the hint, especially having embarked upon a monologue entitled 'Why my children are better than anyone else's'. It was hardly their fault but his niece Tiggy and nephew Harry would do well to avoid becoming the vacuous Aga and school results obsessed type their darling mother was with her 'manic' days being filled with visiting other yummy mummies' spotless south London homes in between 'mad dashes' that involved school-runs, pony-club runs, ballet-runs, in fact an awful lot of running for someone who would never deign to break out even into an undignified jog; Sophie had a private Pilates instructor of course. Try as he could, he just couldn't get excited about their world and his fixed smile was beginning to make his mouth ache.

Everything about her was immaculate, from the beautifully sculpted dyed blonde bob with designer sunglasses always perched on top, discreet but extensive make-up, ruby red nails that she'd have the annoying habit of drumming on the table if waiting for a reply (her 'conversations' didn't usually require one but a call to a local plumber did, ASAP) the Bodens navy style striped crew neck top under a smart blazer, slim fit dark denim jeans over brown boots; well-heeled was an apt description indeed.

He was relieved when Johnnie came crashing into the lounge on all fours with Harry clinging to his back and Tiggy shepherding them both in the direction of her choice, her face the usual mix of amusement and embarrassment. This was just the opportunity he was looking for to break the flow of Sophie's boastful soliloquy and reclaim the day as his own. "It's great to hear all your news Sophie," he said, "But I really must be cracking on, I mean, those essays won't mark themselves." Sophie fixed him with her pale blue eyes in one of her unnerving, unwavering gazes, tilting her head slightly to the right and raising an eyebrow, rather as a visitor to a safari park might if displaying mild curiosity at a caged primate unpeeling a banana skin. He knew as little about her now as when her and Johnnie's engagement was announced ten years earlier, other than she was from an affluent family based in Gloucestershire whose father had led a distinguished career first in the military and then in the Foreign Office. Johnnie used to wind her up about trying to fix Mark up with her younger sister Tamara to which she'd actually recoil. She must see him as being such a waste of space, a part-time sixth form lecturer living in a house he'd inherited but couldn't be bothered to renovate, no wife, no kids, no girlfriend and no hope. He scratched his stubbled chin self-consciously, loaded and then gathered up the tea tray and smiled tightly at Johnnie as he swerved past him and out along the hallway to the kitchen. He was aware of the hushed voices from the lounge and then Johnnie's heavy footsteps approaching for the inevitable 'big brother' pep talk. Sighing, he turned to see Johnnie's sturdy frame leaning on that of the kitchen entrance, red faced, his pale blue 'White Stuff' long sleeved top straining to hide his ever-increasing middle-aged spread and with the obligatory collar turned up. "You look more and more like Jeremy Clarkson every time I see you," Mark said smiling. "Then you must be the sad little prat with the mullet who is far too old to wear leather jackets and Converse trainers," came his witty reply. This was the verbal sparring before the main bout began. Seconds out …

"I had a chat with dad last night and apparently you've refused any offers of a 40th birthday bash."

"That's right."

"So what are you planning on doing then, skulking round here with a Pot Noodle and a jazz mag?" He was trying to keep a lid on his frustration.

"Look Johnnie, I just don't want to make a big deal of it, alright."

"But it's your 40th for God's sake, everyone makes a big deal of their 40th! I've booked you in for a Porsche track day at Silverstone with some of the guys from work, Mum's booked the conservatory at Milanese for dinner and Sophie's lot have had to cancel a long weekend in Vienna to make it."

"Well maybe someone should have spoken to me about it first."

"That's the whole point, you Muppet; it was going to be a surprise! Why do you insist on being so bloody obtuse when we all just want what's best for you?" Johnnie huffed, imploringly.

"But that's precisely *my* point, what makes *you* think *you know* what the best for me is, I mean hurtling around a race track in a Porsche with a load of Hooray Henries then having to go all the way down to Dorset for the routine grilling over dinner by all and sundry as to why I haven't 'settled down yet' under the smug glare of the de Montfords, sounds more like torture to me."

He noticed how disappointed his brother looked and could see they were just going to talk round in circles without a 'cohesive strategy in terms of moving forwards' so decided on a more conciliatory tone.

"Look, I appreciate the thought, I really do, but it's just not me is it? Tell you what, I'll agree to the dinner back home but let's just keep it simple eh, us, mum and dad, you, Sophie and the kids but not the full Cabinet, I'd prefer it that way. And there's still plenty of time for Major and Mrs Major to re-book their Viennese whirl."

"Okay Mark," Johnnie conceded, "if that's the way you want it. But at least treat yourself to a birthday shave and wear something vaguely presentable to dinner. The staff at Milanese won't get the irony of an 'I'm with this idiot' T-shirt."

That's the great thing about big brothers, he thought, as he watched the walking advert for New Labour pile their two kids into the Range Rover Sport, we can have a minor disagreement but can always avert a major fall out. His wave was returned briefly by Johnnie but by the time he'd pulled the gleaming silver beast out onto the road Sophie had her sunglasses pulled down from the top of her head, her mobile pressed to her ear and the kids were both glued to mini screens that glowed from the back of the seats in front of them. Realising they had already left him behind, he let his waving arm fall halfway then completely down to his side as they sped off into the gloom of a late autumn Sunday afternoon, reflecting the motion of the rust coloured leaves thrown up in the wake of the roaring motor, before trudging back inside to see what the future of tomorrow had to say about the poets of the past.

3
November 2007
Mark, 39/40, Lizzie 30

Keep calm and carry on

One of the joys of working part-time in a sixth-form college was the regular late starts, coupled with a lack of dress code that suited him perfectly. Mondays and Fridays were best as he only worked for a couple of periods in the mornings. Wednesday was a full-ish day and so he always got up in the morning full of good intentions to get all his resources in order, photocopying where necessary and generally presenting an organised front. Unfortunately, his love of his duvet and tendency to underestimate the time required to carry out the simplest of tasks often led to an ungainly rush as he'd sling piles of coursework bulging from splitting carrier bags onto the front seat beside him and screech off with a piece of toast and Marmite still hanging from one side of his mouth. On one such Wednesday he was struggling to operate the photocopier in the senior common room; someone had changed the settings to perform the most complex process of stacking multiple sheets in the correct order onto A4 landscape and hadn't reverted to 'bog standard' mode. Why the hell didn't the last person re-set it he thought murderously as he was, ironically, attempting to photocopy a commentary on the early twentieth century pacifists. Whenever he got stressed he would perspire profusely, adding to his sense of anxiety. He knew he'd be late for period three but had to get the copying done in order to lead it so jabbed furiously at the array of buttons on the futuristic looking digital display, hoping that at least one of the many whirring noises he could hear would yield the 16 copies he needed in order to get on. The rapid fire option must have kicked in as a small stack of crisp white pages soon appeared in one of the multiple trays to his left and were still warm to the touch as he strode along the gothic quadrant that linked the admin block with arts and humanities.

As he glanced down one of the grand archways that led to the visitors' car park he noticed a police patrol car with a male and female officer standing to one side, chatting with a woman in jeans and a black puffa-style parka coat with fur rimmed hood, favoured by the Italian students. They seemed to be chatting amiably but there was something about the woman that was familiar that didn't click until he was apologising to his lower sixth for his tardiness and getting them to settle down for a debate on the fairness of the use of the white feather as a way of humiliating a man not in active service during the First World War regardless of their physical or mental state. As the students launched enthusiastically into their respective 'motions' (and he genuinely loved them for their eagerness) his mind began to drift and shift focus. He'd seen her again and couldn't shrug off the image. Time to plan my own campaign he thought.

At lunchtime, he grabbed a sandwich and an espresso, more like a black coffee filled to halfway in the regulation plastic cup from the canteen, and headed for the common room where he'd usually find Pete in a corner chair, head buried in the back pages of the Independent ready to chat through the various Champions League fixtures and connotations for that evening. His disappointment at not seeing Pete was tempered by the figure sitting in their usual spot, a gorgeous, familiar looking young woman wrapped in a trendy parka style coat huddled over a folder, with marker pen poised; it was her. His head was still awash with images of 'lily livered men' being presented with white feathers for cowardice so he strode purposefully towards her, forgetting all about the low table on which her folder was open, smashing his shin on the join between the leg and corner of it, making her jump in the process and spilling coffee on his fingers. Grinning, and trying to ignore the sharp pain in both areas of his body, he blurted, "Ahhh Meeesterrr Bond, I've been expecting you." To which she replied with a frown, "Are you alright?"

"Sure," he said, with a grimace, "At this point you would have swivelled round in your chair, with a manic glint in your eye gently stroking your pussy." There followed an embarrassing pause that lasted an eternity as she took him in. "OOhhh Mrs Slocomb," he said in his best David Brent voice (that was pretty much spot on) as he felt his face redden and a bead of sweat trickle down his back. The opportunity to impress her was fading fast, the moment slipping dramatically through his fingers already so he casually slumped into the easy chair next to her, gathered his composure (and her scattered paperwork) and decided on a more conventional approach. "Hi, I'm Mark, we met at the safe sex seminar the other week, and in the pub after." As usual he felt a quip rising up within him that he failed to suppress blurting, "Actually, we practised safe sex that night, you went home with your mates and I went to the kebab shop."

"How could I forget?" She looked up at him again and he felt his stomach flip, her eyes were such an amazing deep brown colour and her fringe was that bit longer than when they'd met just a month before, it suited her, he thought. A strand of hair had fallen from where she had pushed it behind her ear to read her paperwork and he had to fight an instinct to push it back for her. Maybe sensing this, she self-consciously moved it back in one elegant movement whilst biting gently on her bottom lip. The conversation was already at crunch point.

He'd once considered seeking out an expert on mental health issues as he was convinced he had a form of Tourette's Syndrome or Asperger's where he would naturally make the most inappropriate remark for any given occasion. When he was being interviewed to work as a volunteer at a local homeless shelter a few years before (he was only signing up because he'd fancied one of the staff he'd met whilst she was fundraising in the pub one Friday night) he was asked if he'd had any experience of 'engaging with vulnerable adults' to which he'd replied he'd once had a scuffle with a couple of winos down by the taxi rank outside Brighton railway station one evening and *he* was the one that felt vulnerable that night, adding that no one had pressed charges. Sean, the earnest young Irish manager of the shelter then questioned him on his reasons for wanting to volunteer there and his answer of "Blonde, around 5ft 6" with a bust like Pamela Anderson" saw the interview being drawn to rather an abrupt close with a "We'll get back to you if a vacancy arises." They must have been chocka with volunteers, he'd thought, in the weeks afterwards as they hadn't been in touch since. He could recall countless social and professional situations where he'd been so keen to break ice that he'd end up by burning bridges instead. Dragging his eyes from her Penelope Cruz-esque pout he continued to dig his own grave.

"Well that's considering you didn't get up to anything after you left the pub, I mean this is Brighton after all, one of your colleagues certainly looked as if she'd be up for it and the barman looked keen to show you his didgeridoo."

"As for my colleague, she's simply not my type and yes, the barman was trying to impress me as he was clearing glasses at the end. I can't remember how exactly we got onto the topic of Greek mythology but his offer of going back to his place to 'unleash the Kraken' received short shrift." Mark sighed, "Some men can be so puerile, can't they?"

"Quite," she replied.

He managed to turn the conversation onto her work to find out that she, Lizzie, was employed by Brighton and Hove Town Council as a youth and community worker, focused particularly on female teenagers and young adults (vulnerable of course), running drop-ins and various programmes such as those on drugs and alcohol, self-esteem and peer pressure, all designed to support them within an educational, vocational and social context. She spoke lucidly and passionately about her work, her voice having a slightly husky and sexy tone that he found to be a huge distraction, along with pretty much everything about her. Even maintaining eye contact and nodding sagely as she described some of the projects she was currently running was an effort as he couldn't help but imagine what sort of a figure she had wrapped up in her designer sleeper bag with fur lined hood. As encouraging as it was to be making conversational headway it was also proving a multi-tasker's nightmare as he continued with his nodding and "Ahh, I see-ing," in order to demonstrate a sustained interest whilst simultaneously unwrapping and chewing his egg and cress sandwich and pausing to take regular sips of his coffee, the first of which had scalded the roof of his mouth leaving it feeling like the skin was hanging down, recreating the interior of a Jurassic cavern (mites go up and tites come down was how he remembered the nature of those particular prehistoric rock formations from when he was a lad). He fancied her so much it was all he could do to remain 'cool' as she then talked him through the purpose of her visits to the college but his mind must have meandered ahead to the 'how would you like your eggs in the morning' phase as she had stopped talking and was looking up at him, clearly waiting for a response. "Well I think it sounds like you do amazing work Lizzie, really inspirational."

"I wouldn't quite go that far but thanks. And to repeat my question, *do you* have any students that you feel might benefit from attending a drugs and alcohol session here in college next Wednesday afternoon?"

"It's the lecturers you should be more worried about!" he joked. "Seriously though, I'll get some names together and maybe email some through to you. Would that be okay?"

"So you do serious then do you?" Lizzie replied, holding his gaze before relaxing into a half smile. "Sure, an email will be fine." As she stood to gather up her folder and leave she pulled a business card from a pocket within it and left it on the table in front of him. "See you next Wednesday then." He didn't want his smile to convey just how ecstatic he felt to have her business card as firstly, this might really scare her off and secondly, he was convinced that a piece of cress had wedged itself between his front two teeth, equally likely to render anything more than a passing acquaintance unimaginable. So he opted for a mute closed-mouth smile and nod of the head as he watched her pick her way across the common room and out. Only then did he break into a beaming smile, taking the business card between his fingertips and turning it over and over again, as if it were a piece of newly-mined precious metal.

That evening, and not for the first time in his professional career, he faced something of a dilemma. He knew that Lizzie had given him her business card on the basis that he was going to forward the names of students who might benefit from some hard facts on the dangers of drink and drug abuse (he thought it might be easier to forward her a list of names of those who didn't). On reflection, she could have simply asked him to submit his list to the head of student services and not directly to her. Was there anything about her body language or anything she might have said that may have hinted that she was somehow interested in him? He sipped steadily from a bottle of Becks, feet up on the sofa in his lounge, the TV on low, his mind racing through the gears. Would it be *that* out of order to use the mobile phone number that was on the business card she'd given him earlier to try to arrange a date? He'd once taught a fat, lazy student who hailed originally from Cuba. He'd paid very little attention to him until he met his mum at a parents' evening who was a total stunner. He'd then taken much more of an interest in the lad, asking him casually about his home life to find out that his mother had married a wealthy British businessman who had met her on a holiday to South America when she was a young woman and they had recently separated pending a divorce. He'd called the mother at her home one evening to talk about her son's performance of late, feigning concern and wondering whether there might be something in his home life that was unsettling him thus impacting on his studies and his slipping grades (knowing full well that there had been no more issues with the student's work than any other he taught and that the mother was going through a tough time emotionally). The mother had been understandably tearful on the phone so he'd even suggested that, if 'there was anything he could do' (that included meeting for a coffee to 'talk things through') that she shouldn't hesitate to call him at home. Thankfully she had more sense than to do this, either she was building barriers after a painful marriage break-up or maybe her instincts told her he was looking to gain leverage from his position and her vulnerability in order to get a date. Shocking but true.

He sensed that Lizzie would not be one to play games with, nor would she be easily fooled by his interest in her 'inspirational' work in the local community so decided on a 'halfway house' strategy; a text that read:

Hi Gd 2 talk earlier. Forgot 2 say. A few of us going 2 watch fire wks on S'front this Sat eve. Want 2 join us? Beers after? TB. Mark

He read and re-read the message, written in his mix of full and abbreviated words learned from his students who had ridiculed him for using fully formed words and phrases, his thumb hovering over the send button. Would Lizzie object to this broadening of the boundaries as he liked to call it (stalking was perhaps another way to view it) and ignore his feeble attempts at hitting on her or see this, as he did, as fate that had brought them together? A swig of bottled beer, some of which dribbled down his chin, a sniff, a wipe of his chin with the back of his hand then he pressed send and watched the little arrows depart the in-tray and send this potentially huge message out into the ether. Okay, he thought. What will be, will be.

Nice try he reminded himself three hours later, as he paced up and down the lounge, one eye on the documentary about the Expressionists he was following on Channel 4 and the other on the small screen of his Nokia. He'd never been good at waiting, much preferring a direct answer so he knew where he stood. There was also the fact that there was no group of friends heading down to Hove seafront to watch the fireworks, in fact the thought seemed abhorrent but he'd thought quickly and come up with the safest sounding context for getting together with Lizzie; no dinner for two but a casual invitation to meet up in a crowd; an understatement in itself. He remembered tales of the town's resident former world champion boxer and self-styled Lord of the Manor, famous for riding around Brighton on a Harley Davidson in jodhpurs and for letting off fireworks without going through standard safeguarding procedures. In fact, there were perfectly good reasons why he steered clear of the seafront for most of the year round; the irony of 'Pride' (made up of those who seemed to have left theirs at home that day), the bank holiday weekends full of day trippers sweltering under 'Kiss me Quick' hats and forgetting that it is exactly the same sun that burns bright over Pathos as they waddle back to their people carriers, lobster pink after a day on the beach without sunblock. The great British public en masse; something he avoided at all costs, but for the chance to meet up with Lizzie, he'd brave them. He was half dozing as the Champions League highlights kicked off at 11:30pm but the bleep of an incoming text shook him out of it. His first attempt at grabbing the phone saw him knocking it off the arm of the sofa and behind the coffee table that still contained the empty meat feast pizza box from earlier that evening. Cursing and straining to reach his phone without having to move too far off the sofa or rearrange the furniture he grabbed it, his side stretched to capacity. He read the new message quickly:

Will be on seafront Sat night. Prob see you down there. L

Okay, it wasn't exactly glowing with a burning desire to see him but there again it wasn't a threat to report him to his Principal for misuse of her contact details either. Okay, he reflected, time to drum up some mates.

Fortunes of war

It had been Vaz's idea to grab a beer in the Fortune of War pub right on Hove beach for convenience sake but, judging from the bruisers entering the pub ahead of them, Mark wasn't sure it would be the best place for them. It wasn't a place he visited regularly but on the occasion he had, there had been a mixed crowd either crammed into the inside, with its split level and feature roof shaped like an upturned boat, or spilled out onto the benches and tables that were situated at the top of the beach, but tonight was totally different; it was almost as if they had walked right into a shaved head and signet ring convention. The place was packed so they pushed their way carefully towards the downstairs bar, eager not to spill the pints of any of the assembled gorillas that were packed into the ground floor. As they reached the bar and attempted to get the attention of one of the overworked staff Vaz politely asked the punter in front of him to allow him some elbow room. It turned out that he was one of the blokes who had entered the pub just before them who, along with his mate, bore more than a passing resemblance to the East End's notorious fictional hard men the Mitchell brothers. He turned his thick, tattooed neck in Vaz's direction and fixed him in the type of cold stare he imagined on a Great White just before a kill then he broke into a grin/grimace and, after nudging his equally bullish looking mate (who was even taller and broader) sneered and said in pure Mockney:

"Eh look aaaaaat, mind yer backs, it's my little pony trying to get a Babycham for 'im and 'is boyfriend."

To which they both sniggered before leaving the bar, and a space big enough for half a dozen of Mark's mates (if they had managed to extricate themselves from their domestic duties) and Vaz to fill. They had decided to order a bottle each and not a pint so they could make a hasty exit if needs be; early indications favoured this approach as their fortunes in this war-zone didn't look particularly promising. Whilst Vaz ordered their beers Mark looked around the large interior and was relieved to spot three or four colossal bouncers surveying the scene. He seemed to be the only bloke in the place wearing a winter jacket and scarf, Vaz was definitely the only bloke with a ponytail and pierced nose. He hadn't been aware that there was a boxing event scheduled for that night, nor a Brighton home game but there must have been a reason for such a large number of Neanderthals to have descended on the normally diverse Hove seafront venue that particular evening; probably not for the sparklers and Catherine wheels, Mark thought. Vaz handed him two cold beers and then headed immediately to the loo leaving Mark to ponder their predicament and what else the evening had in store for them.

Getting a group together to go out that night had proved harder than he'd imagined. Pete and his wife had friends round for a 'kitchen supper' and two other lecturers he got on with, Rob who taught politics and Steve who also taught English were taking their families to fireworks displays at their kids' schools; of course, the problem lay with the fact that all his contemporaries, Vaz apart, were all nuclear familied-up and he was the only lecturer who lived more like a student. That thought made him wince for a moment but was counterbalanced by how free he was in life, to get up when he wanted to, not when ambushed pre-dawn by a hyper 3 year- old who saw his bedroom as an extension of the soft play at nursery, how his weekends unfolded at a leisurely pace that he alone determined without the aggravation of chaotic children's parties and freezing trips to the swings with a hangover on Sunday mornings, the sleep filled nights, spontaneous trips to the pub, the list goes on … Vaz had returned from the loo but was still looking uncomfortable.

"You alright?"

"I couldn't go, could I?"

"What do you mean you couldn't go? I thought you were bursting?"

"Well, I was, but just when I was pointing Percy at the porcelain that bruiser came in."

"And?"

"He stood at the urinal next to me."

"So?"

"You know I can't go when there is someone standing next to me, too much pressure."

"So you're saying he was just standing there watching you for jollies, didn't look the type to me, I suppose you just can't tell these days."

"You know exactly what I mean, that I can never go when someone's peeing next to me."

"Well you'd better go back in, you can't cross your legs all night."

"Oh, that's a good idea, they clearly think I bat for the other side so why don't I just cruise back into the bogs, real casual like, and wait for a right good spanking. I'll rephrase that."

"Okay then, let's swig up and go, maybe to the OhSo like I said in the first place."

"For once, we are in agreement."

He really should have left it there, but as was often the case, Mark had to have the last word. "By the way did I tell you how dashing you look tonight Darling?" As always timing is king. The thought that they had survived such an intimidating environment and were about to leave in one piece had enabled him to relax enough to crack a joke just as the said bruiser was making his way back from the loos. Mark had his back to him but Vaz caught the change of expression on his face and grimaced noticeably. Turning slowly, Mark met the Rottweiler's glower and, for a second, the cogs churned and he realised just how it looked. He was about to explain the running gag in Blackadder Goes Forth relating to Captain Darling and how it got him every time but decided they'd better just go forth into the night themselves. "I'll get me coat," he said in his best Brummy accent and they left their barely touched bottles of lager and pushed their way (courteously) through the set of Lock Stock and Two Smoking Barrels extras and out into the freezing night air, ironically, right outside the arches.

It was well documented how Newcastle city centre would be full of young female adults out on the lash on Friday and Saturday nights without a pair of tights or jacket in sight and the same could be said for Brighton. As they meandered along the concrete strip and past the arches that housed the Honey Club and Funky Buddha Lounge they noticed a group of girls who couldn't be much older than seventeen holding the hair back of one who was being sick into a small clinker-built rowing boat moored high up on the beach, revealing her knickers to passers-by. He knew he was getting old when he actually felt cold for those girls who tottered about in vests and miniskirts all year round when on a night out. His instinct as a teacher was to intervene and see if the girl was okay but he'd done this once before and remembered being horrified by the stream of vitriol he'd received, being called a 'perv' and 'paedo' and with threats of the police being called, causing a hasty retreat. A mitigating factor on that occasion may have been that it was on Pete's stag night and the theme was 'characters from great historical battles'; he had looked less than heroic as a drunken and ironic 'Tweedle-Dum' so maybe the girls in question that night were quite within their rights to refuse his offers of help, regardless of how well intentioned they were.

As they were about to cut across the beach to the OhSo bar they were met by a wall of security guards in the obligatory black waterproof jackets with orange hi visibility vests over the top. All of them were over 6ft 2" and all seemed to have spent their pocket money on chewing gum. They joined a long but moving queue of fellow 'revellers' being directed onto the top of the seafront as the main area of beach between the West and Grand Pier had been cordoned off for the display.

His thoughts turned to Lizzie, crushed somewhere in the throng, and how he'd play it if/when he saw her. He'd convinced himself he'd play it cool but knew somewhere deep within was a crass one-liner waiting to ruin the moment. Be yourself he'd thought as they slowly made their way up the stone stairs from beach level, but there again, look where that's got you in life. They shuffled along and managed to get a reasonably good view of proceedings although he wasn't here primarily to watch rockets being launched to the sound of the Ride of the Valkyries. Vaz stood to his right and despite his need for the loo seemed quite happy taking it all in, joining in with the ironic 'oooohs and aaaahs'. He was such a solid mate, dependable and willing, quite selfless when it came to supporting his quest to meet 'the one'. Vaz taught English and Media at a state run secondary school in Brighton; his girlfriend was a primary school teacher who lived and worked just outside Crawley and who was on duty at her school bonfire that evening leaving Vaz free to make up the 'group' of lads out on the town that night. Mark checked the screen of his mobile for the umpteenth time that night and his stomach tightened to see that he had a message. Fumbling his way through the buttons to read it, it was short and sweet but a message all the same:

He liked it. "Okay Vaz, time to roll."

Just how difficult is it to pretend that you're not excited to see someone when you've thought about little else for days? What makes us feign indifference when we really want to make a declaration of love and longing? Okay, the latter sounds a bit melodramatic, but these were the thoughts that he had to contend with as they crossed the decking and entered the bar that was at the other end of the seafront to the Fortune of War and at polar opposites on the cool scale that evening. Grabbing a couple of bottles of Becks and finding a wall to lean on whilst scanning the bar, Mark chatted aimlessly to Vaz and was aware of overdoing facial expressions and responses, grinning and laughing wildly at the slightest hint of an amusing reply to give the impression to an onlooker (as Lizzie was in there somewhere) that they were both having a crazy night out. It just left Vaz with an expression of bemusement. Their match had been much closer that morning but Mark had still had to pay for lunch in the pub afterwards and as much as he loved Vaz he was rapidly running out of things to say.

After a couple of false alerts (thankfully before he had sauntered over to the wrong girl with long dark hair) he spotted her, with her two colleagues and another woman he'd never seen before. Lizzie hadn't seen him and for a few moments he enjoyed being the voyeur, studying her as she listened to the one with the dodgy earrings talk animatedly and gesticulating with one hand, bottle of beer in the other. It was the one with the cropped hair who first spotted Mark, stopping in mid-flow and leaning in conspiratorially to whisper to Lizzie and co, who then all turned, grinning, to look over in his direction. Mark noted Lizzie giving her colleague a playful nudge in the ribs and, smiling, furrowed her brow and gently shook her head as if to prevent her friend from revealing an insight that perhaps would have caused embarrassment. But to whom? Mark flushed as he attempted to interpret and process the nuances of this little mimed exchange, was Lizzie looking to prevent her friend from blurting out an adult equivalent of 'my friend fancies you' or merely reminding her that the 'penis/penii' exchange was fast becoming old hat? Taking a deep breath, he nudged his faithful companion, gesturing with a head movement that they were 'on' and reminded himself of the advice given by many an Oscar winning actor when quizzed on the secret of their success, "get your lines right and avoid bumping into the furniture." Following their exchange in the senior common room earlier that week, this was definitely Take 2 on both counts.

An hour later and it was time to say goodnight as the 'girls' were heading on to a house party in Kemptown. He never knew when it was the right time to stop referring to young adult females as girls and then what to replace this with. Women seemed to apply to those who had bosoms and children and ladies conjured up images of the nineteenth- century upper crust, all brittle and bustle with fans and a propensity to faint due to abominable heat and tight corsets. Anyhow, he was still struggling to keep his sense of euphoria on a tight leash as he hadn't, to his knowledge, mortally offended anyone, spilled drinks down any cleavages, made inappropriate gags (well just the one, but to be fair, he wasn't to know that the fourth woman in the group had just lost her husband in an industrial accident) and to top it all, he had a date with Lizzie for the following Saturday night. He'd been attempting to pluck up the courage all evening but had never found quite the right moment. For once he was grateful for the house DJ ramping up the noise towards the end of the night as he had to lean in close to Lizzie to make himself heard. He'd gone for the casual ''Fancy grabbing a bite to eat sometime next weekend?'' approach rather than the more formal "May I take you out to dinner?' as he lived in an age when a girl/young lady/woman may take offence at the prospect of a man leading them out to dine and then paying afterwards; too controlling, too Edwardian, heck, they could swig beer by the bottle and then go Dutch for all he cared. He'd noticed over the past year or so how many people were now greeting each other and saying farewells with kisses on the cheek, like theatre or media luvvies. He'd observed this etiquette and thought the protocol was a kiss on each cheek on arrival and on one cheek to depart. He'd even tried it on his mother last time he'd visited her in Dorset who had then promptly announced to all her friends gathered for their book club that her son had 'French kissed her' on the doorstep. He was still inwardly stressing about how he was going to close the evening with Lizzie and her friends (would it be kisses all round and if so how many?) when they were off, with a quick 'see ya' and a squeeze on the arm from Lizzie. He watched her as she gracefully weaved her way through the packed bar of drinkers, most of whom were gently swaying due to alcohol, the grooves thrown together by the house DJ, or a mix of both.

A little worse for wear himself and buoyed by the soaring success of the evening he grabbed Vaz in a boozy bear hug and insisted that he bought him a curry for being such a good mate. In the 10 or so years he'd known Vaz, he'd never once turned down the offer of a free curry. Vaz always only drank water with curry, frowning at the Brits who attempted to quench the fire in their throats with copious amounts of Cobra beer, Mark being one such plebeian. The meal passed in a blur for Mark who, amongst the flashbacks of Lizzie's eyes, smile, smell, voice and pretty much everything else, remembered eating, drinking, urinating (in the right place), paying, hailing a cab, urinating again (in the wrong place), dropping his keys, dropping his trousers, finding his keys and stumbling across the threshold and onto his favourite sofa, clicking the TV on with the remote, before falling asleep fully clothed, face down, grinning, muttering to himself and with the front door still a fraction ajar...

A friend indeed

"Are you alright Mark, do I need to call the police?" The shrill voice caused him to wake with such a start he tumbled off the sofa and onto the garish carpeted floor of his front room. Opening his eyes and squinting against the harsh light, another uninvited guest into his lounge this Sunday morning, he could just about make out the outline of Mrs Sheridan peering down at him with a concerned look on her face. "I'm fine, really," he mumbled back. Then, as his senses booted up, along with the ability to process the simplest of facts, he added, "How did you get in?"

"The door was wide open dear," came the alarming reply. "I was just on my way back from Mass and thought maybe you'd been broken into. You can never be too sure these days can you so I thought I'd better pop my head round the door and just check to see that all was well."

"I can't have shut it properly last night, but no need to panic." He paused, not meaning to sound irritated. "But thanks all the same."

Mrs Sheridan lived two doors down and was a good friend of his late godmother's. His godmother had been a Kelly before she was married and, apparently, the Sheridans and Kellys had always got on and so it was that the two widows struck up a firm friendship founded upon their faith and heritage. He was a classic 'CofE' in that it said so on his birth certificate, he went to a CofE Junior School and would always do the honours at Christmas and Easter as well as for births, deaths and funerals. Although he wasn't at all engaged in church life he was aware that it had caused quite a stir in their sleepy little Dorset village that firstly, the live- in maid and gardener/handyman were asked to be his godparents (straddling class divisions) and that secondly, his godmother was a practising Irish Roman Catholic (he's often asked her when she was going to become any good at it as she practised often enough). In later years, he recalled being proud of his parents for being so open-minded, not something he usually associated with them, and had become extremely fond of the chatty cook with her delicious homemade pies and cakes and of her gentle husband who quietly plodded about the place, mending fence panels and tending hedges whilst puffing away at his pipe. They had lived in the small lodge cottage and all those years of rent free employment must have enabled them to retire in some comfort to this conservative area of Brighton, where Mary had grown up having come over from Ireland as a child, only for his godfather to die from a heart attack just a couple of years after they had settled into a more relaxing pace of life.

When his godmother, Mary, passed away and Mark moved into the property, Mrs Sheridan had taken over the surrogate role, regularly looking in on him, more often or not with some homemade cake or 'a nice bit of ham'. As he sat on the edge of the sofa rubbing his eyes, he heard her clatter about in the kitchen, washing the pans that were stacked in the sink, wiping down work surfaces, all the time humming away what he guessed were her favourite hymns. It was at once heart-warming and depressing; sweet to know that she had taken up the baton from his 'Aunty Mary' but sad that at nearly 40 he was still being looked after by a well-meaning old dear. The smell of smoky bacon and the crackle of fried eggs snapped him out of this gloomy introspection and his hunger pangs took over. Shuffling along the hallway into the now clean and ordered kitchen he was greeted by a warm smile from Mrs Sheridan, probably missing the irony of the apron she had donned bearing the image of Michelangelo's David, a birthday present from Johnnie some years before. Mrs Sheridan carefully slid two sizzling eggs onto hot buttered toast that was surrounded by crispy bacon and a mountain of baked beans. Easing himself onto one of the four pine kitchen chairs that surrounded the round table, the plastic cloth having been wiped clean, with bottles of ketchup, brown sauce and mustard all neatly stacked side by side he accepted this lifesaving feast as if a yachtsman facing his first breakfast after spending a week adrift in the north Atlantic. Placing a steaming hot cup of tea beside him she gave his shoulder a squeeze, removed the apron and turned to face him. Her eyes were a sharp pale blue, her grey hair pinned up neatly and her pinched lips moved into a smile, "Sure you could be doing with a good woman now Mark."

"I know Mrs S, it's something I'm working on I can assure you."

"Well I'll be off now and do try and remember to give that door a good shove after you come back in at night, one day you might wake up to find far worse than a meddling old woman standing over you."

"Thank you, and for all this." As he gestured towards the mound of food in front of him and the clear, gleaming work surfaces. "You're a saint."

"Well I don't know about that." She beamed and off she went humming a tune he remembered his Aunty Mary was fond of but, as always, the words failed him.

After breakfast he stacked his plate, cup and cutlery in the sink, squirted some washing liquid over them and left them to soak in hot water. He had an overwhelming desire to soak himself in hot suds and then to get some proper sleep, as crashing out on the sofa after a gutful of beer and curry hardly counted. As he passed the door to the lounge he noticed one of those property makeover programmes hosted by a high energy pretty thirty-something in smart skirt, long tailored coat and high heeled boots wearing a permanent grin as her team descended upon a charming little rustic cottage in the Cotswolds to give it that boutique chic look it was crying out for. That's just what this place could do with he thought, as he re-positioned his body amongst the cushions on the sofa that he'd nestled into just the night before, a proper makeover. He began to imagine a skip outside full to the brim with the green and brown patterned carpets, cream tasselled lampshades, grey Formica kitchen cupboards, white built-in wardrobes, avocado bathroom suite and beige three-piece suite to be replaced by a modern 'bespoke kitchen solution' all steel work surfaces with chrome espresso machine, dark wooden floor that 'flowed' from one room to the next, deep luxurious brown leather sofas, built-in gas effect fires, a vintage roll top bath …

The banging had begun in his dream, as the DIY Doctor and crew were knocking out false ceilings and preparing to sand over the Artex that lurked underneath to present smooth high white ceilings with cornices befitting an Edwardian villa but it continued after the plaster had come tumbling down. For the second time that day he found himself waking with such a start that he'd fallen off the sofa and onto the very carpets he had been dreaming of ripping up. He heard a familiar voice booming through the letter box so headed, gingerly, towards the front door and the source of the commotion. As he opened the front door he was aware of four things that happened simultaneously and all in slow motion; his brother Johnnie, at waist level, bellowing through the letter box, his nephew Harry projectile vomiting into his (Mark's) chest as he opened the door, his sister-in-law Sophie putting a hand to her mouth and his niece Tiggy shrieking with nervous laughter. There followed a moment's silence followed by Sophie's half-hearted attempt at an apology and Johnnie pushing Harry through the door and up to the bathroom muttering something about kids and seafood. He'd been in a daze when he opened the door but it now felt as if he'd been dropped into the middle of a Steve Martin movie as assorted family members trooped past him into his house unexpectedly, him covered in his nephew's sick. Mark, still rubbing his eyes, went upstairs to change out of his sodden top whilst Sophie made a pot of tea, Tiggy hovered by her mother's elbow, once more unsure as to which expression to wear. Just as he was about to pass the main bathroom Johnnie emerged with a sheepish Harry who apologised immediately and reassured him he felt much better for having deposited the contents of his stomach all over Mark's chest. "I'll just change my T-shirt and will be right down, Sophie is making tea."

They hadn't intended on popping in and Mark wasn't sure whether he felt upset or relieved by this. Johnnie had decided just the night before to visit the same friends they'd lunched with the previous Sunday as the 'guy' (who was confusingly actually called Guy) apparently had more money than sense and Johnnie was trying to get him to invest in a property in Corfu he'd bought for a snip and done up for less. They'd taken this guy, Guy and his family out to a seafood place for lunch in an attempt at closing the deal, a meal that Mark had briefly worn before changing. As they sipped their tea and the children sat on the floor skipping through the numerous Sky channels to find something loud, animated and American, Sophie fixed him in her all too familiar 'look'. He had clearly been on the sofa sleeping when they had turned up out of the blue, he equally clearly hadn't shaved for the past few days and, to top it all, the T-shirt he'd pulled on without thinking was one he'd bought as a joke when in Tenerife with some college mates years ago that proudly read 'BIKINI INSPECTOR'. "Sorry to wake you up old boy," Johnnie broke the silence, "Bit out of order getting you up at this unsociable hour eh? I don't know how you part-time college lecturers do it you know, bally heroes one and all. Maybe I'll write to my MP to suggest that you get long paid holidays to go with your 20 hours a week at the chalk face. But hang on a minute ..."

"Yes, hilarious," Mark replied wearily, "I was doing some research into giving this place a makeover actually and must have just nodded off."

"A makeover?" Sophie's ears pricked up at this and her demeanour moved a fraction from contempt to just south of indifference, "Well we can certainly put you in touch with some people who worked wonders with our Barnes place. May I have a look at your plans?" Fearing an action plan being drawn up before his still bleary eyes, (and, crucially, before he had even drawn up one of his own) he attempted to diffuse her zeal and regain control of the situation. "I'm just dipping my toe in the water so to speak, at this point, you know, kicking a few ideas around up in here," (pointing to his head), "but I'll deffo get in touch when I've got more concrete plans, thanks for the offer Soph."

"Well, where else would we expect to find a Bikini Inspector, but dipping his toe in the water?" She reverted to her familiar fixed smile as she realised he'd been lounging on the sofa day-dreaming about it just as she had suspected. "Come along then gang." Johnnie got himself up onto his feet, sensing the ice maiden's renewed frostiness. "How about a nice pukey goodbye to your Uncle Mark, Harry?" The children didn't seem at all upset to be removed from their viewing, maybe the grubby carpet and stack of faded weekend newspaper supplements coupled with the smell of bacon was all far too seedy for the poor little darlings to tolerate for a moment longer, although Harry seemed to be quite engrossed in an old copy of FHM he'd found amongst the pile. For the second weekend running Mark was left to feel like an abject loser whilst the captain of industry, his immaculate first mate and their ship-shape crew motored back to their perfect world in their luxury cruiser. "Déjà vu all over again," he muttered to himself, remembering a football manager making the comment recently after his team had conceded a late equaliser for the second game in a row. He closed the door (firmly this time) behind him and decided to at least run the vacuum around the lounge carpet; a makeover in instalments he thought.

Love is the drug

The following week unfolded in much the same way as any other. He managed to be in late for his upper sixth on Monday, despite it being period 2, so had to rush parts of his lecture on the role that the heath had to play as a backdrop to events in Hardy's 'Return of the Native'. It was rushing to the classroom for that session that had caused him to spill coffee over his jeans and into the carrier bag that contained the marked essays for his lower sixth group on the physical and metaphorical theme of sight and blindness in King Lear. He simply hadn't been looking as the Principal and a group of visitors had surged through the double doors he was struggling to open with his hands full. Some of the lower sixth students were a tad miffed to be handed back dog-eared coffee stained essays after the morning break, making the point that it was usually the student having to give excuses to the lecturer as to the state of their homework. The majority of these more tiresome students would still wear their leaver's hoodies from their secondary school to college, scream and hug each other in between classes and bring pencil cases into lectures so he figured they would learn to loosen up over the next term or two. One or two of the more cynical ones seemed to appreciate the irony of the sight/blindness theme juxtaposed with the not looking where he was going accident; so some hope Mark thought, remembering the look of complete disdain he wore throughout his VI Form years.

On Wednesday lunchtime he managed to catch up with Pete over a coffee and a sandwich in the common room. Pete talked animatedly about various topics including the fixtures for that evening's Champions' League group matches (relishing the use of hammed metaphors as Utd were set to 'stuff' a less than dynamic Kiev side at Old Trafford) and the debate he and his students had over the corn laws when one of the drama students had come into the lecture dressed in the peasant's attire of the period and had given his views 'from the field' as it were. It had turned out that, in his enthusiasm to be creative in his history teaching, he had failed to brief the drama student as to the fine detail of the issues of the day and so he was left to appear as the simplest peasant of the era, struggling to articulate what exactly he and his brotherhood were up in arms against in the first place. Mark did his best to keep up, and indeed contribute, but every now and again his stomach would turn another knot as the minutes counted down to Lizzie's talk on drugs and alcohol in the period after lunch. He had decided to play the 'no texting for 3 days after our last encounter' game despite his fingers itching to hack out a quick 'Hi, how are you doing' message more times than he could remember after seeing her and her friends the previous Saturday night. A few other lecturers started moving towards the common room door so Mark left Pete to finish his lunch, the crumbs of which were scattered over the open newspaper that he was poring over on the low table Mark had collided with so spectacularly just a week before.

There was a low buzz of chatter as the raked seats in the drama studio filled up with students from the lower sixth. He cast his eye casually towards the front to find Lizzie nodding along earnestly to something the head of student services was sharing with her. He had noticed how she always seemed to give her full attention to whoever she was talking to, despite any noise that might be going on around her. Having always struggled to maintain such a focus, he thought it an admirable quality to have. Her hair had been pulled back into a ponytail, with her fringe still framing beautiful almond shaped brown eyes. She was dressed in an open necked white shirt (was it too old fashioned to say blouse?) with a black jumper over it, with the bottom of the shirt untucked and showing under the ribbed bottom of the jumper. He figured that this was an intentional look and not the result of her being either (a) untidy or (b) having washed her wools on the wrong cycle (he could tick both of the above boxes regarding his attempts at domesticity). The studio hushed when the house lights were dimmed leaving just the spotlights at the front of the performance space. After a brief introduction Lizzie spoke for a couple of minutes before nodding to one of the technical assistants, his cue to start the film aimed at highlighting to the students the perils of drink and drugs. The film, a 'gritty drama' depicted the demise of a once popular and promising student into a pale, spotty and paranoid recluse, devoid of friends, hope and his once good health due to an increasing dependency on illegal substances. The scenes were set to a backdrop of pounding dance music and were interspersed with images of how this substance abuse had affected his vital organs ending up with a close-up of a mortuary slab and drawn looking family members attending the funeral of the deceased. All pretty impactful stuff. The D&A film was followed by a Q&A session which Lizzie facilitated with calm authority but at the same time a look of empathy and a clear lack of judgement towards those students whose questions tended to begin with 'A mate of mine has recently begun experimenting with Ecstasy ...'

As the students shuffled out he attempted to catch her eye and managed to do so just as Wiggy, one of his more gobby students (with a nickname that reflected his bushy barnet) sauntered over to her to 'ask a question' but Mark knew he was really trying to get a quick look at her cleavage. He wandered over also, it would have felt odd not to have said 'hi' to Lizzie, just as she was reaching down into her bag to bring out more glossy flyers, inadvertently giving Wiggy just the view he was after. "Alright Wiggy?" he asked. "Yeah, fine thanks Sir," he replied, with a glint in his eye. Many of the new intake were still struggling to call tutors by their first names.

"Don't forget kids, if you drink too much and smoke the wacky stuff," Mark continued, "you'll regret it." (He concluded by raising the little finger on his right hand then closing it to halfway to represent erectile dysfunction.) "Not a problem sir," Wiggy replied, before adding, "Isn't that more likely to happen to a bloke when he's approaching 40?" Grinning he left the studio, larking about with a couple of his mates, leaving Mark alone with Lizzie. "That was great, just the right pitch for this lot."

"Thanks," she replied and, wrinkling her nose, "How was the Q&A?" He was touched by her apparent lack of confidence and felt the urge to encourage her, "Spot-on." He paused, wondering if it would be appropriate to mix business with pleasure, but couldn't help but seize the moment, "You still okay for Saturday night?"

"Sure," she replied. "How about the Cricketers at 8-ish followed by Italian?" he suggested. "Look forward to it." Smiling, she added, "Have you ever thought about going into training or counselling to young people?"

"No," he replied, "what makes you think I'd be any good at it?"

"Just the subtle way you discouraged that young man from drinking and smoking weed implying that it would lead to erectile dysfunction; textbook." With a slight frown and a shake of the head but still smiling she gathered up her bag and went to 'wash up' with the head of student services whilst Mark fast forwarded to Saturday night at 8pm. He had a date with Lizzie, confirmed. "Back of the net," he muttered, grinning, as he ushered the malingerers out of the studio and headed for an afternoon of Chaucer with an extra spring in his step.

*

"Now are you *sure* you don't want us to come with you and sit at a discreet distance away, for *when*, not *if* it all goes belly up?" This was the helpful offer from Janice, her co-worker and the author of penii-gate, who was having tea and cake with her and Lisa, her flatmate, on a typical grey, wet Saturday afternoon of chilling and chatting as they mulled over the week that was and finalised plans for whatever night out was on the horizon. Janice was a divorcee in her early thirties, a fiercely liberal, independent, and bordering on man-hating woman still bitter and raw from an acrimonious divorce and towards a husband who'd cheated on her with their next-door neighbour who, ironically, they'd both been supporting when *her* husband had left her for another woman. She was part of the same team who worked with vulnerable females as Lizzie but in another part of town, including the more challenging Moulescoomb and Whitehawk areas, tackling whatever came her way with a blend of compassion and assertiveness that Lizzie found both compelling and inspiring. Janice had taken Lizzie under her wing when she had joined as a graduate trainee, and she still liked to play the protective role. Her failed marriage coupled with Lizzie losing her mother to cancer the year before increased her maternal instincts towards this pretty, petite and, in her eyes, still in some cases, naïve young woman.

Excusing herself from this gentle banter, with a promise to text her friends if she felt the date was going south, Lizzie ran a hot deep bath whilst perched on the side of it, absent-mindedly watching the exotic fruits bath bomb disintegrate, disperse and froth up before lowering herself gently into it, slowly sinking herself to chin level beneath the scented foam. Laying back and examining the ceiling, her dark hair piled up haphazardly on top of her head to prevent it getting soaked with the sticky suds, she sighed and closed her eyes, allowing the aroma of pineapple and papaya to relax and soothe her senses as she braced herself once more for the prospect of a first date. Janice thought she was mad to be going on a date with 'that grinning try-hard' that had so wound her up on their first meeting at the safe sex seminar. In fact, Mark had wound her up also with his pedantic interjection but she had soon warmed to this slightly disorganised and dishevelled academic, with a part of her wanting to shake him out of his apparent lethargy whilst at the same time reassuring him that he didn't need to be someone he wasn't. Like Janice, she could see that he was trying way too hard, whether to catch her eye, or impress her with a witty remark, but there was nothing flashy or fake about him. She had been with Tony, a retail area sales manager for two years, before finding out that he'd taken the term 'playing away' far too literally when off with his Saturday afternoon football team. Then there was Alex, the model and singer, who was far more in love with himself than he ever was going to be with her, so why not go for an average looking regular guy who wasn't so full of his own self-importance that he wouldn't just pay lip service to all that she found interesting or of value in life. What was it with men, she wondered, her already flushed face warming to the task of, well, taking men to task. They invite a girl out to dinner and waffle on about how amazing they are and expect you to remain gripped, head tilted to one side, eyes wide open in admiration as they describe in detail how they closed the deal, volleyed the extra time winner, stole the show, got short listed for a Calvin Klein commercial whilst all the time thinking, any minute now they're going to ask me about my life, my job, my highs and lows, likes and dislikes, what makes me tick, but no, it transpires that after they had talked at me all evening they then expected me to first fall into a cab with them and then into their bed to be wowed further by their sexual prowess. She can still see the expression on the faces of some blokes as she thanked them politely for a nice evening and hailed her own taxi home. When would they understand that a woman is far more impressed by a man's ability to listen and respond, to take an interest in them and their views rather than harp on about their own bloody sales pipelines and number of crunch sit-ups they can do in a minute?

Somehow she didn't see Mark fitting this stereotype. He had kind blue eyes, short tousled dark hair with a hint of grey creeping into the temples, was under 6ft and maybe a pound or two overweight but after Alex' obsession with his six pack she could cope. At least when she was chatting to him in the common room at the college (after he'd made a complete arse of himself doing Alan Partridge and David Brent impersonations – that would be trying if he repeated those tonight) he seemed to be listening intently to her whilst she described her work, albeit he seemed to wince at his coffee and kept rolling his tongue along the roof of his mouth that was a bit off-putting. She hoped he'd get rid of the slightly aging, scruffy greying stubble as well as a habit of grinning whilst eating, but she would just let the evening run its course and not go out holding any great expectations, that way she could only be pleasantly surprised.

The cold tap dripped its usual beat, reminding him that it had been nearly a year since it needed replacing. He was aching more than usual on account of him actually bringing his 'A-game' that morning and running Vaz close, even winning a set on a tiebreak before capitulating in the third and deciding set. He'd also opted for a salad and a mineral water at the pub afterwards as he felt his T-shirt was just a bit too tight for his liking when throwing the ball up to serve. Admittedly, his diet did include a few too many carbs and he wanted to look as lean as he could for his date with Lizzie; hence the extended soak in the bath/sauna; every little bit counts. Earlier, he'd booked a table for two for 9pm at the Restaurant Donatello, a popular 'genuine' Italian dining experience in the heart of the Lanes, a short stagger from the Cricketers pub, where he was meeting Lizzie at 8pm that evening. Every time he had seen her she had dressed in a sort of urban chic style, with a definite Italian influence, so he'd been mulling over what to wear in order not to look out of place on her arm. He'd thrown a few options out on the bed and was leaning towards a grey Firetrap shirt, untucked over classic vintage style Gap jeans topped off with Converse baseball boots and a black pinstriped suit jacket he'd picked up in a second-hand shop; not too scruffy, not too dressy. As he was that little bit older than Lizzie (he hadn't dared ask but could work that bit out) he'd cultivated the George Clooney look with three days' worth of stubble creating a sense of self-assured maturity and masculinity. It was vital that he looked the part so that she would be struck by his cool, 'hip without even trying look' right from the word go; who dares wins!

She winced as the razor more raked than glided up her shins, her right leg elevated out of the bath that was now more streaky lukewarm water than scalding exotic froth. The things we women do to comply with the media's idea of ideal she thought, knowing that Janice would be nodding along in approval at this observation. She didn't know quite why she was bothering to shave her legs as she was going to wear an old pair of faded blue jeans over vintage tan cowboy boots and would certainly not be taking them off in company at the end of the night, so why endure this torture? It was the same principle with lingerie, however; sometimes the La Senza bra with matching lace knickers made her feel good about herself, it wasn't about trying to look good for a man but feeling sexy in yourself was empowering and bred confidence. Despite the uplifting lacy bra she would opt for the black polo neck jumper, keeping her cleavage under wraps so Mark should be able to maintain eye contact throughout the evening without that added distraction. A short vintage tan leather jacket would top off the look, with hair half up in a quasi-messy style to emphasise the informal nature of this 'date'. She wanted to look good but not that good as it was important that Mark was interested in her personality and life philosophy and didn't major on appearances. Nothing ventured, nothing gained.

First night nerves

For once he got somewhere early. He was determined for this night not to be written off before it had even begun so he'd left himself 'ample time' (a phrase his mum often used) to mosey down London Road past the rows of shabby white goods and second-hand stores that lined this scruffy end of town. On past the Duke of York, the independently run cinema that wouldn't show a movie unless it had subtitles with an audience more inclined to be munching on raw carrots than popcorn, and through the town in twilight. Shuttered stores, garbage strewn gutters, empty bus stops; this was the transition time between shopping, dropping, soaking, preening and once more into the breach dear friends. He loved the rough around the edges feel of Brighton, able to look beyond the Mother Earth dance groups and esoteric workshops to embrace this shabby chic resort that seemed almost defiant in its resistance to the invasion of the capital's flat pack living solutions, with its ready-made luxury apartments, shared pools and clean functional spaces that masqueraded as homes. This was a town with a soul, a heartbeat, a connectivity that had nothing to do with ley lines but a desire to exist within a community that itself sat outside the mortgage fixated career climbing and second home culture that was slowly gripping the nation like social bindweed, slowly infiltrating, almost going unnoticed and then bloody hard to shake off once it had taken root. Bridging the gap between the shops emptying and the bars filling up was the rich and varied café culture that gave Brighton more than just a whiff of the European. He knew of other towns in England that had tried to embrace this philosophy, thinking that simply by placing silver metal tables and chairs out onto the crowded pavement a new way of restrained and civilised continental style socialising would evolve overnight. The reality was, however, that those outside tables would be filled by exactly the same punters that would usually occupy the bar inside; whether red faced hedge fund managers with open-necked pink shirts rah rah-ing over bucketfuls of Pinot Grigio or plaster spattered tracksuit bottomed builders blowing their pay packets on sickly blue coloured vodka flavoured shots; their excesses simply now spilling out onto the streets for all to see. A culture was determined by people rather than town planning or strategy and here the majority seemed to grasp just that, the indigenous set didn't have to try – they were comfortable in their own skins – and if you fancied a latte or pot of Earl Grey over a pint of lager at 7pm then why not? Not for him maybe, but he could certainly appreciate the ambience that the gentle buzz of murmured conversations from open door eateries on street corners generated even at this time of the year, keeping the town's pulse ticking over before the pace picked up once more.

Nestled on the fringes of The Lanes, just off the seafront, was The Cricketers, one of his favourite pubs in Brighton, an honest boozer that effortlessly managed to house a conventional snug bar and saloon with a flag-stoned drinking/dining area without the sense of either being incongruous. He ordered a pint of Amstel and a packet of salted peanuts at the small bar that seemed to him to be some sort of an anti-gastro pub protest; carpeted, with wallpaper of flowery pink and red swirls upon which hung gilt-edged portraits of characters from the Victorian era, small low dark wood tables with black wrought iron legs with matching red velvet topped stools, a cramped or by today's standards, intimate drinking area. He dodged his way through the already busy bar, with some drinkers opting to stand, through to the more spacious drinking and eating area that had double doors that opened out onto a small outside drinking area in the spring and summer. He picked a table that looked out through these glass double doors over the lightly rain stained streets, took a deep breath, unsure as to which direction Lizzie would be coming from and took in the all too familiar surroundings that up until now he had always taken for granted. The floor that he had always seen as cobbled due to their slightly wobbly feel was more akin to large grey slabs of chocolate, more uniform than he had given them credit for (maybe that said something about the state he was usually in when attempting to get a firm footing), from floor to a wooden dido rail about four feet up were vertical wooden panels and above it the brick walls had all been painted a deep red, tying in with the décor of the snug bar.

He liked the retro metal ads that adorned them, Guinness, Coca Cola, Jack Daniel's and even for Brasso and noticed for the first time the wooden beamed ceiling and random bric-a-brac such as an old gramophone and clay cider casks. The distressed bookshelf that was hung on the wall adjacent to where he leaned carried a sign that read, 'There will be no working during drinking hours' that made him smile. He took a sip of lager and absent-mindedly began to grapple with the packet of peanuts whilst looking back on to the streets, his heart racing as he imagined the petite street lamp-lit frame of Lizzie picking her way through the puddles on her way to meet HIM!

The reality was she had entered the pub without him spotting her, for as he was attempting to tear the peanuts open with his teeth, wrestling with the packet as if a lion with a freshly killed antelope, he felt a light tap on his shoulder. This made him jump and the action of suddenly jerking his head up whilst his teeth were still attached to the bag of KPs saw the small bag rip open with the tiny oval shaped salty snacks spewing out across the table and onto the floor below. He looked up, a small slither of shiny bright blue plastic-coated packaging caught between his front teeth, to see Lizzie standing over him, a Greek goddess aglow in vintage leather and denim, smiling nervously down. Let the date commence, he thought wryly!

There was a song, 'Why did it always rain on me' by one of the slightly whiny new wave of indie bands that his students all had on a drip-feed into their brains via their iPods. He felt at times that this song was written for him, and his life. He was just about to get settled into a cool, confident, man about town pose when Lizzie had crept up on him making him jump out of his skin and spill peanuts all over the floor. He was embarrassed and so rushed to get up to greet her, knocking the table with his knee and spilling about an eighth of his pint at the same time. She'd barely reacted to his awkwardness and held her stance, looking ravishing, her dark hair piled up but with long strands teased down either side, tight fitting black jumper and worn jeans showing off a stunning figure, her slim waist emphasised by the short tan leather jacket and her height slightly elevated by some über cool and well-worn Cuban heeled cowboy boots. Maybe she hadn't noticed his fumbling attempts at impressing her after all?

After Mark had apologised for the peanut and lager spillage, attempting to mop the latter up with what looked like a grey pocket handkerchief, he had thrown her by lunging at either cheek, scraping her left side with his stubble before asking her what was 'her poison'. She eased herself into a seat that would place him to her right and the floor to ceiling windows to her left as he went to get her a G&T. It was clear that he would never get the call to screen test for the next 007 as he possessed an unnerving talent for bumping into furniture, a few rungs down the suave ladder that she was sure he aspired to. No wardrobe disaster, however, although she did prefer a man to tuck their shirts in, particularly once they passed the age of 30. Thankfully no earring or ponytail but the stubble that he obviously thought added a touch of the upwardly mobile looked more down and out to her, but he had clearly made such an effort to make it look like he'd made none, that she'd go along with it, refusing to burst his bubble as he was trying desperately not to act like an excitable puppy looking to bestow its affections on a new owner.

"G&T please mate, ice and a slice if you have it."

"Sure mate, large one?"

"Single is fine, thanks."

He was conscious that ordering a woman/young lady a double without her consent amounted to a crime a few short steps from sexual assault in the current climate so decided it was best to play it with a straight bat, he was in the Cricketers after all. Having avoided a potentially disastrous first impression on their first date (he hoped she saw it as a date, despite how

49

casually he'd packaged the offer) he felt confident once more. She hadn't baulked at his outfit, maybe he detected a slight wince as he kissed her on both cheeks (look mum French kissing and I haven't even bought her a drink yet) but that was probably because she worked in the public sector and wasn't used to such flamboyance. The realisation that his life may appear mysterious and arty to the more mundane circles she operated within gave him just that extra swagger as he made his way back through the lounge area and towards their corner table. As he entered this dimly lit space once more he was struck by just how stunning Lizzie was. The soft glow from a street light had illuminated her face as she sat, still, eyes fixed on the various passers-by, their shoulders hunched as a chill sea breeze began to explore the lanes and alleys towards which these diners and drinkers now scurried. He felt like someone had given him a short straight jab to the stomach as he took her in and then strode towards her after being nudged in the back by a bloke struggling to carry three pints without spilling any of the precious golden cargo on the uneven grey slabs. He loved the fact that she wasn't constantly checking her mobile phone; that annoying default mode for so many of his students, as if not checking was to miss out. No, she was just sitting, people watching and waiting for their evening to begin, either not noticing or choosing to ignore something of a false start.

He felt that he made a quick recovery as the conversation slipped comfortably into what they had both been doing since the midweek talk in the drama studio. Sure, he'd omitted to tell her that he had rewarded himself for bagging a date with her by watching back-to-back Star Wars movies all the following afternoon and perhaps had exaggerated how close that morning's game had been with Vaz, but she seemed to take it all in, asking questions and smiling in all the right places. He made sure that he was equally attentive when she described some of the sessions and courses she'd led since the drugs and alcohol seminar and he'd been totally suckered when she suggested they nipped to the loo to do a bag of coke she'd been handed by the head of student services who had confiscated it from a student. As the evening unfurled he came to realise that she had a great understated sense of humour that wouldn't be out of place on 'Have I Got News for You' (witty and dry). His slightly more edgy, animated brand seemed the perfect balance. Over drinks and bread sticks in Donatello's, he wowed her by recounting word for word the scene from 'I'm Alan Partridge' when Partridge is lunching with Tony Hayers from the BBC attempting to impress him and win a new TV contract, even going so far as to asking the waiter what the 'Action Man pasta bow ties' were called and suggesting that Lizzie 'smell my cheese' when the Parmesan was delivered (whilst leaving out 'you mother'). He was chuffed that he managed to seamlessly infuse their evening with classic comedy that was totally relevant to their scenario; the mark of a genius. She was that impressed that she'd smiled coyly and admitted, "I'd never realised until now what an aphrodisiac Alan Partridge quotes over dinner were." This made him choke and he also dropped his spoon clankily into his bowl of spaghetti and spicy meat balls, splashing tomato sauce out onto the tablecloth. He thought he'd got away with that one though, likewise when his fork speared a vine tomato from their shared mixed salad (she had shared, a good sign) and the taught skin had burst sending a shower of pips and juice all over his shirt and even onto his left shoulder. Fortunately, he was a dab hand at concealing these petit faux pas.

Despite the endless overcooked Alan Partridge quotes she found his company easy and for the most part enjoyable. She'd cringed when he'd established that, whilst he wouldn't snort a line of commandeered coke in a grubby loo in a Brighton pub he might be persuaded if she and a four-poster bed in the Grand Hotel were involved (!) possibly the most uncomfortable part of the evening. But equally she found it endearing that he had abandoned the unwritten rules of a first date (other than to suggest naked drug taking in a nearby hotel room) in that he'd chosen the spiciest, messiest and most difficult dish to eat with any shred of dignity from the main course menu. She joked that he actually looked like the Joker with a symmetrical smear of Bolognese sauce on each cheek creating that famous twisted grin and then tried hard not to notice the tomato pips he wore on the epaulette of his designer shirt, like a high-ranking fruit and veg officer. She'd also genuinely laughed at his Hannibal Lecter impersonation when ordering a bottle of Chianti and was touched that he had asked her about her friends and home life as well as her colleagues and work. He talked animatedly about a play he was co-writing with a fellow lecturer that was set in the First World War and his Sassoon and Owen quotes were a welcome break from Coogan and Gervais. She could see that underneath this slightly self-conscious and socially deficient clown there was a sensitive and intelligent bloke bursting to get out and she wondered if she might just stick around a little longer to discover what that might look like.

He thought that, as far as first dates went, this one was text book. No awkward moments or uneasy silences, a steady flow of conversation and laughter, and before he knew it, coffee and the delicate subject of what next. He had been pinching himself all night if he was to be honest, for here at last was a girl as stunning as those he'd seen on magazine covers but with warmth and depth to go with her amazing looks. At first, he'd been struck by her dark eyes and hair but had since been drawn to her mouth, full lips and perfect straight white teeth, a small beauty spot perched beneath her left nostril, her nose totally in proportion with the rest of her features. When she had excused herself to pop to the loo after their second espresso he had gazed, becoming almost trance-like, at her backside as she swayed her hips to move elegantly between the many tables crammed into the heaving restaurant. She had grace, poise and class, so what on earth did she see in him he wondered? He sat back and placed his arms behind his head, slightly frowning as he gestured for the bill from the waiter who, he'd thought, had been a tad too attentive and tactile towards Lizzie, as if to say, 'forget it mate, she's taken'. The evening was now poised on a knife edge. He didn't want to suggest going back to his place as it was a dump and he couldn't assume she'd invite him back to hers, but he'd be kicking himself if he brought the evening to a premature close when she may be hoping to keep it going, for a while longer at least. He moved consciously into a nonchalant pose, stroking his chin with his left hand as he swirled the remains of the thick, black liquid around the tiny white cup with his right, creating the image of the moody artist contemplating his next move as Lizzie made her way back across the crowded room, head tilted slightly down, clearly oblivious to the admiring glances she was attracting, causing one woman who looked to be in her late 40s to elbow her husband in the ribs, making a gesture that he should pick his jaw up from the floor before she closed it for him. She slid back into her seat and smiled nervously. Normally the icebreaker comes at the beginning of the evening he thought, so decided to take the initiative.

"So, now to the bit where we arm wrestle over the bill."

"No problem, Mark, let's just split it shall we?"

"If you're sure."

"Absolutely."

"It's been a lovely evening Lizzie and I'd love to see more of you, I mean, you know, go out again sometime, unless you'd like to go on somewhere from here?"

"I've really enjoyed the evening too Mark, thank you, and yes to meeting up again but I'll grab a cab home now as I've a busy day tomorrow."

For a moment, he had to pause and process the last part of the sentence that over-rode even her agreeing to meet him again. Busy, Sunday, somehow it didn't compute. For him Sunday was the slowest, laziest, least busy day of the week, who was ever busy on a Sunday other than vicars and supermarket cashiers?

"They make you work on a Sunday? Talk about a pound of flesh."

"No, not work, church. I'm part of a prayer ministry team in the morning and a friend is getting baptised in the evening, so it'll be a pretty full on day."

"Sorry, I'm a bit confused all of a sudden. You're a part-time vicar and have a friend who is six months old?"

She laughed at this. "No, I'm not a part-time vicar and my friend is Lisa my flatmate who is 27 and is having a believer's baptism at our home church, I've been her sponsor." For Mark, an occasional member of the good old solid CofE she was talking a whole new language and he was surprised to hear that the church she 'worshipped at' was also part of the Church of England. Apparently, it was a charismatic evangelical church planted by HTB (a bank, he had joked) just a few years earlier. It turned out that, according to Lizzie, these 'new-fangled' churches had young vicars who didn't wear robes or swing incense (some were even women), ordinary people without dog collars who led 'prayer ministry' and adults who got baptised in what she described as 'full immersion' in a huge pool, as Lizzie had earlier that year. Despite the subject matter being of a religious nature, Mark drifted off momentarily, picturing Lizzie in a white bikini, rising up through the water like a modern day, holy Ursula Andress whilst he waited, Bond like, to wrap her in a towelling robe. In order to claw himself back to some semblance of reality he shared a little about his church back home, or 'home church' as he'd now call it, of his mum's involvement in the flower arranging and church fetes but he couldn't help but feel that it all sounded incredibly Dibley-esque in comparison to her edgy church or place of worship as she referred to it, with its worship band and worship leader and street outreach team, a far cry from raffles, homemade cake stalls and renditions of 'Jerusalem' that he remembered thunderously concluding Sunday Communion services when he was young.

In a way, her involvement with this church came as a huge relief to him. At least that would mean she wouldn't be out drinking or clubbing every Saturday night, the object of desire to hordes of beery, leery blokes.

On the other hand, being so gorgeous would mean she'd stick out like a sore thumb in a church so she must be fighting those oily bible bashers off with a stick. He decided to keep these musings to himself until he worked out which was the most favourable scenario for him. They left a neat pile of crisp notes fresh from the cashpoint earlier that evening on the small saucer that held the bill, decorating it with a scattering of coins to help console the waiter as Mark gently placed an arm around her shoulder and led her towards the door, being held open by Luigi's ogling twin brother. He shivered involuntarily as they stepped onto the street outside as the air had turned icy, a chill wind scattering raindrops with every gust. They wandered up towards North Street, her arm now linked through his, to where the garish green taxis snaked around the block, red eyed drivers weary from daytime chit-chat and endless word searches, bracing themselves for the rowdy Saturday night crowd. Despite the freezing cold he'd decided to walk home so he waved her off, still glowing from her delicate peck on his cheek, soft touch on his arm and agreement to meet the following week. Turning the collar on his suit jacket up he plodded, head down, along the rain splattered street lined pavements once more, looking every bit a Billy no-mates when the reality was, he felt more like Charlie Bucket on finding the last golden ticket.

Life begins at forty

He always had mixed feelings about the drive back to the family home in Dorset. Okay, he loved the route from Brighton, along the A27 bypassing Portsmouth and Southampton before picking up the A31 towards Ringwood, the New Forest and the Dorset coast, but the joy he felt as he passed such picturesque land and seascapes was tinged with the apprehension felt of yet another year deemed as a failure in the eyes of his parents. They hadn't voiced it in so many words, not in recent years anyway; in fact his mother in particular was always incredibly sweet and listened intently as he talked about college life, the students, the bars, festivals and comedy clubs in Brighton, Mrs Sheridan, his writing with Pete; but he always felt like he still had something to prove, and that he had never quite grown up in their eyes, especially that of his father's, who still seemed to be waiting for him to get a 'proper job'. Parental expectation can be a killer. They say they want what is best for you in life because they love you but when you *know* what's best for your life differs considerably from what they *think* they know is best for you the cracks begin to appear.

He was never going to go into the world of business or finance and despite his father's lectures on the value of solid commercial and fiscal foundations he shuddered at the thought of suits, collars and ties, of handshakes and high fives, of joint ventures, alternative stock markets and share prices, diversification, organic growth and that through acquisition, despite this being the language of the breakfast table when he was growing up. He'd preferred the worlds of the Silver Surfer and the Dark Knight, complex, brooding characters and bold stories with dramatic outcomes. He could still recall the look on his father's face when he'd raced home from a comic convention to exclaim proudly how he'd been to London to invest the money he'd been given for his 16th birthday. His father's glowing look of pride on the mention of the word investment (he can still remember his mother beaming as she leaned against the Aga) had swiftly turned to one of utter disbelief and despair as he had produced an early original copy of Marvel's The X-Men, still in its cellophane wrap and declared it a snip at £95.

He'd long since given up competing with Johnnie, the apple of his father's eye, and zoned out when their after-dinner conversation turned to boardroom battles and the cut and thrust of the commercial arena, or 'space' as they now referred to it. The broad evolution of language interested him though. Who had decided and when, for example, that a war zone, or killing field would now be termed 'the theatre'? And since when did the innocent civilian casualties of war become classed as 'collateral damage'? Rather than engage with their talk of punchy investors and ballsy sales predictions he would make obtuse comments designed to challenge but usually with the effect of causing irritation. At one Christmas dinner, when he was at home from university, and when the maritime heritage of the family business was being saluted yet again, he had questioned if he was the only one who had felt uncomfortable that the family empire had been founded partly upon the shipment of slaves from African colonies to the New World in the 18th century, and that the bricks that had built their grand Victorian villa that overlooked the very sea that transported these unfortunates were, fittingly, red. Did they not feel that they had blood on their hands? That had gone down well. Suddenly the party hats had seemed to wilt and the party poppers were overshadowed by this party pooper who had so many chips on his shoulders he was in danger of sinking in the gravy boat as silence descended and all that could be heard were the sounds of forks screeching on the best family dinner service.

The older he got the less antagonistic he felt towards his family. He'd felt frustrated as a teenager and young adult that for his father in particular there was only one way, and that was his way. He had loathed the chummy relationship between father and eldest son and how he assumed the role of the runt of the litter, slinking off to record shops and gigs in Weymouth whilst Johnnie earned his stripes in the family business at its Head Office in Poole. He'd even managed to avoid the potential ice-berg when he informed the 'old man' that he was leaving the world of shipping to embrace new media and multi-channel marketing (whatever that was) by agreeing to remain on the board and to give assurances that he would take over as Chairman when dad stepped down. It was about this time that Mark had gone to his father cap in hand as he had written off the classic Mini Cooper that he'd been bought for his eighteenth birthday after wrapping it around a lamp post on the way home from a festival on the Isle of Wight. He had learned over the years to carry and then release this burden of expectation, experiencing the liberation that comes through the realisation that he was his own man, capable of making independent life decisions free from the weight of guilt and shame that he was not living up to the Woodford name. He was determined to strike out and make a new name for himself, to leave his mark through literary greatness, something that would resonate with society in a way an import/export business never could. He had first moved into a shared house in Bournemouth before gradually migrating east via a seafront flat in Southsea and finally a waterfront apartment in Arundel before inheriting the house in Brighton. He had found the discipline of writing more challenging than he'd imagined and began to drift, without anchor, through weeks and months, eating his way through his allowance with very little to show for it. He was fast approaching crunch point, a financial ground zero, when his lovely godmother, who cared little for big business, finding fulfilment in the smallest things (such as picking the first primroses of spring or freshly laundered sheets on a 'good drying day') had passed away, leaving him her retirement home and saving him from the humility of having to ask his father to bail him out yet again.

"Penny for them, dreamer," Lizzie smiled as she stretched out her long limbs after an extended catnap in the passenger seat wrapped in her quilted coat, the bright winter sunshine pouring in through the passenger side window. If he was on his own he would have had the hood down and the music turned up but, given the options, he'd happily be in the position he was in, with Lizzie, now wearing her inquisitive expression, by his side. "Where are we?"

"Just heading past Dorchester, not long now." He grinned and put his left arm out towards her, she gave his hand a squeeze before he returned it to the steering wheel, keeping his eyes on the road ahead despite the lure of her just woken flush. "How long have I been asleep for?"

"Oh, just the entire journey, but don't worry, I'm used to it."

"What rubbish company I am." She smiled apologetically. "Lizzie, this journey has been just perfect, the sun is shining, I have you in the passenger seat and I'm allowing the usual thoughts to wash over me as I cover the miles and the years as I head for home."

He had shared some of his teenage angst with her in the days preceding this visit, once he'd got over the shock of her having accepted his invitation to join him for his forced family fortieth birthday celebrations. They had begun dating regularly after their dinner at Donatello's, mixing trips to the cinema with open mic comedy nights, walks along the beach, pub lunches, in fact everything he'd ever dreamt of doing once he had found the right girlfriend to do it with. In fact the one thing they hadn't done was, well, it. She had said kindly but firmly that there would be no 'hanky-panky' in the foreseeable future so he'd better get used to the idea. Somehow this only served to make her even more ethereal and desirable in his eyes; that she was so confident in herself and her beliefs that it didn't bother her that she was flying in the face of the accepted norm. He'd never been one to swim with the tide so had respected her even more for making her boundaries clear, despite fantasising about waking up to her. She had pulled down the sun visor and opened the vanity mirror that was set within it, the mirror squeaking when she lifted the cover, through a lack of WD40 and use. He could see her out of the corner of his eye, running her fingers through the side of her hair that had become tangled from her nap, then dabbing a finger under each eye in turn and lifted it gently to remove any smudged mascara before applying a thin film of lip balm to her full lips. "Got to make a good first impression." She smiled, sensing how she was distracting him, feeling a mixture of flattery and anxiety as they were now on a busy A-road in single file traffic. She had surprised herself by accepting his offer to celebrate his fortieth with his family, as they had only been seeing each other for a few weeks, but she felt safe in his company and was warming to him more with each date. He was funny, charming in a roundabout way and had layers which she was gently unwrapping, especially where his family were concerned. She felt that, whilst she would never act out of a sense of pity or duty, it would be something of a strike for the underdog for him to arrive triumphantly with a girl on his arm for such a milestone celebration, and felt delighted that she could play her part in helping to banish some of the ghosts that still haunted him.

"So, remind me of the agenda, your Lordship?" She grinned, gently winding him up. "Well, of course we'll start with a rousing rendition of the national anthem before lunch as we raise the family flag above the turrets," he replied with a smirk, knowing full well what she was up to. "Lunch should be a quiet affair with mum and dad then Johnnie, Sophie and their little darlings down for tea and cake, late afternoon. Tonight, we'll all be dining at a local Italian restaurant at 8pm, that most predictable of time for Brits to sit down for their evening meal, regardless of where on the planet they are." He recalled the first time he was on a Spanish island without his parents, with a group of mates, and how they dared to go out to eat at 9pm, but it was still way too early for the locals, with the restaurant heaving with English couples fanning themselves with their menus whilst ordering their desserts and coffee. "Well let's hope there are no rogue flying tomatoes tonight like the ones in Donatello's, as it may just be an Italian thing," she added, still smiling. "You noticed that?" he replied, his voice going up a pitch or two so he had to cough to clear it. "Why didn't you say?"

"What, and break the illusion of the masterful man about town, wooing yet another maiden with his impeccable storytelling and dining skills? Oh no, I thought I'd wait a while before letting you down gently. And I don't think we'll even mention contraband cocaine and the Grand Hotel, unless it just comes out after a couple of glasses of bubbly of course." He was just about to mention that he would actually have gone up in both his father and Johnnie's estimation if she had mentioned it when the turning to Charlestown off the A354 came into view. "Would passengers please brace themselves for a sharp descent into another era, with the warning of turbulence and a possible bumpy landing." He allowed himself to laugh half-heartedly but the old nerves had gripped his stomach once more.

Charlestown Manor was a handsome red brick villa built at the turn of the century on the site of the former manor house that had fallen into a state of disrepair. Situated at the end of a narrow private drive it balanced formal front gardens awash with conservative shrubs and rhododendron bushes with uncomplicated sweeping lawns to the rear allowing stunning uninterrupted views out across Chesil Beach and up towards Lyme Bay. The dark green painted front door was covered by a red tiled porch, held up by two now weathered white pillars, either side of which sat a leafy bay tree in large terracotta pots with assorted cracks and chips. To the right of the porch as you looked face on was the familiar black wrought iron boot scraper and faded cream metal garden bench. To the left was the neat white milk bottle container with the arrow now pointing to 3 to represent visitors, his mother being one of the few who still ordered their daily pinta/s. The wheels of the Z3 crunched their way slowly across the gravel towards the 'ample' parking area where his mother's shiny blue Suzuki Swift was parked, with frost still on the windscreen. His father's Aston would be tucked up in the garage for the winter and he would have taken the Range Rover to the nearby golf club for a round or two before lunch. Two large helium balloons, one a bright red 4 and the other a 0 looked out of place tied to the bay trees, bobbing in the late morning breeze. He felt a familiar lump in his throat as he parked alongside his mum's modest motor and turned off the ignition.

He'd barely opened the car door when his mum was scrunching her way across the gravel to greet them, arms open, warm smile, hair immaculate after her weekly appointment at the hairdresser's in the village. She was in her usual smart trousers, flat shoes, blouse, scarf and red cardigan combo with matching lipstick giving her the appearance of a minor royal. "Darling, how lovely to see you!" she exclaimed, hugging him, the familiar scent of Chanel No5 wafting in the sharp air of a winter morning. "And you must be Lizzie, my, let me have a look at you." As she made her way round to greet Lizzie like an old friend. "Aren't you gorgeous, what a catch!" as she flashed a grin towards Mark. "Now let's get you inside for a nice hot cup of coffee my dear." And with that she had linked arms with Lizzie and, with head bowed slightly to one side conspiratorially, she continued chatting and laughing her way inside. Mark smiled to himself, he loved the way his mum was as accepting of his girlfriends as his dad was disapproving, often gently chiding her husband as he mumbled a stock set of comments just out of earshot such as "Is that a skirt or a belt she's wearing." Or "That top doesn't leave much to the imagination." At least he'd have no cause for concern with Lizzie as she was the kind of girl that everyone took to immediately. He dragged their overnight bags out of the small boot, his a scruffy Quicksilver rucksack and hers a neat patterned Christian Dior with gold clasps, along with the winter arrangement he had picked up at a service station en route. (Lizzie had raised her eyebrows at this and told him never, ever to present her with a bunch of flowers that still smelled of petrol.) With rucksack over one shoulder, bag in one hand and flowers in the other, he glanced up at the rows of sash windows before setting foot across the familiar threshold once more.

He'd not remembered such a relaxed and enjoyable day at home since the summer of '76 when they had ignored the hosepipe ban and spent a long scorching summer leaping and whooping through the sprinklers in the garden. His father, ruddy cheeked from a round of golf and a large G&T in the clubhouse was on fine form, making a big deal of "No, no, please call me Henry," as Lizzie addressed him as Mr Woodford. Smart girl, Mark thought. His father had given him a firm handshake and a genuinely warm smile, addressing him as William, leading him to explain to a vexed looking Lizzie that his son had been christened William, Henry, Arthur, Mark Woodford in memory of his grandfather, father and great-grandfather but he had rejected the first three names as they were not deemed 'cool' enough and liked to be known as Mark. The difference here was that his father had no trace of bitterness or sarcasm in his voice but a new-found playfulness that Mark could only put down to winning his earlier game of fours, the effect of the Gordon's and, of course, Lizzie. She had an effortless charm, managing to say all the right things without a hint of insincerity, admiring the house, the portraits of the former Woodfords that adorned the walls of the entrance hall and the sweeping wooden stairway, his mum's furniture and best morning china, her soft furnishings, all evenly paced, not gushing but measured and genuine; Lizzie to a tee.

Lunch, a homemade game pie with new potatoes dripping in butter and piles of fresh veg, washed down with a bottle of St Emilion, had been an informal affair taken at the large scrubbed pine table in the huge kitchen, with the conversation flowing as easily as the wine. A combination of the pie, the warmth from the Aga and the effect of the Bordeaux red had left him feeling slightly woozy so he suggested that he and Lizzie got their overnight bags unpacked and then freshened up before Johnnie and his troops descended. His father even ventured into the unfamiliar territory of innuendo with a gentle nudge to his mother and a wink. "Freshen up eh June, that's what they're calling it nowadays." His mother, beaming, mock scolded him whilst ushering Lizzie and Mark out of the kitchen, not hearing a word of Lizzie's offer to help clear the table.

"Alone at lassht Mish Moneypenny," he said in his best Sean Connery accent, closing the door to her guest room behind them and turning to face her. "Oh James," she whispered breathlessly, fluttering those long eyelashes and continuing the charade. "We'd better leave the door open as I would hate for your family to think I am just like all your other girls." She flashed her winning smile at him as she opened the door to reveal the polished floorboards of the landing outside, decorated with a faded red patterned oriental rug, before striding into her room (or guest suite) and lowering herself into one of the armchairs that sat to either side of the tall, elegant, sash windows. "You have totally won them over," Mark began, "They both love you, I can tell!"

"And I think they are both charming," she replied, "Nowhere near as intimidating as you'd made out, not to undermine your childhood of course," she added, ever the sensitive. "Now I could do with an hour to unpack and put my feet up, do I ring a bell or something to call the butler when I want the bath run?"

"Very droll," he groaned, "But if you're looking for someone to scrub your back ..." At which point she had leaped out of the armchair to march him slowly back and out onto the landing, grinning all the time and, to him, looking more beautiful as ever before. "Just in case you change your mind, I'm in the red room at the end of the corridor, just knock three times and I'll know it's you." He grinned in vain as the varnished wooden door gently clicked in his face, sighed and, shaking his head playfully made his way along the corridor that was punctuated at every few feet by bright shafts of winter sunshine containing dancing particles of dust.

She pulled her feet up underneath her and took in her surroundings. She had known of but never experienced such wealth first hand. Growing up in the small village of Funtington her family knew the local landed gentry, with their Land Rover Defenders, shoots and rugby tournaments but they had always been on the outside looking in. Her dad had worked in the planning department for the Town Council in Chichester and her mum, God rest her soul, had been a part-time librarian so although comfortable enough in their three-bed flint cottage, holidays were saved for and were an annual rather than seasonal occurrence. But this, this was something else. From what she could gather from a quick scan as they came in, and from interrogating Mark on their way up the stairs, there was a kitchen, boot room, drawing room, study, dining room and even a library on the ground floor, with wine cellar below. The first floor boasted three double bedrooms, two with en suite bathrooms, a further family bathroom and a huge lounge with open fireplace. She and Mark were billeted to the second floor where there were a further two guest suites along with a sewing room and at least one single bedroom (probably for a maid). The enormous attic had, apparently, been boarded out and contained the usual mixture of packing boxes stuffed with children's toys, metal trunks full of old letters and yellowing photographs and, she suspected, a vast wardrobe crammed with fur coats that just kept going back and back towards a magical snowscape ...

Her room (the yellow room) had walls painted in a matt lemon colour that was stylish and soothing. The two deep armchairs were upholstered in broad yellow and white stripes and the brass bed was made up with crisp white linen under a pale yellow spread specked with pale blue cornflowers to match the material of the curtains. The floors, like those in the landing, were of dark oak, highly polished and finished off with rugs in various sizes and states of disrepair. This is how she had imagined a moneyed family home to look, austere in places but lived-in throughout, with no need to re-furbish with every new interior design whim or celebrity sofa launch. She pulled off her boots with a sigh of relief and made her way gingerly towards the open door to the rest of her quarters, careful not to slip on the floorboards that seemed more prominent than rug. Pushing the door open fully she was taken aback to find a small lounge, complete with open fire, made up, an occasional table, small sofa, bookcase and a writing desk with views across the lawn and the bay, the same views that she would wake up to in the morning. Letting out a small 'wow' she moved on into the bathroom, again the same polished wooden floor and lemon walls with a quaint white roll top bath dominating the room. The fixtures and fittings were all modern but in a Victorian style, with a high cistern affixed to the wall, with the chain hanging down to a wooden handle. The taps were wide at the bottom with the handles the type of design that Mark's brother probably had in cufflinks. Time to make myself at home she thought, turning on the taps to the bath and then heading back to the bedroom to find her toiletry bag and soak essentials.

He lay back on the black wrought iron bed and stared at the crisp white ceiling that met the deep red walls with dramatic effect and let sleep creep slowly upon him. He had set his alarm for 3:30pm knowing that his brother would be down at 4pm so time for a kip and a shower before the peace was shattered. Outside came the familiar and haunting sound of a solitary gull, drifting high above the breakers that crashed and foamed upon the rocks below. Despite some difficult moments when he was growing up it was still comforting to be at home, the reassuring smell of polish, wax jackets and wood smoke, the creaking floorboards, the warmth of the Aga, the homemade pie, the rhythm of the ocean, he nestled his back deeper into the plush eiderdown and let his heavy lids close.

"Happy Birthday Uncle Maaaaaaarrrrrrk," was what he heard in his dream but then he felt a small figure using him as a trampoline and woke with a start to find his nephew Harry bouncing up and down on the bed, Johnnie leaning on the door frame. "Hold the front page, Mark Woodford in sleeping away the afternoon shock," he mocked. "Hello Harry, hello brother dear," Mark mumbled, still attempting to recover from such a rude awakening. "What's the time anyway?"

"Just after half two, managed to get away early as Sophie and Tiggy only packed just the one Louis Vuitton case each as opposed to the usual four." That meant that Mark had enjoyed all of 20 minutes sleep. "So, where's the totty?" Johnnie blurted, comically pulling up the bedclothes from the bottom and pantomime peering under the bed, "she's got to be around here somewhere, where have you hidden her you rogue?"

"Very good, but she had to cancel on account of a last-minute swimwear photo shoot in Barbados so Elle McPherson is flying into Bournemouth airport at 5pm to take her place for dinner. Couldn't take Harry and pick her up for me could you?"

"Okay we get the hint, come on little man, let's leave Hugh Hefner here to get into his silk dressing gown. See you for tea and cake in a bit." Mark sat up on the bed and scratched his head. What was it with his brother's family and waking him up? He thought he'd grab a hot shower and go face the music, as they always insisted on a hearty rendition of happy birthday, regardless of age and ageless repetition.

Refreshed and changed into dark blue jeans, a crisp white Ted Baker shirt that Lizzie had bought for him, along with the black V-necked woollen jumper, he descended the stairs two at a time, partly out of habit and partly as Lizzie hadn't answered when he'd knocked on her bedroom door and he dreaded her being left in the clutches of Johnnie. As he bounded into the lounge (he refused to call it the drawing room) he was relieved to find just Sophie, poised elegantly on the edge of a chaise longue, Blackberry in hand, regulation sunglasses pushed on top of her blonde bob despite it being November and Tiggy reading the latest Harry Potter on a rug in front of the fire, kicking her legs in the air absent-mindedly. Johnnie and Harry were apparently in the library fiddling with something with his father and his mum was getting the afternoon tea ready. In the far corner of the room was a pile of brightly wrapped presents, one of which was tied with a piece of ribbon that had a Spider-Man helium balloon attached. He was just thinking of what to say to Sophie that wouldn't result in the temperature of the room plummeting when he felt two hands around his waist and a peck on his cheek. Despite his mother boasting to her book club friends that he'd 'French kissed' her, she would never have put her hands around his waist like that; thank the Lord above, it was Lizzie, looking and smelling divine, fresh from her long soak. Not waiting for Mark to make introductions Lizzie strode across to Sophie, hand extended, "Gosh, Mark told me his sister-in-law was a stunner and he's not wrong there, I'm Lizzie, lovely to meet you." Sophie didn't know quite how to react, repulsed at the thought that Mark might have described her in that way (he hadn't) but flattered that a woman a few years her junior (and quite a knockout herself) greeted her with such a compliment. "And delighted to meet you also." With one deft movement Lizzie had taken Sophie's hand and perched next to her. "And you must be Tiggy of course, no please don't get up, you carry on with The Deathly Hallows, it's quite brilliant, isn't it?" If the government ever made cuts in the public sector there was always a career waiting for her in the Diplomatic Corps, Mark thought, glowing with pride at how naturally Lizzie was ingratiating herself to all and sundry.

"Well hello, what have we here?" came the booming voice of his brother as he strode into the room, Harry trotting along behind with a mischievous look in his eye. "Tell you what, Lizzie, if that is your real name, whatever he's paying you I'll give you double." Johnnie had a habit of roaring with laughter at his ribald comments but was cut short by a laser look from The Duchess (as Mark referred to Sophie when she was out of earshot). "Ahem," he continued, smiling apologetically at the two ladies whilst also nodding at Harry who dutifully switched off the lights, leaving just the glow from the fire to light the room. "Birthday tea is served."

His mother looked like a glamorous land army girl, lipstick freshly applied and face beaming as the candles on the huge cake lit up her still youthful face. She placed it on the mahogany sideboard and ushered the assembled group to gather round. His father, who had recently and after years of resistance 'gone digital' was poised to capture this one for the family album, or desktop folder as he now joked. Lizzie gently nudged Mark forwards for the obligatory candle blowing and he smiled at this nod to his past (not distant enough as Sophie would no doubt be thinking) as the writing read, **Fantastic 40**, decorated with the iced superheroes themselves. Mr Fantastic was hanging upside down from the end of the 4 and The Thing smashed his way through the 0. There was even room for the Silver Surfer, he was impressed. "Mum, you shouldn't have," he started, "but as you have, where did you get the ideas for the characters from? You used to get them all muddled up when I was a kid."

"Well, dear, there was a stack of your old magazines up in the attic and I used those for inspiration. Apparently, it took Alison at the bakers ages to get their dimensions right."

"Blimey!" exclaimed Johnnie, "good job it wasn't the other stash of his favourite magazines you found up there or we'd have a different set of dimensions to get right on the cake altogether, although I can see where the glazed cherries would come in useful." Mark didn't even have to respond as Sophie, smile still fixed, delivered another withering look that cut him off in full flow. Mark dutifully blew out the blazing array of red and blue candles to their chorus and then they all settled down, his mother busying herself serving tea and squash whilst Johnnie moaned that Mark had a bigger piece of cake than him, to which Mark had told him he was watching his waistline for him as Johnnie was clearly unable to see it any more. Johnnie always had an answer and usually a smutty one at that, now making proud reference to his 'balcony' that overlooked the 'playground', one that saw far more activity than Mark's ever did. Lizzie sat back into the deep-seated sofa and quietly took it all in, the grand but lived-in surroundings, the boyish banter of the two brothers, the quiet, deft touches of his mother and the suppressed pride of Mark's father as the gentle abuse continued to be handed out along with the birthday presents. She knew just how much Mark had been dreading this weekend and she felt strangely privileged to have been let into his private world and to have made such a positive impact on it; the Lizzie effect as Mark would come to call it.

From his parents, an array of household appliances including a Dyson upright, a wallpaper steam stripper and a cordless drill; quite a hint, along with a more light-hearted gift of china mug with 'Life begins at 40' emblazoned across it. The children had clubbed together to buy him a retro game of 'Blow Football' (that Harry immediately had taken back, unpacked and set up) and a set of Marvel Hero Top Trumps whilst Johnnie had presented him with a Sat Nav so he could stop 'buggering about' with AA Road Maps and start fantasising about Joanna Lumley whilst he was stuck in traffic. This raised a wry smile from Sophie who then handed Mark an envelope that contained two tickets to see the highly-acclaimed play 'War Horse' that had just opened at the National, with a night at a 'top London hotel' part of the package. Mark was genuinely taken aback, touched and grateful, not just at the generosity but at the fact that Sophie, who had chosen the gift, had done so knowing that he had a keen interest in theatre and in the First World War. She winced and stood still as a board as he hugged her and waved it all off as 'nothing really' just in time for Johnnie to lower the tone once more with his final offering, a DVD of the comedy '40-Year-Old Virgin' a film, he alleged, that was based on the true story of a scruffy part-time English teacher based in Brighton, but with the names changed 'to protect the innocent'. He laughed so much at his own gag that he choked on his last sliver of cake, needing a swig of Tiggy's squash to regain a semblance of composure to which his daughter stared disdainfully at both his antics and at the backwash that her red-faced father had left around the rim of her glass. Like mother like daughter, Lizzie reflected, whilst she grasped that with this family there clearly had to be a fair dose of humour amongst all the sincerity in gift-giving, otherwise it might all become a bit 'too American' as his Father had so succinctly put it at lunch earlier when describing some of the 'new money' members of his golf club, whooping it up after a fours, what with grown men hugging each other, whatever next. She wondered what he'd make of the Pride festival on Brighton sea- front and decided to make sure their dates to visit didn't clash. So, thinking of inviting them down already, she checked herself, don't get too carried away girlie, it's still early days.

Lizzie had bought him a copy of 'Up the Line to Death' an anthology of First World War poets along with a smart shirt and woollen V-necked jumper (that Mark was wearing with new jeans and looking good in she thought) but was ruing not topping it all off with a whoopee cushion so as to truly fit in. "Penny for 'em?" Mark said as he slumped onto the sofa beside her, perfect whoopee cushion territory. Tiggy was sitting on the other side of her, still reading whilst steadily consuming forkfuls of cake, but clearly comfortable nestled in next to Lizzie. She was about to respond with a 'touché' when the lights were dimmed once more, the fire now crackling with discarded wrapping paper and ribbon, as Harry cleared his throat with music hall theatricality, to announce, "Ladies, Gentleman, and Uncle Mark," (with a pause for the inevitable laughter), "you are all invited to join us in the library for a trip down memory lane." A frisson of excitement rippled through the room and Lizzie squeezed his arm in anticipation whilst Mark simply groaned. As he dragged himself up off the sofa Johnnie caught his other arm and, grinning from ear to ear, whispered, "I do hope they've got the right film loaded, because I got hold of some of those old mags of yours and the chaps in the media suite at work put together the adult version, 'A trip down mammary lane'." In the words of the great Alan Partridge, Mark thought, 'unbelievable'.

The library always reminded him of those countless BBC adaptations of Jane Austen novels that always seemed to be on TV on Sunday evenings before the news; vast bookshelves from wall to ceiling, even with one of those sets of portable wooden steps to help you select those tomes in the upper reaches. He imagined Lizzie, sitting in one of the easy chairs, fanning herself modestly, as he, in breeches and riding boots, manfully climbed the steps to reach down a copy of Fielding's raunchy 'Tom Jones'.

Then another image sprung to mind, that of Rachel Weisz as the pretty and accident-prone antiquarian who attempted to re-classify the entire set of library books in the film 'The Mummy' with disastrous effect. Despite the gorgeous actress in question this caused him to wince inwardly at the prospect of him inadvertently sending his father's extensive literary collection tumbling in domino fashion whilst attempting to court Lizzie. As it was, she was all wide-eyed with anticipation and gave his hand another quick squeeze as they gathered round a table upon which sat a laptop and projector, surrounded on three sides with chairs, all facing a large screen. Johnnie had waffled on earlier about needing help with his erection in the library and now he could see what all the fuss was about. A glass of champagne was served to the adults and yet more squash for the children. Flushed from his hastily swigged first glass and still from the warmth of the lounge Johnnie addressed his expectant audience rather predictably with, "Unaccustomed as I am to public speaking," before embarking upon a clearly pre-rehearsed soliloquy extolling the virtue (he had made a point of emphasising the singular) of his kid brother before, with no further ado, he clicked the play button and the entertainments commenced.

The show-reel began with assorted images of a bashful looking toddler playing in the huge empty boxes of Christmas presents, dwarfed by a colossal tree, or pedalling tentatively on a new tricycle, his eyes occasionally looking up at the camera then averting his gaze once more as he focused on steering his way around the formal dining room wearing a frown of concentration. So many of the images contained the turn-ups of tweed trousers and the polished brogues of his father, who was holding the Super 8 that flickered unsteadily as it captured distant memories on grainy reel. Next a beautiful spring morning as his mother took him for a toddle in the manicured gardens and held him up to look out at a huge ship that seemed to be inching its way along the horizon ("one of ours," his father had interjected proudly). His mother looked like a Hollywood actress, with a scarf over her wavy blonde bob, dark glasses and red lipstick, looking elegant even as the little Mark wriggled to free himself from her affection. Lizzie made this point (about how amazingly glamorous she looked and June just blushed and said, "Oh I don't know about that dear"). So Mark's life continued to unfold on film, leaping through the water sprinklers with Johnnie during the drought of '76, picking apples in the orchard one autumn with Aunt Mary, Uncle Bill in the background looking on and smoking his pipe, football goalposts and nets with balloons tied to the crossbar, superhero themed birthday parties followed by a leap of over half a dozen years to a self-conscious frowning teenager looking every inch the lead singer of Tears for Fears with a crimped fringe, long black overcoat and a smudge of eyeliner as he headed out to a VI Form gig. "Bally woofda," was Johnnie's helpful remark, "I always did wonder which side you batted for, until now of course that is," as he smiled apologetically at Lizzie. Mark took all the ribbing in good spirits, feeling so much more confident with the stunning Lizzie at his side whereas without her he would have succumbed once more to the loser tag.

A burst of applause rang out as the film came to a conclusion, a freeze-frame of Mark looking as if he couldn't wait to remove his gown and mortar on Graduation Day, followed by bellows for "speech, speech." Mark slowly got to his feet and obliged. "Well, what can I say?" he began, "People may describe family as the friends you would never have chosen but I guess you're not all that bad, with the exception of old Jeremy Clarkson over there," as he nodded towards his brother. "Seriously, I am touched at how much thought everyone has put into this weekend, the great pressies, the cake and even being woken up after just 20 minutes of my afternoon kip to find myself transformed into a trampoline, but at least you weren't sick all over me this time, eh Harry? Sophie, I was particularly touched by your thoughtful gift and am so looking forward to seeing War Horse up in town, and yes Johnnie, I really did like the film but no I don't want to see the over 18 version. Finally, I'd like to thank you all for the warm welcome you've given to Lizzie and I hope this is the first of many visits we'll be enjoying together. So, everyone, bottoms up." After the glasses were drained, the applause faded, and the three cheers rang out, Johnnie announced their departure time for supper. Mark and Lizzie exchanged a fleeting glance, both seeming to have sensed that their feelings for one another had shifted, becoming deeper, more rooted during the course of what felt like a significant weekend; with neither one of them resisting the sensation.

*

Why did she go through with it, knowing how repulsed she was at the thought of sex? And, looking back, just how friendly was her father to her on all those trips away without her mother that she had thought so innocent at the time? She was sitting up in the blissfully comfy bed, pillows puffed up behind her head and the covers pulled up as high as they could go as the ancient central heating system slowly creaked and groaned into life. She

68

had stayed up late and then woken early to read the book that was sitting on the bedside cabinet, a relatively thin work with a beautiful, delicate pale blue cover depicting Chesil beach after which the novel was named, a beach that lay at the foot of the very cliffs that stood just beyond the walls of the sloping garden that was still shrouded in heavy early morning mist. She had just finished the final page and the book remained in her hand, lying open at the spot where the narrative concluded, as she took in the overwhelming weight of the conclusion, a tide of emotions washing over her. She had a certain amount of sympathy for the young lady in the novel, a university graduate and musician living in the early sixties, married young, excited at her life ahead but dreading the wedding night itself due to a paralysing fear when approaching the expected and inevitable physical intimacy, despite the love she felt towards her husband, a young man she'd known since she was a girl growing up in Oxford. Lizzie had squirmed when reading of their disastrous attempts at consummating their marriage and, though futile, urged them to set their pride aside and work through the issues that had consumed them at such a significant point in their lives. The incredibly well written novel powerfully addressed the potentially devastating impact of silence within a relationship and the importance of couples working towards shared expectations rather than retreating into separate worlds of unspoken fears. She had slept with just two of her former boyfriends and had decided that the next bloke she slept with would be her husband. She allowed her mind to wander and to imagine Mark being in bed beside her and whether or not that felt right. She smiled as she imagined him suggesting the cap as a possible form of contraception whilst grinning and putting on a Kangol hat. No, there would be no risk of uncomfortable silences in that department. She stopped this flow to track her chain of thought. She was usually so cautious when it came to relationships and had a reputation amongst her girlfriends for being overly guarded and quickly dismissive when confronted by potential suitors, so what was it about this affable part academic part comedian that she found so compelling? For a start it was his complete lack of pretension. She was tired of men who practically listed their CV on a first date in an attempt at impressing her and found his ability to be fully in the here and now, rather than the now and then refreshing. Sure, his buffoonery and flippancy took some getting used to but she had seen a much more reflective and sensitive side to him, particularly of late, for her to wonder whether his constant need to conclude each conversation with a quip was some form of nervous tick. He hadn't even attempted a joke after her lingering kiss goodnight, the first and only time she had ever seen him speechless.

She knew that she wasn't being seduced by the trappings of affluence and admitted to feeling rather embarrassed to be whisked off in a convoy of Range Rovers to dine at the most exclusive Italian restaurant in the area, despite a fabulous meal and amazing selection of wines. The more time she spent with Mark's family the more she saw how he had been shaped by them, by their expectations and perceived sense of failure when he failed to measure up to them. He could see how his mother adored him regardless and how his father seemed to view him with greater respect now that he had a 'decent' girl on his arm. Their value system did seem outdated to say the least, especially when you consider Johnnie, the blue- eyed boy, who couldn't take his eyes off the pert little backside of the waitress in the restaurant and who could barely get through a sentence without making reference to some part of the anatomy. But he had 'knuckled down' and learned the family business, married into 'good stock' had earned well and invested wisely and was therefore set up for life. But what if he keeled over from a heart attack tomorrow she thought, how would his legacy be viewed then? Don't become too morose or retrospective Lizzie, she corrected herself, it's not often one gets to stay in such luxury so why not indulge oneself in another of those hot, deep baths?

Mark had woken up with a start from a reoccurring nightmare where he is at the head of the long table in the boardroom at Woodford & Conville Ltd.'s head office (they had bought out a rival firm a couple of years previously and added their name to the company's) where he was about to present to the board who have all turned to face him but he was dressed only in his underpants and had no idea what he was supposed to say. Mouth dry, he slumped back into the mountain of pillows he had nestled deeply into late the night before and tried to regain his senses. The house was in that pre-breakfast state of quiet, except for the familiar sound of the thick pipes clanking under the strain of heating the network of bulky radiators and industrial size water tanks that would soon be drained by the demand of a small army looking to bathe and shower before descending on the kitchen for their regular fare; scrambled eggs and freshly percolated coffee. All in all, he could look back on a hugely successful weekend. The family had clearly taken to Lizzie, even Sophie had dropped her sullen veneer and shifted up through the gears, being positively chummy with her over dinner, at one point even laughing loudly, all this being taken in by the awestruck Tiggy who now had two aspirational women in her life. Mark usually had problems concentrating on his Tagliatelle Carbonara when at Milanese due to the short, tight fitting skirts worn by Maria, the owner's eldest daughter, who he used to fantasise over when growing up.

Last night, however, he only had eyes for his woman. The same couldn't be said for Johnnie, however, whose booze bleary eyes seemed permanently on stalks as Maria shimmied and swayed her way around the rows of minimal chic dark wood tables. Ordinarily Mark would be waiting for one of Sophie's acerbic put downs to create a wall of ice but she ignored her husband's leering, clearly content to enjoy Lizzie's company and not allow Johnnie's indiscreet lechery to ruin yet another evening out. Lizzie was enchanting, seeming to have time for everyone around the table, making eye contact, turning her head to one side to hear above the background din, and proving equally charming whether chatting to one of the other adults or helping Harry or Tiggy twirl a forkful of spaghetti.

Back at home, after coffee and brandies, Lizzie followed Sophie and his mum's lead, announcing that she was to retire for the night. Johnnie blurted. "Fifth, eighth, thirteenth and seventeenth if I remember rightly."

"Go on," she replied. "The floorboards that creak on the corridor between the yellow and the red room, at least that's what he used to tell the occasional other girlfriends, hoping they'd pop down and give him a quick hand-shandy before lights out."

"Oh, I'm sure this lady has far too much class for that sort of teenage carry-on but I will allow the birthday boy to escort his lady to the door of her boudoir and no further." With that she bade the chaps a good night, linked arms with Mark and headed for the stairs. Fortified by the Barolo from earlier in the evening and with the warmth of the brandy still lingering in his throat, he remembered meandering up the wide staircase telling her what a hit she'd been with the family, how amazing she'd looked and how grateful he was for her making such an effort to make his birthday so special when, as they reached the first floor landing, she had stopped him by placing one of her fingers on his lips before removing it and looking up into his eyes then closing hers to give him the slowest and most sensuous kiss he'd ever had; 40 years old to the day and going weak at the knees after a kiss from a new girlfriend may sound tragic to some but for Mark it was the perfect ending to a perfect day. He was smitten with the sweetest, kindest, most beautiful woman he'd ever known and there was even a chance that she might just be falling for him too.

71

4
January 2008
Mark, 40, Lizzie 30

A good year for the roses

He was in heaven. The day stretched out before him as he stretched out on his trusty old sofa, TV remote in one hand, hot mug of tea in the other, Radio Times on the nest of tables beside him and huge plastic tub of Roses chocolates within arm's reach on the floor. It was an old habit of his to go through the festive edition of the Radio Times and circle stand out films or specials with a red pen so he could plan his viewing in advance and not miss out on some of those classic repeats due to them being either tucked away in the morning listings or equally late at night. These were the days he had always loved, even as a teenager back in Dorset, post-Christmas and New Year and pre-term starting, those non-descript days that many would fill with shopping in the sales or visits to aunts and uncles that were too distant either by geography or relationship to feature in the turkey filled main event or sausage roll laden Hogmanay parties, where the New Year would be seen in with a boozy shouted countdown with Jools Holland on the TV. His New Year had been seen in clutching a glass of champagne in one hand and Lizzie's in the other, as he joined her, Janice and Lisa as they pushed their noses to the large window in their lounge and watched the fireworks hiss and puff their way skyward lighting up the black starless sky before descending gracefully into the mass of sea that gently washed the shoreline. The way she squeezed his hand before turning and smiling up at him, eyes wide and alert, gave him the sense that the year they were ushering in would be the most significant in his life so far, that forces were already on the move, powerful forces that he felt would run their course regardless, with him clinging on for dear life, scared in many ways as to the direction it was taking him but even more frightened to let go for fear of missing out on the ride.

For Mark, these in-between days had always represented the ideal opportunity to take stock of his life in a purely passive, hypothetical way, happy to allow random thoughts to meander alongside the steady murmur of the television and to consider life's 'ifs buts and maybes' but with no particular conviction to alter the status quo. Once more, he prepared to immerse himself in the non-descript viewing on this non-descript day in the company of Pike, Mainwaring, The Grace Bros, Del Boy, Indiana Jones and of course, James Bond. Popping another strawberry-centred chocolate into his mouth and washing it down with a healthy swig of tea, he realised that, this year, a warm sense of contentment had crept into his annual performance self-appraisal, a rare intruder into a process that had often left him reaching for the consolation of a pre-noon beer and slice of cold foil wrapped turkey as yet another year had passed him by with neither literary nor amorous aspirations fulfilled, but now he had Lizzie (a fact that still caused him to pinch himself) and that made life a joy to live.

She was in Chichester visiting her dad and brother, whom he'd met briefly in between Christmas and the New Year, leaving him to spend a blissfully quiet few days at home, 'planning sessions' for the new college term. A turning point in their relationship had been the trip to Dorset for his 40th and the 'Lizzie effect' on him and the rest of the family. What touched him more than anything was that it wasn't an act; there was no sudden switching on of the charm to make an impact and gain popularity but simply the sweet nature of Lizzie extending to all reaches of his complex family cast. There was the gentle charming of his father by her taking an interest in their family heritage, with all its pomp and portraits and his mother with her soft furnishings and village life, nodding earnestly as changes to times of choir rehearsals or the new vicar's like of modern hymns were recalled in some detail. There was how she deftly avoided Johnnie's 'playful' gropes and innuendo, and then how she effortlessly conquered the ice cap that is his sister-in-law Sophie by asking questions about her home(s) and children's schooling, her outfits and accessories, all perfectly natural and, to him, just adorable. She had even joked in the car on the way back from their maiden voyage to Dorset that they'd better make sure they avoided a 'Chesil Beach' whilst on theirs, as it were, a comment that had confirmed to him that maybe she was in this for the long haul also, a fact reinforced by another hugely successful trip to the family for Christmas, only partially ruined on Boxing Day by Mark who accidentally smashed the rear lights and open tailboard of Johnnie's Range Rover when a shotgun he thought was empty must have still had a cartridge in it. He'd made the point that it could have been a lot worse, although for all the fuss Johnnie made Mark thought it might have been less of an inconvenience if he'd accidentally shot one of the children.

One of the countless qualities that he loved about Lizzie was her insistence that they didn't 'sell' out on their existing friendships just because they'd found each other. To be perfectly honest he'd been more than prepared to drop Pete and Vaz like the proverbial stones in order to spend every waking moment with the object of his desire, but he didn't have to, instead feigning loyalty and a newfound maturity, telling them that there was no way he was going to bale on them, his mates, just because he'd found the girl of his dreams, although he had an inkling that neither were convinced by this show of solidarity. She would often spend a Friday evening in with her flatmate Lisa and co-worker Janice, watching a movie or just chatting through their respective weeks over takeout Pizza whilst he continued to sip lager with Pete and keep up the pretence that, once they had completed their script, they could even push it to the Beeb who had a great track record in adapting period drama. Lizzie would enjoy a 'mooch' around antique and charity shops on a Saturday morning whilst he sweated it out on the tennis court with Vaz and then he and Lizzie would meet after lunch for coffee and cake and an amble through the Lanes before maybe heading out to the cinema or for an early bite to eat, with Mark always going home afterwards. He would usually call for her on a Sunday mid-morning and they would stroll along the seafront, pick up the papers (he The Independent and her the Express although he tried not to hold this against her) and trawl through them at their leisure over a decent brunch that would extend into the mid-afternoon. He would then walk her back to her flat and would return home to catch up on some marking or preparation whilst Lizzie attended an evening church service with Lisa. His weekends had taken on a perfect pitch, still time for the rituals of his bachelor existence such as the occasional kebab on the way home from the pub on a Friday night, lazing in front of sport on the telly or soaking for an hour in the bath listening to the football on the radio but without the downsides, the quiet Saturday nights and Sunday afternoons in that could drag, even if he liked to convince himself otherwise.

A glance at the wall clock told him that Lizzie would probably be in her family kitchen preparing a snack for lunch whilst her brother and father would probably be finding needless jobs to do that involved taking things apart, such as carriage clocks or old computers. He'd met her dad, Trevor and brother 'Stu' along with Lizzie for a pub lunch at the Black Rabbit in Arundel, roughly halfway between Brighton and Chichester, albeit nearer to her home turf. They were both pleasant enough but also extremely dull, her dad harping on about proposed out of town retail developments, whilst shaking his head and muttering on about local business, whilst her brother seemed to be speaking in fluent Klingon as he described at length the coding he wrote for the software company he worked for that specialised in customer relationship marketing, or CRM. Lizzie had subsequently shared with him that she was far more like her mother, a 'people' person, whilst the men-folk preferred the solidity of things, often servicing household items such as the toaster or vacuum cleaner just as her or her mother was about to use them. It struck him that they both needed to learn to relax a little, as, after questioning, they seemed to know little about The Fast Show, Blackadder Goes Forth or even The Office. What a waste, Mark thought, to be tinkering with a soldering iron when you could be sprawled out in your traccy bottoms in front of Journey to the Centre of the Earth with Spartacus to follow; their loss he shrugged. As another commercial break loomed he shuffled down to the kitchen to assemble his own lunch, an easy foray into the fridge for cold sausage rolls, a couple of slices of ham, a dollop or two of coleslaw, a hunk of Cheddar and an ice cold can of Coke then to the cupboard for a rummage through a multi-pack of crisps, settling for roast chicken and back to the sofa in time for more toxic, volcanic eruptions; time for one of my own, he thought, before Kirk Douglas leads the slave uprising against the Roman Empire; how he loved his life.

*

Pete was mightily relieved that Mark had agreed to resume their Friday evening Stella and script night ahead of the new term starting. He had a two-year-old that resisted sleep at any cost and a wife at her wits' end. He felt somewhat guilty in leaving a scene where his son, Barney, was doing his level best to ensure that there were equal amounts of water on the floor as in the bathtub and his wife, Emma, rapidly losing all patience. Help was at hand in the shape of his mother-in-law, however, so he felt the waves of guilt ever decreasing as he settled down to his second pint of the evening. Until now, Mark had always viewed Pete's world as distant and alien, a Tatooine with its twin suns and barren landscape, hopeless and bleak, but now he viewed it with far more interest almost as if it could be a sign of things to come. He questioned Pete on the number of hours he and his wife slept, how they decided on who would get up in the middle of the night and how they managed to recover, on delegation of chores and number of weekly rows (and sex) and whether or not he'd ever regretted starting a family. Pete was quite taken aback at first, grateful for his mate's concern but with it the realisation that Mark wouldn't be asking these kinds of questions out of the goodness of his heart but only as a form of research. "You must have got it bad mate," he said, between a slurp of lager and a crunch of steak flavoured crisps, "to be even thinking about it. For the last two years you've winced, glazed over or done both at the slightest mention of my domestic demise." Mark, not wanting to give the game away as to how his thoughts had meandered over his previous two sofa based days, said that he was just curious and that nothing should be read into him simply enquiring as to how his colleague and friend was faring when secretly he was thinking 'the only way I'd be up three times a night is if I'd had one pint too many'. Time to move on, he thought. "Hey, how about we research into just how well Owen and Sassoon knew each other and use their shared love of poetry to explore how, during the Great War, the class divide was bridged through a need for survival and how the troops and officers all seemed to accept the inevitability of certain death." Pete held Mark with a searching stare, "If I didn't know you better, I'd think you're finally getting serious about this."

*

It wasn't the only thing Mark was getting serious about. For the first time in his life he actually felt like making a plan, not just a daydream on the sofa in front of a TV property makeover programme whilst nursing a hangover (although both décor and drink were to appear on the list) but an actual commitment to (a) putting words on paper and (b) plans into action. He eschewed trite New Year's resolutions but had had time enough to reflect on how his relationship with Lizzie was developing to contemplate at least embarking upon a process of change and improvement. He was sitting in the room on the top floor of his three-storey house the Sunday night before a new college term began in what he referred to as his study, a huge sprawling room with views out across the town and down towards the sea, but a space badly in need of some TLC. The faded patterned wallpaper was peeling in areas, the polystyrene tiled fake ceiling was stained and sagging, and the cheap dark wood shelves heaved under the strain of text books and A4 files full of teaching notes. His desk was, ironically, an old wallpapering table that had been set up years ago and his chair a portable garden chair that he'd found out in the shed. The light from the main bulb was too harsh, as he still hadn't got round to fixing a shade so a pool of light from a dated white metal desk lamp was the only illumination, giving him the effect of a shoe string private detective mulling over his latest case load. Beside him a paint-stained wooden step ladder acted as a primitive filing system, with each step holding the folders of each group he taught. He really should have been planning revision sessions but was totally distracted, particularly after the weekend he'd shared with Lizzie.

The previous afternoon, the first time they'd seen each other since New Year's Day, they had finally taken the hood down drive to Lewes that he'd dreamed of the first time he'd met her. Bright winter sunshine, thick woolly jumpers and scarves, teacakes washed down with Earl Grey tea, arm in arm meandering along the quaint narrow streets; exactly as he'd imagined it, even down to the detail of them listening to Faithless en route. The fact that he'd got fresh dog crap across the sole of his right Converse boot and subsequently smeared across the driver's side carpet, something that once would have been enough to ruin any excursion, failed to dampen his mood as they were both giddy with the exhilaration of the sunlit drive, the bracing wind whipping off the coastline and the catching up after a few days apart. That magical day had been followed by showers and changes in their respective homes before an early curry at the Polash where they both enjoyed a Cobra beer or two. Walking her home afterwards Mark talked about this and that on her doorstep before pulling Lizzie close to him, kissing her deeply and passionately before whispering, "I am so in love with you Lizzie Wilson." She had held his gaze, her deep brown eyes angled up to meet his and replied, "Well you'd better be careful with that Mark Woodford, because it might just be catching."

As they took their usual morning after hand in hand stroll along the seafront before picking up the papers, nothing was mentioned, nor did it need to be. Every now and then Lizzie would just pull gently on his arm, turn inwards towards him and smile coyly before gazing out across the water once more. The day had then unfurled as most of their Sundays did but they both knew another milestone had been reached. He knew it had only been four months since they'd first met but the intensity of his feelings, and it appeared of hers, was such that the time was irrelevant. He took a sheet of A4 from the printer that was perched precariously on the end of the table and began to write his list:

1) Cut down on booze and crappy food – especially kebabs on the way back home from the pub

2) Clean the house and tidy up – then Lizzie might actually agree to coming round for dinner

3) Check bank account and write budget of monthly income/outcome

4) Reminder to do number 3 – it's bound to get overlooked

5) Plan work more effectively to make best use of time off

6) Reminder to do number 5 – it's bound to get ignored

7) Plan for weekend in London to see War Horse

8) Sort problem of double room – yikes!!

9) Propose romantically to Lizzie

10) Live happily ever after!

He didn't want to be getting all premature but why not finally kick the habit of a lifetime to embrace decisiveness? He knew he only had eyes for her, only ever wanted to be with her, so why wait just because convention said that anything under a year was 'whirl-windy'? He continued to mull over his list and brood as to what the future might hold until the darkness closed in around him and his piles of unmarked coursework, the small pool of light from the desk lamp ever diminishing as rain drops began to tap gently against the top floor window panes.

5

February 2008

Mark, 40, Lizzie 30 approaching 31

Winter offensive

As they settled into the plush velvet seats and took in the hushed bustle before curtain-up, he took another gulp of his bottled mineral water and subtly dabbed his perspiring forehead with the back of his hand as he felt as nervous as he'd imagined the lead role might be. He'd planned this trip with military precision and, he'd learned, when a military strike is imminent you had to be prepared to deal with rogue elements that hadn't been factored in, always with your mission goal in mind. He recalled a discussion between two lecturers he'd once overheard in the senior common room, one, a female, was explaining why, historically, it was always the woman who chose the dates for the family summer holiday and the man, unquestioning, took the dates off work he's been given by his wife. Mark had only been half tuned into this conversation, as he'd been reading the paper at the time, but wished now he'd taken more notice, especially in the light of this 'surprise' weekend away in London as he noticed Lizzie rubbing her tummy once more and turning to give him a sympathetic smile.

After a late night spent ruminating in his study at home a month or so before, he had decided on a master plan that got him so excited he wondered how he was possibly going to be able to keep it from Lizzie. He was going to cash in on his weekend for two to London, inclusive of overnight stay at a top boutique hotel and tickets to see War Horse at the National, culminating with a proposal of marriage! He felt that the trip had all the right ingredients to be a resounding success, being away from familiar surroundings, the elegance, style and comfort of the classy hotel, the buzz of a trip to the theatre, the romance of the Thames at night-time, how could she possible fail but to fall into his arms, and be swept up by the occasion to exclaim 'yes, yes, yes!' Okay, there would be the tricky question of sleeping arrangements, but surely they could overcome that for just one night, knowing that they'd have their whole lives ahead of them to share a king-size bed in the way he intended? He had nothing but respect and admiration for Lizzie's stance over no sex before marriage, with him anyway, and it was only on the odd occasion when perhaps the wine or beer had been talking that he'd made reference to those 'lucky other blokes' who had found themselves fortunate enough to be sampling the goods before she had found God. On the whole, they rarely argued but this was the main source of his frustration so he'd have to make sure he got his bed protocol script right and stick to it in order to avoid a potentially trip ruining performance.

In the weeks leading up to this potentially life changing weekend, the last that the War Horse was playing at the National before being transferred, he had been liaising with Lisa her flatmate who he had convinced to become a co-conspirator, despite some early misgivings, particularly on sleeping arrangements. With Mark's assurances that it was to all be above board she had agreed to pack everything that Lizzie would need for the weekend in town whilst Lizzie was out enjoying her usual Saturday morning mooch around the Lanes. Mark had turned up in a cab to meet Lizzie for their two o'clock coffee date, only to be kept waiting for over 20 minutes (at a cost of an extra £15 and plenty of 'come on mate, it's a Saturday, I can't sit here all bleepin' day') from the burly taxi driver but he couldn't blame Lizzie as she had no idea what he had planned (although he was quietly getting hot under the collar at managing the stress levels of the taxi driver). There were only so many conversations one could start that hit a dead end after a minute or so. He had even scraped the barrel with "have you ever had to pick someone up who was famous?" Eventually Lizzie had turned up looking pale and strained and, it seemed, rather begrudgingly allowed herself to be ushered into the waiting taxi and whisked off to the station. The reality was less of a whisk and more of a traffic snarl up to add to the already dark mood of the taxi driver, resulting in an ungainly dash along the platform to make the train up to town, with Lizzie smashing her travel case against her shins and howling in pain and Mark attempting to display sympathy whilst simultaneously urging her to hurry for just that bit further.

Clearly, Lizzie loved spontaneity, so long as she was the one revealing the surprises; she wasn't quite so enthusiastic when on the receiving end. Mark had attempted to inject some energy and enthusiasm into the trip but had been deflated by Lizzie's lack of spark and her general moodiness, something he was not used to seeing in her as she was usually so full of verve. Maybe she had already worked out what was going on and her thoughts had raced ahead to the possible sleeping arrangements, could that be what was rendering her detached and pensive, nervous almost? They hadn't even reached Haywards Heath when the silence and tension had caused him to retreat into something of a sulk, chin resting on the palm of his hand as he gazed out of the window at the alternating rural landscapes and suburban sprawl with the latter more prevalent the closer to London they got. It was on this and other such rail journeys in the UK that he loved to sit back and reflect upon the changing face of this once great nation and it struck him that the label 'a nation of shopkeepers' was no longer necessarily a fair reflection on the contemporary British society, no it was more 'a nation of garden shed keepers'. Practically all of the gardens that backed onto the railway sidings, many shaped like pizza slices with what seemed like arbitrary boundaries marked by rickety fences or thin lengths of steel wire sagging between rusty posts, had at least one if not two wooden sheds, all in various states of disrepair. He could see the inherent value of such structures, he even had one himself, they were cheap and easy to install and maintain, great for bundling away all manner of garden related machinery, tools, furniture and toys but he wondered if some of the owners had considered the space to shed ratio pre their purchase of said storage unit as many of the gardens seemed to display an imbalance of 'all weather storage solution' to grass or patio, as if the shed was erected in spite of the space it was to inhabit. We have a garden therefore we must have a shed!

He was nudged out of his random musings by Lizzie sighing and shifting her position on the aisle seat next to him. He had offered her 'window or aisle madam' when boarding the carriage to which she had replied with a thin smile. He had even pointed out to her the emergency exits and where the loos were in his best and extremely camp air steward accent (he didn't know why but when he imitated a camp bloke he always did it in a soft Scottish accent). He decided he could bear the silence no longer so turned in towards her and, attempting to mask his agitation, "so what do think of it so far folks?" She opened her eyes and returned his eye contact. "I'm sure that whatever you're doing is with the best of intentions Mark, but I do wish you would have consulted me first."

"Well it wouldn't be much of a surprise then would it?" he countered. "Remind me how you felt when your brother had organised a racing track day for your fortieth, Mark?"

"Well that's totally different and despite owning a high-performance vehicle, I've never even been vaguely interested in racing it or any other car for that matter, and besides, I've planned something special for us as a couple, stuff I know you'd like, so why the long face?"

"Because, darling heart, at this time of the month I could pluck yours or anyone else's out with my bare hands such is the quiet PMT rage that burns within me. You keep telling me that with comedy it's all in the timing, well here's a newsflash lover-boy; with romance it's no different." 'Okay, Mark,' he thought to himself, 'just keep calm and carry on.'

The short cab ride from Victoria, along Whitehall and the Strand towards the hotel at One Aldwych passed in a blur of light rainfall and more silence punctuated by Mark's attempts at lightening the mood. He was back at attempting joviality, falling into a Mockney accent when giving instructions to the cab driver and pointing out various buildings of interest to Lizzie as if he were an East End tour guide. Her demeanour seemed to have shifted from one of frustration to 'trying to make the most of it' but she was clearly in some discomfort as she would automatically release her left hand from his and move it to rub her stomach, so he ceased his chatter and sunk back into his seat once more. After tipping the cabbie generously but refusing help with their luggage from the stylish looking all in black suited and booted doorman at the hotel, something that left them exchanging knowing smiles, he led Lizzie by the hand into the impressive lounge of the chic boutique hotel. He was struck (not literally) by its large marble statue of the rower, with oversized oars and the neatly placed high backed chairs and fabric sofas creating a sense of comfort but also of space. They checked in and he took Lizzie in the lift up to her room and left her there to unpack as he dropped his rucksack into his (for which he'd had to pay) before heading back down to the Axis at Number One restaurant that adjoined the hotel and where he had booked a table for after theatre supper. The maître d', a pretty woman in her mid-late 20s with an accent that sounded Middle-Eastern, was hugely sympathetic to his plan to propose to Lizzie later that night and assured him that they wouldn't be seated in a table for two next to the swing doors to the kitchen or to the loos. Satisfied that he'd done all he could by way of preparation, and picturing Lizzie stretched out on the double bed resting, he decided to stop for a gin and tonic in the hotel lounge, well, when in Rome and all that.

As he got comfy in one of the high-backed chairs with a window view onto the insipid looking street outside, to sip his over-iced and over-priced drink (served with a complimentary bowl of mixed nuts) he reflected on a trip that was already panning out so differently to how he'd imagined it. He had anticipated a 'difficult conversation' over sleeping arrangements but was going to assure Lizzie that he'd keep strictly to the rules of 'you can't touch what you haven't got' but didn't think this would be necessary in the light of current circumstances. He'd imagined them splashing about in the hotel's indoor pool, the closest he'd have got so far to seeing her in her underwear (he'd made sure Lisa had packed a bikini) but that also wasn't likely to happen now either. This had all come completely from the left of field, leaving him feeling deflated and quite helpless to remedy the situation. Maybe a long rest followed by a deep bath would do the trick and she'd perk up a bit. He continued to sip his G&T fearing that his meticulously planned weekend of a lifetime had already hit an iceberg and was in danger of sinking without trace.

Lizzie was struggling to get comfortable on the king-size double bed adorned with multiple pillows and in a room that seemed to be roasting her one minute then chilling her the next. She had done her best not to be angry with Mark for whisking her off to London on the day when it was the last thing on earth she'd have opted for as he was a bloke and had no idea how some women have to plan their diary around the stabbing pains and chronic cramps that herald the onset of their dreaded monthly cycle. Despite her chic and sumptuous surroundings, she longed for the comforts of home, for her own single bed with the eiderdown she'd had since she was twelve, her Shaun the Sheep hot water bottle, familiar bath robe. What she missed most of all, however, was those reassuring hugs from her mother whenever she was feeling under the weather. She thought that maybe her flatmate Lisa would have been alert to the timing of this romantic excursion but maybe she, like Mark, had become so wrapped up in the excitement of it all that she had overlooked the significance of the 9th February, a day when, such was the intensity of pain that she experienced that she felt she couldn't be held responsible for her own actions. As she was due on she hadn't bothered to shave her arms or legs that week, so felt pretty grim as a result, neither did she have any pain killers with her and had just the single 'emergency' tampon in an inside pocket in her handbag. For now, she was prepared to surrender to sleep as everything else would have to be dealt with later. Curling her knees up towards her chest she allowed her heavy lids to close, against the steady background whirr of the air con.

Mark slid Lizzie's key card into the slot next to the door handle and when the tiny light flickered green gingerly put his head round the door to see her fast asleep, knees curled up to meet two huge white pillows that she hugged with her right arm, the remote control to the air con in her left hand, that dangled near the edge of the king-size bed. 'Bloody hell, it's like a freezer in here,' he thought as he gently prised the remote control from her, causing her to stir faintly, as he steadily increased the room temperature. Feeling just a touch woozy from his boozy mid-afternoon refreshments he decided to climb onto the bed beside her and grab a kip himself and so quietly undid the laces of his (now clean) Converse baseball boots and eased up onto the luxurious thick duvet giving in to a wave of tiredness and deep, dream free sleep. He awoke with a start and to the sound of the bath taps running and Lizzie humming through the closed bathroom door. Stretching out, he saw a note containing a list of items that Lizzie required and had hastily scribbled on a page of the branded hotel notepaper so he scratched his chin, put his trainers back on, grabbed his phone, wallet, key-cards and jacket and headed out once more.

He'd asked for directions to the nearest 24/7 store from one of the suave hotel doormen, knowing that it was too late to find a high street pharmacist. Pulling his trusty army style jacket about him he strode, head down, into an icy wind that was whipping up strips of waste paper in the doorways of gloomy empty office blocks and coded entry apartments. He soon found the all-night corner shop and purchased all of the items on Lizzie's list, blushing ever so slightly as the po-faced cashier scanned each one and placed them into a carrier bag. He had been wondering if the word 'super' before the tampon made reference to the woman's size or the flow of the period but decided this was definitely a question for another day. Lizzie had already mentioned that the stomach cramps she had been experiencing would rule out a mid-afternoon snack so he scoffed a cold chicken tikka slice whilst on his way back to the hotel, leaving a little trail of crumbs behind him.

He entered the room to find Lizzie perched on the edge of the bed reading the in-house magazine dressed in a grey crew neck woollen top with long matching light weight cardigan over the top and her black skinny jeans tucked into heeled brown suede boots. Her hair was worn the way it was on their first date, mostly piled up on top of her head with some longer parts teased down at the side that served to emphasise her amazing bone structure and huge brown eyes. She may have been in some discomfort but still managed to look a million dollars, so he told her so. Lizzie managed one of her winning smiles and took his hand. She explained to him how touched she was that he'd gone to all the trouble of planning such a wonderful weekend away and that she'd do her best not to ruin it. This immediately made him feel guilty and he admitted that he had allowed the romantic impulse to totally overrule all sense of reason and of course he should have checked that the weekend he had in mind was okay for her before booking it. They were both relieved to have had the 'clear the air' conversation and, looking up into his eyes through her fringe, she opened her arms and said "Come here you." To which he replied, "Are you sure, I mean we've got to be out of here in an hour." Both laughing at his audacious line of humour she whacked him on the arm with the magazine and pointed to the door. "Well you'd better get a move on then."

Under an hour later and they were in a minicab taking the short drive back over the river towards the National Theatre. Mark was in his Lizzie bought outfit of white shirt tucked into smart blue jeans with a black V-necked jumper, finished off with black brogue style shoes and a vintage dark brown leather jacket. Considering how scruffily he usually dressed he felt particularly sophisticated, particularly with the gorgeous Lizzie nuzzled up next to him. He thought they looked like a cool urban couple on their way out, with perhaps a whiff of Soho media about them. "Is it me or does this cab stink of curry?" Lizzie whispered. Mark had been regretting the chicken tikka slice he'd wolfed down earlier as it had been repeating on him ever since but was in no mood to ruin the image he had created for himself by coming clean. "Have some discretion sweetheart," he said, gesturing towards the back of the turban wearing driver. Lizzie pulled an 'OMG' face, putting her hand over her mouth just as the cab pulled over in a side street amidst a stream of theatre goers all swarming towards the theatre entrance, they paid, thanked the driver and joined the throng.

And so there they were. In great seats with a fantastic view of the soon to commence action, he anxious as to what was to come later that night, and she, anxious to overcome the regular stabbing pains in her stomach and take in everything else in between. Whilst never having the confidence to be on the stage she still loved theatre nevertheless. Her mother was an avid theatre goer, regularly taking her to the Festival Theatre seasons in Chichester and was also a member of the Funtington Players, an amateur dramatic society based in their village that had the reputation for being one of the best in class. Her mother was not beautiful in the traditional sense, neither was she flamboyant in any way but she seemed to come alive when on stage in a way that made her, to Lizzie anyway, striking and elegant whilst at the same time capable of generating a subtle sexuality that was rarely exhibited off stage. One summer she was playing one of the wives to a keen amateur cricketer in the Alan Ayckbourn play 'Outside Edge' and Lizzie was in attendance at one of the final rehearsals. In one scene, her mother had to sit on a bench next to her stage husband who was the next one in to bat. She remembers vividly the conversation between her mother and the director as to how she should be reacting to her stage husband who was distracted by nerves as he waited to be called in to the crease. He had responded with the simple stage direction of acting naturally. As her stage husband wittered on about fast bowling and defensive batting techniques she simply smiled, turned in towards him so that their knees almost touched, made eye contact, reached up, turned his collar down and straightened it, leaving her hands on his chest for a fleeting moment. Some of the other male actors sitting watching did a sort of shudder and exchanged glances, as if to say 'Wow, that was sexy even if she didn't mean it to be'. That was her mother, Rose, in a nutshell.

As the house lights dimmed and with it audience chatter, she replaced her hand on his and smiled expectantly. Her eyes widened as the performance began with three actors moving on stage, each holding what appeared to be thin bamboo sticks affixed to a slight, jerkily moving wood and fabric structure that they appeared to be controlling. Before long she was entranced at how the first faltering steps of a new-born foal were portrayed so beautifully through the puppetry, ignoring the puppet masters and seeing only that fragile pony embracing its first moments on earth. Just stunning. As the narrative unfurled, Mark too was drawn into the heart of the drama, allowing his imagination to embrace the power of the performances, the deep love and loyalty that ran between man and horse, the heart wrenching circumstances surrounding one separation after another, the resilience of both in surviving the conflict to seek each other out and, ultimately, their emotional reunion and return to the rural scene of their first encounter, 'closing the circle' as a theatre critic may have written.

By the time the cast came back on stage for their second encore the tears of emotional relief worn on the cheeks of the majority of the audience members were now glistening alongside beaming smiles of pure admiration for such an innovative and profoundly engaging piece of theatre. Mark couldn't help but see himself and Pete on stage, huge bouquets in hand, taking bow after bow as the audience's applause thundered as powerfully as the shells had rained down in their Somme re-inaction. He felt deeply moved by what he had experienced and compelled to up the ante with regards their collaboration, thinking that they ought to cash in on this groundswell of interest in the Great War before the moment was lost. *Carpe diem* to go with *Dulce et Decorum est* he mused, already awash with pretentiousness despite having only spent one evening at the theatre and lacking even a completed first draft of a first script.

He was considering suggesting a stroll back across Waterloo Bridge and then a meander along the Embankment but the icy rain had increased rather than abated and Lizzie looked perished so they walked towards Waterloo, away from the direction they wished to travel in but towards a cluster of cabs with yellow lights on and a swift journey back to the hotel. Lizzie was enthused by an amazing theatrical experience but equally exhausted by the relentless pain she had endured since lunchtime and couldn't wait to take some more painkillers, crawl into bed, curl up and sleep it off. This rather rained on Mark's proposal parade but he knew that resistance would be futile and so he escorted her up to the room once more and excused himself in order to undo the arrangements he had earlier made for dinner. The restaurant was still a third full when he strolled in, despite the late hour. On the whole the atmosphere was subdued, with murmured conversations and the occasional clatter of cutlery on china punctuated only by a roar of laughter or clap of hands from one lively group of four. He was pleased to see the maître d' who he'd booked the table with that afternoon surveying the scene from the bar from where she directed operations so he made his way over to her and explained how, unfortunately, his wife to be (who remained blissfully unaware as to the prime motive for this weekend away) had become unwell when at the theatre and had taken to her bed (a description straight out of a Jane Austen novel he thought). She responded warmly, putting her hand on his arm to demonstrate that she was less concerned about losing a table for two and more worried that his romantic plans had failed to come to fruition. "Don't be too dejected Mr Woodford," she said with a smile, "there will be plenty more opportunities for you to propose. In the meantime, perhaps you could enjoy a glass of champagne on the house." She gestured to a member of her staff who was polishing glasses behind the small bar to pour a glass out for Mark and he took it gratefully. He sat at one of three seats, sipping the delicious, ice cold fizz, holding the glass by the stem, remembering his father stating that 'only a complete oik' would clutch the main body of the glass, thus warming the liquid that should be served chilled. The maître d' went back to her rounds, moving methodically from table to table, checking with her customers that all was well, nodding discreetly towards service staff to remove a plate here or replenish a glass of wine there. She had a deft touch, clearly experienced in her craft, managing to appear friendly without being intrusive and with those customers she clearly recognised familiar but without being flirtatious. He sighed as he saw precisely these qualities in Lizzie, always looking to make people feel at ease, to listen to whatever was concerning them, to make them feel valued, and this caring approach was not just restricted to her working life, it spilled out into everything she did, all those whose lives she touched. Lizzie hardly had a bad word to say about anyone, always seeing the good in people and giving them the benefit of the doubt whereas he was a natural born cynic with an acerbic tongue and a tendency to brood for longer than was necessary, or healthy. He was on his second glass when she returned to the bar. "You seem to enjoy your work," he commented.

"I do," she replied, "and it also benefits my family back in Turkey that I work so hard."

"Well good on you," Mark replied, draining the glass and leaving it on the polished counter, "talking of family, I had better look in on the future Mrs Woodford."

"Well, good on *you*." The maître d' smiled and turned to one of her staff who had presented a bill that a table had questioned. He dismounted the bar stool with less style than when he had mounted it an hour or so before and made his way out of the restaurant, up the sweeping stone steps and back into the hotel lounge. It was still fairly busy, with a third of the spacious open-plan area occupied by couples and groups having a nightcap after a night out in town generating a low buzz of conversation. He and Lizzie should have been one of those couples, basking in the glow of being newly engaged, instead she was curled up in bed alone and he was the lone bar fly, drowning his sorrows and sinking into the depths of self-pity.

He wasn't in the mood for sleep and was still feeling hacked off that the ring he'd carefully selected for Lizzie from an antique shop in the Lanes was still nestled firmly within the red silk interior of the velvet display box, itself buried amongst his change of socks and underpants in an overnight bag, still unpacked and sitting, crumpled in the corner of his deluxe suite. He took a seat on a bar stool and ordered a large Jack Daniel's on the rocks and, nursing it in his right hand, allowed his thoughts to drift, mulling over how real-life events played out so radically differently to those portrayed in the movies. If this episode had been scripted for film then his character, played by Johnny Depp, would have excused himself at the first encore in the theatre, feigning the need to pop to the 'bathroom' but instead would have quickly made his way backstage to where his great friend, the impresario and director of the award winning production would have greeted him warmly before giving the technical director the nod to dim the house lights once more, only to bring them up once 'he' was centre stage, small velvety box in one hand and microphone in the other. He would then have charmed the audience with a witty anecdote before reciting by heart a poem he'd written summing up their romance to date before ending, down on one knee of course, with, 'and so Lizzie Wilson, sitting in seat 14, row G, will you do me the greatest honour of marrying me?' Lizzie, played by Rachel Adams/Anne Hathaway/Rachel Weisz (either of whom could carry off playing Lizzie) would stand, grinning from ear to ear, hand over mouth before running down the aisle yelling, 'Yes, yes, yes' to which the orchestra would strike up a stirring but uplifting piece as Lizzie was helped up onto the stage by a number of the soldiers from the cast and then into his/Johnny Depp's arms to the rapturous applause of the audience as they kissed passionately to the sound of the huge velvet curtains closing and their perfect life together just beginning.

He was jolted out of this daydream by an elbow into his ribs and turned with a start to see the back of a broadly built bloke talking animatedly to two women and another man, his right arm leaning on the bar whilst his left arm gesticulated wildly, nudging Mark's side with varying degrees of ferocity. He recognised the group as being the more raucous diners in the restaurant next door when he had gone down to cancel his booking. They looked just like the sort that Johnnie and Sophie socialised with; the women immaculately groomed, one blonde the other dark, looking perhaps more mummy-ish and slightly less sharp chic than Sophie but still displaying the brands and winter tan of the great and the good. They also knew their roles, to stand in awe of their husbands, throwing heads back to laugh enthusiastically at every anecdote, regardless of having heard them all before. Probably worth it, Mark thought sullenly, to have free rein of the Landrover Discovery 3 all week whilst the Ruperts were off in the city gambling away the life savings and pensions of the retired. The men were of the Jermyn Street by week, Ralph Lauren at the weekend ilk, one in dark cords and stripy shirt, the other, the one with his back to Mark, in light chinos and pink shirt with red jumper tied around his neck in that casual European 'strolling along the marina after dinner look'. He was extremely loud and, to Mark's mind equally obnoxious. Mark left the dramatic, climactic scene of him/Depp proposing to Lizzie/Adams/Hathaway/Weisz and re-tuned his frequency to pick up what was being said in his immediate surroundings. From what he could make out, Pink shirt was telling a long story about some lost baggage, a luxury ski resort and the owner, who he knew, concluding with "and the general consensus was, accept the offer of a free week on the house so I bit his hand off, literally." Before he knew it, he was also speaking aloud, adding with a sigh, "You don't need to prefix consensus with general as consensus means the majority viewpoint."

Pink shirt, whose cheeks matched the colour of his jumper, had swivelled to face Mark and wore a look of utter disbelief. The wives kept smiling, perfect white teeth being emphasised by the glow of their skin, but with a hint of bemusement at this unexpected interruption whilst Stripy shirt looked irked. "Who asked you to butt in?" Pink shirt began, his face now twisting into a sneer. "Well you nudged me that many times," Mark replied, "I thought maybe you were trying to get my attention." Ignoring this clever reply Pink shirt continued, "And what the hell are you going on about anyway?"

Mark decided to expand on his interjection, "You said *general* consensus and I was merely pointing out that you don't need to use the word general and consensus together as one would do, it's a bit like saying collate together or reflect back, one negates the other." At this point Mark should have left it but he never knew when to stop, adding, "And I must say you don't look the Hannibal Lecter type, so are you sure you didn't mean that you bit the hand off the resort owner *figuratively* and not literally speaking."

Stripy shirt, who looked thoroughly lost by Mark's impromptu tutorial on basic spoken English but also furious that his chum had been interrupted so rudely whilst in full flow, stepped in close to Mark, grabbing him by the lapels and, with what smelled like brandy on his breath, spat out a threat to teach him some manners. Whilst Pink shirt removed Stripy shirt from grabbing Mark and gently turned his chum back towards the ladies, Mark just kept the insults going by informing Stripy shirt that "saying it not spraying it" might be a good start which, in hindsight, was probably not the cleverest reply. What happened next was something of a blur but he did remember feeling a sharp stinging pain in his bottom lip followed by a numb sensation that didn't really kick in until he was being helped up off the floor by one of the doormen who had been quick to intervene. Pink shirt, whose face and neck were now as red as the sweater that had tumbled free from his shoulders in this one-sided fracas, stood over him, yelling at Mark and telling him in no uncertain terms what a loser and a prick he was (as if he didn't already know) was being pulled back by his wife, who gave Mark the 'Sophie glare' whilst Stripy shirt remonstrated with the other doorman, who had asked the party to kindly leave. Mark decided to take the advice of the doorman who had picked him up and call it a night. "The general consensus is for you to leave, literally," he said in the direction of the Putney posse as he attempted to smile, wincing at the effort, and headed for the lifts.

90

*

"You did what?" Lizzie was the animated one now, opening her arms, palms up, her mouth wide open, the picture of exasperation. They'd decided to head back across Waterloo Bridge for their breakfast before checking out, both needing the air and preferring a less formal environment to the hotel restaurant, particularly after Mark's performance the previous night, one that Lizzie was now anxious to hear about in great detail. They'd settled into wrought iron seats at an outside table adjacent to a silver trailer that had a fixed pitch serving hot and cold drinks and snacks to regulars and passers-by down towards the Blackfriars Bridge end and overlooking the river. Lizzie and Mark were not the only ones looking to make the most of a bright, fresh winter Sunday morning with just a hint of a breeze coming off the water, as a steady stream of garishly clothed joggers and more casually attired, sedate moving couples added a sense of movement to this calm city still life. As soon as he had woken up, Lizzie (who was already showered and dressed) had knocked on his door and, not surprisingly, demanded an explanation as to why Mark's bottom lip was split and swollen like a defeated boxer's and he'd promised her one after he'd taken a shower and changed his clothes (he'd slept on top of the bed in the outfit he'd worn to the theatre, complete with bloodstains splattered on his white shirt collar). With breakfast on the way he was able to compose himself and recount the events that led to the altercation at the bar. Lizzie was lost for words, struggling to reconcile the charming if not a mite touchy boyfriend who had escorted her to the theatre with this rather pitiful looking individual who had managed to goad what she imagined to be a perfectly respectable couple of men into a bar brawl. His explanation that the weekend hadn't exactly gone to plan seemed a feeble excuse at best.

"How many times do you want me to apologise but I can't help the fact that (1) I get killer PMT with stomach cramps that would reduce most men to blubbering wrecks and (2) that you had planned on whisking me off for a romantic weekend for two without consulting me; if we'd have done this in a week or two then it would have been totally different. I can understand your disappointment to an extent Mark but don't you think that getting drunk and into a fist fight is just a bit OTT?"

"Well, firstly, in a week or two the play would have been transferred and this deal was specifically for War Horse at the National so we'd have missed out altogether if I'd delayed booking it. I had originally wanted us to see it on its last night but that's this Thursday and as well as being a school night there was no way it could happen on February 14th."

"Why not – I'm sure I could have got the time off. I think being treated to a night out at the theatre on Valentine's Day would have been quite a sweet gesture as it happens, but I guess that's just too obvious and cheesy for you, isn't it?"

"Well yes, to be honest, but it wasn't just about the night at the theatre, Lizzie, it was about what came afterwards that's been weighing on my mind."

"Don't tell me you were going to use it as an opportunity to try to get me to sleep with you, Mark, you wouldn't sink that low surely?"

"God no. Well, I'd hardly have turned you down if you were in the mood, but there was no way I was going to try and force the issue, I have way too much respect for you for that."

"Well, what then?"

"For this."

Mark had taken a deep breath and reached into the pocket of his army style jacket to pull out the small dark blue velvet box that left no room for ambiguity the world over. Inside it, nestled in rich, red silk, was a vintage white gold engagement ring with inlaid diamonds that had cost him the best part of a month's salary. Just as he was about to click open the box, his heart racing, mouth dry, the waitress arrived with a tray that she settled down on the adjacent table, unloading each item at a time onto theirs.

"Latte for you madam," she almost sung the words as she placed a glass of warm, milky coffee in front of Lizzie, "and double espresso for you sir," as she did the same for Mark. He couldn't believe her timing. He was frozen, one hand on the base of the box and the other on the lid, ready to reveal the ring to his sweetheart and ask the biggest question he'd ever asked anyone in his life but the waitress, who had a gentle Caribbean lilt, carried on as if oblivious to this timeless and romantic act that was unfolding before her eyes. "Bacon roll with ketchup?"

"Um, that'll be mine," said Lizzie, her eyes fixed on the box in Mark's hand, letting out a small giggle at the ludicrous nature of this scenario. "And with brown sauce and mustard for sir. Can I get you anything else at all?" she concluded with a smile but still no acknowledgement of what she had walked into. "No, no that'll be fine for now, thanks," spluttered Mark, as he too was struggling to maintain his composure. The waitress then departed and the pair of them spurted out with laughter, leaning forwards over the steaming coffee and bacon rolls so that their heads touched. Tears streamed down Lizzie's face, a mixture of the hilarity and poignancy of the occasion. Reaching across to place her hand on Mark's she said, "I don't care what is inside that box, nor does all this matter," gesturing with a sweeping arm movement to the iconic sights of the capital's skyline from where they were sitting, "all you ever needed to do was to ask."

"Then will you," Mark almost stammered, "marry me?"

"Yes, Mark, I will marry you," Lizzie replied, her eyes still wet, "if we can agree that your bare knuckle fighting days are well and truly over?"

Later, as they sat on the train home, utterly content, hand in hand, her head leaning on his shoulder (in marked contrast to their body language on the upward journey) the towns and villages passing in a rainswept blur, they reflected on how for other couples the ambience surrounding a proposal might have been enhanced by the scent of fresh flowers in a tropical paradise and the sounds of the waves gently caressing a moonlit beach but for them by the side of the gently lapping Thames, that bright but still chilly Sunday morning, it was to the aroma of fresh coffee and bacon butties and the sound of their uninhibited laughter.

6
August 2008
Mark, 40, Lizzie, 31

Wedding belles

He knew that, when he sat in this very room just eight months earlier to draft a plan as to how he could play his part in altering the direction his life was to take, the subsequent pace of change may prove exhilarating and scary in equal measures; he was not wrong. As if to emphasise the sheer breadth of evolution that had transpired in the months after that eureka moment had lit up that deep mid-winter night, the large wall mounted pine framed mirror that reflected a neater, clean-shaven Mark was itself a recent fixture to the newly re-furbished top floor, one that now looked far more boutique hotel than Steptoe's den. In two days' time he was getting married, relinquishing the long-held title of bachelor for good, and tonight was all about seeing it out in style.

Not surprisingly, the news of their engagement was met with a chorus of approval from his family who still couldn't quite believe that he'd managed to hook let alone catch and net such a prize; his father often reverted to analogies that were rooted in country pursuits. His mother was absolutely thrilled but even she was taken aback at the speed of developments with a February proposal and August nuptials, secretly fearing a 'shotgun' wedding. Johnnie was his usual boorish self, stating, "It's simple, she's playing the virgin bride and he can't wait to get his leg-over so the sooner the better for my deprived and depraved little brother, a ring on the finger means nookie on tap, that's something he's only ever dreamed of." It was a slice of good fortune that saw Johnnie up north on a new business pitch that would mean him missing out on the stag do, a low key local event that had been planned by Vaz, as Mark was sure that the presence of his older brother would have lowered the tone by several decibels. He shuddered at the thought of being spanked by a stripper dressed as a schoolgirl or other such 'treats' Johnnie would have in store for him, trusting in the balance that Vaz, Pete and the others would strike.

Johnnie's stag do had comprised a weekend in Amsterdam where a cohort of cocaine snorting city boys seemed intent on fulfilling every conceivable cliché in the book as if they were doing it all for the first time. These included (hilariously) paying an eastern beauty to perform a lap dance for a groom so drunk he could barely stand only to then reveal the dancer was a lady boy, (Mark's Alan Partridge recollections of lady boys fell upon deaf ears), throwing Johnnie off the boat into the canal fully clothed after a long liquid lunch and, of course, leaving him tied, stark bollock naked to a lamp post in an area full of gay bars with a sign around his neck reading, 'Free man sex, queue here'. It was one of the most excruciating weekends he'd ever had to endure. Bizarrely, Johnnie thought it all a total hoot, despite him being the butt of all the pranks, as it were.

Looking around him he struggled to take in the just finished study and 'guest suite' as he and Lizzie liked to call it, where he'd been sleeping whilst the assortment of plumbers, plasterers, electricians, and painters worked their way downwards, putting the finishing touches to the family bathroom and three bedrooms on the second floor before tackling the lounge, dining room and kitchen whilst they were away on their honeymoon; Lizzie's idea, of course. The weekend after his proposal she had shifted from blushing bride-to-be to flip chart wielding project manager, determined to ensure that the dump that Mark was happy to inhabit had the Laura Ashley/Habitat makeover prior to Lizzie making it her home also. Mark was more than happy to go along with her plans, rarely objecting, and offering enthusiastic endorsements of her choice of olive, pistachio and mushroom painted walls downstairs with mocha corner sofa and armchairs and the vanilla painted master bedroom with raspberry feature wall commenting that, by the time she'd finished, they'd have a house that was good enough to eat.

He was in awe of her energy and tenacity as she devoted her days off to wading tirelessly through brochures of kitchen appliances or through piles of fabric, tile or colour samples. She negotiated rates and dates with suppliers, organised work schedules and task priorities to coincide with the college summer break and even produced typed sheets of instructions for Mark to follow whilst he project managed in her absence. He soon began to enjoy this change of scene from white board to clipboard, enduring the gobby Chris Moyles and co each morning whilst making his bacon buttie

95

and coming off his high horse to embrace a whole new vernacular, engaging in the banter with the workmen whilst being careful not to correct their grammar, especially if the response to a question was, 'he done the undercoat on the ceiling yesterday', or 'we're having to turn off the electric, guv'. Keith, the burly foreman of the firm, who was managing the small army of sub-contractors brought in according to their speciality, was a south Londoner who could and would talk for England if given the opportunity. He possessed a strong view regardless of the topic, from whether Jordon should have a breast reduction to the moral dilemma surrounding the issue of assisted dying. A die-hard Chelsea fan, Mark took great delight in reminding him of that night in Moscow in mid-May, when Manchester United beat 'the Blues' on penalties to claim their second Champions League title in a decade set against the pouring rain; a fitting backdrop to a dramatic climax as 'JT' the Chelsea captain could have sealed victory with a penalty kick but slipped on the sodden turf and hit the post instead under the gloomy watchful eye of billionaire owner Roman Abramovich. Utd's keeper van der Sar then saved a tame effort from Nicolas Anelka to cue a red celebration in the former red state. Keith's reply would always be, "I won't be goaded by a plastic Manc mate, find me a real one and we'll talk football."

On one occasion, Mark caught a glance between Keith and Dave, one of the plumbers, as Lizzie made her way up the stairs from the main bathroom where they were working up to the third floor, with cups of tea for the painters who were decorating the guest bedroom. Rather than feel angry as they were clearly ogling her bum, Mark experienced a smug sense of pride, 'that's my girl,' he thought, 'yes she's hot and yes she's about to become my wife.' He wouldn't have known where to start without Lizzie and still got into the occasional fix when asked a direct question from one of the tradesmen, "Your Mrs asked us to order the dimmer switches for the landing lights in burnished steel but the closest they've got is the mock pewter, shall we go ahead and order them as we can have them 'ere by the morning." He wouldn't have a clue what to do and would come out in a cold sweat, not wanting to annoy Lizzie by making the wrong choice but equally he didn't want to appear the hen- pecked drip, indecisive in the face of these testosterone filled white van men. He'd usually opt for "Sure mate, go ahead, no worries," hoping that Lizzie would then agree with his decision so avoiding the embarrassment of having to go back to them the next day and ask them to cancel his order and try other suppliers for Lizzie's preferred choice. "Women, eh?"

It wasn't just the house that was having a makeover either. Lizzie had contracted a landscape gardener friend of her colleague Sue's to draw up plans to maximise the modest garden space and they had duly signed off on plans for a decked outside seating area and to open up the main patch of lawn, removing some of the shrubbery and replacing the dilapidated old shed with a new dual shed and summer house combo, complete with wooden veranda. In order to fund the considerable work to house and garden, not to mention furniture, fixtures and fittings, they had agreed for Mark to take out a loan using the house as collateral, that they were both contributing towards paying off, cementing a sense of the property becoming their home, one barely recognisable from that which Mark had lolloped about in for the previous decade or so. Lizzie had even turned her makeover magic to him, letting him know that she felt his stubble aged him and hurt her chin when she kissed him, gently suggesting he shaved and had his hair trimmed more regularly. She had also been through his wardrobe and tutted at some of his T-shirts, holding the offending articles up to him and frowning, as if to say, are you really intending on wearing a bikini-clad Princess Leia with the line 'Hello Boys' after we're married? He smiled to himself when he remembered how he'd defended that item and even attempted to convince her that, along with his Bikini Inspector T-shirt, it was post-modern and ironic and how she refused to be taken in by his waffle. She just had this way of putting her point across without being pushy, of suggesting rather than ordering that he should take a different (her) view. She was usually right, there comes a time when all men must recognise the need to grow up; tonight, however clearly wasn't that time as he checked his hair and tucked in the Mr Tickle T-shirt for perhaps the last time.

There was something about being in education, an elitist approach, a sense of superiority at times, that could package five grown men all sporting Mr Men T-shirts as clever, funny, precisely the post-modern irony that Lizzie rolled her eyes at. If Keith and the workmen at the house had 'done it' then Mark would probably have rolled *his* eyes as the burly tradesmen would strain to heave the humorous garments over their beer bellies with whoops and laughter that would usually break into wheezing coughing fits due to the amount of cigarettes they got through in an average working day. But as an assortment of teachers and college lecturers they'd pitched it just about right. Mark had been quite explicit when discussing plans for the stag night with his best man Vaz; no different to any other good night out in Brighton other than all to be wearing witty T-shirts. They had mulled over Star Wars, Marvel super heroes and classic TV shows such as the A-Team and The Dukes of Hazard before settling on the Mr Men, with each member of the group asked to purchase a T-shirt that reflected their personality. As Mark was the stag it was only fitting that he should wear the cheekiest of the lot and one that, hopefully, should generate the most interest when out and about. He was nearing the end of the first Stella of the evening, sitting outside the Park Tavern whilst Vaz (Mr Grumpy) and Pete, who at 5ft 9" and around 11 stones in weight was the perfect Mr Strong, had gone to the bar to get the next round in. It was one of those balmy early summer evenings after a long hot day, when a cold pint and a packet of peanuts whilst sitting outside a pub with his mates seemed everything a man could need. Mark felt a wave of contentment wash over him as he closed his eyes, his face turned up towards the source of the now slowly fading warmth. He allowed the animated after work chatter from other benches and the occasional laughter that rang out from inside the pub to merge into a gentle background drone as he lost himself in the moment and tried to take in the enormity of how his life had been turned on its head in less than a year through a chance meeting at a training seminar he almost failed to attend. No more the sad loser, no more Mr Untidy, no more Mr Lonely on a Saturday night and no more Mr Uncomfortable on his family visits, for he was Mr Tickle and he was about to marry his very own little Miss Gorgeous.

The hens were all up at Sue's, a workmate of Lizzie and Janice's, in Kemptown opting for a cheesy evening of takeaway, sparkling wine, homemade face masks, popcorn and a movie fest featuring as many male heart-throbs that they could cram in. Lizzie was never one to maintain hordes of girlie friends, she instead preferred a smaller, more intimate circle where she could really get to know the people she cared for, in this case Lisa, her flatmate and close friend from church, Janice and Sue from her team and Vicky, an old school friend from Chichester with whom she'd never lost touch. As her adopted guardian, Janice had expressed concern at how quickly things had progressed from vague interest through steady boyfriend to potential life partner, feeling that perhaps the loss of her mother the year before may have triggered a subconscious desire for security, hence the rather premature extent of her attachment to Mark. Rather than getting defensive, Lizzie had respected her all the more for voicing these concerns and had taken the time to reflect upon them, tracking her emotions in the wake of her mother's loss and reassuring Janice that her feelings for Mark had evolved independently of her grief at losing her mum. Yes, that loss still felt raw, and even more acute at a time like this, but she was unwavering in her conviction that Mark would be the right man for her. She loved that he liked to wander aimlessly with her along the beach on Sunday mornings, listening as well as talking, asking questions and taking a genuine interest not just in what she was doing but in how she was *feeling*. She felt so relaxed in his company that she could lose herself in her own thoughts with no awkwardness. They could flick through the papers together and exchange views as they went, despite him dismissing her choice of reading material as jingoistic propaganda. They'd animatedly discuss movies they'd seen over a curry or pizza, him teasing her as she always saw the potential for romance and happy ever afters whilst he'd see betrayal and disappointment or expand upon some deeper lying moral truth. Above all, he never pushed the boundaries regarding physical intimacy that she'd set from the beginning of their relationship, nor had he ever belittled her faith. She knew that many Guardian readers and so-called members of the intelligentsia dismissed religion as outdated superstition with a sneering sense of superiority and an alarmingly self-assured belief in their own non-belief but her faith meant everything to her, it was the source of great comfort, hope and strength, something she wore every day, not just on Sunday. Sure, Mark asked questions and challenged her on many theological and moral issues but never in a provocative or antagonistic way but always with balance and respect. She knew deep down that, despite his sensitivity towards her, he still yearned for the retention of some of his bachelor ways and strongly encouraged him to keep up his scriptwriting with Pete as that seemed important to them both. She probably never would, however, understand his desire to waste a whole afternoon or evening hollering at the telly as 22 overpaid, over pampered metro-sexuals chased a ball around in front of a baying crowd of grown men or quite how he got so emotionally involved in film adaptations of fictional comic book characters. She wasn't a huge fan of late night kebabs (or at any time for that matter) and could only take Partridge or Brent in small doses but was touched at how his language had been toned down and his stomach muscles up without her suggesting or requesting that he do either. And yes, he did have a worrying habit of making the wrong quip in the wrong company at precisely the least opportune moment but when all was said and done, he was a good bloke, he adored her and she knew that she could trust him no matter what.

*

"Okay then, you're shipwrecked on a desert island, and you have to choose one companion that (a) isn't male and (b) who isn't your wife or girlfriend. Who would you go for?" Rob, a politics lecturer and Mr Bump wiped his glasses with a tablecloth and put this weighty issue up for consideration as they all tucked into Cobra beers and a pile of spicy poppadoms with chopped onions and mango chutney. Steve, a livewire from the English department who had made up the party, suitably attired as Mr Happy, was first to engage in this challenging debate.

"Easy," claimed Steve, "Carol Vorderman, beauty and brains, she could draw pie charts in the sand to demonstrate your rate of survival by day and then dazzle you with her vital statistics by night."

''Very good, Steve, and with a level of wit we come to expect from the English department, but isn't she a bit, well you know, mutton dressed as lamb?" suggested Rob.

"Sorry mate," Steve replied, "Didn't I make myself clear, I was choosing someone for Mr Grumpy over there, he likes the primary school teacher types and is the least likely from round the table to choose himself a girl Friday on account of him being far too mature for such nonsense."

"If that's how you want to play it," replied Vaz smiling, "who could we choose for you, a man more of words than of action … got it, the sexy sultry queen of TV based literary chat, Mariella Frostrup. You could drool over her husky reviews by night and she could eat you up for breakfast."

"Touché," conceded Steve, "but what about the man of the moment, who would you take with you to keep you warm on Paradise Island, Mark? The lovely Lizzie not being available for selection."

"Well, it's quite a dilemma, isn't it?" said Mark, thoughtfully through a mouthful of poppadoms. "You could go for a bombshell like Kelly Brook who'd look knockout lounging about in a bikini all day but might be somewhat lacking in the conversational stakes. Charlie Dimmock would be a dab hand at digging out the foundations and constructing a sturdy lean-to but who'd honestly want to cosy up to a Ray Parlour look-a-like every night? So, we're probably looking at someone like Halle Berry who could use her Catwoman skills to sniff out and snare that night's supper whilst looking superhot in leather at the same time."

"Hang on a sec," interrupted Pete, "who said anything about fantasy figures, we're talking real women here surely, not the characters they play?" The others nodded sagely. "Halle Berry is a hot chick in her own right but not as Catwoman. Hot in more senses of the word by the way as just how impractical would black leather be on a desert island? If superheroes *were* allowed then I'd go for Jessica Alba as Mrs Invisible from the Fantastic Four, she could catch fresh fish without them seeing her coming then pout and make big eyes at me whilst we cooked them slowly over a beach fire at sundown."

"Mrs Invisible," spluttered Mark through his lager, "It's Sue Richards, the Invisible Girl, you pleb."

"Are you gentlemen ready to order?" The waiter arrived to interrupt the clash of heavyweight thinkers as they turned their attention back to their stomachs before continuing their debate; as if there was any likelihood of either one of them being shipwrecked on a desert island and of Kelly Brook, Halle Berry or Jessica Alba cosying up as a breeze rustled through the palm trees, head resting on their shoulder as they watched the fire on the beach flicker and crackle as the sun set over paradise.

*

She applied an extra layer of lip gloss before sliding it back into her make-up pouch that was inside her fake Chanel handbag, running through the usual checklist before heading out to work; fags, purse, phone, perfume, rape alarm, condoms, chewing gum. She took a long look at herself in the cheap pine framed mirror hanging on the wall of the same cramped bedroom she'd had since she was a girl, cursing her estranged dad for her corkscrew hair, flat nose and flared nostrils; hating the sight of them. The term 'half-caste' had long since been consigned to the history books, replaced by the softer and friendlier sounding 'mixed race', but despite the political correctness of her label, a label it remained and one that, ironically, had prevented her from mixing well at school, leaving her on the fringes of the cliques that inevitably form, particularly with teenage girls. Men now described her as stunning and exotic but she certainly didn't feel that way. Sure, she had a figure that many women would die for and looked pretty fit in her black tights, denim hot pants and white vest, but most men didn't realise that it didn't matter how a woman looked from the outside, if they had never felt truly loved by their father and as a result struggled to even like themselves, then accepting love from a guy was almost impossible. Anyway, most of the blokes she met in her line of work rarely looked beyond her figure and features and she accepted that, it somehow gave her power, a hold over them and she felt secure behind her mask. She pulled her favourite grey hoodie with Burberry trim from her chest of drawers and up over her head, took one last long critical look at herself before flicking off the light switch and heading downstairs and out to meet Tia, one of the other girls, for a drink before their shift began. Stopping at the foot of the stairs she called out, "Off out to work now Mum." She didn't wait for a reply, glancing down the hallway and through the open lounge door she saw her mum slumped in front of the telly, snoozing after a takeout, a couple of glasses of Chardonnay and a long day on the checkout. She stepped out into the still warm early evening air and clicked the glass fronted paint-flaked red front door shut behind her.

*

"Shall we dance?" The girls all squealed at this line, barely able to contain their delight as Richard Gere, suave and handsome in a dinner suit and clutching a single stem red rose, had taken the escalator up to where Susan Sarandon was working in the department store, to the envious gazes of her co-workers. Yes the outcome was predictable, and the gesture was as cheesy as a night of fondue but Lizzie was totally lost in the moment (despite the fact that the businessman he played had only taken up dancing in the first place as he spotted the smouldering instructor played by J-Lo from the window of his commuter train one evening and fancied his chances). "He's so gorgeous," Vicky sighed, as the credits rolled, "Manly and sensitive, why do I only ever get one or the other? A real looker who takes great pride in being able to burp the word bollocks or the gentle type who has more late-night headaches and emotional issues than I do."

"Which category would you put Mark in then Lizzie, the over manly or over sensitive?" chimed Janice with a sparkling wine induced look of mischief in her eye. "Neither fully, I guess," was Lizzie's honest reply, "and I take great comfort in that fact. He acts like he's Bruce Willis when I ask him to do something I'm not strong enough to do, like open a new jar of marmalade but will then struggle to open it without breaking out into a sweat and resorting to placing it between his knees whilst donning a Marigold 'just for the grip'. He also thinks he's Keats whenever he pens a love sonnet that I find amusing in areas where I don't think he intended them to be. Mark genuinely tries hard to understand what a woman wants

102

and responds accordingly. He doesn't always get it right, but gives it his best shot and I love him all the more for it."

"What a woman wants!" shrieked Lisa, "you genius, let's watch it next!" Sue refilled the wooden bowl perched on the low smoked glass table in the middle of the lounge with a fresh bag of popcorn whilst Lisa rifled through the stack of DVDs toppling onto the wood effect floor and Janice topped up the glasses with fizzy wine. Lizzie took a moment to sit back and take it all in; Vicky, her oldest friend, pretty and studious, with designer glasses that she kept pushing back up her nose, whether out of a need for them to sit right or just out of habit. She was ever the romantic but yet to find her match, always seeing the potential but just as often let down by the reality, by men who were emotionally stunted and/or incapable of monogamy. Lizzie admired her resilience, for whatever the knock-back she always came back for more, believing that her perfect match could be a train seat opposite or next in supermarket queue away. Then there was dear Sue the team administrator, older than the rest of the group and still struggling to come to terms with the tragic loss of her husband Roy to an industrial accident on a building site the previous autumn, still waiting for compensation owed her despite the verdict of negligence being found against his employer at a tribunal that seemed to take an age to announce its findings. It would have been understandable if she'd decided to pull out of the evening altogether but she was adamant that she hosted it, joining in as best she could. How must she really be feeling thought Lizzie, to be mourning the loss of her husband whilst helping me to celebrate finding mine? Lisa, her flatmate, was her usual open and accommodating self, quick to find common ground in whatever social circle she found herself in and a natural at making people feel at ease in her company. You really could take Lisa anywhere, thought Lizzie, and she'd find her way. Janice, with a warm smile and furrowed brow as she searched to gauge Lizzie's mood, stepped over Lisa's outstretched legs and knelt down in front of Lizzie, who was perched on a cushion on the floor with her back leaning against the sofa. "You okay kiddo," she asked gently. "Of course," Lizzie replied smiling, "I'm just taking you all in, wondering how different it will be when I'm married. I've always maintained that it would be friendships as usual, regardless, but I hear of so many women who immerse themselves in their husbands and home lives to such an extent they drift away from the women who have helped to keep them afloat for so long." Janice filled her glass with more of the cold Australian fizz that reflected the upbeat mood of the evening, light, bright and bubbly. "It's only right that your priorities change, lovely, but you've always been good at balancing relationships, and have great intuition, more so than the rest of us put together. The bonds that men and women make outside of physical relationships are different, ours seem somehow deeper, more rooted, not to belittle the friendships that Mark has but we've all been through so much together that there is an emotional thread that runs through our collective experiences, binding us; that will never be broken. Never." The two women exchanged a hug as best they could, one balancing a bottle, the other a full glass. Turning to the other girls Janice boomed, "Okay, what other mush do we have to endure, insulting my feminist credibility." They'd already had Gerard Butler and Richard Gere with Mel Gibson up next, not to mention Brad Pitt and Johnny Depp still on the pile. It's going to be a long night, thought Lizzie, but she wouldn't change it for the world.

*

The cool sea breeze sent a shudder down his spine, it was cool now, away from the benefit of the heated patio at the OhSo as they'd rounded the evening off with more beers, sprawled on the scruffy outdoor long black painted wooden tables and benches. Not for the first time he and Vaz were leaning on the railings gazing out to sea and philosophising. "How come it's always me and you left standing, Vaz? I mean you're a lightweight so how can you last the course when others fall at the final hurdle, do you really drink every beer bought for you or do you discreetly pour it into the nearest plant like in that Mellow Birds advert from the '80s?"

"Whether you like it or not, your best man is irrep, irrep," he struggled. "Irreprehensible," helped Mark. "Irrepressible," finished Vaz. "I am da man, and unless someone says otherwise, I shall remain so." He smiled and adopted a stance, mimicking a famous locally based super middleweight boxer. Mark was weighing up a suitable quote of his own, his brain just a tad slower than usual, when the air was punctuated by an overpowering waft of citrus perfume and a voice that seemed to sing as much as say, "You two look like you don't have a clue where you're going so you're coming with us." Out of nowhere had stepped two absolute babes, the one who had announced their arrival verbally, was tanned and toned, with long salon straightened blonde hair and bright pink lip gloss; Barbie goes to Brighton he thought. The other, taller, afro/Caribbean, with an amazing mass of black corkscrew hair and deep brown eyes framed by bronze eye shadow flashed perfect white teeth as she broke into a smile. Both were wearing frayed denim hot pants with black tights underneath and white vests with something sparkly written across the front. Mark restrained from leaning in to get a better look or pointing at this writing as the girls were both pretty well endowed and he didn't want a slap across the face to end this chance encounter, but how cute, he remembered thinking, matching outfits. Suddenly the air was charged with a heady mix of designer fragrance, cigarette smoke, salty sea spray and sexual energy, they could have been on a night out in Ibiza and Mark felt totally thrown by this change of tone and direction to the evening. The two girls, both of whom seemed to fit the description of desert island girl Fridays perfectly, linked arms with Vaz and him and marched them off along the seafront back towards the Grand Pier before they could put up any resistance.

Talking about taking the initiative he thought, but what's going on? He 'whoooad' the procession down, un-linked arms and took Vaz a few feet away from them, back to their original pose, leaning on the seafront railings, whilst the girls fiddled with their hair, rolled their eyes at each other and waited expectantly. "Come on Vaz," Mark stuttered, "this is going too far, we don't know them from Adam, well Eve, and where did they suddenly appear from, and why us?"

"Mark, you ask too many questions," Vaz replied, "just go with the flow knowing that I've got your back. What harm can a stroll and a chat along the seaside with two pretty girls do, eh? You know and I know that you wouldn't get up to no-good – you're too besotted with Lizzie and besides, I wouldn't let you mess it up even if you were too dumb to self-destruct." Mark reluctantly consented, after all, Vaz was his best man and the most sensible bloke he knew. Feeling more reassured he allowed the link up to be re-linked up and the unsteady procession to resume. They chatted about their night so far, their clever 'stag' T-shirts, the curry, how they then regretted jumping to House of Pain in the OhSo, fumbling for their wallets as they paid to get in to wherever the girls had taken them. "It's The Zap I think," Mark mumbled to Vaz. As they made their way through the foyer towards the dark double doors that led to the bar and dance floor the blonde girl, (Bond girl) who with her friend had followed them this far, announced brightly, "You're on your own now lover-boys," as the two greeters smiled once more doing that annoying half-hearted Mariah Carey wave before turning on their heels, well in their UGG boots, and heading towards the exit and back out into the balmy night air to attract more unsuspecting punters.

Vaz collapsed against the wall laughing whilst miming the act of an angler reeling in a huge fish. Sure, they'd been had, hook, line and sinker, flattered into believing that two girls both half their age with glamour model looks would be vaguely interested in anything other than their wallets, but Vaz had been equally duped so why was he mocking Mark? Mark shook his head as the reality of this sting sunk in. He was actually more relieved than hurt, there might have been at first the realisation that there existed women that simply wouldn't view him as being an attractive proposition, seeing through him as if he didn't exist in any other way than as a route to a potential commission payment but the overriding feeling was the sheer joy that Lizzie did, and what's more he hadn't blown it by flirting with the notion of flirting with such dolly birds. The combination of relief and surge of love for Lizzie was exhilarating and so he shouted over in the direction of Vaz, jerking his head towards the pounding Balearic beats that throbbed and pulsed from the other side of the doors. "Come on then Vaz, when in Ibiza and all that." They pushed through the double doors and were at once hit by a wall of euphoria, the DJ whipping the trance-like crowd into frenzy as Energy 52 by Café del Mar reached its spine tingling, epic break out. Within seconds Mark and Vaz were losing themselves in this sea of swaying bodies, arms all raised to the roof as the revolving lasers illuminated the scene, one that could almost be taken as a joint act of worship. To some, God might well be a DJ.

*

There was still a beat pounding relentlessly in his head as he was woken by his landline ringing, and ringing. He sat up with a start and wished he hadn't, his head was swimming and waves of nausea rose from deep within. Struggling to orientate himself, he groaned and hauled himself up from the sofa, shuffling gingerly towards the source of such piercing irritation, knocking over a pint glass of water in doing so then promptly squelching through the liquid as it ran in the direction in which he was blindly lurching like the Mummy in an episode of Scooby-Doo. Fortunately the carpet, yet to be replaced by expensive oak floor, absorbed the impact so no broken glass to add injury to insult. He got to the phone just as the caller was about to ring off. "Errgghhhh hello." His voice sounded full of gravel, smoke and dry ice, of lager, late night and curry and, judging by the paper wrappers that curled around his bare feet, kebabs. "At last," came the anxious voice of Lizzie, "Where have you been? I've been so worried, I tried your mobile and left I don't know how many messages. I thought you'd been tossed naked off the pier or something."

"Stag night or not there was no tossing going on last night beloved, off the pier naked or otherwise." He heard a deep sigh and could detect the exasperation in her tone, "Now is not the time for your puerile humour Mark Woodford, it's nearly lunchtime, my dad and brother are due to check into the seafront Thistle in an hour and you and Vaz are supposed to be picking them up from there at 2 to collect their suits, I do hope you've remembered?" She was trying hard to mask the irritation that had quickly replaced the relief at hearing that he was okay, albeit not successfully. "So, how was your night last night?" Lizzie asked, more out of a sense of duty than genuine interest as she could have easily predicted the outcome; too much beer and junk food and a flop on the sofa in the early hours with the TV still on in the background. "Oh, so, so, well more OhSo actually," he replied, quite capable of attempting weak puns even when in a comatose state. "And what about you sweetheart, how was it with you and the girls?"

"It was okay to a point but I was mortified when a burly young policeman came to the door asking for me only to announce that he was going to have to 'take down my particulars' before ripping off his uniform to reveal a six pack and a thong and ordering me to smother his naked torso with baby oil." Silence. "You're kidding me, right?"

"Of course I am you idiot! We did just as we'd planned to, we drank wine, put on face packs, ate popcorn, watched cheesy movies, shared some pizza, you know, all very civilised, as you'd expect from the more mature sex. Listen, we're off to do some last-minute shopping and then head over to get our hair and nails done, you will promise that you won't go back to sleep and leave my Dad and Stu in the lurch?"

"Of course not, go on, have a great afternoon my love and I can't wait to see you tomorrow at the altar, my gorgeous wife to be."

"Oh, leave off you charmer." Lizzie's voice had begun to soften."

"Missshhh Moneypenny, at last I am going to make an honest woman of you."

"Goodbye Mr Bond."

As he replaced the handset on the receiver he breathed a sigh of relief that he was still in one piece and that he could tell that Lizzie signed off with a smile. Slowly, he took in the scene around him; the battered sofa with crumpled cushions and an old blanket hanging over the side where he'd thrown it back to get up so abruptly, an equally tatty old armchair in which Vaz was still sprawled, asleep, half covered by an ancient picnic rug, his mouth open, gently snoring. Looking down he realised he'd trodden in the remains of the previous night's kebab and had a piece of cold red onion stuck to the sole of his foot. Why on earth did we have a kebab after consuming a curry he wondered? Shrugging, and still battling the nausea, he lowered himself down slowly, his back upright, to remove the offending articles and an empty bottle of Becks beer that must have accompanied this late-night feast. How often had he had to piece together the events of a night out by analysing food stains on his clothes or the carpet the morning after? Pretty gross really. Well that was all soon to change as Lizzie rarely allowed herself past the tipsy stage, where he would often and readily hurtle past it towards a boozy oblivion. There again, with Lizzie he rarely felt the need to, as being in her company was stimulation enough. As he stepped over Vaz' outstretched legs and into the hallway, meaning to take the rubbish to the pedal bin in the kitchen, he was aware of a draft around his ankles. Not again, he sighed, as he pushed the front door closed with his hip. Now that's another thing I'm going to have to tighten up on when Lizzie's moved in, home security.

He let the cold tap run for a minute before filling another pint glass with water, that he promptly downed in one, topping it up again before sitting on one of the pine chairs in the kitchen to draw breath and bridge the gap between leaving the curry house the night before and waking up on the sofa, with Vaz snoring in the armchair. Slowly and painfully it all came trickling back and he filtered events in chronological order, the rest of the lads leaving after closing time at the OhSo, he and Vaz wandering up onto the seafront to gaze out across the ocean, the two girls 'picking them up' before depositing them at The Zap club, more drinks there, switching from beer to Vodka/Red Bull, losing themselves in the sweaty Balearic euphoric crowd, the long walk back picking a kebab up on the way, chucking the salad out as they walked, leaving a trail of lettuce and tomato all the way up London Road. He vaguely remembers sitting slumped on the sofa pressing the TV remote over and over before admitting defeat and crashing out. That was weird, as usually it wouldn't matter how much booze he'd consumed, he'd always managed to operate the Samsung widescreen; he could do it in his sleep. Steadily placing the half empty glass of water on a cork coaster (a gift from Mrs Sheridan bought, ironically, in Cork) on the kitchen table he made his way gingerly back down the hallway and into the lounge only for the mystery to be resolved in an instant; there was a gaping 42" gap between the bookshelf and the fireplace where the flat screen would normally sit on top of its stand. "Shit!" he exclaimed, "Vaz, wake up, we've been burgled!"

*

As she sat at the walnut dressing table and gazed into the mirror that her mother had done so for many years before her, she wondered if any woman ever truly felt happy with the hand they'd been dealt. She detected small purple patches under her eyes, the result of too late a night, and wrinkles around them, laughter lines her mother would have called them. Growing up, she had always been incredibly self-conscious of her eyes that she felt were too big for her face, along with lips that looked too puffy. As a seven-year-old you only ever concerned with fitting in, totally unaware of the 'Bardot' effect that, apparently, she had as a late teenager. Peering so close that her breath left a small mark on the mirror, she examined her skin for any blemishes, thank the Lord, she thought, no pocket of blackheads on the end of her nose, as sometimes happened when she felt anxious. Her skin was normally smooth and clear, albeit a touch on the oily side, and she needed to guard against becoming lapse with regards maintaining a regime of sorts. Reaching for a cotton ball pad, she squeezed some moisturiser out and enjoyed the cool sensation of it gliding over her skin. She had a vivid recollection from when she was a girl of standing alongside her mother, transfixed, as she carried out precisely the same procedure early one summers evening as she prepared to head out to a drama rehearsal. She saw her mother's smile in her own, the same shaped fingers moving across her cheek that was now stained by first one tear and then another. The grief had stolen up on her like an early morning mist, enveloping her and taking charge of her emotions. Now sobbing, she placed her arms across her chest, hugging herself as there was no one else there to do it for her; rocking gently back and forth on the worn pink velvet topped wooden seat she whispered, "Oh Mum, why aren't you here?"

*

Mark and Vaz, both in Mr Men T-shirts and boxers, stared at where the flat screen TV should be, as transfixed as if they were watching a big game or a movie. Vaz briefly disappeared only to pop his head back around the door to say, "No sign of a break-in, have you checked the back door?"

"No need," sighed Mark, "we didn't close the front door behind us, some bastard must have stolen it from right under our noses." But something didn't quite add up, a thought kept nagging at him but struggled to make itself heard against the maelstrom of others that made his already delicate head spin all the more. Vaz, the most sensible bloke he knew, went into crisis management mode and, sounding more like Jack Bauer than a school teacher with a hangover, announced. "Okay, so let's do a floor by floor sweep to see if anything else has been stolen." As quickly as their sluggish state would allow, they made their way up through the house, the freshly painted show home feel of the second floor in marked contrast to the ground floor that was all shabby with none of the chic that was evident elsewhere after the recent transformation. The three bedrooms and family bathroom were exactly as they had left them, with no sign of any intrusion so Mark headed to the top floor with a sense of relief that was soon to turn to utter despair. Another noticeable absence, but this time from the vintage desk that sat beneath the window with views out across the roads that ran parallel to Preston Park down towards the town and the sea; his laptop had gone, along with his passport, the flight tickets, hire car confirmation, the wedding rings and £900 worth of euros that he'd only picked up the day before. "She's going to kill me," was all he could whimper feebly.

*

Lizzie was shaken out of her mournful mantra by a knock on her bedroom door. "Hot, deep bath all ready for you Lizzie."

"Thanks Lisa, I'll be right there." She dabbed her eyes with the cotton wool ball and blew her nose, drawing a soft scented tissue from a box on the dressing table. A good soak, she thought, that'll help me get things straight in my head. She waited until she could hear Lisa humming whilst tidying in the lounge before heading into the steamy bathroom, shutting the stripped pine door behind her. Hanging her robe on the hook on the back of it she piled her hair up and tested the temperature with a toe before wincing and adding more cold water to the tub that was brimming with scented foam. Satisfied that she wouldn't scald herself, she eased herself down into the oily froth before submerging almost to her neck. Bliss. Lizzie was a lover of baths, doing much of her deepest contemplation when in this floaty state. She recalls such a soak before her first date with Mark, how Janice had predicted a disaster and was offering to be her get out of jail free card. To be fair, Mark hadn't exactly swept her off her feet, instead spilling peanuts across the floor before knocking his pint over the table that he'd hit with his knee when getting up to greet her; taking half her face off with his stubble in doing so. She smiled as she considered his tendency to decorate any situation with comedy, whether intentional or not, even suggesting that he may even be on the autism spectrum due to his emotional disconnection with certain situations, manifesting in the least appropriate comment or gesture. He'd agreed that the thought had even crossed his mind. She wondered what her Mum would have made of him. She had opted for the sensible choice after her 'first love' broke into the acting world with a touring theatre company and had asked her to go with him. She decided it was just too much of a risk, remaining in rural West Sussex where she met and married her father, a good sort, hard-working and reliable but ultimately without the spark that had been ignited by the one that her Mum had let go. She was too loyal to ever admit it, but Lizzie did often wonder whether or not her Mum ever regretted her decision, secretly pining for the more adventurous life her former leading man would have offered as her father suggested yet another visit to the Wildfowl Trust at Arundel or insisted that they waited until after 6pm to make a phone call as the rates were cheaper. Lizzie had experienced her fair share of the more showy blokes but still didn't feel that she was making a compromise with Mark as life was never dull with him around.

She knew that he had a tendency to err on the side of procrastination, to favour going with the flow to actually ever having a plan, but she had seen a genuine change in his attitude since they had been together, getting to grips with the responsibilities that had for so long seemed to have eluded him, with his privileged background affording him the time and the money to continue avoiding the day to day chores that the majority of people had no option but to get on with. She recognised a glazed look that would come over him whenever she mentioned topics such as home and contents insurance, warranties, savings accounts and APR, as if the shutters were firmly coming down, but he had made a go at getting to grips with the work they were doing on the house, managing the assorted tradesmen that she'd organised to come in over the past month or so and he had even taken responsibility for booking the honeymoon villa in Rhodes, complete with the flights, hire car and spending money. Johnnie had kindly offered them his place in Corfu for a fortnight but, rightly, Mark wanted them to go somewhere that neither of them had an association with for their precious first two weeks of married life so, having jettisoned a number of viable options due to one or both of them having already holidayed there with friends or family, they had settled on a delightful looking whitewashed villa with a small pool enclosed within a walled garden nestled within the low hills overlooking the Med on the south-east coast of the island. She pictured them sitting at the rustic wooden table under the covered porch area that overlooked the pool, nibbling on freshly picked olives and sipping an iced G&T whilst listening to the crickets as the sun slowly set on another day of swimming, sunbathing and that all-important siesta.

As excited as she was at the prospect of sexual union with Mark it also caused her stomach to tighten and her cheeks, already flushed by the sauna of a bath she was soaking in, to deepen a shade or two as her body temperature rose. When it came to sexual relations, she was someone who was quite prepared to swim against the tide of opinion held by many in contemporary society with 'try before you buy' almost a standard approach. After a couple of instances where she had felt pressurised to sleep with boyfriends she had decided firmly that she was going to save herself for her future husband. So many young females that she worked with assumed that if you had had sex once then you automatically entered into a sexual relationship with the next lad that came along and there began a cycle that remained unbroken. She was proof that, if you wanted to step off that path then you could, but she also appreciated that the weight of peer pressure could make that an extremely difficult and potentially alienating choice for the individual concerned and strived to give the best and most supportive advice to all those who came to her from it, free from any judgement. She'd had many conversations with Janice and Lisa on this topic over pizza and Pinot and Janice had assumed that the other girls' stance (Lisa was saving herself for marriage) had been forced upon them by their church that she described as outdated and unrealistic and was surprised that it was purely down to individual choice.

She would miss these talks with her close friends and made a mental note to do all she could to maintain these precious friendships. Lizzie suspected that Mark didn't view sex in quite the same way as she did but that he was not the experienced lover that his bravado conveyed whenever the subject arose. She felt at once bashful but also excited at the prospect of embracing physical deep unity within the context of their marriage. As was often the case with Lizzie, however, a moment of clarity and transcendence was quickly followed by one of reality and practicality as she visualised them on their wedding night; what if they were too tired from the day and the travelling to make love, or if it was clunky in some way? What if he snored? What if *she* snored? How would they cope with the inevitable flatulence that nerves, coupled with a change of climate and food may bring on? What if he stank the loo out before she showered or bathed and this repulsed her? What if *she* had an upset stomach on her honeymoon? This wasn't helping her pre-wedding nerves so she dragged her thoughts from toilet arrangements on a balmy Mediterranean evening in a sun soaked villa to more immediate matters to consider in a fragrance soaked bath; the wedding day itself.

She had deliberated at length over the venue for the service, torn between the traditional flint stone church in her home village in West Sussex, with all its childhood associations, and the much bigger, vibrant contemporary church she currently attended in central Brighton. Her mum's passing two years before had changed her feelings towards that ancient and familiar little place of worship that used to engender such a sense of warmth and comfort. She could still hear that thick, worn, solid, studded wooden door creak open, unlocked with a huge wrought iron key the likes you only saw nowadays in *Midsomer Murders*. She could picture the dust dancing in multicoloured, diagonal shafts of light cast by the stained-glass windows of knights and saints of old (the Archangel Michael being her favourite); she could feel the sensation of sliding across the polished dark-wood pews in her light cotton summer dress, smelling wafts of mustiness from the thick embroidered kneelers and she could still taste the communion wine, sherry-like with a metallic tang from the old silver chalice.

But she could also still hear the first few handfuls of earth thud and scatter across the lacquered lid of her mother's light wood coffin, after it had been lowered gently into the neatly dug hole alongside the low moss covered grey flint wall that bordered the fields, now vivid yellow with rape flower. She could still feel her feet almost giving way beneath her as she reached out for her father's left arm for support, his shoulders crumpling at the same time, with his right hand going up to his face as they stared in silence, subduing their sobs, until the other mourners had solemnly gravel-crunched their way back to their cars and they were the only sentinels remaining, along with the skylarks and the wood pigeons. She could still smell the inside of their cottage on the shoulder of her father's jacket and remember the enormity of the rupture that now ran through their rural idyll. The joy that she had always associated with that place, scuffing through the snow towards a candlelit glow for carols on Christmas Eve, weaving excitedly in and out of the tombstones on Easter egg hunts on bright spring mornings, stopping beneath the sprawling canopy of the thousand year old yew to briefly inspect a worn inscription before chasing the next clue, had been replaced by a deep, cold, hollow, sadness. For her mother's name had now been added to the list of deceased that lay in that small insignificant corner of England, just another obstacle in a treasure hunt for the new generation of village children, many of whom had known her mother, but none any near rocked to the bone by her departure as her only daughter.

She had been dreading the trip home to discuss her wedding plans and had put it off for as long as she possibly could, proving elusive when on the phone to her dad each week and simply delaying the inevitable fallout. True, she had dreaded every visit since losing her mum, but there was an extra heaviness in her heart as she could predict the deep disappointment and abandonment felt by her father and the local vicar at her decision not to uphold tradition and have her wedding at the parish church of her home village. The dear old Reverend Poe had become a closer family friend with each passing year, having presided over her Baptism and First Holy Communion as well as her mother's funeral. A tall, broad, slightly stooped academic, and a relative of the writer Edgar Allan, he was a softly spoken man with a deep honey-smooth, educated voice that managed to convey both authority and compassion. She would hate to hurt his feelings in any way as he had been so supportive of the family during her mother's illness and since her death. She had been so distracted at the prospect of difficult conversations and being the cause of such disappointment as she drove west along the A27 towards Chichester and 'home' one Friday evening in early spring that she'd had to exit the dual carriageway, heavy with rush hour traffic, at Arundel to sit for half an hour on a wooden bench overlooking the River Arun, that gently coursed over weeds and pebbles, her fragile nerves becoming smoothed by the water just as the stones had been by that steady mesmerising flow.

But her anxiety had proved to be in vain. The following afternoon, she had sat patiently, nervously in the study at the flint built vicarage, sipping tea from bone china cups, waiting for the Reverend Poe to attempt in vain to create some semblance of order amongst the precarious piles of papers and reference books that had threatened to overrun his dark wooden desk, with its scuffed green leather surface quite buried from view. The window was half open and she could hear a flurry of swifts noisily flitting and flirting amongst the ancient eaves of St Mary's. He had given her advice that had surprised her as they munched their way through a plate of digestive biscuits, on the menu in the vicarage since time immemorial, removing his glasses and sitting back in his worn leather chair, saying that her wedding should be a day of celebration and not of mourning, lit by the light of a bright future and not shrouded in the dark clouds of the past and that she should forget tradition if it was to remind her of the great loss that she had suffered when her mother had been taken from her. He had suggested that if we held on too tightly to the past then we would not be free to fully embrace our future and that was where she had to look now. She was full of admiration for that creaky old chap, with his kind watery pale blue eyes, unruly eyebrows and grey hair that sprouted prolifically from ears and nostrils, for he had put her feelings and their roots above tradition and ritual, the very elements that she thought in some cases threatened to strangle faith like bindweed around a garden rose. But today was a good day and had gone some way in restoring her faith in the institution, because one learned, wise old man, had put compassionate reasoning and the love of another before religious tradition.

He had also put his heavy pear soap scented hand upon her shoulder, referred to her as 'my dear girl' and nodded gently as she reached the end of that familiar hallway, the smells of baking wafting out from the kitchen, as his wife dutifully made her famous Victoria sponge cakes for the coffee and chatter that took place in the church room after Sunday Communion. Maybe there might be some traditions that aren't so bad after all she thought as she made her way towards the heavy wooden gate across the smooth worn paving slabs that were overlapped by luscious thick licks of long grass and bordered by primroses, the occasional hyacinth and heavy headed daffodils that nodded to her in the breeze. Turning her face up towards the pale sun that was not yet fully exerting itself, she smiled to herself as she heard the reassuring late Saturday afternoon sound of lawnmowers that heralded the arrival of spring to the village. She pictured her dad plodding methodically up and down their small back lawn in his old green wellies, leaving perfect, straight lines in his wake. So, one down, two to go she thought.

As she prepared a huge dish of homemade lasagne with salad for 'the men', Radio 4 murmuring in the background, she thought how odd it felt, doing what her mum would usually do with all the familiar utensils and ingredients she would deploy, as she would be watching on. Her stomach tightened once more as she anticipated her talk with her dad after supper. She was less concerned about Stu, as he rarely expressed any passion, other than for a new piece of code or Red Dwarf memorabilia, and avoided confrontation like he avoided people; it was her dad that she dreaded hurting. He was a simple but proud man, upright, his life based on solid principles, be the best you can with what you've got, be punctual, courteous, treat others as you'd like to be treated, don't judge people, don't be wasteful, either with words or money and respect others, especially your family. As with all 'talks' timing was king and she knew that the best time would be after he was full with homemade lasagne and apple tart and before she made some of that 'posh coffee' to be taken into the lounge and sipped by the open fire. However, she was a woman, and no matter how hard she attempted to prioritise this domestic efficiency over any potential emotional outpouring, the latter would often refuse to be compartmentalised and would invariably find a way to spill forth at an unscheduled moment.

How could she possibly articulate her sense of loneliness and loss, how could she even begin to reconcile her twin senses of relief and guilt? She could no longer face walking the narrow high hedged lanes and dusty woodland paths where she and her mum would stroll at dusk, arms linked, chatting or simply taking in the birdsong or evensong as the air here was always thick with the reassuring sounds of rural England. Nor would she ever wish to sip Earl Grey and nibble carrot cake in the cosy tea rooms in Chichester that would provide welcome rest after a browse amongst the boutiques and cloisters of that elegant city. But she didn't have to face those daily physical reminders of their family life, her father and brother did. They couldn't escape it like she could and how did they feel that she had barely returned to the family home since the funeral? And now, on top of it all, she was about to drive in another painful wedge by getting married in Brighton? They must despise her!

Her father was not relaxing in his favourite armchair, full from a delicious homemade supper and pud, but he was, instead, standing in the kitchen, trousers still tucked into thick socks, holding his Wellington boots in one hand, mouth agape as Lizzie, hair tied up, face tear stained, wearing her mother's flowery cooking apron and waving a wooden spatula in the air when it wasn't being used to smooth the white sauce over the top of the Bolognese, poured her heart out. He was not a man of speeches or soothing, more of quietly doting and 'doing' and so wasn't used to having to console his hysterical daughter, he always had Rose to do that, whilst he pottered away, fitting new washers to the bathroom taps or fixing the latch on the garden gate. But Rose was not here, and the house was diminished by her absence, duller, quieter, lacking the sparkle of her presence, the lightness of her touch and warmth of her voice as she sung or hummed her way through the daily chores, always smiling, always bright. He placed his boots on the doormat and moved towards Lizzie, opening his arms and inviting her into his hug. He rested his chin on the top of her head, her hair smelling of exotic fruit and fried mince and he of grass and two-stroke petrol and patted her back gently as her body convulsed into deep sobs, soon joining her so it would be unclear to an onlooker as to who was consoling who. And there they stood, as the dusk drew in, and the wood pigeons co-cooed, needing no words to convey the depths of their loss and of their love for one another.

She wiped her eyes as she recalled the tenderness of that moment, of all the things that could have been said but equally that didn't have to be. Later, as they sipped their mugs of coffee before the glowing embers in the hearth he had reassured her that he understood fully why she had stayed away and why she wanted to get married in Brighton, he told her that he was proud of her strength, of her faith, of her independent spirit, and that she was just like her mother, lighting up a room like a beam of sunshine. He said that leading his beautiful, clever, caring daughter up the aisle would make him the proudest man alive and that her mother would be smiling down on them all, whilst at the same time wishing that someone would straighten his buttonhole and remind him to keep his hands out of his pockets. She went to bed that night relieved that they had shared, that she had been understood and forgiven, but racked by the unspoken grief that he must carry everywhere with him, particularly through the long dark nights, alone and at each solitary first light.

He would be arriving in Brighton soon; not going a mile over sixty on the dual carriageway, his silver Astra immaculately cleaned, waxed and vacuumed on the inside, despite the fact that no one would see it apart from him and Stu, but that wasn't the point, it was a matter of personal pride and not for show. She exhaled, her quiet fondness and deep respect for her father being replaced by a pang of tension, as she pictured a hung-over Mark still shuffling around at home looking for some jeans to throw on. She had trusted him to look after her father and brother whilst she and the girls went for their pre-wedding day pampering session, a present from dear Sue, and would be furious if he let him down. At the same time, she thought of how much he had grown up in the time they had been together, of how he'd become far more organised with all his planning and marking before the end of term, of how he'd mucked in with managing the workmen during the re-furb and of how he'd taken on the responsibility of booking the honeymoon villa and everything associated with it to enable her to focus on the service and the reception. Maybe it was time to release those doubts, relinquish control and begin trusting unreservedly in her future husband who was proving far more capable than she had given him credit for.

"She'll rip my balls off, wedding or no wedding, correction, there'll *be* no wedding, so how the hell can I be calm and think clearly Inspector Vaz!" Mark was now back down in the lounge, dressed in last night's jeans, complete with curry sauce stains, and still wearing his Mr Tickle T-shirt, as dress code was the last thing on his mind. Ironically, it should have been the first thing on his mind, as Vaz pointed out, that in less than an hour they were going to pick up their wedding suits, but Mark wasn't in the mood for wit; he was up to his neck in something else and could see all the good work of the past few months evaporating before his eyes.

"This is what we'll do," said Vaz, assuming control of the situation, "We'll meet Lizzie's dad and brother as planned and keep schtum about all this, otherwise they'll only flap and will bring Lizzie into it. After we've sorted the suits out we'll come back and work this out."

"Work it out!" Mark squeaked, "What's there to be worked out, this isn't a crossword puzzle, I've been robbed of a laptop and nearly a grand's worth of euros, not to mention a villa, a hire car and probably a wife."

"Listen," Vaz continued, "let's keep our heads here. Maybe Lizzie came by for all the tickets and money because she knows you're such a Muppet you'd probably lose them, I know, I know, that doesn't explain the TV, maybe you have been burgled, if so we'll call those PCSOs you know and they can get on to it discreetly, you know, no flashing lights and sirens."

"Okay," Mark nodded, "let's just take a deep breath and keep our cool. I AM GOING TO DIE!" he yelled as he pulled on his Converse, picked up his wallet and keys and headed out into the early afternoon heat with the ever unflappable Vaz.

*

The Thistle Hotel is one grim looking building, he thought, it looks like a giant breeze block had been dumped indiscriminately from a great height within spitting distance of the sea, and had windows and doors chiselled out symmetrically, a sort of concrete pumpkin, dimly lit from within. Stuart had pulled his suitcase on wheels behind his father who had walked upright into the reception area, trying not to let on that he was struggling to carry his ancient, battered dark brown suitcase that bashed against his legs with each purposeful stride; he wouldn't have dreamt of buying a new one, especially not if it had wheels. His dad was wearing grey 'slacks' (he hated that word) with a shirt, tie and blazer, looking like a war veteran on the way to a regimental reunion. He'd had what was left of his sandy haircut and had trimmed his moustache, respectable, was another of his favourite words. Stu knew his dad didn't approve of his black jeans, white trainers and AC/DC T-shirt, but he'd promised to have a 'wash & brush up' before they tried on their suits, and assured his dad that he'd look the part on the day. He felt that his dad was trying that bit too hard to assert himself, to demonstrate that he was the man of the house, and that he looked lost without his mum by his side. He had warmed to his dad increasingly since his mum had passed and in no way resented his correctness, his precision, his immaculate timing and appearance, as he knew full well that they acted as crutches, a support mechanism, without which he would keel over, curl up and cease to function. He'd been surprised to find Mark and his best man waiting for them as they checked in, although they looked like death and stank of beer and BO, as if they'd come straight from a night out/a prison cell; of course, he reflected, their stag night, no wonder they looked so rough, and no wonder I sent my apologies he thought. But Mark also seemed agitated; he was sprawled across one of the bucket seats in the reception area, twitching his leg up and down and checking the screen of his phone in between taking deep swigs from a large bottle of Volvic. Stu put it down to pre-wedding nerves, relieved in a way that the groom looked even scruffier than he did. He'd noticed his dad do a double take at the two of them, unshaven and in crumpled Mr Men T-shirts, but maintained a formality with warm handshakes and apologies for having kept them waiting (they were 5 minutes early actually but that was his dad for you). After they had dropped their cases off in their adjoining rooms they'd followed Mark and Vaz the short distance to a boutique menswear shop in the Lanes 'to get suited and booted' as his dad kept saying nervously, taking in the various groups who meandered through the narrow streets, his brain working overtime to process the complex nature of the relationships between those who had arms draped over the other, looking a bit like George minus Mildred from the popular '70s sit-com as he plotted his course gingerly through twenty-first century Brighton.

The menswear 'boutique' seemed straight out of Grace Bros., thought Trevor, as a scrawny twenty something Mr Grayson bustled around them, stepping back to clap his hands together when he felt they were making progress. He was feeling more uncomfortable and out of his depth by the minute, struggling with the effusive language as if he were trying to understand a waiter in Tenerife. He had no idea what 'working a waistcoat with cravat' meant nor did he grasp the significance of a classic morning coat with a modern twist. The formal suits were smart but not as he had imagined them to be; for example, the trousers were black, without a pinstripe, and the matching jackets were three-quarter length but didn't have tails, and there was not a top hat in sight. He thought paisley cravats were something that would be worn to a reel dance and not a wedding and certainly would never have imagined wearing brown shoes with a dark suit. He kept his concerns to himself, however, as Mark, Vaz and, to his surprise, Stuart all seemed fluent in this surreal language, and comfortable in the hotchpotch attire. Finally, they were 'done' as the assistant exclaimed, seemingly exhausted by it all; *he* certainly was. As the suits, shoes and accompanying paraphernalia were all boxed and bagged up, his thoughts turned to how reviving a stroll along the front and a pot of tea would be.

Mark had struggled to keep his cool, in more sense than one, throughout the suit fitting; as if being wound up like a coiled spring over the burglary was not enough, he regretted wearing his Mr Tickle T-shirt from the moment he crossed the threshold, as he was greeted by a giggling Graham Norton wannabe who thought Mark's top was HI-LAIR-IOUS darling. It was bloody hot in the tiny cubicles they were squeezed into, with just a loose curtain separating him from the gay cavalier, making him sweat all the more. He needed a hot shower and time to think; instead he was in a cramped humid changing room surrounded by fuss, being prodded and poked, tightened and loosened, until he was ready to explode. Not for the first time that day, he was relieved to see Vaz take control, dealing effortlessly with all the details and ensuring that all four blokes would look a million lire on the day, he had to explain that one. Lizzie's dear old dad looked mortified, especially as Quentin Crisp Jnr approached him with a tape measure and asked him which side he dressed on. Stu was taking it all in his stride though, and seemed on pretty good form. He was all right, Mark thought, the type of nerd who would still crack in jokes with his geeky mates about The Hitchhikers Guide to the Galaxy or Red Dwarf and would do the "Excuse me, pardon I" from the Harry Enfield Show but he seemed to take this bizarre experience in his stride, unlike his poor dad; what was he wearing though? He was still wearing the original clumpy white trainers with Velcro fastening much favoured by soft rock bands such as Bon Jovi before they went right out of fashion and then back in again, unnoticed by Stu probably, with dark skinny jeans and a faded denim jacket adorned with metal badges. There was nothing at all ironic about his dress sense either; just a complete lack of style. At last, they returned to the shade of the Lanes, a lazy breeze greeting them, just as it had the previous night, moments before the two pouty poppets had linked their arms and then led them a merry dance. He shivered at the thought before saying their farewells to Lizzie's dad and brother, until the rehearsal that evening at least.

He was still tense as Vaz eased his Mini Cooper into the space still available from earlier, around the corner from where Mark's Z3 sat right outside the front of the house. Mark had nearly been punched once when he stopped to argue with a driver of a Renault Clio who had cut him up one Sunday afternoon when on his way back from Lewes. In an attempt at injecting some humour into a tense situation he had asked the bloke, all crew cut, red face and casual sports attire, what time his Mrs had wanted her car back by, to which, once the penny had dropped, he'd nearly blown a gasket. When Mark had asked Vaz a similar question he remained deadpan and had replied not until after the rehearsal. Number 83 Waldegrave Road was situated on the corner of Stanford Avenue, and Vaz usually found a space right under the huge beech tree that spread its branches from Mark's garden, a spot Mark avoided due to the bird crap he invariably found on the hood of his soft-top. Just as they rounded the corner they were greeted by a red-faced Mrs Sheridan, who had evidently just popped to the shops and back. "My it's another hot one," she commented, "warm work for your builder fellah now, in and out last night and just now, but they were all a bit rowdy so they were." He couldn't quite piece it all together, maybe it was the heat, the tiredness, the anxiety, as he thought Keith and Burly Inc wouldn't be back in until the following Monday, to complete the work downstairs whilst they were on honeymoon. He was still scratching his head as he turned the key in the door and entered the welcome cool of his hallway to find his front room full of blokes sprawled out in his lounge, drinking beer, eating crisps and watching cricket on his plasma screen; his turn now for the penny to drop. "You *wankers!*" he yelled, closing his eyes and stifling a smile as the waves of relief washed over him as he was greeted by a sea of grinning faces and raised beer bottles; there they all were, Pete, Steve, Rob and Keith the builder, resplendent in a blue Chelsea top with Samsung stretched to the limit across his chest. Ironic really, as his had been the van they'd used to shift his own Samsung TV the night before, along with his passport, laptop, honeymoon tickets and money. After much banter, pretend punches (his to them, apart from Keith, who might have hit him back) and having a cold beer placed into his and Vaz's sweaty palms they sat back to listen to how his marriage threatening jape had unfurled. Apparently, it was Keith who had come up with the idea, as exactly the same thing had happened to him before he'd got married, so why re-invent the wheel? He had the keys to the house and the perfect getaway vehicle so a plan was hatched. Hardly the A-Team and a far cry from Ocean's Eleven but, according to the perpetrators it had all gone like clockwork, with Keith even creeping back round early that morning to unlock the front door and leave it slightly ajar to make the burglary story seem more realistic, as Mark was renowned for not shutting the front door after a heavy night out. They had banked on Mark being so mullered when he had returned from the stag night that he wouldn't have noticed that the TV had gone missing until the following morning; they were bang on the money with that one.

What hurt as much as the deception and the crushing sense of day-before-wedding-day-disaster was the fact that the lads had even bought the two dolly birds from The Zap club a couple of rounds of drinks in the OhSo by way of a bribe to keep Mark and Vaz occupied whilst they carried out their derring-do. Amazingly Vaz had been complicit throughout (Mark made a note, never play poker with Vaz) so no wonder he had gone along with their 'seduction' and then stalled on going to the police. The ice-cold bottle of Becks he'd been handed had never tasted better as he answered his mobile to his wife to be, who was calling whilst her nails were drying.

"Of course, we met up with your dad and brother … yeees sweetheart everything's fine, suits and boots all sorted … uh-huh, they've gone back to the hotel to get unpacked and Vaz and I are just chilling here before the rehearsal … I told you, no probs and no last-minute panics, I'm a changed man." A lucky man he sighed as he finished his beer and strode upstairs to pack, leaving the lads all lounging on the ancient sofas and armchairs hurling abuse at the umpire.

Flight of fancy

He hated flying. Seriously hated it – not just a dislike but a slowly suffocating all-encompassing paranoia that brought him out in a cold sweat at the mere thought of it. It wasn't just his fear of being in a tight space with other humans with no way out but the physiological impact that take off, in particular, had on his body; his stomach being twisted and turned inside out, his ears pounding, shirt or top usually stuck to his back due to the sweat, face a grey/green colour as he would gulp water that more often or not he dribbled down his front, not the most flattering image to present to your new bride on the first day of your honeymoon. Ahhhh. The honeymoon, the newlyweds, he was still getting used to the idea that the stunning brunette on his arm that was attracting admiring glances from fellow travellers as young as late teens up to the early retired was actually his wife. He walked that bit taller, exuded just a tad more confidence and assertiveness when with Lizzie, he had a glow, a new-found aura that said, 'this is me, Mark Woodford, and who's laughing now?'

"Ouch! Look where you're going you little shit!" Mark exclaimed as a young lad of around 11 with tram lines cut into the sides of a crew cut rammed a metal trolley packed high with assorted cases and holdalls out from its stationary position in the departures lounge into the gap between the rows of brightly coloured plastic seats that Mark and Lizzie were cutting through on their way to boarding, crashing into his shin and causing him to howl with pain and hop, melodramatically on one leg. The boy's dad, red-faced and barrel-chested, in blue shorts, white trainers and a Bolton Wanderers FC club shirt who already looked as if he'd gladly about turn and head back up t' north-west looked up sharply and made a move to get up but Lizzie gave him a smile and put her hand out as if to say, it's not a problem, and my husband does tend to overact, linking her other arm through Mark's and guiding him on his way, so the dad glared at Mark for a few seconds before slumping back into his seat, continuing to bite his nails and stare ahead as his wife yelled at the boy's two sisters who were fighting over a comic that had a brightly covered glittery free gift attached to the front cover, whilst the boy grinned at Mark and casually waved two fingers in his direction.

"Sweetheart, you really must learn to be more tolerant of people, I'm sure it was just an accident," Lizzie said, her smile a little forced as they headed towards Gate 23 and the flight to Rhodes. "That little prick knew exactly what he was doing," a limping Mark replied, "and, in the words of the great Alan Partridge, I just hate the general public."

"That's a little strong, Mark, listen, we're going to encounter people of all shapes and sizes over the next fortnight, the wonder of the Brits abroad along with Germans, Dutch the indigenous population and who knows who else, so just chill out, try not to get agitated about others and concentrate on your wife, and our honeymoon eh?"

Mark grinned, as he always did when he put the words 'Lizzie' and 'wife' together. She gave his arm a gentle squeeze and briefly rested her head on his shoulder, relieved not only to have averted a possible scuffle in the departure lounge but also that she had dissuaded Mark from making jokes about weapons of mass destruction when they were having their cases weighed.

*

He knew he'd left it too late to take the travel calm pill but took it all the same; the placebo effect. They were seated, strapped in, man/hand bags safely stowed away in the overhead locker, in fact, everyone seemed to be ready for the off so why the delay? The cabin crew were huddled around the still open door and seemed to be deliberating whether or not to close it when the sound of a family running for their flight whilst shouting at each other loudly drew nearer. Across the threshold stumbled three kids with a generously proportioned mother in a strapless flowery dress waving boarding passes and an agitated looking father attempting to get his breath back. Once on-board they huffed and bumped their way up the aisle checking their tickets for seat numbers as they went, knocking passengers with their hand luggage and clinking carrier bags full of duty- free until they found their seats behind and across from Lizzie and Mark. He took a deep breath as he recognised the family from the departure lounge and closed his eyes as his seat was bumped repeatedly by the mother who barked instructions in a harsh Lancashire accent as to where her brood were all to sit, whilst easing with some difficulty into the middle seat of three. "Bluudy tight squeeze this," she muttered, "are t' seats made for bluudy Kate Moss or what?" Lizzie just smiled whilst placing her hand on top of Mark's, both of which were flat on the little fold down table that held his book and bottle of still mineral water. "It takes all sorts," she whispered into his ear, pecking his cheek and settling back for take-off as the sweat that had soaked his forehead, trickled down his now stubbly cheeks.

Yesterday had been such an emotionally draining day, and only now was she able to reflect and take stock, whilst Mark, now a pale shade of grey, attempted to get some sleep as they banked up over Crawley and headed out across the Channel. Her dad and brother had looked so handsome, her dad choking up the moment he saw her, as did Mark, who did the same. The church had been full of family, friends, church members; such a joyous occasion. Her pastor had delivered a moving talk that was pitched perfectly at the mixed congregation of those with faith and with none, heartfelt, inclusive and typically free from any starchy sanctimony, people were still talking about it as they waved them off, showering them with confetti as they were chauffer driven to their hotel in a vintage Rolls that was a treat from Johnnie. Mark's brother had been on top form, gregarious and flirty as the night they were all out in Poole. Sophie had simply glistened, hair sleek, body tanned and toned in a fitted cream sleeveless dress, as if someone else had given birth to her children for her. She had really warmed to Sophie, she saw her as less the ice maiden that Mark did and more the woman who built up a wall around her due to potential anxiety or insecurity that compelled her to project the opposite, a calm assurance and cool detachment, a self-protection mechanism that she had seen in so many women, regardless of their social standing. She'd like to get to know her on a deeper level and looked forward to building a relationship with her on their return, seeing the potential in Sophie rather than pigeonholing and writing her off as she felt Mark had done.

Janice had been her maid of honour, complete with white Doc Martin boots, with Vicky and Lisa the more conventional bridesmaids. Vicky's romantic aspirations were further underpinned when she caught her bouquet amidst a chorus of squeals. She had seemed to be getting on well with one of Mark's colleagues at the reception, so she would expect a full report on her return. The huge void in the day was of course the absence of her beloved mum that, despite Janice's thoughtful, caring, attentive nature, she would never be able to fill. Her dad's voice cracked as he spoke so tenderly of the joy that both the women in his life gave him, and of how proud his Rose would have been at how their beautiful daughter had blossomed. Mark seemed genuinely moved by her dad's speech but then moments after did his level best to ruin the mood with an ill-timed gag about condoms but, thankfully, managed to avoid doing any serious damage to inter-family harmony; her major fear for the day. His father seemed slightly reserved at first, reminding her of Tim Henman's dad, sitting still and emotionless in the royal box wearing a fixed smile whilst his son bared his soul yet came up short once again for millions to witness just below as he willed him to win without getting too carried away with the occasion thus letting the side down. He soon relaxed, however. He did raise an eyebrow at Janice's 'punk princess' take on a maid of honour's outfit, but was later seen taking to the dance floor with June Woodford, her new mother-in-law, who beamed throughout the entire day, so no worries there.

Lisa was, well Lisa, quietly making sure that everyone was okay, ducking into an empty chair here and there after the meal to chat to any guest who looked like they had been left on their own, a truly wonderful friend and witness. She'd miss their 'deep and meaningfuls" over hot chocolate and muffins whilst curled up on armchairs in their flat after the Sunday evening service, and the girly Friday nights-in with her and Janice. She really must maintain a balance in her married life, making sure that she still had plenty of time for these girls who had been such great comfort in her life; and great fun too. Vaz' best man's speech was a warm and witty rough guide to Mark and his foibles, not too harsh, nor too crude; relief all round. Johnnie, true to form, requested that he kissed her garter, request denied, to which he promptly responded with an offer to make up for any of his brother's deficiencies in the bedroom department with a crash course when they came back from honeymoon, suggesting that Mark might be 'a bit quick out of the blocks' as it were. Even though she was not a 'little princess' type of girl, she would, perhaps, have expected the Hilton over the Travelodge at Gatwick but, as Mark was at great pains to point out, their honeymoon proper, would begin once they were in the villa on Rhodes. They were both weary after such a long day, and had jaws that ached from all the smiling and talking. She had enjoyed a glass of champagne with the speeches and another with the meal but Mark had polished off multiple glasses of both and quite a few beers with his colleagues at the bar afterwards; she'd have to keep an eye on that. Maybe it was a way of him coping with nerves, as he was nowhere as near as confident as he liked her to think. She would have been furious if he had 'just crashed out' when they got to the hotel room (as he had threatened to) a cramped, overheated room along a characterless corridor decked out in hideous patterned carpet. Hardly the trail of rose petals leading to the spacious suite with polished wooden floorboards, four poster bed, roll top bath and sweeping views over the formal gardens (where the peacocks strutted and rutted) that she'd always imagined. But he was right, they had an early flight so it made sense to stay at the airport; a head over heart decision that she would have applauded in any other situation than on their wedding night. Once in the room, he had talked nineteen to the dozen, she thought, sweetly, to avoid the act that would truly make them man and wife but had then been touched at the way he had held her as they gazed into each other's eyes, hers wide and expectant, his slightly bloodshot and bleary before tenderly undressing each other and making slow, harmonious love, both instinctively in tune with the other. As she lay in his arms afterwards, her head resting on his chest as he drifted off, she felt a warm glow of absolute happiness and relief as she then allowed sleep to catch up and envelop her.

She turned her head to the left and smiled warmly at her frowning man as his head rhythmically lolled forwards then shot upright as he now slept fitfully across mainland Europe. She felt a huge wave of affection towards this one-time loafer and dawdler who was determined to at least explore if not fully reach his potential with his writing and teaching and to (with her gentle encouragement) become a part of the world around him and not to be *apart from it* as was his natural inclination. She was impressed that they'd got this far already, that he hadn't made a mess of the hotel and flight bookings, nor forgotten his passport or their spending money, so she relaxed into the flight, despite the bickering from the family behind her and the occasional snort from Mark. To have and to hold, she thought.

*

No matter how many times you've been abroad nothing quite prepares you for the blinding light and suffocating heat of a continental airport at midday. After the usual stretch then shuffle off the plane to the waiting buses that transport passengers to the main terminal, the snaking queue at customs and the lottery of the carousel they made it to the Europcar desk to collect their Fiat Punto. Mark had been staggered by the lack of 'cool' in the range on offer, all reasonably priced family cars and 'people carriers' and not a two-seater sports car in sight. Well, there was a Ford Mustang but he reckoned that someone who was quite content with a Peugeot 207 would consider this too flash an investment so settled on small and sensible. Lizzie could tell that Mark couldn't relax as he was wearing a fixed smile that resembled more of a grimace. He had told her once before that, if he had walked into the bank or a post office and was confronted by a queue, he would about turn and go, regardless of the urgent nature of his business. He had expanded at length of his contempt for the general public and how he had as little contact with the masses as was humanly possible; so to have felt so sticky and queasy sitting in such a confined space with total strangers for two and a half hours followed by the inevitable queues that airports throw up must have been quite an ordeal. Lizzie just took it all in her stride, or, on this occasion small step, and remembered her Dad's maxim about never worrying about something that you had no control over. She didn't blame the staff at passport control or at the hire car kiosk for being impassive/borderline surly as they had to deal with hordes of holidaymakers on a daily basis but smiled warmly all the same as she found this approach often proved disarming to the recipient. Mark, still sweating profusely, had pulled a bundle of crumpled paperwork out of his Firetrap 'man bag' that he still insisted was designed to carry vinyl, therefore qualified as hip. "So, you're an international superstar DJ then are you?" she'd enquired with a grin. "Does Paul Oakenfold have competition?" To which he had just rolled his eyes. She knew full well that she was not as plugged into the trendy dance scene as Mark but resented ever so slightly the way he was almost possessive about the music he was into and she wasn't, a bit like a teenager, but we were talking about Mark so in many ways that was to be expected. If she had been the one responsible for organising their honeymoon she would have presented a folder with the paperwork pressed in pristine condition inside a clear plastic punched pocket behind a brightly colour coded tab labelled 'Car Hire' but again, this was Mark and organisation wasn't his strong point. The rather striking young woman with beautiful thick dark wavy hair (I'd love hair like that Lizzie had thought) frowned as she attempted to straighten out the ball of printouts that Mark presented to her, finally nodding, clicking her beautifully manicured nails on the keyboard of a dated computer terminal before loading a wad of crisp white A4 paper into a printer and running off the forms for Mark to sign. With a (surprising and pleasing) minimum of fuss they were handed the keys and pointed in the direction of an underground car park where the black Punto was parked in front of a garish looking Europcar sign. Mark loaded the small boot with the two cases and threw the holdalls on the back seat before easing into the driver's side and turning over the engine. Pausing to check the mirror position and whack on the air conditioning, he took a deep breath, turned to Lizzie, and said,

"Thish isssh your Captain sshpeaking Misshhh Moneypenny, are you ready for take-off?"

"Now look 007," she replied in a serious tone, "have you ever driven an automatic before?"

"A piesssh of cake my flower," he replied confidently, "piesssh of cake, it's just ssshhtop and go, like driving a dodgem at the funfair."

Mark selected the gear before putting his right arm around the back of the passenger seat and craned his neck to see if there were any other cars in the vicinity. He was still peering out of the rear window as the car lurched forwards and the sound of plastic crunching against metal rang out in the basement car park.

"Maybe you'd like a fork with that cake sweetheart," Lizzie joked, stifling a laugh, "it seems like you've made a bit of a mess of it." Mark swore, flung off the seat belt and got out to inspect the damage. It sounded worse than it looked but the plastic front bumper was dented and cracked in the middle as it had been forced against a small metal pole that was part of the low metal fencing that ran along the interior walls. He held his now sweaty head in his hands and swore again before sitting heavily in the front seat (after instinctively attempting to get in Lizzie's side) and letting out a huge moaning sound. Lizzie put a hand on his knee and suggested that maybe they should wait until the end of the holiday before reporting the damage, just in case they had any more scrapes in the meantime, to which Mark felt put out and undermined, as he maintained that he was at least at advanced driver's level but was hot, tired and unfamiliar with left-hand drive cars, let alone autos. They finally agreed to get going, albeit at a steady pace.

Mark breathed a huge sigh of relief as they left the heat and noise of the main town and headed out on the coastal road towards Lindos, driving like an old man in a flat cap and Rover. He was aware of the glare from the early afternoon sun, despite wearing his vintage Ray Bans, but of little else as he gripped the steering wheel and repeated in his head, 'drive on the right and overtake on the left' but there would be little chance of the latter after their less than auspicious start. Lizzie, meanwhile, had relaxed, leaning back against the headrest and either closed her eyes to absorb the heat, or gazed out across the scrubland and farmland to the stunning blue of the ocean, a map spread out on her lap and grin written across her face. Mark allowed himself a glance at his beautiful bride, hair scraped back, sunglasses pushed to the top of her head, summer skirt hitched up above her knees and one strap of her vest tantalisingly falling down off her right shoulder as she leaned back, eyes closed. He remembered the drive to Dorset for his 40th, as she stretched out in the passenger seat of his Z3, and would have pinched himself at bagging such a stunning wife if it wasn't for the fact that he was gripping onto the steering wheel for dear life. Her eyelashes were dark, thick and long, her lips just a fraction apart and glistening from where she had just swigged from a bottle of Evian. He could be in a TV commercial for a designer fragrance, he contemplated, powering along the treacherous coastal roads to a cover of the Roy Orbison track 'I drove all night' and wondered if 'I drove all day (in the blistering heat on the wrong side of the road in a reasonably priced hire car') would have the same dramatic effect, before concluding maybe not. He was shaken out of his fantasy by the blaring of a horn as he had failed to spot a dust covered van joining from the right-hand side and had to swerve out pretty sharp-ish to avoid a collision. Better just concentrate on the road he thought as he relinquished filmic fantasy featuring Lizzie. One by one the road signs to Koskinou, Faliraki, Afantou, Kolimbia and then Archangelos came and went and finally that to Lindos came into view.

He had been really chuffed at the luxury villa he'd found online and subsequently booked through the Lindos Villa Company. A few years earlier this would have involved an arduous trip to a local travel agent where, under pressure to make a decision under the bright strip lights and the gaze of an over made up consultant with a wide grin and one squirt too much of her overpowering perfume, he would feel that all too familiar trickle of sweat running down his back and would either abort the mission whilst halfway through the consultation or hurriedly book the first half decent destination that guaranteed sun that he was presented with; hence trips to Tenerife and Minorca when he'd had Tunisia and Morocco in mind. This time, no such panic, or early folding as before, doing it all with a click of a mouse from his top floor study whilst sipping a cold beer, even enjoying a virtual tour of the villa, complete with balconies and heated pool set amidst well kept low walled gardens that boasted sweeping views across farmland to the Med; perfect for the newly-weds. They were to visit the offices of the Villa Company in Lindos to pick up the keys and then a rep was to give them local directions to their sun-drenched love nest. Mark allowed the car to slowly crunch its way over the uneven surface as they turned off from the main road and down towards the picturesque town of Lindos; postcard perfect with its little white sugar cube houses and streets wide enough only for a donkey and cart or moped, a squeeze for most cars and some of the more generously proportioned older ladies of the town (one of whom they trundled past) who still favoured the black peasant skirt, headscarf and fear of anti-wrinkle cream or dentist look, hardly Greek-chic he mused.

Not surprisingly the town lacked the bustle of an early morning or late afternoon as they were approaching the 'only mad dogs and Englishmen' time of the day where any sensible local, or tourist for that matter, would be snoozing on a swing chair on their verandas after a light lunch of bread, cheese, cold meats and olives washed down with a glass of locally produced wine. Mark loved the idea of all things rustic, sneering at those Brits abroad who insist on fry-ups for breakfast and burger with chips for tea (despite sometimes longing for one, the snob in him wouldn't allow him to relent). His status as college lecturer and pretensions of him being a writer afforded a type of smugness, a sense of superiority that would see him distance himself from the hoi polloi with their sunburn and Midlands accents and ingratiate himself with the indigenous folk by immersing himself in their culture, embracing their cuisine, altering his body clock and way of doing things to theirs, thus broadening his mind through this full immersion into time, place and experience.

"Crisp?" Lizzie asked cheerily, thrusting a huge open bag of sea salt and vinegar in his direction. "When's lunch Mark? I'm starving?" Lizzie mock groaned, holding onto her stomach and pulling a face. "Not long now my love," Mark replied, as he parked the car up outside the small brick built office of the villa rental company that was situated conveniently just on the outskirts of the town, adjacent to a dusty car park and a sandy path that seemed to snake its way down towards the beach. "Just got to pick up the keys to the love nest and then, let the honeymoon commence," he grinned. Lizzie had said once that a man needs to be aware of the three most critical stages in any day of a woman; that if not acknowledged and resolved, could be the difference between a good day and a horrendous one; namely:

1) Being too hungry

2) Being too tired

3) Being too hot/cold

Mark was increasingly aware that at least one/one and a half of these boxes had been ticked so far and so resolved to getting a move on. "You wait here and finish your crisps my treasure, I'll pick up the keys and get the directions." With this he left Lizzie to step out of the car, stretch her legs and munch her way through the overpriced and upmarket snack and made his way towards the rentals office, his gateway to paradise. He'd spent quite a lot of time before their honeymoon whilst in the bath or the shower, or in the car, or anywhere in fact, trying to conjure up images of Lizzie semi-naked. In her underwear, of course, and if the lacy combo that she was wearing under her wedding dress was anything to go by, then he was about to enter seventh heaven. In a skimpy bikini (maybe topless, why not?) in the blazing sun next to their private pool, showering afterwards, head turned up towards the outdoor shower, that had a head like that of a watering can, the cold water meeting the glistening sweat drenched body; easy tiger, he thought, snapping himself out of this fantasy, just focus on the task at hand.

Inside the rentals office it was dim and cool, with two portable fans perched precariously at either end of a counter, behind which a burly man in his mid-fifties with slicked back grey hair and a quite incredible thick black moustache that was peppered with grey was struggling to insert a strip of tiny staples into a stapler, his thick sausage fingers making the task even more impossible than for an averagely finger sized mortal. He glanced up, frowning with concentration and, rather than taking a break from this fiddly but Herculean task, he gestured with a flick of his head for Mark to take a seat on one of the tired looking four bamboo framed seats that were set in a circle around a glass topped table, itself stained by two almost perfect coffee mug rings. After a full three minutes (according to the clock on the wall behind the counter that had hands that glided silently past gold Roman numerals) watching this stationery mis-match Mark attempted to break the ice with a gag, "Why did Helena Christensen spend an hour staring at a carton of orange juice? Because it had concentrate written on the front." The man looked up wearily, frowned even more, and replied with a scowl, "We not sell orange juice here." Mark ignored this deciding to capitalise on this sliver of acknowledgement afforded him by leaping up and moving towards the counter. 'No, no, I haven't come for orange juice but for the keys to the villa I've hired." This seemed to do the trick and finally, admitting defeat, the surly assistant put the stapler down noisily on a desk beside a computer terminal and placed his thick, hairy arms on the counter, interlocking his fingers and giving Mark his full attention, as if realising at last he was behind the counter in a villa rental office and not a general store.

"My name is Woodford, Mark Woodford," he announced, surprisingly not in his Sean Connery accent, "and I've come to collect the keys for the Villa Aiges. We're on honeymoon and looking forward to getting cracking, well, you know, starting our holiday." The man, who was wearing an open-necked white polo shirt that was straining across his barrel chest, stomach and shoulders, tapped on a well-used PC keyboard in front of him, the monitor of which was placed on top of the wooden counter, angled so that it was visible to both the operator and the customer. Looking more closely at the thick wiry hair spiralling its way upwards from the top of his chest towards his cleanly shaved neck and chin, Mark saw a name badge that read Kostas. He was about to fill the silence by blurting out a joke about how the villa had certainly 'kost-us' an arm and a leg but didn't even have time as a podgy finger directed his gaze to the screen.

"You not get email?" Kostas started. Mark gulped. "Whaaaat email?"

"Thees email, from my daughter Mikkaella." Mark turned to the screen and saw an email dated just two days before with his email address at the top. With the final preparations for the big day along with the fiasco over his 'stolen' passports and holiday money the last thing he was doing was checking emails. "Villa Aiges no longer available. All bookings cancelled and money to be refunded."

"But, but," Mark stammered, "It's our honeymoon and my wife left me to make the booking." The beads of sweat that had prickled his forehead at the mention of 'thees email' had now formed a steady trickle that ran down from each temple and from his neck down to the small of his back. "She'll bloody kill me! Don't you have anything else?" Kostas shrugged non-apologetically and shuffled towards a door in the far corner of the front office that opened into another smaller back office into which he spoke in a fast paced but low tone with an unseen female who answered as quickly but in a softer tone and who then emerged, placing one hand on his broad shoulder and smiling in Mark's direction. She was petite and cleared not much over 5ft high and that was in heeled open-toed sandals that click-clacked on the lino floor as she approached the counter. She was wearing fitted black jeans and a white shirt, the sort that was rolled up at the midriff and tied into a knot. Her hair had been badly dyed, with long dark roots reclaiming the peroxide invasion and was worn down and she wore thick eyeliner, in the style favoured by the ancient Egyptians. What drew Mark's gaze, however, was a nose that was as impressive and imposing as her father's moustache, totally dominating her pretty high cheekboned smooth olive-skinned face. It would mean that she would forever be described as striking, but never beautiful, but if she could resolve this living nightmare that Mark now found himself in the middle of, he would love her forever.

Mikkaella took over from her father, who resumed his losing battle with the stapler, explaining in a sympathetic tone that the villa's English owners had decided at short notice to sell the villa and so it had been withdrawn from the rental market and that they had informed him of this by email, sending him details of alternative accommodation in the area to a similar specification and price bracket. Despite Mark's protestations, aimed at the owners of the Villa Aiges, there seemed no alternative but, well, to check out the alternatives. Mikkaella clicked through to a few average-looking villas but nothing like the one he had set his heart on, until at the bottom of the page was an almost identical property, if anything marginally larger that was situated just slightly further from his original choice, outside the comically sounding village of Afantou back in the direction from where they had just come. "That looks perfect!" Mark practically squealed, automatically putting his hand on her left arm to make her stop the cursor on the link. The photos showed a villa of an equal spec with huge open-plan downstairs space, red tiled veranda over- looking the pool, the front facing bedrooms with balconies and far- reaching views to the ocean, available for the next two weeks so what was the catch? "The villa is called Villa Eirana," Mikkaella smiled, "which means place of peace. Oh, and the pool is to be shared with the couple staying in the villa attached, is that okay sir?"

Mark was so relieved that he didn't really take in the last line. With the help of this little Greek goddess he had managed to salvage what was looking increasingly like a TV Holiday from Hell. What's more, her uncle (Kostas' brother) apparently ran a little taverna just a stone's throw from where the villa was situated and she was going to arrange for them to have a free meal on the house/taverna to compensate for all the stress that the change of villa had caused them. Such were the emotions that overwhelmed him that, without thinking, he reached across the counter and grabbed her in an ungainly bear hug, just as Lizzie walked in to see what was taking so long.

The Villa Eirana, or Villa Fiasco as Mark had christened it, was a 45-minute drive back towards Rhodes town and was situated down a dusty track on the outskirts of Afantou off the main road between Kolimbia on the Lindos side and Faliraki. Mark chatted almost non-stop on the way, anxious to turn the situation round after the 'grope-gate' that had threatened to de-rail the rest of the day at least. As they approached

Afantou Mark burst out into a rendition of the Black Lace classic 'Agadoo' with the word Afantou replacing the original but this failed to bring a smile to Lizzie's strained face. Eventually she broke the silence, "Mark, I spend my wedding night in a cheap hotel with the noise of the aeroplanes taking off and landing the only thing louder than your snoring, I am tired after the wedding, after not the best night's sleep – don't you *dare* snigger – and the flight, I'm hot after the drive and hungry too and, to top it all, I walk into the villa rental office to find you in a clinch with the first Greek girl you can get your hands on!"

"Now listen, Lizzie," Mark began.

"No, you listen, Mark," Lizzie sighed. "I might not wish to be spray-tanned to within an inch of my life with a 30ft train and a desire to be treated like a princess *but I do want to be made to feel special*, as if I am the only girl in the world that you have got eyes for, so to find you groping a local on the first day of our honeymoon is hardly reassuring. That poor girl looked mortified and I felt so humiliated, so just *think* of the repercussions before you act so gung-ho in future and please don't make me feel so uncomfortable again."

"Left turn Clyde!" Mark yelled as he leant over towards Lizzie, the car veering across the left-hand lane cutting across another shabby looking delivery truck, the driver responding with the obligatory blast of its horn and shouted abuse aimed at him, as they hurtled past the small wooden sign to Villa Eirana and onto a dusty track off the main road.

"Sorry about that," Mark conceded, "just came right out of nowhere." Lizzie rolled her eyes and, turned to look out of the window at the small parched looking shrubs that dotted the lane, small white stones pinging off the tyres, as they bumpily made slow progress towards their honeymoon destination. As the track curved round a tight right-hand bend the villa came into view. They drove through a rather grand stone pillar and wrought iron gated entrance and parked up next to a black 4.0 litre Wrangler Jeep that still had the hood down. Mark felt his stomach tighten as he recalled Mikkaella mentioning something about another couple but this had not registered until now. He turned off the engine and they both got out of the car to stretch their limbs once more, the action lifting the bottom of Lizzie's vest top to reveal her beautiful flat stomach.

To their right, just 20 feet from the villa's veranda, the late afternoon sunlight danced across the beautiful cool turquoise of the swimming pool that was being cleaned by a tall, blonde, tanned, fit looking thirty-something in vest and rolled up jeans who clearly wasn't the only one to admire the view as Lizzie pulled her vest top down. Looking up, he waved over at them, flashing a smile in Lizzie's direction. Lizzie turned to Mark and, across the roof of the car, said with an eyebrow raised, "Time for me to hug a total stranger now, don't you think?"

Trouble in paradise

And so it began. The couple in the villa next door insisted on welcoming the newlyweds to early evening drinks, just as Mark had ideas of his own involving a large bag of tea-lights and some massage oils that he'd bought especially to create a certain ambience on their first night abroad together; ever! He and Lizzie had unpacked, showered (separately, he was disappointed at that) changed and were back out on their neighbours' veranda within the hour for cold beers and a selection of Mediterranean snacks. With a huge plate of cold meats, cheeses, tomatoes and cucumber and bowls piled high with olives, Lizzie returned to her old self, relaxed and charming and enjoying the still warm early evening air.

Their hosts turned out to be, so Mark was to comment bitchily to Lizzie later, a perfect his and her media Ken and Barbie who were on their second week of a two-week holiday and, as they'd pointed out, had enjoyed having the place to themselves all the previous week. Well that's just bloody typical thought Mark. Chris King, was a smooth ultra-self-confident Client Services Director (whatever that was) with a big ad agency in London. Like Johnnie, he liked to talk in 'Ks instead of 'thousands of pounds' but unlike his brother, Chris seemed to be smothering his home counties accent and affecting a mock-cockney drawl that had become popular in some circles since Lock, Stock and Two Smoking Barrels and a whole raft of other East End based gangster movies had hit the screens. He clearly looked after himself, perhaps too much, thought Mark, a bit 'metro-sexual' as his skin seemed to be moisturised and even his eyebrows looked as if they'd been plucked. He looked annoyingly good looking dressed in a tight fitting white designer V-necked T-shirt and rather clichéd loose fitting black drawstring trousers, like a slightly aging former boy band member, with a week's worth of tan in the bank (on top of what he'd had sprayed on before their holiday by the looks of it, Mark scoffed inwardly). His girlfriend was not affected in the same way, less eager to impress and more relaxed in allowing the conversation to ebb and flow, rather than stubbornly forcing it along a route of his choice as Chris seemed determined to do, as if in a sales pitch. An attractive slim blonde with an equally tanned and toned gym fit body and dressed in their uniform tight white top, but with a short denim mini skirt, she had introduced herself simply as Jo, not with the surname, as if at a business meeting or a conference. Her smiling blue eyes were small and piercing and her hair was pulled back into a ponytail that revealed a small scar over her right eye; the result of her love of kick-boxing, they were to find out later. Her evident competitive nature was well suited to the world of media sales as she worked for the London Evening Standard selling advertising space to recruitment advertising agencies. They spoke with the assurance of two professionals who were heading towards the top of their game and conversed knowingly about the local region, restaurants, bars, cuisine and customs, as if they were locals or well established ex-pats and not merely sun seekers here and gone in a fortnight.

Despite feeling initially on edge in the company of Chris, this confident and dominating smooth-talker (everything that he wasn't) and by the disconcertingly short skirt worn by Jo, that at one point revealed her knickers, Mark soon relaxed into his second then third chilled bottle of Amstel and took in his surroundings. The crickets reached fever pitch and the night cloaked them all in darkness, save from the glow coming from the villa's lounge, the slim solar powered lights that lit up the path to the pool and gardens and those dim and distant shafts from the small flat roofed houses dotted along the surrounding countryside and down towards the ocean that pierced the night sky like pinpricks in a black canvas. Chris got louder with each beer he consumed and continued to regale them with endless stories featuring acts of drunken debauchery, some of the major restaurants and bars in the capital with a cast list of minor celebrities. At one point Mark mockingly pretended to bend down to pick something up saying to Chris, "Just another name you've dropped there, mate." (Getting more than he had bargained for as it was right in front of Jo, hence her unintended knicker-flash) but Chris carried on, oblivious to Mark's less than subtle dig and Jo had seemed blissfully unaware of his eyes fleetingly on a level with her crotch. Lizzie was sweet throughout, listening attentively and laughing appreciatively, making as much eye contact with Jo as she was with Chris so as not to give the wrong impression, putting her hand onto Mark's arm as a sign of reassurance. He appreciated this more than she could imagine as he was feeling increasingly uncomfortable at the glances that she was getting from the Cuprinol man. He'd got his Lizzie back he sighed; what a relief that was.

*

She had felt bad for making Mark suffer for hugging the girl in the holiday villa office especially when presented with the full facts about how his original choice (of villa) had been withdrawn from the market at such short notice. She actually felt a huge debt of gratitude towards the girl who had so efficiently found them an equally luxurious alternative and harboured no ill feelings towards her whatsoever but felt that Mark just had to take more responsibility *for* and understand the potential impact *of* his actions. On more than one occasion she had saved his bacon in a pub, café or even once in a local supermarket when he had commented loudly on someone's poor use of grammar and they had reacted, quite understandably, vociferously. It saddened her that he took such a dim view of the rest of mankind and that he existed in a self- created little elitist bubble that she thought was a sign of insecurity and not of strength. She had always been taught to treat others as you would like to be treated yourself, not to judge by appearance or accent and to just accept the rich diversity of the human tapestry with all its flaws. She looked forward to getting deeper under the defences that Mark had built over the years with his flippant, dismissive attitude, and to gently try to understand the root of such a cynical and aloof approach to life; for which she had her theories. She was sure he felt more pain at the closeness of the relationship between his father and brother than he would let on and that he struggled with the tag of 'drop out/family failure' despite claiming proudly that he'd embraced this label (he'd once said that he and his small group of friends, when overlooked for the role of school prefects, had made their own badges in metalwork that read 'defect'). He talked little of his family life and formative years and, to her mind, was just a bit too quick to resort to flippancy or sarcasm at the first sign of a potentially emotional recollection. She knew that everyone carried some form of brokenness within them but her female friends were open to acknowledging and discussing their issues, viewing them as baggage to be unpacked and dealt with in order to move on in life, lighter and free from the constraints of past hurts and regrets. She feared that Mark was less likely to be open to expressing his vulnerability and more inclined to see his insecurities and anxieties as character flaws that needed to be padlocked inside a large wooden chest, the type that housed his teenage comic book collection and was stored in the attic of the family home where perhaps he had been conditioned to manage emotions that way; there to remain for the rest of his years, dust gathering on the lid and rust to the padlock. She wondered how she might unpick this lock over time, and help her husband to be released from whatever was the cause for an undercurrent of bitterness and resentment dressed up in throw away humour and a pretence that nothing of any great substance really mattered to him; she knew there was more to him than he let on, part of the reason she had fallen for him. She had time, she wouldn't rush in.

They soon established a routine around lie-ins, leisurely breakfasts on their veranda, a trip to a local town or beauty spot in the morning, light lunch of cold meats, cheese and olives with a cold beer or two before heading back to the villa. There they would swim, sunbathe, read, chat and enjoy the type of siesta that Mark had only ever imagined happening in films. They'd decided to alternate between taking supper at 'home' and heading out to one of the local tavernas, most of which were within walking distance and one that was, indeed run by the uncle of the girl who had found them the villa. They were to spend a memorable evening there with the owner, Georgis, his brother Kostas and his daughter Mikkaella (from the villa rental agency) with all of them extending genuinely warm hospitality, although Lizzie noticed that Mikkaella sat as far from Mark as was possible and seemed to be avoiding eye contact. At a point halfway through the evening, when Mark was getting more beers (he seemed to be getting carried away with the fact that he was the guest of the owner and appeared to be showing off to the other Brits who were dining there. They were simply a small group sitting around white plastic garden furniture outside a modest hostelry; hardly the VIP lounge at the Sanderson but it may as well have been the way he was lording it). Lizzie leaned in to the striking looking Mikkaella with her hair up that emphasised her big kohl enhanced eyes, prominent nose and white-teethed smile to thank her sincerely for all her help in finding them such wonderful accommodation. She also apologised for Mark's 'over enthusiastic' demonstration of his appreciation explaining that, as it was left to him to find the honeymooners a villa in the first place, he had gone from deflation to elation in a matter of minutes so could barely contain his sense of relief when she had found such a perfect resolution. It was a quiet moment that emphasised that global sense of sisterhood; in just a few short minutes all residues of discomfort had been erased and a sense of balance had been restored. Well, for them anyway, Mark was still struggling slightly on that score as he returned shakily to the table from the bar with yet another tray containing huge litre glasses of ice cold beer for the men and half the quantity for the ladies, swaying slightly and slopping the froth from the tops of the beer over the sides of the icy frosted glasses and onto the ancient metal tray, grinning widely as if a returning hero from an ancient trial of strength and endurance. Let's just pray that this marriage doesn't come to represent a trial of strength and endurance, Lizzie sighed, as her hubby raised yet another noisy toast to their humble hosts.

*

During the sweltering afternoons, there was no getting away from Chris and Jo as they were both devoted sun worshippers and spent hours soaking up the scorching rays, their already tanned bodies glistening with oil and a light sheen of perspiration. They didn't swim much but adorned the surroundings, like those ancient gods of old in a region so steeped in mythology. Lizzie had thought there might be some unspoken protocol around the girls not sunbathing topless when in the company of the other couple but Jo seemed quite at ease in nothing but a skimpy thong that left nothing to the imagination. It seemed to stir Mark's as he didn't quite know where to look thought Lizzie, as he strained to maintain eye contact in the face of her tanned breasts, smaller than hers but perfectly rounded with large pert nipples. Do try not to stare she thought, a rebuke as much aimed at herself as to Mark; he gawked, however, because he was a bloke who seemed to retain an almost adolescent fascination with boobs, she because she was a woman, who would always manage to see good points in the figure of others whilst finding fault in her own. Lizzie felt quite self-conscious, even just in her black two-piece, let alone alongside this bronzed goddess and despite the natural olive tone to her skin but even more so when she caught Chris taking in every inch of her figure with more of a leer than a smile on his face. It wasn't quite what she had envisaged as she counted down the days to their wedding and honeymoon, a time for her and Mark to discover each other's bodies, she hadn't factored in the added distraction of a scantily clad female nor the lascivious attention of her muscle-bound beau. To be fair to both Mark and Jo, there had not been even the hint of any inappropriate interaction, with Mark almost falling over himself daily to reassure Lizzie that he only had eyes for her, but it was difficult to act normally and relax fully with the added pressure of having to look good in the company of someone who seemed

140

so confident in her own body and sexuality and was quite happy to have it all out on show.

On one of those searing hot afternoons when it was so stifling that even Jo had lowered herself into the pool Mark thudded along the white concrete surround to the deep end, hopping from foot to foot due to the heat and bellowing that Jo had no need for concern as he was not about to transform himself into a swan and violate her whilst she bathed (a poorly chosen mythology reference that went way over her head, leaving her staring blankly at him in his bright flower patterned Hawaiian board shorts). He then proceeded to yell 'dive bombers' before jumping out over the calm, clear water and pulling his knees up to his chest before plunging deep into the pool causing a huge plume of water to arc up, covering Jo in the resulting spray and causing her to shriek and recoil whilst wiping away the streaking mascara and push her soaking fringe back out of her eyes. Mark clearly thought her cries were playful but Lizzie could see that she was pretty hacked off. As Mark spluttered and splashed his way up and down the length of the previously millpond calm water (why can't men swim the crawl gracefully without leaving a wake the breadth of a cross channel ferry) Jo had climbed up the metal ladder to grab a towel and head back up to their villa whilst Chris wandered over to where Lizzie was reclining and broke out into some kind of slow motion martial arts routine that was clearly designed to impress her. Lizzie looked up, shielding her eyes from the sun, despite wearing her sunglasses and smiled briefly before returning to her new copy of 'The Shack', anxious not to give the slightest hint of encouragement to this lecherous show-off but at the same time not seeming to appear rude.

"What's that you're reading Lizzie? 'The Shack' eh?" Chris leaned over at a right angle to read from the cover of Lizzie's paperback. "What's that all about?"

"Well," started Lizzie, "it's about this chap in North America who goes to his mailbox one freezing winter's day only to receive an invitation to go and spend the weekend with God in a shack up in the mountains. He accepts the invitation and finds that the place they are to meet was the last place his little girl was traced to after being abducted by a child murderer. He gets the chance to vent his anger on God for not preventing the death of his child and, throughout the course of the weekend, manages to find some peace in the situation and in the knowledge that his little girl was now safe in God's kingdom."

"Phew," Chris exhaled, flopping into the sun lounger next to Lizzie's and pushing his sunglasses up to rest on the top of his head, "that's pretty heavy going for a holiday read, isn't it?"

"I guess you might think that, but this book is all the talk in Christian circles as the author has taken some liberties with the three persons of God and has personalised them to an extent that few have done before. I couldn't wait for it to be published over here so got together with some friends from church to have a bunch of copies imported from the States."

"You believe in all that stuff then. God, good, evil, sin?" asked Chris, rather lazily.

"Maybe not that God is a large black African woman as portrayed in this book," ('with good reason,' she added, as Chris had raised his eyebrows), "but certainly that God is relational and wishes to be known by us and to us intimately. It's great as it deals with so much stuff that Christians and non-Christians wrestle with and it's got people talking about God at their dinner parties."

By this time Mark had hauled himself out of the pool and was drying himself off energetically with a beach towel. Jo had returned from their villa with ice cold Cokes, having taken care of the streaky mascara and soaked fringe that was sleeked back stylishly and, thankfully, she was now wearing a loose-fitting T-shirt. The four of them joined in a conversation about religion and faith based belief systems that lasted for almost an hour. Lizzie loved the opportunity to share her faith in this way and gladly answered some of the more rudimentary questions that non-believers routinely asked, (if there is a God how come rapists and 'kiddie fiddlers' get to live and decent people get cancer and die, where do dinosaurs fit into the Creation story and did Jesus even exist)? Even Mark seemed interested as she talked animatedly about free will, intervention, fact, authenticity, love, forgiveness, hope and salvation.

When pushed about the authenticity of Jesus she had explained that his existence had never been up for debate as records showed he was as much alive in the early years AD as was the Roman Emperor Caesar Augustus (who had actually initiated the census that had led Jesus' earthly parents to be in Bethlehem at the time of his birth in order to raise more taxes to fund his huge empire) but that the debate centred around *who* he was; prophet, teacher, healer or all these and more as the Son of God as Christians believed? She explained that the Bible contained over 60 books written by over 40 different authors on three different continents over a period of

1,600 years and that this alone was compelling evidence of universal truths, a shared spiritual consciousness, along with the mind-boggling number of prophecies that Jesus had fulfilled. Lizzie totally engaged the other three with her calm, articulate explanations and as they lounged under the huge stripy parasols, there seemed to be a shift in the mood, a sense of interest if not understanding in the concept of God and His plan for the world and each and every one of us.

As always, Mark could be relied upon to break such a moment, commenting on the book he had seen Chris read called 'The Guv'nor' about a giant of a bare-knuckle fighter from the East End of London to which Mark had commented about a rival (someone called 'Roy Pretty Boy' that didn't sound at all right for such a 'sport') who he reckoned was the better man. Their afternoon then descended into a testosterone filled debate about who was the toughest ranging from football players, actors, wrestlers to superheroes. Men, she thought, do they ever really grow up?

*

Boobs! Was the thought on Mark's mind, years without much of a sniff and now more than any man could cope with; like London buses, he reflected. Any other time he'd be quite happy to get an eyeful of someone like Jo who was as fit as a butcher's dog and seemingly without inhibition as she lounged practically naked in the searing Aegean heat, but on his honeymoon, well that was hardly fair was it? It would be a tough one to explain to Lizzie because, when faced with a topless woman in a thong asking a routine question such as whether or not you fancied a Diet Coke in the afternoon it was difficult to maintain eye contact because somehow, despite your inward protestations, your eyes were drawn precisely to the bits that should really be covered up and where a married man shouldn't really be looking. It was weird how uninhibited people could be when out of their natural habitat. If they were all ever to meet up in London for a beer (although highly unlikely) it would be difficult to maintain a level conversation without imagining Jo in her thong and nothing else. It wasn't that he was being lustful towards her, heaven forbid, not only was he on his honeymoon but with a woman who could just as easily be a Bond girl, but, as he would respond to his ribald, red faced, half-cut brother every Christmas when the turkey was being served, he was definitely a breast man.

He loved Lizzie all the more for her modesty. As someone who had never been anywhere near heart-throb status (he always got the most drunk and least attractive girl to snog at the end of the school disco, and pretty much ever since), he was in awe of just how stunning Lizzie was and how humble she was about it, almost as if she hadn't noticed. He had, of course, fantasised for months about how she'd looked in various states of undress and was still pinching himself every time she came out of the shower or eased herself into bra and knickers or her bikini. As his eyes widened she would smile and look down or away, never flaunting her amazing figure but seemingly happy for him to take it all in. How blissful he'd thought that afternoon, as he was stretching out on a sun lounger after a swim in which Jo had found his dive bombing hilarious – she was even crying with laughter – everything a honeymoon should be except for Mr Media and his lusty glances at his wife. At least, they'd learned, the Ambre Solaire twins were off back to Blighty at the end of the week and, according to Mikkaella, the following week they would have the place all to themselves. Maybe, when alone at last, he might encourage Lizzie to dispose of her bikini top, when in Greece and all that.

"Are you thinking what I'm thinking?" whispered Lizzie leaning over the reclining Mark, as, despite the shade given by the parasols, it was a degree or two off unbearable. "Probably," replied Mark, "that if we do go ahead and buy Berbatov from Spurs we might have to change the way in which we set the team up." Never before had a handful of ice cubes thrown down the back of his neck felt quite so good, and been so well deserved.

*

That evening, after another 'golden hour' as they had come to know it, Mark and Lizzie had dozed then took turns to shower (Lizzie still enjoyed her privacy when in the bathroom). Lizzie took the first shower whilst Mark lounged, pillows propped behind his head in the antique metal framed double bed, the shutters and windows wide open to let all the sounds and smells of an early Mediterranean evening in. He was a huge fan of these afternoon encounters and they seemed all the more illicit as they gently made love with the shutters pulled almost together, stray shafts of light cutting rays of dust as they tenderly lost themselves in the other. In addition to the heavenly experience shared inside avoiding the suffocating heat outside, there was a welcome by-product; that all pressures around nocturnal performance of a sexual nature were eradicated as they headed out for supper; lovemaking at midnight was a bonus and not an expectation. Many a time in the early days (before Lizzie spelled it out in capital letters that she was not going to jump into bed with him or do anything vaguely similar) before marriage, he had felt quite sick with nerves during a dinner out, sometimes ordering a lighter dish than he'd fancied just in case the offer of sex was forthcoming. This way, with the sex all sorted in the late afternoon, he could eat and drink to his heart's content (although his arteries might be complaining somewhat with the high volume of carbs he was putting away), viewing all other male diners with an inward swagger that said, "yes she's mine and yes, she's well taken care of in that department, hence her glow, it's nothing to do with bronzer and everything to do with my prowess at lovemaking."

As the lukewarm water trickled over her shoulders and ran down her back she shivered but with relief at the cooling sensation. Closing her eyes she looked upwards and allowed the flow to run over her hair, smoothing it back before gently lathering it up with her exotic fruits shampoo and moisturiser. She recognised relief from another quarter as her body tensed then relaxed as the water ran hot then back to tepid (Mark must have gone to the kitchen for a glass of water) as she reflected on their intimacy over the past, most significant week. Her suspicions were confirmed with regards how inexperienced a lover Mark was and they had had to overcome a couple of less than harmonious moments when they had to readjust to the other's intentions but they had soon found a rhythm that brought them close in all ways, deepening their bond as their bodies lay entwined out of the oppressive afternoon heat. She had surprised herself with her appetite for lovemaking and could easily have managed a couple of times each day but Mark seemed hugely self-satisfied with their afternoon discovery and allowed himself an indulgence of an altogether different kind each evening with two or three pints of ice cold lager on top of the bottle of wine they would share with their meal and the brandy he'd like with coffee afterwards. She had detected a new-found swagger in her hubby these past few evenings and thought it typical of him to have ticked the box of 'lovemaking to my wife on honeymoon each day – check', as if it was a job well done and that his reward was to gorge himself on booze and lamb kebabs. She had come to accept early on in their marriage that there would be no road to Damascus moment with Mark regarding a revelation or even a shift in attitudes and behaviour 'just' because they were married and that, if there were to be such a transformation it would more likely be gradual in nature, as a rocky spit that juts into the sea becomes gently eroded over time through the constant attention of the tidal ebb and flow.

They dressed and headed out for an evening at one of the little eateries that could be reached after a leisurely stroll along a dusty path that had been cut into the hill that overlooked their villa where they would stop to take in those breathtaking and uninterrupted views across the dry ploughed fields and down to the still, calm, vast ocean where once the prows of those distinctive wooden ships surged in search of adventure. On each of these alternate dining out nights Mark would deploy ninja type stealth in an attempt at avoiding the attention of Chris (in particular) and Jo who (a) had the villa nearest the driveway and (b) always seemed to be sitting outside drinking. As they strolled hand in hand past their veranda the familiar greeting of "'ello lover-birds" punctuated the balmy night air and they felt obliged to stop and chat. As the following night was to be the last night on their holidays for Chris and Jo they felt they were obliged to go out on 'a large one' that would comprise trawling round the bars of Faliraki, a notorious nightspot within a taxi drive of their rural retreat. Not surprisingly, they wouldn't take no for an answer when inviting Mark and Lizzie along, and arrangements were made to meet for drinks outside their villa the following evening at 8pm whilst they waited for the taxi to pick them up. Mark proceeded to grumble his dissatisfaction at this arrangement all the way down the rocky path to the restaurant, now a sharp white in the twilight, whilst Lizzie smiled and reassured him that it would be one night to see Chris and Jo off in a way they saw fit before they had a week of peace all by themselves. Put like that, Mark thought, what's the worst that could happen?

*

"It feels like déjà vu all over again," Mark sagely jested (it was one of his favourite ever quotes from a football manager) as they headed out for drinks with Chris and Jo for the last time. He was in smart black jeans, his white Ted Baker shirt left untucked and light slip-on suede shoes with no socks. Lizzie opted for slim fitting white jeans with heeled sandals and a black top with straps, hair up and just a minimal application of mascara and lip gloss that both slipped nicely into a tiny vintage black beaded clutch bag along with the villa keys and her phone. Her already olive skin had turned an even shade darker whilst Mark sported a mixture of early tan and late angry redness, the latter a feature of his temples and neck, areas that he'd frequently missed with his slapdash application of sun block; to the outsider they looked like a Brit abroad with exotic foreign wife. Mark was getting used to the looks they, or rather Lizzie, would get from other men when they were in restaurants or bars with the gaze usually going from them as a couple (brief) to Lizzie (lingering) then back to Mark (incredulous). It wasn't that he was ugly it was just that she was so drop-dead gorgeous and looked out of his league. Mark got the impression that other men must imagine him to be minted to have landed such a catch, an image he was quite happy to foster with a knowing smile.

They found Chris and Jo in their usual spot outside their villa both preened to within an inch of their lives already well into their first drink of the evening, ice cold lagers. Chris had his thick hair slicked back and was in designer jeans with a black shirt undone practically to his navel to show off his plastic looking pecs (and, typically for someone who professed to have no Christian faith, a large silver cross hanging from a chain), his look finished off with expensive looking leather sandals. Jo was in a tight white top with a complicated looking arrangement of slashes and straps arranged to show off her cleavage and skimpy black satin hot-pants with shimmering legs ending with some bejewelled high heeled sandals with a further complex looking strap scenario climbing ivy like towards her glistening shins; Brighton meets London thought Mark as he braced himself for an evening of Mockney mayhem and wind-ups. Another beer later and they were rattling along the dusty road heading north to the town that the tired looking, unshaven taxi driver described as 'the Blackpool of the island'. Mark, sitting in the back with the girls, like Freddie from Scooby-Doo, had the window down so didn't hear clearly. "God, the black hole of the island, what are we letting ourselves in for!" he exclaimed, to be met by a raucous chorus of correction from his fellow explorers. A few hours later, as he lay on the plastic couch of a brightly lit Medi-Centre, he reflected that his description was actually far more accurate.

The evening got off in predictable style, sipping garishly coloured cocktails topped off with huge umbrellas and fluorescent straws whilst sitting around plastic tables outside neon lit bars watching more and more drinkers spill onto the main strip that ran through the town. Mark and Lizzie raised an eyebrow to the other at the speed at which their 'hosts' managed to consume one luridly named cocktail after the other as they struggled to keep apace. Mark felt on edge as there was an air to the place that made him feel uneasy. He'd noticed that the hordes of earring, vest and tattoo wearing males that were hungrily roaming the vicinity vastly outnumbered the similarly attired females who were to provide the focus for their boozy lust, willingly or not. Even by 9pm there was a sunburned shaven headed youth sitting on the pavement outside a nearby bar, head in hands, feet surrounded by a pool of vomit with a white T-shirt ripped to shreds (not intended) and splattered with (presumably) his own blood. Further down the street a group of girls all in heels and miniskirts were shrieking in hysterics as one of them had pulled up her Lycra top to flash her boobs at a police car that was prowling the litter and lout strewn streets. Their attention was turned by the shriek of cat-whistles as a six-foot tall blonde with peroxide hair and bright red lipstick wearing a latex nurses outfit and precarious looking black heeled boots tottered up the middle of the road with an extended arm ushering a pasty looking bespectacled man a few years older than her on the end of a lead and wearing nothing but his underpants into a bar opposite. Mark actually felt less unnerved by this than the others, much preferring the prospect of a freak show to a fight club.

Mark couldn't fail to notice that with each goblet of sex on the beach or long slow screw against the wall that he guzzled, Chris' drawl had become more slurred and innuendo laden and his glassy eyes were falling more and more upon Lizzie and her chest. Mark and Lizzie had colluded and had given up attempting to keep up with a couple who were clearly more practised than they were in the art of alcohol consumption and, though pacing himself, was already beginning to feel the wear and tear of a heavy nights drinking. Shouting above the din inside a tacky bar that boasted all manner of lime green shots for the price of a pint of milk, he asked them how long they had been together as a couple and whether or not they had plans to marry. "You must be joking," Jo replied immediately. Mark was taken aback by this and asked why she was so adamant. "No, Mark, if we did ever get hitched that's what I'll face for the rest of my life when people meet me for the first time. So, you must be Jo King."

"Ahh, now I see. Well what about Chris taking your name then?"

"He would be better off I reckon," Jo grinned, "Imagine how many restaurants would reserve him the best table when they hear that it's Chris Martin on the blower, he'd milk that one for sure." Jo's voice had a huskiness to it that came from her love of all things Marlboro, this addiction working in direct opposition to her gym routine – how to prolong and reduce your life expectancy in one fell swoop thought Mark.

They had decided to stroll down through the scenes of Dante's inferno towards the welcome breeze of the beach, clutching one another to avoid

148

the unpredictable lurches of the swaying hordes, more of whom seemed to be perched unsteadily on the edge of the pavement with fast food wrappers and the regurgitated contents strewn and spewed around them. Lizzie gripped Mark's arm as they passed yet another group of girls who must have been 17 or 18 years old, propping one girl up as she heaved into an alleyway off the main drag, revealing her DKNY knickers in the process. "These girls are putting themselves into such a vulnerable position," Lizzie whispered into Mark's ear, "I really should do something to help." Mark suggested otherwise and that, in his experience, trying to help a group of well-oiled young females often ended in being on the receiving end of abuse. That said, whenever he had been the saving hero he'd quite understood why he'd been told to do one, or 'jog on' as the contemporary parlance seemed to have evolved as he'd invariably been drunk and/or in fancy dress at the point of intervention. But Lizzie seemed insistent, "I just can't let it go, Mark." And letting go of his arm she weaved her way towards the group of girls.

Mark and the others held back a few paces as they watched Lizzie approach the girl who was caring for the knicker-flasher, who, on feeling Lizzie's arm on her shoulder, looked up, held Lizzie's gaze for a moment then flashed her a beaming grin revealing a perfect set of white teeth, even more evident as a result of her smooth brown skin. The two embraced like old friends and then began talking, the younger of the two animatedly so, gesticulating and pointing at one of the bars nearby before resting her arm on the back of her mate, who had come back up for air. As Lizzie offered her a bottle of water the rest of the gaggle moved a few feet away to light cigarettes that they blew upwards into the cooling night air, leaving Lizzie with the two at the centre of the puking incident. As the two young women, both in white vests, one in denim miniskirt and the other in denim shorts listened earnestly to Lizzie it felt as if a punch had landed flush in Mark's solar plexus. Turning away to look back up towards the carnage they'd just left behind he muttered an expletive out loud, exhaling loudly and then running his fingers through his hair. "You alright mate?" Jo queried, "Just you look a bit peaky all of a sudden." Mark muttered something about the drink and the noise but how could he explain just how he and Vaz had ended up in The Zap club on his stag night? Lured by two flirty sirens who had then dropped them like stones once they had paid their entrance fee; the very two denim clad babes that were now being looked after by Lizzie. Sure, nothing untoward had happened but it might take a bit of explaining as to how he had become acquainted with the two pouting little poppets. Mumbling again, he mentioned something about giving Lizzie more space to work and motioned for the three of them to move off further away from the huddle of hussies as he had put it, pointing to Lizzie the direction in which they were going to which she nodded briefly in acknowledgement. Chris and Jo shrugged and consented and they were soon out of view, heading back towards the ocean.

As they neared the point where the beachfront sprawled on both sides before them, Chris stopped short and said, "I don't feel so good about this, we shouldn't have left her, it's mayhem up there and a pretty woman like that making her way down here on her own, well, it doesn't bear thinking about does it?" He had a point thought Mark, who was in a quandary about what to do next, to protect his wife or his dignity but had barely time to formulate a response before Chris had taken control of the situation. "I'm the biggest one here so I'll go back, you two find us some sun chairs and we'll meet you in a bit." And with that he had turned on his heels and waded back through the throng. "Alone at last then lover-boy," said Jo, linking arms with a flustered Mark and leading him in the direction of a row of white plastic sun chairs that were situated in front of a huge cactus plant that must offer a welcome shade in the midday heat he thought. What was it with him, the seafront late at night and scantily clad females linking arms with him he thought, through a haze of cheap lager and garish cocktails? Despite the alcohol consumption, Jo managed to sit side-saddle on the edge of the first seat then elegantly lift her legs up and swivel into a sitting then reclining position in one motion to gaze up at the night sky. Mark remained standing, shuffling from foot to foot, cursing his bad luck at spotting those two girls here, of all places and also at his inertia when faced with the dilemma of fight or flight; of course he should have gone back for Lizzie, whatever the consequences.

He was just about to underscore his lack of chivalry by leaving Jo and running back for his wife when she turned the corner, walking at pace looking flustered, with Chris grinning a step or two behind. "Are you okay sweetheart?" Mark asked, with one eye on Chris. "Sure," replied Lizzie unconvincingly, "let's all call it a night, shall we?" Mark, who had begun to sober up the moment he'd recognised the greeters from The Zap club ignored the rational inner voice that told him to leave it at that but put his hand on Chris' shoulder as he had brushed past him in the direction of Jo, spinning him around to face him. "What have you done? Have you put your grubby little mitts on my wife you Mockney wanker?" Chris sneered and put his face down into Mark's, stinking of rum and tropical fruit, "Thought she might like to cosy up to a real man for a change, no offence." As he stepped back, Mark calmly replied, "None taken," before lunging forward and throwing a looping right hook in the direction of Chris' smug smile. Jo wasn't the only one who practised martial arts and, with a deft movement (remarkably well executed, Mark had later thought, after all that booze) that comprised sinking his hips, swivelling ninety degrees and placing one palm on the small of Mark's back and the other between his shoulders, Chris simply guided Mark and all of his drunken aggression off the concrete walkway and through the decorative foliage, where he plunged head first into the giant cactus. Both girls shrieked, and threw their hands up to their faces; Mark did likewise but, despite his best efforts at absorbing the impact he emerged shakily with a face full of short spikes embedded into his forearm, forehead, cheeks and nose.

Two hours later, he lay on a plastic couch, staring up into glaring lights in the nearest on-street Medi-Centre rather than a sun lounger admiring the night sky, having each little spike removed and the tiny puncture wounds cleaned with stinging antiseptic by a male nurse around the same age as him. He had breathed a huge sigh of relief that the nurse in attendance had not turned out to be the woman he'd seen earlier tottering up the main street in the skin-tight rubber costume and smiled to himself (wincing as soon as he had done so) as the way his life seemed to go he wouldn't have been at all surprised if it had, only to then find out that it was a transsexual who had migrated from Hove and who recognised him as his former VI Form tutor. Lizzie had been, well Lizzie, annoyed at Mark for resorting to violence (for the second time since she'd known him, both times he had come off worst so he might begin to consider learning from it) but thankful to him for reproaching (she actually used that word) Chris for his inappropriate behaviour, without going into any details. It would be some years before he got Jo's side of the story. By the time they had returned to their villa just before dawn and had a long lie-in until midday, the two Londoners had packed up and departed for the airport, having shoved a brief, handwritten note of apology for their drink fuelled falling out under their door. Mark had deduced that, owing to the loopy script and fat circles that sat atop each 'i' on the faded, lined paper that must have been torn from an old notebook found in one of the drawers in the kitchen dresser in the villa next door, the writing was hers. Well, at least they could relax and enjoy the second week of their honeymoon in perfect peace; some consolation.

7
February 2010
Mark 42, Lizzie 33, Isaac 3 weeks

Breast is best

He felt quite guilty at getting such a thrill out of watching Lizzie breast-feed and had to pretend this wasn't the case as he guessed she wouldn't be too impressed. As he hadn't had anywhere near as much breast action in his life as he liked to make out, he was mesmerised every time she casually removed one, firm and milk-full from one of her now regulation smock tops, for little Isaac to latch on to. She had just *the* perfect breasts and he pinched himself on a daily basis that they were all his for the pleasure, or they were until the suckling, dribbling little Isaac came on the scene. It came as little surprise that Lizzie began to view her body differently after Isaac was born, that firstly she was unconcerned as to who saw what (Mark would get overly-possessive if she had to breast- feed in a park or a café, scowling as he scoured the immediate area for any blokes trying to get an eyeful) and second that two of her (to Mark) most prized physical assets were now purely for practical use and ceased to become sexual objects to be ogled and fondled at will. (Mark certainly took liberties and groped at every opportunity, not always leaving Lizzie feeling particularly flattered in the process if she was bending over to unpack a shopping bag or standing at the kitchen sink.) He would smile and say, "First she used to sink into my arms, now she is up to her arms in my sink." Thankfully for both of them, although exhausted beyond belief in the first few weeks of parenthood, his trusty sense of humour hadn't deserted him and, he felt, had helped to carry them through the worst of it.

Pete had taken great delight in painting the picture of a parent's pathological desire for peace and rest in those first few weeks post-birth and had verbally assaulted Mark with a barrage of language that would have been at home in the trenches, informing him that it was all about just surviving, of the fatigue that he'd experience like never before, the vertigo inducing range of emotions, of feeling shell-shocked and disorientated; Mark had laughed all this off as scaremongering but, less than a month in, had to agree unreservedly with every sentiment. Even the birth itself, immortalised in the world of Hallmark and Pampers, had been nothing like as glossy as he'd been led to believe it was going to be. Lizzie's waters had burst at 2am and, despite having been present at all the pre-natal classes, Mark's mind had gone completely blank and it was Lizzie who'd called the maternity ward and arranged for them to go in. He was feeling both drowsy and stressed and had left the yellow plastic folder containing all the pre-natal notes in the car on the floor behind the passenger's side and so had to leave Lizzie bent double and groaning at the reception area of the maternity ward to retrace his steps, at a half jog. He felt a curious sensation, or rather range of them, as he huffed his way back out to the car park; the stark sense of 'this is it' coupled with an unreal sense brought about by the current situation and the time of day, usually associated with a stumble home after a curry and a club or an early start to catch a flight. His mind was awash with the most sobering thoughts possible yet at the same time he moved in a dreamlike state, about to play his part in something truly monumental whilst simultaneously being a passive onlooker. Strange that, despite all the talk, the jokes, the classes, the documentaries on TV, nothing, but nothing, had come close to preparing him for the emotions that threatened to overwhelm him at this point. Despite the fact that little puffs of his breath were visible in the early morning chill, he felt a trickle of sweat run down his back, partially induced by the fact that he'd been 15 minutes in retrieving the folder owing to the fact that he had trawled the car park looking for his beloved black Z3 before remembering they now owned a silver VW Touran. The whistle had been blown and they were going over the top – out into the dawn and the no man's land of parenthood. This was it, there was no going back. There was also no Lizzie in reception as a porter had taken pity on her and taken her up to the maternity suite in a wheelchair where she waited wearing a strained expression as Mark flustered and blustered in with the folder.

Untypical for a first labour, it was a lengthy and messy process lasting over 24 hours. As pathetic as it may sound, Mark wondered if perhaps more might have been done in the classes to prepare the father as it was totally unnatural to be awake around the clock and expected to remain fully coherent and engage with every step of the marathon that Lizzie was going through. He had begun to share this theory at the latter stages of the labour and just one look from the midwife who was responsible for seeing Lizzie through to the birth was enough for him to shelve his thoughts. He had, however, given himself two private challenges, to remain awake throughout and not to faint in the delivery suite at the crucial moment.

In order to achieve goal one, Mark had arrived at the hospital equipped with a book (Regeneration by Pat Barker, from a trilogy going by the same name that focused on the mental and physical regeneration of troops who had seen action at the front in WWI, a subject that had become of increasing interest to him of late) and, whilst off sorting out his parking permit, he had stopped off at the small 24 hour 'grab and go' shop near the reception area to stock up on a 'Meal Deal' (sarnie, crisps and a drink for £3.50) and The Guardian newspaper for the sports pages and the crossword. He had already ensured that Lizzie's overnight bag was well stocked with breakfast bars, a multipack of Kit Kats and some of the old skool classics that he and Lizzie both still loved (Star, Dime, Lion, Crunchie) and so had 'hunkered down' in a dated looking green cloth covered armchair with worn wooden armrests in the corner of the delivery suite nearest to the top of the bed, waiting for battle to commence. He hadn't had to wait for long. As he rubbed Lizzie's shoulders with the palms of his hands (as instructed in the pre-natal class) and listened in awe to those amazing unearthly cries that the early contractions caused, deep groans that seemed to rise up from the very bowels of the earth itself, he pondered on just how ancient and primeval an act it was to conceive, carry and give birth to a child. He wondered if there existed a subconscious link that all women might experience; a connection that transcended time, race and status, as peasant girls and queens alike had felt the onset of those indescribable waves and braced themselves for the single most gruelling and rewarding experiences of their lives. His earthy birthing musings had been cut short by Lizzie screaming for him to let go of her shoulders and to get her the gas and air but he felt that he was somehow 'with her' on her journey now as the midwife returned to Lizzie and he returned to the sports pages for a preview of that weekend's fixtures.

He had never been comfortable in and around hospitals and illness, although Lizzie wasn't strictly sick, getting that familiar clammy feeling at the mere sight of an H sign indicating a hospital and immediately feeling light-headed and fearful; similar sensations to when he was faced with a flight. On the rare occasions when he had been on a hospital visit he had been mistaken as a patient and asked if he was okay by a sister who might have noticed his ashen pallor or the vacant expression in his eyes as he attempted to make sense of the multitude of lurid signs and arrows denoting the various wards and departments. The last time he had had to spend a night in a hospital was when on honeymoon in Rhodes after he had locked him and Lizzie out of their villa and, ignoring Lizzie's objections, had attempted to climb up the vine onto the balcony only for it (the vine not the balcony) to come loose resulting in a fall, concussion and broken collarbone. Thankfully, he'd had the good sense to arrange for travel insurance as it's a costly business having an accident abroad. It didn't do much for their planned second week of passion though as they had been so looking forward to having the place all to themselves after having to share the pool with Chris and Jo during the first week. He was also useless at retaining the medical terms that accompanied childbirth and had confounded Lizzie during her labour by staring into her eyes as, he explained, he was waiting for signs of dilation. Lizzie, however, had blossomed and bloomed during pregnancy, embracing it and positively glowing in it. How could anyone possibly continue to be so sexy being so pregnant Mark remembered wondering along the way, and similarly as he wandered along the dimly lit corridors on the night of Isaac's birth. He had just returned from the loo in time to hear the first little high-pitched bleats from Isaac, so called because Lizzie had burst into laughter when her pregnancy had been confirmed by their GP, such was her delight at receiving the news (as had Sarah in the Bible, she told Mark, when hearing that she had conceived albeit later on in life, with the name Isaac being derived from the Hebrew word for laughter). Mark remembered the sense of utter helplessness, both in that newborn little miracle wrapped in a regulation green blanket and in himself as he struggled to comprehend what had just passed and just what the future held, as Lizzie held that very future in her arms and nuzzled into his soft, crinkly skin, weeping tears of joy mingled with those of relief as her ordeal was finally over. 3:40am, Friday 12th February 2010. The moment the rest of their lives began.

*

How was it possible to love someone from the very core of your being but want to shake them and throttle them at the same time? These were the oscillating emotions felt by Lizzie towards Mark in the run up to childbirth and in those trying early weeks afterwards. She had never once regretted her decision to marry him and loved their life together utterly despite his many foibles but, and this was a big but (Mark hilariously referred to these as a 'J-Lo') he just couldn't seem to stop himself from saying something either flippant or stupid or flippantly stupid at precisely the wrong moment. Add to that the fact that he was an absolute liability in a crisis, either mislaying the pre-natal notes or wandering back from the loo in the middle of the night to head for the operating theatre rather than her room (just being headed off by a less than impressed ward sister as he had one hand on the theatre door handle as an emergency Caesarean was in process). His overall presence, far from calm and reassuring, just added to her sense of anxiety; what would he do or say next? That he meant well was one of the most demeaning epithets afforded to any man, but he just didn't know when to put a sock in it. Beaming to Sally, the midwife who took her through the uncomplicated first 8 hours or so of labour, that it was a 'Carlsberg labour', was funny the first time, but by the time he was informing Claire, 16 hours and two midwives later it began to grate. Even Lizzie was confused when, at 1am, 23 hours into her marathon, he put on the gas mask and barked, in an upper class voice, "Chocks away and beware the Hun from the sun." And yes, he probably was the only person to leave the maternity ward heavier than when he arrived, on account of eating too much during her labour but again, a gag repeated endlessly is a gag diminished in her eyes. But then, when all was said and done, he was there, like a faithful hound throughout, fighting his tiredness, battling with his fear of their sterile, medical confinement and, in his own clumsy way, offering his love and support when what she needed most was gas and air.

Contractions, and the labour itself, must surely be considered the greatest secret unknown to woman until that point of no return when the only one who can get you through it is yourself. It remains one of the few indescribable experiences left to man, well, woman, with words proving utterly futile and lacking the depth and breadth to capture the gripping, tearing, searing, relentless, all-encompassing brutality of it, nor the desire to embrace it and hold onto it; like a prisoner who falls for their kidnapper such is the bond forged through a shared trauma and entwined sense of being. She remembers the overwhelming sense of exhaustion that consumed her immediately after Isaac had been born, replaced quickly by the euphoria at holding, smelling and kissing him for the first time. She was relieved that Mark had readily agreed to go home to get some rest at 6am and that she had, although reluctantly at first, accepted his parents' offer of a private room. As sleep gently overpowered her, her eyes strained to stay open, not leaving that clear plastic tub within which her greatest achievement lay, himself content to sleep, after their day long ordeal. Lizzie and Isaac. Mother and son. Thank you, Lord.

*

In the weeks that followed, one day merged with the rest, a blur of visiting friends and family, sleep snatched wherever and whenever possible, a birthday (Lizzie's 33rd) endless washing, new and unpleasant smells, bags of disposable nappies, bags under their eyes, piles of new soft toys, piles full stop. When they had just settled Isaac for a mid-morning nap and crawled under their crumpled duvet for the same and the bloke delivering the flowers had ignored the sign not to ring the doorbell but to knock gently on the back door instead and Isaac would wake at the repeated ringing and cry and cry and refuse to return to sleep and Lizzie's nipples would be leaking milk ... Mark would simply grin and whisper 'living the dream'. 'Oh to dream, perchance to sleep', but sleep seemed to have been murdered.

Mark's family mercifully staggered their visits, his mother bustling about the place being delightful and gushing and replacing flowers on the wane with those freshly delivered whilst Mark rued the fact that his home resembled that of Elton John's with lilies everywhere. His usually restrained father didn't attempt to conceal his pride at another Woodford grandson and even placed a hand on Mark's shoulder, uttering a sincere "well done." Lizzie's dad had a major wobble as he held Isaac for the first time and didn't have to mention how Rose would have felt to have done the same. Her brother seemed indifferent to their new arrival but Lizzie didn't take offence as Isaac could neither speak nor hold a plastic light-sabre so wouldn't prove his usefulness for a few years yet. Johnnie made the obligatory remark that Isaac was the spitting image of the milkman (despite them not having had one since living in Brighton) and Sophie had clearly warmed even more to Lizzie now she had joined the club, but retained a sense of emotional decorum and quietly offered practical advice as well as a number of junior Boden outfits for Isaac to grow into. Then of course there was Mrs Sheridan to buzz in and out almost at will with an assortment of homemade cakes, biscuits and home cooked meals, all extremely generous and thoughtful but exhausting at the same time for Mark. Lizzie had given up entirely on any idea of modesty as every time she was breastfeeding someone or another seemed to turn up with well wishes, gifts, cards or even more flowers. At one point, and he had put this down to sleep deprivation, Mark had even invited the postman in to see Isaac (after the postie had commented on the number of cards he had delivered that week) only to find Lizzie on the sofa, breast out and Isaac suckling merrily away. The poor postman immediately made his apologies and backed out, looking quite flushed and Mark's Partridge quip 'if there is any left after junior's finished', warranted that cushion flung fully into his grinning face at the very least. Yes, you did have something to do with it my darling husband but do please stop acting as if you are some kind of stud to any other male within earshot as it was me that really did all the hard work thought Lizzie. And continues to do so.

Two weeks in precisely and after yet another lengthy visit (this time from Janice and Lisa) Isaac was safely tucked up in his Moses basket, the monitor registering the occasional coo but nothing more and one of Mrs Sheridan's cottage pies was browning nicely in the oven. Mark and Lizzie flopped onto their corner sofa, sighed, and breathed in the silence. Lizzie had always been at peace with a total absence of sound but Mark preferred the hum of a radio or TV somewhere in the next room but right there and then it was just magic. The two of them, Lizzie with her head on his chest, the little one asleep, the phone unplugged, the promise of a meal they hadn't had to prepare and a large glass of red (for Mark anyhow, Lizzie was still abstaining owing to her breastfeeding). They reminisced about the night that Isaac was born, scrolled through the countless photos they had taken on their phones in awe of his breathtaking fragility and beauty and laughed at what a complete eejit Mark had been when push had come to shove. As it were.

"I really had no idea that I was that annoying," Mark said, pulling a hurt face and rubbing his gum.

"Oh yes," replied Lizzie, "but loveable with it, just not at the time. Are you okay sweetheart?"

"Just feeling run down and I rubbed some of that gel you recommended on my ulcer but it tastes weird and doesn't half sting, is it supposed to?"

"Bring me the packet of that gel a minute Mark would you, and we'll just check something."

Mark returned from the bathroom brandishing a small rectangular cardboard box not unlike those that carried toothpaste that had Bonjela in lower case printed on the outside but that contained a metal tube branded Germaloids on the inside. Apparently the two look quite similar and it was an easy mistake to make, for once Lizzie being the one in error and collapsing into fits of the giggles whilst Mark howled with a sense of pain and injustice. "Like you said Mark," Lizzie spluttered in between laughter, "it's your sense of humour that's got us through this."

Half an hour later and they were settling down to homemade cottage pie with broccoli and carrots on trays (well, on plates, on trays) something they'd been doing more of during these early weeks when in survival mode. They had, as usual, deliberated over a choice of movie, with Mark leaning towards Iron Man and Lizzie pushing for Cold Mountain before they eventually agreed on Elizabeth: The Golden Age satisfying their respective need for action, narrative and romance. It was at times like this that it all seemed okay, manageable even, and it wasn't as if they were in a minority as just how many people did they know who had gone through exactly the same upheaval?

It never ceased to amaze them both just how much power this tiny little mite held over their lives, dictating when they ate, slept, even their moods and ability to register a smile. They reflected that even after so much preparation (that Lizzie had thrown herself into with typical vigour) nothing had truly braced them for the moment when they had carried their newborn from the hospital in his tiny expensive new car seat and tentatively strapped him into their sensible family car to head for home for the very first time as parents; as a family! They were both a jitter at every hiccup, every puke, every bout of tears, constantly attempting to retune their frequencies to interpret each cry, was it one of hunger, of tiredness, surely not another nappy change? And the poo! Checking the colour chart as it went from black to green to a yellow-brown. And so much of it! They had proudly bought a set of 7 vests that had each day of the week alongside a farmyard animal embossed on the front and had used the lot up on the first day along with a mountain of muslin and an ocean of energy and emotion. Having prayed that Isaac would settle for his regular naps (Lizzie was adamant that a routine would prove the secret in retaining their sanity; not for the first time she was right) they would get him settled then hover anxiously at the door of his nursery only to tiptoe back in when convinced that he was sleeping to check that he was still breathing and then count down the minutes when he would be in their arms again. It really was the strangest, mind-bending dynamic of co-dependence that either of them had ever experienced. Or ever would.

Mark returned to work but his timetable allowed him to give Lizzie regular breaks during the day to enable her to catch up on her sleep/the laundry/housework/replying to the multitude of texts that had flooded in in the aftermath of Isaac's birth. Managing these was almost a full-time job in itself (for Lizzie, as Mark just deleted most of his). After Sunday lunch he would insist that Lizzie took a nap for an hour or two as she would be heading out to church that evening. He loved to wrap himself and Isaac up, drive down to the seafront and push him along the promenade regardless of the weather. He'd grab a coffee from one of the beachfront cafés that remained open all year round and would lean on the railings and just gaze out across the sea, never tiring of it. At this time of year there wouldn't be many people to mire his view; a few hardy joggers and dog walkers, all suitably attired, might pass behind him from where he stood with Brunswick Square to his back. Occasionally a post-pub lunch couple huddling into each other, confirming affection and seeking warmth would make their way uneasily across the pebbles, with each step displacing the smooth stones ahead and around them, adding to the effects of the alcohol and increasing their sway. Otherwise just him, a snug newborn, and the occasional gull screeching and wheeling overhead.

When gazing out across the sea on one such promising Sunday mid-afternoon when the skies were suddenly growing darker, he was struck by the linear nature of the view, something many may have noticed but was captured beautifully by John Banville in his short but evocative novel 'The Sea'. His eyes traced the horizon, comprising such a clean straight line as if ruled in, where a huge expanse of crumpled churning green met powder blue; so clearly defined. From this sharp green border the pale Wedgwood hues rose to slate grey where it met an ominous mass of slow moving sludge coloured low hanging cloud, all bulk and density despite its softly rounded edges; threatening to engulf all below in a gloomy squall. Growing up overlooking the sea he had such an affinity with it that he had withdrawal symptoms when too far inland, even Preston Park wasn't close enough. He was also used to its sudden shifts in mood. The one thing from Dorset that he had never tried to escape or outrun and had remained a constant in his life was how comforted he felt when breathing in the salt air and hearing the familiar pounding, booming and whooshing of the waves on sand or pebble beach. He closed his eyes and let the cool breeze wash over him, smiling even as he felt the first few spots of rain that dappled the hood of the buggy within which his snug little newborn gently snored. Life is good, he thought – I get it now. I can do this.

*

"Mark, what *do you* think you are doing!" screeched Lizzie, above the wailing of little Isaac. A quick glance at the kitchen wall clock told him that it was 2am, that he had only been asleep for two hours and that attempting to make up a bottle of formula when still suffering from the effects of five pints of Stella wasn't a good idea after all.

Mark and Lizzie had agreed that they would both have a night out by themselves each week, as well as one together at least every fortnight as they attempted to recreate a semblance of normality and not retreat into the monastic, monosyllabic solitude that many couples seemed to after having had a baby, where the world outside almost ceases to exist. Lizzie went out to her church cell group on Wednesday evenings and then had a hot chocolate and a natter with Lisa afterwards. (Mark thought this sounded like some sort of a punishment, nothing against Lisa, but the whole cell thing, correction for naughty Christians), whilst Mark resumed his Friday nights down at the pub with Pete; it was hard to gauge which of them was most relieved at this. In order to manage this regime it was agreed to introduce formula into the equation to supplement the breast milk that Isaac was still receiving from Lizzie and that she would also pump into sterilised bottles when she had surplus. After a typical Friday night of beer, analysis of the latest Man United squad and season to date (neck and neck with Chelsea) fastest 0-60 speed for cars under £30K and rounded off with a kebab (although Mark now no longer drowned it with mayonnaise and had passed on the chips) he had returned home entering through the side door, totally overdoing the tip-toe-ness and with the general exaggerated movements and shussing and giggling to himself of a man who (a) knows he has had one too many and (b) was well aware of the consequence of waking either Lizzie or Isaac at the midnight hour. Maybe it was this pressure, or the effects of the alcohol, or a bit of both, that made him trip on the top of the low step that led into the small utility room. Hurtling head first towards the washing machine he instinctively reached for the nearest item to prevent a heavy, noisy fall, managing to twist and grab his old combat jacket that was hanging on the coat rack pulling it and the rack clean off the wall in the process leaving a mess of exposed plaster and wall plugs. He'd sort it out in the morning he thought (or rather Lizzie would as he would take longer in getting round to DIY related tasks in the home as he would to completing his income tax self- assessment forms). With a deliberate, surgeon's precision he drew then downed a large glass of water, clinking the glass against his front teeth in the process, refilled it and shuffled wearily into the sitting room, slumping onto the sofa and switching on some late-night TV. He could feel his head getting heavier and heavier, along with his eyelids so stretched out and submitted fully to the oncoming advances of sleep. He was violently jolted out of this glorious, deep and welcome slumber by the sound of wails coming through the little monitor that was perched on top of a rustic pine bookcase that stood to one side of the fireplace, accompanied by the sounds of Lizzie soothing their hungry/wet/smelly/needing a hug little bug.

He'd heaved himself up from the sofa in a flash, and in doing so had whacked his knee on the corner of the small table upon which he'd left his glass that he had topped up with fresh water before he'd crashed out, spilling the contents over the rug that had absorbed the impact of the glass, so thankfully no breakage just a puddle; we can deal with that later he'd thought, not for the first time that evening. Wanting to demonstrate once more his prowess as a hands-on dad to Lizzie he had made his way unsteadily to the kitchen, hit the switch to the kettle and had reached for the large tub of formula and pre-sterilised bottle. The problem was that Mark, not the most agile nor in possession of the greatest dexterity at the best of times (and still trying to shake off the effects of the booze and the snooze) had managed to completely miss the mouth of the bottle with the little level scoop and had scattered the powder into the bottom of the washing-up bowl that was empty apart from a ring of foamy suds still clinging onto the sides. It was moments after this point that a bleary-eyed Lizzie had entered the kitchen with a distressed Isaac, only to find her hapless hubby clumsily attempting to scoop up the now congealed (and soapy) powder out of the washing-up bowl and into the feeding bottle of her hungry newborn. Even the calm, even-tempered Lizzie would occasionally lose her composure, as was the case at this point; apparently, according to Pete, it happened to the best of 'em. Lizzie, more huffily than he was used to, thrust Isaac into Mark's arms and started the formula operation from scratch with a freshly sterilised bottle and new scoops of powder. Once this had been cooled and tested on her wrist she took Isaac back from Mark, who had perched himself on a kitchen chair and Isaac on his knee and made her way down the hallway to the lounge to feed the little one.

"Mark!" exclaimed his exhausted wife, "why do I find myself standing on a sopping wet rug?"

"Maybe it's because you hadn't stepped around it, my sweet," was his less than helpful reply.

"Sometimes, Mark Woodford ..." she continued, "You would try the patience of a saint!"

"Well then, it's a good job that I married one then, isn't it my darling?"

As mother and babe nestled into the sofa and Isaac suckled noisily on the bottle, his eyes slowly closing, Mark took in the scene, with conflicting emotions. On the one hand, here was his gorgeous wife and newborn son, the perfect picture of contentment, with Lizzie looking effortlessly sexy in a grey T-shirt with her dark hair ruffled by the few hours she had spent in bed as she gazed dotingly at her peaceful little tot. Future – perfect.

On the other, this was now his life. Gone were the carefree days of meandering aimlessly through the evenings and weekends, the lazy lounging in front of Sky Sports or the Dave channel, the pub lunches followed by a live game on the big screen, afternoon kips on the sofa, lie-ins, fry-ups, hood down days. All gone, vanished almost in an instant. Well, over the course of three and a half years.

He'd got swept up in his crush on Lizzie, the dating, the falling in love, the proposal and subsequent planning and transformations – and what transformations! To the house, his wardrobe, his mindset, his financial management, his image (less paunchy and stubbly than when they first met, although a slight thickness to his midriff was beginning to creep back, leading to breathing in moments as soon as Lizzie would enter the bedroom or bathroom to find him in his Calvin Klein's) but did he hanker after this 'before' or was he still fully committed to this 'after'. He felt torn. He felt guilty for doing so. He felt knackered, permanently. Past – tense?

8
August 2010

Mark 42, Lizzie 33, Isaac 6 months

Some like it hot

August bank holidays always meant converging on the family home in Dorset for barbecues, cream teas, crabbing in rock pools, French cricket on the lawn and competitive boules matches, in fact '5 Go Mad in Dorset' with the addition of Pimms, hangovers and Johnnie's smutty one liners. Mark and the family (he was still conscious of this label and struggled with the sheer ordinariness of it on the one hand and the absolute uniqueness of his little family unit on the other) had stopped off in West Sussex on route to see Lizzie's dad and brother which wasn't anywhere near as trying as Mark had expected. For Lizzie it proved poignant, at times painful but ultimately reassuring.

Her dad had clearly been working overtime to make the place look as homely as he possibly could without a 'woman's touch' a phrase he repeated frequently during their brief stay. Freshly cut roses were set in the modest crystal vase that sat in the hallway on the small round table underneath the coat hooks and alongside the ancient mahogany grandfather clock that had metered out the time in Lizzie's early years with such unfailing consistency that she had stopped noting its steady rhythms in childhood, only registering its metronomic presence since returning as a visitor. There was not a speck of dust anywhere (spick and span was how her dad would have described it) and the scent of Mr Sheen was evident but not overpowering those other familiar but elusive smells that were vying for her attention. The narrow hallway and open staircase retained a timeless musk of mustiness and wax with notes of her father's cologne flirting with the summer roses and wafts of home cooking. What was it about the smells of a family home that could take you back across the decades at a sniff or a whiff she thought?

She had come back into the relative gloom of the cottage hallway after the piercing light of the early afternoon to grab a sun hat for Isaac who was being walked around the immaculate back garden by a proud but cautious grandfather and a more relaxed looking father – someone who was increasingly growing into the role. Lizzie had gently reminded her father that Isaac wasn't made of china and wouldn't break as he handled him with such trepidation; each movement was measured and mechanical, lacking the lucidity of a parent. This was understandable she thought, as she leaned on the sturdy Belfast sink in the kitchen, the scrubbed pine work unit alongside it overflowing with the piles of paraphernalia associated with a baby and watched the three generations of men explore that familiar scene.

From her vantage point she surveyed them, taking in the immaculately kept lawn, mossy, dry flint walls bordering the garden and the hanging baskets bursting with geraniums and pansies. The old wooden wheelbarrow had been strategically placed with the effect that it had just been left at the exact spot where its squeaky wheels had finally refused to turn another rotation and her Dad had planted it out with the same precision and traditional flora of the baskets now that it had outlived its usefulness. The small apple tree provided shade in the bottom right corner with the rope from their childhood swing twisted and frayed, hanging on by a thread, and the recently creosoted, padlocked tool shed standing guard at the bottom left corner, where every last wing nut had its place. This had always been his territory, ordered and planned, methodically pruned and maintained. Her Mum had added her flair to the banks and borders, planting bulbs that would burst forth with blasts of colour just as others were on the wane; wild daisies, poppies and foxgloves, all lending a more natural country cottage sway. Her approach was spontaneous, something that often left her father smiling and shaking his head as he consulted his notebooks and weekend supplement tips sections whilst she moved gracefully from one spot to wherever took her fancy, trowel and trug in tow, straw hat in place, humming to herself, occasionally looking up but rarely looking back at the piles of weeds left in haphazard piles in her wake.

As Lizzie moved her right hand along the work surface to change her posture and stretch her back from the slight stoop that allowed her to keep up with Isaac's progress, her hand alighted on the page of her mum's well worn recipe book, open on the classic country cottage pie double page spread much favoured by her family over the years. Whilst her mum would often take liberties in order to save a bit of time or add her own personality to a dish, her dear father would have pored over this with a furrowed brow, measuring out each ingredient with meticulous accuracy, double, treble checking before proceeding. She pictured how he would have prepared everything before beginning to cook, chopped onion on a saucer, carrots washed, sliced and in a small dessert bowl, potatoes scrubbed, peeled, halved and sitting in a saucepan of cold salted water. Her mum took a totally different approach, gliding from hob to cupboard to larder, tossing used mixing spoons aside, leaving piles of peeled potatoes around which she would chop the other ingredients on impulse, all to the sound of classical music blaring, not booming, from her small transistor that she kept on the deep windowsill near to where Lizzie now leaned. She closed her eyes and conjured up the scene, complete with the haunting melodies of Madame Butterfly or the rousing crescendo of The Planets as her mother, lost in the harmonies would almost conduct the supper into being whereas her dad would have steadfastly manufactured its existence. She had such warmth, such soul, such a glow and lightness of touch, for her nothing was ever a problem, nothing was insurmountable, until she went toe to toe with breast cancer and after a brutal battle, had to concede defeat. Through misty eyes Lizzie looked down at the recipe book once more and traced the outline of her mum's elegant hand where she had added her own notes to the printed process; a combination of this downward turn and the waves of emotion that had engulfed her as she reached into that void that had been left by her mother's untimely departure acted as the floodgate to release a torrent of tears. Soon she was sobbing, uncontrollably, doubled over with her left hand supporting her, before sinking onto the smooth flagstone floor, arms wrapped around herself and wailing with grief for her beautiful and remarkable mum, who had not been alive to see her get married, nor to hold her grandson in her arms. She wept for herself, for her dad, for her brother, for the situation, for the past, for the future, and was so lost in her sorrow that she failed to hear a familiar voice calling from the open doorway. She jumped at first to find strong arms gently picking her up before allowing herself to be embraced. She buried her face into the shoulders of a well-worn black T-shirt, comforted by the familiar scent of fabric conditioner, the brand of which was another reminder of home; still clutching Isaac's sun hat whilst holding on to her precious memories.

"Hey, hey sis," Stu whispered, "I know I've never been one for displaying emotions but we all feel it you know, we all still miss her so much."

And there they remained, in a comfortable silence, brother and sister, listening to the encouraging sounds of her father and husband as they watched Isaac being bobbed from one side of the garden to the other, until Lizzie, still sniffling, apologised for leaving snot trails on his Iron Maiden T-shirt to which Stu had remarked that it had actually added some authenticity to it and muffled laughter rang out in that little cottage kitchen once more.

*

With Isaac bathed and settled it was the adults turn to relax. Mark had fixed everyone a generous G&T served over mountains of ice and fresh lime (despite Trevor and Stu's protestations that it was a slightly effeminate drink) that they had enjoyed with dry roasted peanuts and olives sitting at the circular metal table situated underneath an overhanging jasmine bush that seemed as one with the wisteria that sprawled across the rear walls of the flint stone cottage. The sun cast a warm glow on the stubble fields and reflected from the chalky hollows nestled into the downs just a mile or so to the east. It was blissful. Mark felt an affinity towards Lizzie's family like never before and could not attribute it to the large gin alone. In her father he saw the honourable, upright (and uptight) head of a household who had crumpled inside at the loss of his wife. Everything he did seemed tinged by an inner turmoil, clouded by the presence of absence (if ever there was quite an oxymoron) the joy at being able to hold his grandson underpinned by the sorrow that Rose was not able to share in it, a garden bathed in a late summer's early evening glow, but without that which his late wife radiated, a home cooked supper warming in the range but one that lacked her influence, her finishing touch; but never articulating these feelings and stoically ploughing on even though all those close to him could see the full weight of the yoke that he carried. Never had he seen the living so haunted by the dead. It had profoundly impacted Mark, stirring in him feelings towards his own father, a man who was similarly restricted by a generational fear of expressing emotion and equally diminished in part as a result.

Stu, on the other hand seemed to be enjoying something of a renaissance. Mark had put him in touch with Johnnie, who in turn had connected him with one of his 'IT Walla's' as Johnnie referred to them and Stu had done some coding for them that had been well received leading to a shed-load of further contracts. Whilst this source of revenue seemed to be drying up, it had led to Stu 'hooking up' (romantically – in their own strange way) with another IT consultant employed by the firm, who was equally fluent in Klingon, loved Sci-fi and playing on gaming consoles (called Suki no less, the girlfriend not the console). Mark had been reassured by Lizzie that she did actually exist and was not some Japanese Manga style avatar or cyber girlfriend – she was real! To Stu he was in some sort of seventh heaven as the young lady in question lived down the coast near Southampton so he had plenty of time to hideout in his room/lair with the curtains drawn doing whatever he did on his laptop, part of which involved teaming up with her to zap other nerds from all over the globe in some bizarre other world online adventure. Whilst Mark would never understand a grown man's love of computer games, as a one-time full-time slob, he could fully appreciate the value of 'me only' down time.

Supper proved to be an easy, informal and dare Mark thought enjoyable experience. Trevor was quietly thrilled that his cottage pie had gone down so well, Mark delighted that Stu seemed as keen as he was to polish off the couple of bottles of Rioja he had brought and Lizzie was beaming at the thought of all the men in her life being under the same roof. Lizzie had brought an apple crumble with clotted cream for them to finish with and they retired, full and happy, to the lounge for coffee and a brandy for the chaps. Despite the season, a chill had crept into the cottage and so Trevor had lit the fire and they all withdrew slightly into their own thoughts, stuffed by the food and alcohol and mesmerised by the crackling in the grate. So this is contentment, thought Mark. Until this point in his life he had underestimated the value of this feeling, he now embraced it, reaching out and taking Lizzie's hand in his. There was no need for words, they all seemed to sense this, and stayed in this reflective state until the piercing cries of a little one with night terrors punctuated the still night air.

*

The drive to Dorset no longer represented the fraught, painful road of self-analysis it once did before Lizzie entered the scene. Not only had Lizzie encouraged Mark to become a little more focused on his career, on getting his house in order (literally) and wardrobe less reflective of a pot noodle guzzling bachelor but just by her being with him, before they had even reached the point of discussing marriage, had given him such a confidence boost that he felt a new and unfamiliar self-assurance when about to re-enter the family fray. No more the embarrassing silences when gently pressed by his mother about his teaching or writing or whether or not he was 'courting' or 'stepping out' (only for Johnnie to yell 'coming out more like', a comment that even his father had chuckled at, making it hurt all the more). They were always so natural in each other's company, his father and brother, seeming to be able to pick up whatever thread the other had been weaving, and Mark had always felt the outsider, the boy with his nose pushed up against the glass, watching the grown-ups drink whisky and talk of the sorts of things that grown-ups did whilst he seemed stuck in a world of top trumps, catapults and conkers. It was hard to believe that there were only a couple of years separating Johnnie and he. But despite his older brother's boorish buffoonery, non-politically correct innuendo and questionable political leanings he couldn't find it in him to dislike his sibling, not least for the fact that he was married to a woman who made the White Witch of Narnia seem affable by comparison.

"How's it going there driver?" Lizzie asked, turning her head to the right and shielding her eyes from the bright midday sun with her left hand, despite wearing dark sunglasses. Mark was making steady progress down the A31 towards Ringwood and was confident of them making it in time for Sunday lunch. He loved her intuition, her caring heart. That simple question was aimed at stilling any last-minute anxieties that he might be carrying with him, an act of reassurance, reminding him that he no longer had to step into the Dragons Den without backup.

"Do you know what, these visits are nothing like as intimidating as they once were," Mark reflected, "Sure there will be the uneasy silences with dad, the winces at Johnnie and the 'what on earth do I talk about to the Ice Queen and her perfect offspring' moments but with you, I really do feel that I can face all of it, and more. I guess it also helps that they think of you as a saint/angel for putting up with the runt of the litter when others might have had me drowned in a sack at birth."

Again, thought Lizzie, he is hurting, despite the forced grin. Yes, things had changed almost beyond recognition since that first visit not yet three years ago but there again how could three good years possibly remove the hurt of all those that preceded it? Fresh from her own family retrospective, she understood the tangled emotional weeds that lay beneath the surface of any reunion, moving on the undercurrents of sadness and bitterness, a past that threatened to choke the life out of the present at any moment. This empathy was extended to Mark as she moved her right hand from her lap and placed it gently on his left leg, glancing over her right shoulder at the same time to check on Isaac who, although in a baby car seat turned to look away from them would be sitting contentedly, with those big brown eyes taking in the sky and tree tops as they passed in a blur; these were her two concerns now, man and boy, and at times it seemed that Isaac was the least vulnerable of the two.

Mark had come such a long way in a relatively short space of time though, thought Lizzie, smiling to herself at the under confident but over-powering bachelor she had first met at a conference, where he had fallen foul of Jan's withering sarcasm. She really hadn't had him down as boyfriend material at all and had been as taken aback at her willingness to go out on dates with him as Janice, and Lisa in particular, as she was fully aware of Lizzie's 'ideal man profile' since they shared theirs regularly.

Since her late teens she had carried with her a clear picture of how married and family life would play out and Mark had, to a large extent, shattered this image. Her 'dream' husband was always going to be a strong, clean cut, decisive man of faith, maybe a talented worship leader or overseas missionary, someone with whom she could explore their faith and put it into practice, reaching out to the poor and needy, maybe on trips to Africa or South America together or as a family. She had imagined them working shoulder to shoulder in constructing a wooden school or chapel that would then ring out with the sound of singing as they all praised God for His abundant blessing. Mark seemed more interested in singing out of tune along to old David Bowie CDs or offensive football chants aimed at the opposition during live games on Sky. She longed for the opportunity to at least attend services together as a family in Brighton and had begun taking Isaac to morning worship and then returning for the evening service alone. Mark was never hostile regarding her faith but he had remained indifferent to it. She remained mindful of the fact that it was her choice to become Mark's wife and that she married him fully aware of all his idiosyncrasies and it would be wrong of her to attempt to change him beyond all recognition and mould him into her perfect partner. She had fallen in love with this dishevelled, disorganised, unambitious layabout because there was so much more to him than this initial impression. He remained witty, charming (in his own way), loyal and devoted to her and Isaac with a big heart and generous spirit. At times she would hold herself in check, not wanting to appear disapproving, suffocating or controlling, fighting her impatience and trusting in her instinct that he still had more growing to do and so much more to give, with fatherhood adding a greater sense of perspective and maturity into the mix.

"Move over you spotty little Muppet – you're only in a Citroen Saxo for God's sake!"

Lizzie was jolted back to the present by Mark's explosive outburst towards a couple of young lads in a souped up (she hated his expression 'chavved up') metallic blue hatchback that was hogging the fast lane on the A31. Mark was driving too fast and too close so Lizzie turned to him once more and said softly,

"It's okay sweetheart, we've still got plenty of time and, after all, we're in a family car now and not a two-seater sports car. Would you consider letting the boy racers off the hook? They're probably not as grown up as you are and might take your pressure to overtake them as some sort of Alpha Male challenge, to which, of course, they'd come up short. And please don't use God as an exclamation for your frustration Mark, goodness sake would do."

Mark sighed, indicated and moved over, slowing down to 80mph, more than fast enough in Lizzie's book. He loved how well she knew him, how she managed to turn an instruction into a suggestion, giving him the final say, allowing him to reply rather than comply.

"As you wisshh missssshhhh Moneypenny," he replied, "They'll jusssht have to thank their lucky schhtars that the Ashhton is in for itshhh MOT. And why is it that when I start out as Sean Connery I always end up sounding like a Dutch tour guide? Over here schee, the heeshtoric doorsh and da windowssh. Ant across the schquare the barschh and de reschtaurants."

Equilibrium had been restored. The exit from the A31 and the final stretch on the journey home was approaching.

*

After the usual flurry of greetings; hugs, kisses (actual) air kisses (Sophie) handshakes (the chaps, who still held the view that it seemed odd that men would ever want to embrace) banter (Johnnie) and reassurances to his mum that everything was fine with them all, just a few hold-ups on the A31 that was all, they settled into a more natural rhythm of drinks on the terrace before lunch. His dad seemed pleased with himself when serving 'newfangled' crisps that impressed Lizzie and Sophie (Mark thought them foul, some mash up of root vegetable flavour, no doubt overpriced at the local Waitrose) but it remained very much out with the new and in with the old when it came to Henry's choice of Scotch as an aperitif, as did Johnnie, with the ladies enjoying an iced G&T (Mark used to flush with humiliation whenever he was included in this group, as he still was by his brother, but simply smiled on this occasion and raised his glass to join in the toast for 'happy bank holidays'). Johnnie had clearly had a couple before they arrived and was red faced, from the Scotch and the ever-rising temperature. They were sitting at a huge worn outdoor teak table over which sat a vast green canopy providing shade from the early afternoon sun. Down the broad stone steps that led onto the lawn were Tiggy and Harry half-heartedly batting a shuttlecock over the ancient net that was dragged out every summer along with the boules and an assortment of warped wooden tennis racquets and, Mark cringed, the well-worn croquet set. Johnnie was shouting less than helpful hints at his children, much to Sophie's disdain, he finding his comments as hilarious as she clearly didn't. Mark felt for him as he always seemed to feel the need to fill a silence and so would end up on the wrong end of a withering glare or put down that made everyone uneasy. Johnnie choked on a crisp and pulled a face as he must have tasted the beetroot, before grinning and blurting,

"I was in my club the other day having a Scotch with an old school chum of mine when I asked him, do you ever talk to your wife after you've made love? To which he replied, yes of course old boy, if there's a telephone handy."

Johnnie couldn't contain his mirth at this gag and laughed so heartily that he started coughing again, spitting bits of soggy crisp over the table. Sophie pushed her chair back sharply and marched off, announcing that she was going to help June in the kitchen; Lizzie smiled and went with her, taking Isaac and leaving the three men 'to it'. Usually at this point, with the women in the kitchen, his father and brother would either slip effortlessly into business speak that excluded Mark or ask him some pointed questions as to how his career was progressing (or more than likely regressing) but Mark decided to buck the trend and asked them about their commercial interests instead. Johnnie frowned and glanced in the direction of their father before shrugging and grumbling about how his business faced a huge downturn in demand as a result of the international financial crisis and loss of confidence in the banking sector (financial services representing a huge slice of his corporate pie), how they had frozen all expansion plans (whether organic or through acquisition) in order to consolidate their existing market share and faced tough decisions regarding the workforce, with redundancies inevitable and other asset stripping a likelihood. Whatever all that meant, thought Mark, but now was not the time to 'do a Johnnie' and make a flippant remark as to how his brother always seemed to enjoy strippers with assets. His father, always the calm and measured Chairman of the Board, gave no more than a sound bite with regards the family business, citing the huge expansion into the mining of natural minerals on a global scale by the Chinese as having serious implications for the family shipping firm's traditional markets but they were exploring other untapped markets and left it at that.

Before Mark could ask any further questions, the wives reappeared in procession with the honey glazed gammon pre-sliced and served on the best family china, accompanied by huge bowls of steaming, buttered new potatoes adorned with fresh mint and rosemary picked earlier from the garden complemented by a beautifully crafted salad platter. With Isaac settled for his afternoon nap (Lizzie had fed him in the kitchen whilst chatting to Sophie and his mum) and the children making their way up from their ill-tempered racket games, the wine was poured and lunch was taken, with no more talk of downturns, upturns or investment returns. As Mark devoured far too many potatoes than perhaps was healthy and maybe a glass or two more of Sancerre than was advisable, he was left wondering whether or not he had been introduced to the tip or the mass of the financial iceberg that seemed to have drifted firmly into family waters.

*

The noise from the applause was almost deafening as he gazed out across row after row of black jacketed and frock wearing theatre goers all on their feet delivering this thunderous endorsement of their first night. The lights glared harshly adding to the stifling heat in the auditorium, he could feel his shirt sticking to his back and the stiff collar rubbing on his neck but no amount of physical discomfort could detract from his crowning moment. He had finally arrived and was fully deserving of the plaudits with every clap, every cheer, proving more euphoric to his ears. He attempted in vain to take it all in, the monumental significance of this end-point in what had been an arduous journey; a long, slow haul to his own personal summit. He remembered all the doubters (including himself he had to admit) the obstacles (self-imposed and those out of his control), the late nights drafting, the exhausting days grafting, the final push to get the thing over the line. All of it, every bit of it was worth it as he surveyed the delighted recipients of his endeavours.

Out of nowhere, he felt something hit his chest hard, taking his breath away and causing him to gasp aloud. He put his left hand up to shield his eyes from the blinding lights and his right to cover the blow, fired from an unseen assailant, liquid now soaking his shirt; being assassinated by the critics was one thing he'd been braced for but in reality was certainly not in the script. Another shot caught him on the shoulder and he lost his balance, falling to his left. He instinctively put out a hand to break the impact on the unforgiving, polished wooden boards but was surprised to find something softer to the touch. Turning once more into the glare he was aware of the shrieking laughter of a young boy and the raucous roar of a male nearby. Shaking his head to relieve the grogginess, he found that he was not lying wounded and prone, centre stage in a West End theatre but straddled half on and half off a sun lounger in a south Dorset garden, the fingers of his left hand groping wildly for the sunglasses that had been perched on top of his head before his white wine induced siesta; his right hand still clutching his side. As his bleary eyes became accustomed to his now familiar surroundings and single vision was restored he was confronted by a grinning Harry and a doubled over Johnnie, both armed with ridiculously oversized high-powered water rifles coloured in garish lime green and purples, looking like a couple of characters from a computer game. Welcome back to the real world.

For the rest of the afternoon Mark joined in the 'fun' chasing Harry around, whacking a football, a shuttlecock, a croquet ball, breaking only for a cup of tea and slice of homemade lemon drizzle cake, one of his mum's specialities, or 'signature products' as it would probably now be described, before continuing the onslaught to his father's lawn. His mum was in her element, beaming to have all her family around her, effortlessly managing to attend to everyone's needs whilst never looking tired or flustered. His father had retired indoors away from the heat, probably to read the business section of the Sunday Times whilst catching up on the cricket scores. Mark noticed how relaxed Sophie appeared in the company of Lizzie and June, breaking into regular smiles and even a peal of laughter or two. This family caper really is okay, he thought, right before catching a tennis ball full in the crown jewels and falling, groaning to his knees once more. As always Harry and Johnnie were the guilty culprits, hooting with glee, although not even 'KP' could have hit a cover drive with such unnerving accuracy, according to his brother.

"The batsman's Holding, the bowler's Willey," Johnnie boomed, imitating a famous commentator's immortal line with a grin. "Just think yourself lucky we weren't using the proper cricket ball," he added ruefully, "with that full toss caught mid-wicket you would be out for just the one."

After thoughtfully deciding to 'bundle' him, further reducing his ability to breath, the afternoon of outdoor endurance testing came to a natural close as talk of tea for the children, baths and bed loomed. Mark seemed unconsciously to allow a more traditional division of labour when amongst his family as both his father and brother seemed quite clear on what a role of a father was, and bathing children certainly didn't fall into it. Johnnie put a heavy arm around his shoulder and steered him towards the patio chairs and some cold beers that were nestling amongst a mountain of ice in a champagne bucket with a grin that boasted 'here's one I made earlier', as Sophie managed the two children with her usual forthright precision. Lizzie was happily singing softly to Isaac as she carried him on one hip, her left hand extended to Tiggy who clasped it tightly whilst gazing up in adoration at this tanned goddess, hair loosely tied up with a few strands falling down in haphazard waves (as if she didn't have a glamorous version of her own to admire) but to Tiggy, Lizzie was everything a woman and mother should be and she hung on her every movement, smile and encouraging word.

"What a sight," Johnnie said admiringly, shaking his head in wonderment.

"I know," agreed Mark, "it really does evoke powerful emotions to see a mother with their child, doesn't it? So earthy, so timeless – I never thought I'd experience it for myself but Lizzie has unlocked so much in me that has taken us both by surprise, especially since having little Isaac."

"What *are* you prattling on about?" said Johnnie with irritation, before offering him the binoculars that their father used to use to check the tidal swells morning, noon and night, "get an eyeful of that little dish Maria from Milanese still sunbathing topless on her father's boat, what a minx, her nipples are like bullets, no wonder the old man likes to spend so much time out here gazing across the bay, tidal swells indeed, something else is on the move down below I can tell you!" He turned to Mark beaming with a lascivious grin across his jowly face.

Mark's spirits sank. He actually thought that he was on the verge of sharing a meaningful moment on the joys of fatherhood with the buffoon of a big brother of his, but instead he was being urged to ogle the bare breasts of a childhood fantasy through his father's binoculars. This was puerile even by Mark's Viz rooted standards. Having seemed surprised at Mark's resistance to what he thought was a perfectly reasonable offer and dismissing his use of Lizzie and Isaac as evidence that he was not the 'gay boy' that his brother was fond of calling him, Johnnie suggested that they drained their beers and headed out into the town to pick up fish and chips for the grown-ups.

"Man hunt fish!" Johnnie bellowed whilst getting up and making a Tarzan impression, thumping his chest only for a window on the first floor to be thrown open and Sophie to hiss a shushhhhhh at him with as much venom as she could muster (and she could muster a lot). Un- perturbed, Johnnie led the way around the side of the house (turning suddenly to grab Mark in a headlock and cajole him into a mock boxing match) to where the Range Rover was waiting, complete with the obligatory Chris Rea CD that boomed Road to Hell out of all 76 speakers as the engine roared into life and the gravel crunched and pinged under the sheer weight and power of the silver V8 beast.

Supper was a relaxed affair, with the adults consuming their plaice and chips out on the patio as the sun slowly set across the linear horizon. Another family evening meal, another breath-taking sight thought Mark, reflecting on the beauty of the rural scene they had witnessed in West Sussex just the night before and what lay before them now perched on the edge of the Dorset cliffs. To the west, they could trace a string of lights dotted along the coast up towards Bridport and Lyme Regis, villages and hamlets aglow in the soft evening light, to the east the familiar flash of the lighthouse on the headland spit at Portland, loyal sentinel over these waters for over a hundred years and ally to generations of the Woodford family. The atmosphere around the table reflected the calm waters out over which they gazed, with no underlying tensions, not even between Johnnie and Sophie, but probably as a result of the seating arrangement akin to in the canteen at the House of Lords with the men and women segregated by the ice bucket (with a Chablis replacing the beer), salt and pepper and bowl of tartar sauce.

Lizzie was feeling equally relaxed, loving the tingle on her skin from a day in the sun and the ebb and flow of conversation, allowing the whole experience to wash over her. Still managing to give the impression of fully engaging with Sophie and June in the chatter around school fees and the cost of living (she was yet to become fluent in affluence) she too reflected on her evening at home with her family in Funtington just 24 hours earlier and the modest, earthy environment that she was so used to. She was neither repulsed nor overwhelmed by the wealth that hung over Charlestown Manor as a sea mist over the rocks below, as she had always placed value on people and relationships over material acquisition. As the darkness encroached more boldly around the alfresco diners, creeping up and over the walls and spilling across the manicured lawns, the outside lights on the side of the house and those set along the neat stone paths and patio around them automatically clicked on. Lizzie shivered and reached for her cardigan, her skin just beginning to bear the bumps of late evening. Placing her elbows on the table, regardless of etiquette (they were out of doors after all) and her chin on top of her hands, she tilted her head to one side and gazed down to where Mark sat, nodding at something his father was saying, his kind face, slightly sunburned, lit up further by the soft glow from the candles in weathered period style holders, all adding to the historic presence of this place and family line. Mark must have felt her eyes latch onto him as he turned and returned her affection in a look that words would have failed to do justice to as love, reassurance, solidarity and respect embraced this unlikely couple, though they were out of each other's arms' reach. Within the hour, he was stretched back on the huge wrought iron bed of the red room, Lizzie on top of him, as they made slow, beautiful love to the sounds and rhythms of the waves gently exploring the cracks and crevices of the rocky cliff base far below.

One of the frustrations he found after love-making was the fact that he would stand for what would seem an age over the loo, seat up, waiting to pee. He thought he had given it long enough before slipping quietly out of bed, anxious not to disturb Lizzie, who was already sleeping soundly but he had clearly underestimated the time required before normal service had resumed. Giving up he gently lowered the wooden seat and tiptoed back into the bedroom before deciding to pop on a T-shirt and make his way stealthily down the two flights of stairs to refill his glass with tap water. He detoured to the little single room along the landing where the door, slightly ajar, cast a shaft of light into where Isaac was sleeping deeply in a travel cot. He adored gazing at this little miracle as he slept, on his back, tiny arms above his head, dainty fists clenched with his favourite rabbit draped across his chest. His blonde hair was tussled and he breathed steadily, pouting his tiny lips to suck at regular intervals on the dummy, despite it lying beside him. Mark carefully leaned in and lifted the glow in the dark pacifier and slipped it back where it belonged before whispering a barely audible 'goodnight little one' and backing silently out of the door and onto the landing once more. All was quiet, all was still. It was the midnight hour. A gleeful Tiggy had been allowed to avail herself of the yellow room, on the same floor as Mark, Lizzie and Isaac, whilst Johnnie and Sophie, Harry and his parents had a room each on the floor below.

Taking care with each step, he moved with a newfound sense of grace down the creaky stairway, avoiding the steps that he knew would squeak under his weight. Pausing at the foot of the landing on the first floor he could hear the restrained fury of a woman's voice, clearly Sophie, tearing strips off his beleaguered but deserving brother without wishing to disturb the household. He remembered commenting on a conversation a couple were having in the queue in front of him in a supermarket in Brighton where the man had moaned about their daughter 'waking the whole bloody house up' late the previous night. Before he could help himself, Mark had blurted, "Technically you can't wake a house up as it is an inanimate object, but you can, of course, wake a household." The man, still wearing the high visibility jacket of his building contractor employer, turned on him, face reddening with rage, "In-an-a-f*****g what you little prick?" Mark had gulped and responded, "Inanimate, as in not living," to which the burly six-footer had replied, "which is exactly what you'll be unless you keep your nose out of our bleedin' business. Got it?" Mark looked down whilst the man handed a multi-pack of smoked bacon to his Mrs, who looked at Mark with a sneer then turned to unload the trolley of food items, an advert for obesity and coronary thought Mark, but this time just to himself.

Wanting to be spared the details of Sophie and Johnnie's tête-à-tête, he pushed on, to the ground floor and the familiar smell of wax jackets and furniture polish that was also a reassuring constant in Lizzie's family home but it seemed at odds with the whiff of battered fish and chips that still lingered around the door frame to the family kitchen. He was just about to stride towards the kitchen when he noticed that the lamp on the main table must have been left on and another hushed conversation was being held between two adults, the only two left unaccounted for being his mother and father. Another late night whispered exchange, this is turning into an Agatha Christie, Mark thought. He froze, and strained against the crushing silence of the gloomy hallway in order to pick up whatever snippets he could.

"But Henry, please, this has gone on for long enough now darling, the dear boy has a family of his own to think about now and has a right to know."

Despite stretching as far as humanly possible, with one hand still on the polished banister, he could not hear a word of his father's reply, he thought fleetingly and enviously of Reed from the Fantastic 4 and his amazing stretch capabilities before just preventing himself from falling head first into the mahogany settle that ran along the left-hand side of the spacious terracotta tiled corridor that led to the kitchen and boot room beyond, a right to know what, exactly? His heart pounded so loudly he swore they'd be able to hear it. Time for a dignified retreat, he thought, despite a thirst that had failed to be quenched by downing a full pint of water, thus precipitating his trip to the loo in the first place. He made his way back up the stairs (Sophie's anger must have since abated as there was not a sound coming from their room now) and to his bedroom as silently as he had descended, and lay, staring at the ceiling for what seemed like hours, as he pondered exactly what it was that his parents were keeping from him.

*

He practically leaped up into a sitting position, one hand covering his aching eyes and the other outstretched as if attempting to turn back the deluge of bright light that poured in through the open bay windows, with Lizzie raising the sluice of the heavy velvet curtains and tying them back with the matching ties. "Morning lover boy, my, we must have over-exerted ourselves last night."

Mark groaned as he allowed his head to sink back into the soft thick white pillowcases, "What time is it?"

"Half nine,' replied Lizzie chirpily, "Your mum, Sophie and I are going to take the children for a walk so you need to get yourself mobilised as you and Johnnie have a barbecue lunch to prepare for."

"And dad?" enquired Mark. "Golf course, of course, bank holiday weekend or not. Come on d'Artagnan shake a leg or shall I ask Harry to come and do his trampoline wake up call?"

"Alright, alright, I'm there, really," protested Mark, pulling back the eiderdown and light summer duvet and waving his right foot around as if about to test the temperature of the icy ocean with his toe. Lizzie placed one hand on each of his cheeks and he closed his eyes, now accustomed to the warmth of the morning sun and of her love for him. She kissed him lightly on his forehead and then she was gone, leaving a swirl of dust twirling in the sunbeams.

After a pee that would have made a racehorse proud, Mark showered in the en suite and then towel dried quickly; leaving his hair damp he pulled on a navy blue Superdry T-shirt and the same brand khaki army style knee length shorts only to then crawl around for a minute or two as he struggled to locate and then reach his flip-flops that had ended up strewn right under the middle of the bed and agonisingly beyond his grasp until he lay flat on his stomach. Cursing as he caught his shoulder on the iron bed frame on the way out and petulantly shoving the metal edge with his left hand in angry retaliation he was aware of a presence leaning on the door frame behind him. Turning to look over his right shoulder, that he was rubbing furiously, he saw Tiggy, hair in a plait and wearing a pretty floral summer dress, observing him with the same cocked head and aloof/inquisitive air that she had inherited from her mother.

"Morning Uncle Mark," she chirped, "sleep well did we?"

"Oh hi Tiggy, yeah, fine thanks, and you?" he replied absent-mindedly, still nursing the pain.

"What is that mum says about the couple who live next door to us in Barnes? Oh yes, too much bed and not enough sleep. Is that why you look so tired Uncle Mark? Too much bed and not enough sleep?"

For a moment Mark thought it uncanny that Tiggy could have been aware of his sleepless night, as he had turned his parents' short but loaded conversation over and over in his mind. But he had been conscious of lying still so as not to disturb Lizzie, so how could Tiggy have known of his fitful slumber? Sure, she was on the same floor as them but the yellow room was some way down the corridor. Sensing the cogs churning, Tiggy helped him out.

"I couldn't help but overhear you two love birds 'at it' late last night, you weren't the only ones with your windows open. Mind you, Lizzie is quite the most exquisite creature, but you, Uncle Mark, quite the dark horse, or should I say stallion."

Flabbergasted, Mark stammered a response, "B-b-but you're only ten, what do you know of dark horses and stallions? Your equine reference point should be Black bloody Beauty or My Little Pony!"

"Eleven actually, you forgot my last birthday. Anyway, don't be so naïve Uncle Mark, I'm not a kid anymore," Tiggy said with a smirk, clearly enjoying the fact that she was in complete control of this exchange. "Besides I have perfected the art of pretending to have my head buried in a book or in a movie whilst overhearing more of what Mummy and Daddy say than they think, particularly when on long car journeys or when they think I am asleep and they are discussing other family members."

"And what exactly do they think of me and Lizzie then?" asked Mark, totally drawn into Tiggy's gentle ambush, once more being reeled in by a female, despite the 32 year age gap …

"That she is way out of your league and can't imagine what she sees in such a scruffy waster. (Mummy).

That she's only jealous because Lizzie's younger and fitter (Daddy) but despite your lack of ambition and drive then you must have some redeeming qualities in the bedroom in order to keep Lizzie fed and watered (Mummy again). Apparently one woman can tell whether another is 'getting it' or not."

"Getting it!" Mark spluttered, simultaneously staggered at the worldliness of his 11-year-old niece whilst understanding the need for all the safe sex seminars banded around in Brighton; maybe we are delivering these 6 years too late he groaned inwardly.

"Sex, of course," Tiggy continued. "Hadn't thought I needed to spell it out."

"But you shouldn't be talking about sex at your age Tiggy, you should still be doing colouring in and playing skipping and hopscotch." Mark was beginning to sound like such an old fart now, he could just hear himself in 10 years' time trying to tell Isaac the facts of life. Tiggy jolted him back to the uneasy conversation of the present.

"It's a simple fact of life. And in Mummy and Daddy's it appears that she isn't getting any whilst he is." Tiggy paused for dramatic effect (clearly all those brattish after school and Saturday morning stagecraft classes were paying off Mark thought cynically). "Oh yes, it's common knowledge, he chases any little tart in a skirt (Mummy) the reason being that she is too cold and uptight (Daddy). He 'bangs' that little slut on reception whenever he can get his grubby little mitts on her (Mummy again) and she wonders how much he has to pay for the pleasure and whether or not it is listed as a monthly bonus or cash payment? Mummy of course. If cash, could he please get a receipt as it might prove to be tax deductible, as we need every penny we can get thanks to his, and I quote, piss poor record in financial management."

Mark, still kneeling on the rug, must have resembled a guppy fish, floundering in a landing net as he could not vocalise a response to any of Tiggy's revelations, despite searching for the right one, any one. He was saved by Sophie calling up to Tiggy to announce the imminent departure for their cliff top walk and for her not to forget her sun hat. "Coming Mummy," she replied brightly over her shoulder before turning to smile at Mark once more. "Toodles," she said, as if butter wouldn't melt, and then was off skipping down the landing, sun hat in hand, like any 11-year-old might.

After struggling first to process what had just occurred then to get up and finally to locate his sunglasses case, Mark made his way downstairs to the cool quiet of an empty house, until he heard the groans coming from the kitchen. As expected, Johnnie was sitting at the kitchen table, head in hands, the half-eaten remains of a bacon and eggs breakfast pushed away from him and the fizzing of an Alka-Seltzer clearly the equivalent of a marching band to his sensitive ears.

"Morning dear boy," Mark announced, imitating his brother in phrase and volume, "in the dog house and with a hangover, my we must have been a naughty boy. And you don't 'arf look rough."

"So would you be if you were on the prescription I'm on," Johnnie replied, struggling to raise his head to even make eye contact with Mark, "combination of Viagra and laxatives, really don't know whether I'm …

"Coming or going," interjected Mark. "I used that one in the common room at college and it got a laugh out of everyone apart from the Principal's PA who said she didn't get it – the cue for more rib nudging. Mind you neither did she get the one about not having to buy Viagra online any more, you know the gag: You don't need to buy online, because you can get it over the counter. Really? Yes, if you take two. I thought I was going to be given a verbal warning after I tried to demonstrate the punchline in a charades style."

Johnnie managed to raise a smile before resuming his hung-over stance, staring at the effervescent tablet as it whirled and swirled, reducing in size, whilst Mark began to rustle up some tea and toast, not quite feeling ready for the full shebang of an English breakfast. As he waited for the teabag to infuse he took a munch of a piece of toast and Marmite before relaying to his brother the snippet he had heard from their parents' conversation the night before and if he knew of any skeletons in the closet that had yet to be revealed. Johnnie's gaze remained steadfastly on the glass before him but Mark did detect a flicker of something, then gone. "Maybe they were going to tell you that you're not quite the total loser they always thought you were," he shrugged before glugging the milky looking liquid in one go, some of which dribbled down his unshaven chin and onto his un-ironed open-necked pink shirt, and slamming the empty glass down on the table. Gesturing to the plates and mugs he suggested that they got the lot into the dishwasher before getting cracking with the BBQ grub.

"Usual drill," chirped Johnnie, with his uncannily remarkable powers of recovery now kicking in, "the men will prep the meat whilst the ladies get on with the salad." He chucked an apron in Mark's direction and placed the salad drawer from the fridge on the worktop in front of him before turning to rifle through the freezer for the assorted sausages and burgers whilst singing, 'I'm an Easy Lover' and to Mark's disgust, actually gyrating as he did so.

*

Lizzie always drove at a much steadier pace than Mark, pointing out to him that the slow lane was technically the lane that all vehicles should travel in until the point of overtaking and it wasn't at all helpful that he kept straining to lean across and check the speedometer then twist and look out of the rear window as if to say 'go on then, overtake now'. Whilst she was behind the wheel he would just have to sit back and enjoy the view. Mark slumped back into the passenger seat and actually turned to look out of the window to gaze out across the scorched landscape of the New Forest in high summer as they headed back towards the M27, his right hand bandaged and facing up, and resting on the wrist of his left arm. The afternoon had been going great guns until he had picked up a saucepan of new potatoes, the handle of which had been allowed to sit over a live flame giving him in his view 'third degree burns' but the consensus of the womenfolk was that they needn't be another clichéd BBQ burn victim clogging up the A&E on a bank holiday afternoon but that a good rinse under the cold water tap, the application of some cream and a bandage would do the trick. His mother had taken charge of the repairs, nodding with sympathy as he had hissed at the pain when the cold water hit the scalded weal across his right hand and then winced as she administered the cream and yellowing bandage from the First Aid kit that was stored under the kitchen sink. Johnnie was, unsurprisingly, less sympathetic, making innuendos on Mark's love of 'red hot pan handles' whilst suggesting with a nod and a wink that he tried doing it with his left hand that night so it felt more like someone else was doing it for him. Mark smiled to himself as he reflected on time spent with his brother over the weekend and how somehow he felt better disposed towards him, actually feeling something approaching compassion despite his lack of appropriate behaviour that extended to practically every area of his brother's life. Maybe Mark wasn't such a failure after all, and maybe his upsurge in acceptance of his brother combined with that of his own self- confidence. Anyway, there would be time enough for introspection, for now though, rest. Lowering his sunglasses he allowed himself to drift into a shallow sleep, still aware of the steady hum of the motorway traffic and the motion of the onward journey whilst being gently cradled by the late afternoon sun's glow.

9
December 2010

Mark 43, Lizzie 33, Isaac 10 months

Nice work, if you can get it

As she woke she lay still for a moment or two allowing her senses to boot up before turning slowly to look over her right shoulder. The duvet was bunched up on the other side of the bed, leaving her less of a half share, beneath it a still sleeping Darren (Aaron?) snored rhythmically. Shivering, she dangled a foot out and then down on to the carpeted floor below. Unusual for these types of gaff she thought, as most of them went for wood effect flooring, but she welcomed it for the warmth and soundlessness. She never managed to get over the awkwardness of waking up next to someone who's name she had either forgotten or not known in the first place and knew full well they would hardly wish to sit across the breakfast bar from her now that her sparkle and their drunkenness had both worn off. With a stealth perfected from too many of these inauspicious early morning starts, Hope gathered up her clothes that had been left in a heap beside the bed and tiptoed across and out of the bedroom, silently closing the door behind her.

She made her way unsteadily down the steel spiral staircase to the open-plan kitchen diner and got mechanically dressed whilst taking in her surroundings. One of those split level mews apartments favoured by the professional types. Full of clean surfaces, chrome gadgets and white walls but with some exposed brickwork to give it a sense of being lived in. From the look of the hob and oven this seemed hardly the case as they looked as if they had never been used. A huge canvas adorned the main wall of the living space, a riot of yellows, reds and oranges, a kind of sunset on speed she thought. This, presumably overpriced painting was marginally larger than the oversized plasma screen that was fixed to the adjoining wall, a mushroom coloured corner sofa running the length of the space left by what would have once been the fourth wall provided a natural partition beyond which she stood beside the breakfast bar. Opening the fridge door and peering inside she noticed a proliferation of white wine and champagne, ready meals, expensive looking cheeses, cold meats, yoghurts, low fat spread and Italian beers. What was it he said he did again? Estate agent, that was it. She helped herself to a carton of orange juice and took a few swigs, wiping her mouth on her bare arm and replaced the juice in the inside rack alongside the wine and champagne. In the middle of the breakfast bar sat a ceramic bowl into which had casually been slung a bunch of keys and a wallet. Handy, she thought, opening the black leather wallet and peeling out three crisp £20 notes. Cheap at half the price she smiled wearily. Using the hazy reflection from the steel fridge door she put her hair up and made for the front door. Bracing herself, she stepped out into the icy morning air that immediately took her breath away. As predicted, her hot pants, leggings, vest and cheap faux fur coat didn't provide adequate protection from the bitter chill that hit her full in the face. Stepping around the obligatory silver Audi TT she clutched her coat around her, hitched the strap of her handbag up onto her shoulder and clickety-clacked her way, head down, along the cobbles on what she and Tia called the walk of shame.

*

"Not a bad result last night eh?" Pete glanced up from The Independent that was spread out across the low table in front of him as Mark eased into the seat beside him, steaming black coffee in hand.

"Not bad at all," Pete replied, "what odds on a Michael Owen hat-trick in Europe. Mind you, he still doesn't look right in a United shirt to me."

"After that winner against City back in September he could retire now and still be a cult hero in my mind," Mark concluded.

"So, how did it go last night?" Pete enquired. Mark had gone out for a couple of beers with Vaz who had recently proposed to his girlfriend Nicki and the two were to be wed in the spring of 2012. Vaz being Vaz though, he had insisted on an initial planning meeting with Mark, his best man to be despite the wedding being over 16 months away.

"It was all going well," Mark began, "Vaz sketched out his 'vision' for this and that whilst I nodded and agreed with basically everything he said and then we went on to the Funky Buddha for a few more beers when in came those two young greeters, you know the two from my stag night and our honeymoon."

"Blimey," Pete responded, "but not altogether surprising, Brighton's not the biggest place, is it?"

"I just feel so on edge when I see them, and although nothing ever happened, I still feel guilty for being lured into The Zap by them in the first place. To make matters worse, Lizzie is seeing one of them for 1:1 mentoring sessions so their lives edge closer to mine." Mark sighed and shrugged his shoulders.

"Why don't you just tell Lizzie, casually, that you know the girls from being out and about, no need for any further explanation," Pete advised.

"Trouble is," Mark continued, "I should have said something to Lizzie when we bumped into them in Rhodes, the fact that I didn't then and still haven't made the connection makes it seem more as if I have got something to hide. What's more," (turning to see if anyone was listening in), "don't tell a soul but Lizzie wants us to start trying for another and I don't want anything to jeopardise the run in ... to think, weeks of nookie on demand, I've been waiting all my life for this!"

"That's great news," blurted Pete, perhaps louder than intended, whilst patting Mark on the back. Mark responded by spraying his mouthful of coffee all over the sports pages before digging his mate in the ribs and frowning as if to say 'what part of don't tell a soul don't you understand?'

"Anyway," Mark composed himself and wiped his mouth on his jacket sleeve before heaving himself onto his feet, "I need to copy some work sheets before the next period. Little darlings in lower sixth are working on the difference between a Romantic hero and a noble savage. I guess I should just hold us up as an example of each."

Pete smiled before adding, "Never had you down as a noble savage mate, just a savage full stop."

Mark had his back to the rest of the common room so didn't hear or see the Principal come in with a group of local town councillors who were touring the college. The group were greeted by a staff member backing slowly in their direction whilst repeatedly flicking the V-sign at a colleague who sat on an easy chair wearing a look of total disbelief.

Mark simultaneously clocked the look on Pete's now pale and panic-stricken face and heard the clearing of a throat behind him. He turned slowly to be faced by the Principal and a group of grey haired business looking types, all in suits, the majority of whom were also wearing chains, medals and confused frowns. Mark froze mid-gesticulation, not for the first time at a withering look from the head of the college who opened his mouth to speak but couldn't form the words. He remembered reading the memo that a group of councillors were giving a civic welcome to their counterparts from the French town to which Brighton and Hove was newly twinned (he couldn't remember the name) and that the party were going to be given tours of local commercial, cultural and educational centres. This was a situation from which Mark knew he could only emerge with a P45 and a mountain of explaining to do to Lizzie. Time seemed to stand still until it was punctuated by one, solitary word.

"Agincourt."

All eyes, the majority of which looked startled, turned towards Pete who had uttered the iconic word that, to a visitor from across the Channel, might be taken as an undeserving and nationalistic insult of the highest order. Pete continued, stuttering at first but quickly gaining confidence as he formed his explanation, "My upper sixth history students have been studying Anglo-French conflict and key turning points in pursuit of power and peace, Mark's literature students are studying Shakespeare's Henry V so we thought it would be a powerful cross curricular idea to bring both groups together to celebrate and debate the importance of England's strong alliance with France and to discuss the impact this has had on social, political, cultural and commercial diversity from the Middle Ages to the present day. We simply used the Welsh longbow-men as an example of the numerous cultural references that still exist in our language as a direct result of interaction with France and how much richer our heritage is for it."

Once of the suits translated and there was a ripple of understanding nods from the delegation who in part appeared satisfied at this explanation if not the inference allied to the palpable awkwardness of Mark's partially obscured but instantly recognisable two fingered salute that greeted them. Mark breathed a huge inward sigh of relief and shuffled his way towards the door, deliberately avoiding making eye contact with anyone but smiling and nodding in their general direction as he went, even muttering a quiet 'bonjour'. He could feel the sweat sticking to the back of his T-shirt and now soaking into his zipped woollen top, accompanied by a trickle down each temple as he hastily removed his jacket and leaned back against the cool wall of the corridor outside the common room that led towards the open-air quadrant. You total Muppet, he thought to himself, when will you ever learn? He knew four things straight off the bat: that (a) Lizzie would go ballistic when she heard of what had transpired, and she would find out somehow (b) the Principal would be having words with him and a disciplinary might not be out of the question (c) he would be laughing at this in the pub tomorrow night after the shock had worn off and (d) that he owed Pete big time and that a pint of Stella and a packet of crisps might fall short of his expectation; a curry at the very least might now be in order. As Mark made his way to his next teaching assignment he admitted to himself that he just had to accept that he was far less Heathcliffe and much more Frank Spencer.

He was right with all four of his predictions, in no particular order:-

1. That Friday morning he was summoned to the Principal's office and was met by an ashen-faced head of college, flanked by his PA and the head of HR to be read the Riot Act. He escaped with a verbal warning that would go on his HR File (didn't sound quite as sexy as the 'X Files' but thankfully he kept this one to himself, as he didn't want to become an ex-employee). He felt thoroughly chastised but relieved to still be in a job. He had Pete to thank for this.

2. He did indeed laugh about it that evening whilst in the pub with Pete, sharing the whole episode in some detail before getting down to their scriptwriting, even acting out an embellished version for some of their colleagues including Steve who was one of many who had heard of his Anglo-French gaff (or F-Gate as Pete had christened it) and were keen to hear it from the horse's mouth and were in stitches as a result. Unfortunately for Mark, also within earshot was the head of HR who happened to be in another part of the same pub but was intrigued by the raucous uproar from the corner around from where she was sipping a G&T with the bursar and had caught Mark in full flow, complete with V-signs.

Crucially, it was the first time in ages she had gone for a drink after work and it coincided with this clear demonstration as to just how seriously Mark had taken his reprimand of that morning. As a result, she felt that she had no option but to schedule a further meeting with Mark and the college Principal the following week that in turn was followed by a written letter to warn him of his future professional conduct underlining the fact that he remained an ambassador for the college whilst on site and in the vicinity. Another such incident would result in his instant dismissal.

3. He did end up in the curry house with Pete.

4. And the dog house with Lizzie.

The latter meant that any 'practice' at baby making was to be put firmly on the back burner as a furious (and exhausted) Lizzie left Mark to stew over this latest debacle, apparently one in a long line of him totally misreading the situation and ending up with egg on his face. He had applauded her clever mix of kitchen based metaphor and added that he would certainly try to keep out of hot water, not wishing to stir things up any further to which she had responded by making a sound like a throttled banshee, throwing a wet J-cloth at him, that hit him on the shoulder, before storming out of the kitchen and up the stairs in tears. He had bitten his lip and sat for some time, the kitchen cloth dripping steadily into his lap, thinking what would be his best course of action before deciding that doing nothing was probably the safest option all round, especially at this time of night and with him suffering from heartburn and suppressing lager and lamb bhuna belches.

*

Sometime she really felt like screaming. On this occasion she actually did, albeit on mute. Here was an intelligent, articulate man, an English teacher (sorry, *lecturer* as he was always at great pains to point out, no less) who would pride himself on his quips and witty one-liners and who maintained an absurd and infuriating snobbery at the 'plebeian masses' and their failure to grasp and apply even the rudiments of grammar whilst displaying a complete lack of awareness at how to apply *himself* appropriately in any professional or social situation. And why was it that he would automatically and needlessly speak when it wasn't required whilst remaining silent when his words were just what she needed? Words of acknowledgement at him being such a complete arse, of humility and remorse, reassurance, of a desire to learn from his mistakes, she would have taken anything, apart from the silence that seemed to descend at every moment of crisis, pushing at the walls of their home from the inside, the very walls that seemed to be closing in on her. She was lying on their bed, curled up, sobbing into a pillow whilst being aware of not waking Isaac; she couldn't even have a proper wail these days! She was hormonal and aware of how up and down emotionally she always was at this time of her cycle whilst simultaneously feeling powerless to stem the tide of tears and rage that threatened to overwhelm her.

*

Usually when Mark told her to 'wake up and smell the coffee' it was regarding her views on global poverty or sex trafficking and her sense of hopelessness coupled with a desire to do something, anything to help to make the world a more fair and just place. He remained a cynic, quoting an endless stream of statistics about corruption within the hierarchies of most developing countries and how futile it was to even send money in most cases. That said he had relented when she all but insisted they gave away 10% of their combined income to charitable causes both home and abroad as this was Biblical. Mark had resisted at first, suggesting that in first century Judea they probably wouldn't have had such things as emotive advertising campaigns, celebrity endorsements, chip and pin and direct debits, before conceding to fighting a losing battle and allowing her to make the arrangements as she firmly but calmly argued her case. On this occasion, however, his request was a literal one as he nudged their bedroom door open and tiptoed in, carefully carrying a tray of fresh coffee and pastries; a Saturday morning treat.

"What time is it?" Lizzie enquired. Her heavy eyes struggled to focus on her familiar surroundings.

"And where is Isaac?"

"Up, fed, walked, changed and now napping, your highness," Mark grinned proudly, as if to have accomplished once what a stay at home mum would routinely manage multiple times a day was worthy of some form of recognition/decoration. "Let me plump up some pillows for you my darling."

Mark made sure Lizzie was quite comfortable before bringing the tray across from where he had balanced it on her dressing table. She couldn't help but notice the glint in his eye as she leaned forward to allow him to prop her pillows, with him predictably staring down at her cleavage as the front of her nightdress gaped. She was at once appreciative and mildly suspicious at this over the top attention. Okay, he was on his usual early Saturday morning shift (her two-pronged attempt at gaining some 'me time' whilst also curbing his Friday night excess as she often reminded him

191

that babies 'don't do' hangovers) but he would usually mumble a good morning and leave the breakfast tray by the door before heading out to play tennis mid-morning.

She blew the steam off the coffee and tentatively took a sip before replacing it on the tray, tucking hungrily into an almond croissant, her absolute favourite. She noticed that Mark was in a T-shirt, jeans and an old V-necked jumper and not his sports kit. "You and Vaz not on court this morning then McEnroe?"

"The big wuss is going to a wedding fair somewhere in Kent so you have me all to yourself my princess. I thought a light breakfast followed by some baby making might be in order, all before Isaac wakes and joins me for Football Focus before lunch."

"Sweetheart, for someone who teaches poetry you can be pretty unromantic at times. Basically, you want to have sex with me before the football comes on."

"But surely practicality comes into the process my darling, I mean love isn't always a candlelit dinner for two."

"That maybe so, but this really is a breakfast for one so let me enjoy this in peace. Come back in 20 minutes and we'll see how I feel then."

Mark left compliantly, singing 'Heaven is the back seat of my Cadillac' by Hot Chocolate as he skipped down the stairs. If he had a tail it would be wagging Lizzie thought as she told him to pipe down or he'd wake the baby; the very baby that he had just put down for a morning nap. Men!

She closed her eyes and took in the wafts of freshly percolated coffee whilst savouring the sickly sweet paste found underneath the flaky pastry of the croissant along with the silence and solitude that she now embraced. Just a quarter of an hour to herself, to think her own thoughts, or none at all, was a newfound bliss as the rest of the day was dominated by the needs of her two boys, her actions dictated to by the appetite and bodily functions of Isaac or whimsical requests from Mark. This, she whispered, is a little slice of heaven.

She had never been a fan of their morning sex, always feeling under prepared for the onslaught and much preferring love-making before lights out. She had been surprised at how keen Mark was considering how long it would normally take him to shake a leg in the morning; but there again she supposed that grappling with her naked body was a greater motivation to getting him up and about than a morning teaching seventeen year olds

Chaucer (although he did love the ribald content and language, naturally, and would often describe a celebrity who had been cheated on as a withered cuckold). Despite showering, he had still smelt of the pub and curry house from last night and no matter how many times he brushed his teeth on a Saturday morning the taste of onions remained entrenched for the best part of the day. She loved Mark deeply for all his faults and foibles and he was giving family life his very best shot. She managed to see the funny side of most of his attempts at fatherhood, for example leaving Isaac on his changing mat earlier that week when running into the kitchen to celebrate a United equaliser only to trot back a minute later to find Isaac sitting in the corner of the lounge having left a trail of poo along the floor that was also on his hands, bare feet and up the sides of the surrounding walls.

It wasn't a case of lying back and thinking of England as she was still attracted to Mark and keen to start trying for another child with the man she loved but she was just focused on being totally lost in the moment, wanting to think of nothing more than the bitter taste of the coffee and the sweetness of the almond croissant. Her thoughts turned to her appearance and the need to brush her hair and deal with her smudged mascara but just another 5 minutes she thought, keeping her eyes firmly closed and smiling to herself once more, just another 5 minutes.

10
August 2011

Mark 43, Lizzie 34, Isaac 18 months

Once more into the breach

He loved the way little Isaac explored their back garden, his first unsteady steps were all jerky and unpredictable with both hands flapping wildly in the air. Mark had commented that he looked like an old drunk at closing time insisting he was sober as the landlord ushered him out of the bar and into the cold night air. They had, for once, broken with tradition, and decided to spend the bank holiday at home quietly, away from Dorset and all the tensions that would no doubt be simmering. Johnnie had endured another awful year with his business turning in some atrocious results and there was talk of them having no option but to sell both their second home in West Sussex (their third home in Corfu had already gone, sold to the guy called Guy in Brighton the previous year) and to seriously batten down the hatches and ride out the storm. He could always rely on members of his family to fall back on solid seafaring analogies such was their rich maritime heritage. Sophie had responded to the crisis by reducing the number of sessions she had with her personal trainer and on one occasion even picking up some essentials (chicken liver pate, fresh trout, chilli infused olive oil, baby new potatoes, mangetout, fromage frais, Green & Black's chocolate and a bottle of Oyster Bay Chardonnay) from their local Sainsbury's no less. Never again, reported Sophie who had clearly been traumatised by the experience. According to Tiggy her mother spent the whole time clicking her fingers impatiently at staff members (and even other customers) due to her frustration at failing to know the 'lay of the land' often huffing or tutting before cross referencing where they were with the layout at Waitrose. Eventually she had pushed in at the basket only checkout, despite having more items in her basket than permitted, thus annoying the elderly couple who she had swept past en route on two counts. Tiggy thought it all mildly amusing and commented on the poor grammar at the checkout, "Surely as a teacher, Uncle Mark, you can appreciate the error in 'five items or less'. Anyone with a half decent education would tell them it should be 'five items or fewer'." Mark couldn't disagree and was impressed by his precocious niece and her grasp of the English language.

He also had a modicum of sympathy for Sophie who had invested so heavily in her social stock that seemed to be plummeting at the same rate as their financial status. She had been in a permanent strop since the previous August and had threatened to walk out on Johnnie (taking the kids with her) on more than one occasion partly due to the sheer embarrassment of having to tighten the purse strings so publicly and also in coming to the end of her tether at his string of infidelities. The stress of their plight and of the economic downturn in general now seemed to be taking its toll on his father also, someone who had seemed almost immune to the impact of modern market forces. He had looked pale and tired on the past two occasions they had visited. They had endured such an uncomfortable Christmas and Easter break due to the palpable atmosphere of bitterness that engulfed his brother and sister-in-law that they felt that they would give them all some breathing space this summer. Mark was particularly keen to avoid any unnecessary stress on his blooming wife as they had suffered the heartbreak of a miscarriage back in February followed by much soul searching and praying (Lizzie) before deciding to try again that summer. Ten weeks into her third pregnancy was just too delicate a time to be subjecting her to the family feud. They just wanted to get to 12 weeks, have the scan and then tell the world.

*

Mrs Sheridan had kindly agreed to come round and sit with Isaac whilst they went for the scan. She had been extremely supportive of their relationship from the moment Lizzie had come into Mark's life, often hugging her spontaneously before stepping back to hold her at arms' length and tell her, with a tear in her eye, what an absolute blessing she was to the family and how she had made Mark the happiest man in all the world. Lizzie had taken to her immediately and, not being a woman who was overly possessive of her domestic environment, was more than happy for 'Mrs S' to bustle around with the duster or do some vacuuming (always wearing an apron and humming hymns) whilst Mark took Isaac to the park and she was ordered to put her feet up for half an hour. Yes, Mrs Sheridan did chat a lot, often in that gossipy way older women did, particularly about other women in the parish who might, for example, be showing just a little bit too much flesh at holy Mass or talking too much before the bell was rung for Mass to begin (a delightful irony in her highlighting those who had far too much to say for themselves). Lizzie listened and nodded as Mrs Sheridan wittered endlessly in that little sing- song southern Irish accent whilst Mark would always sigh and head for cover after five minutes at the most. As for Isaac, he loved this genial next door neighbour but one and the feeling was clearly mutual as she would gather him up into her strong, wiry frame to kiss him repeatedly until he giggled then wriggled to get free and totter off to the next distraction.

Lizzie had been fascinated at the 'back story' of Mrs Sheridan's links with the Woodfords and in particular with Mark's deceased godparents. She had agreed that his parents had demonstrated real tolerance towards the Irish Catholics that was not always consistent with upper-middle-class Church of England families during the post-war years and, shamefully, not even in the present day. Mark had agreed but had grown used to being around the equally chatty Mary and quiet and steady Bill as a backdrop to their youth. Lizzie loved hearing people's stories and was keen to hear more about Mrs Sheridan's close friend Mary, how they met, growing up in Ireland, coming over to England after the war but this was one area where Mrs Sheridan remained tight-lipped, "Oh the past is the past Lizzie dear, we have the present to concentrate on now," was her usual refrain that left Lizzie wondering whether this was just a case of letting bygones be bygones or if there was more to this narrative than she cared to let on?

They left Mrs Sheridan perched on one of the garden chairs whilst Isaac toddled about the garden tentatively kicking a sponge ball whilst holding up a bright red plastic toy train which he would look at frequently and exclaim loudly (and proudly) "Toot toot." They left through the side gate whilst he was crouched over a snail in that amazing way a toddler can when they notice something of interest and just drop down, peer and balance perfectly on their haunches. The drive to the hospital was conducted largely in silence, with Lizzie requesting that Mark turn his Aphex Twin CD off in order for her to feel calm before the scan. On the one hand she had taken the miscarriage in her stride, on the other she had grieved for the life that could have been, wondering if they had conceived a boy or a girl, but at the time of the miscarriage it was too early to tell. Her faith told her that this little soul had not been lost and there was a reason why he/she (she couldn't bear 'it') had not come to term. Her humanity, however, left her with a deep sense of loss that at times seemed too great to bear. She had blamed herself for being too stressed, too intense, too keen, too uptight but ultimately knew this was a fruitless course to take. How could she possibly face trying to conceive again when she was still grieving for the little life lost? It had taken time, prayer and the support of her close friends before she was in that place emotionally to contemplate beginning the process again.

Mark had been as gentle and understanding as he was capable of, bless him, but through no fault of his own lacked the emotional tools to deal with such a tragedy and its aftermath. Thankfully he hadn't fallen back on his flippant default mode or she really might have strangled him but instead he tended to tiptoe around her, as if she were made of glass and surrounded by a sea of eggshells, smiling sympathetically and making far too many cups of tea. Thankfully, he was sensible enough not to suggest 'getting back into the saddle' too soon and had given her the time and space that she needed to recover emotionally. Lisa and Jan had been absolute rocks for Lizzie as she had expected but a surprise factor in this healing process had been some of the many conversations she had shared with one of her former clients, Hope. Once a troubled, headstrong adolescent she was now a beautiful independent young woman whose stunning appearance and overt confidence camouflaged a deeply rooted vulnerability born through a childhood that lacked a father (unknown to her) and a mother (who had to work all hours to make ends meet). Now 18 and officially 'off the programme', Hope was free to meet Lizzie on an informal basis and they would have coffee at one of the seafront cafés every couple of weeks to catch up. Hope seemed absolutely besotted with Isaac and he in turn was totally mesmerised by her amazing corkscrew hair, huge made-up eyes, full lipstick painted lips, huge hoop earrings and heaving copper-glitter brushed bosom that always seemed unfairly squeezed into a top at least a size down from that that might have been required. Lizzie thanked God for these diverse friendships, the support from her church family and all those close to her, thankful for so many listening ears and helping hands whilst remaining painfully aware of just how many young women went through what she had experienced, and far worse, without anywhere near the love, care and support that she had been blessed with.

*

197

Mark prided himself on always having saved enough change for the 'pay and dismay' at the Royal Sussex on Eastern Road and had managed to find a parking space to the front of the main building of the hospital where Isaac had been born less than two years earlier. Anyone would have thought he had just downed a charging Rhino with a toothpick such was his glowing sense of achievement.

Lizzie had her appointment letter clutched in her hand as they sat on a row of bright orange plastic chairs in a busy corridor of the ultrasound wing, waiting to be seen. Next to Mark sat a huge hairy biker with multiple piercings and forearms the size of Mark's legs, the chair he was squeezed into seemed to be straining at its seams to contain him. Mark, in his usual 'I'm feeling anxious so will speak without thinking' way nodded to this bruiser and asked him if he had paid the extra eight quid for a photo. The Viking had growled and sat upright in his chair, his huge torso turning slowly and deliberately in Mark's direction, oozing menace, just as his girlfriend, a much slimmer, petite, more manicured looking version also bedecked in leather and denim but tottering on stilt like red high heels returned through a door marked 'Gynaecology' that was situated along the same corridor to the ultrasound. Thankfully before Giant Haystacks could address and/or destroy Mark, Lizzie heard her name being called from the opposite end of the corridor; quickly grabbing Mark's arm she pulled him away from a potentially life-threatening situation and straight into a life giving one.

The jelly always came as a shock to the system; she knew it was coming but always forgot just how cold it was as it was liberally smeared across her smooth skinned belly, forcing a sharp intake of breath. Mark sat to one side, holding her hand as the sonographer wriggled herself into her saddle style seat, satisfied that enough of the gel had been applied and began clicking on various buttons with her other hand whilst her assistant asked Lizzie the statutory questions required at this stage of the game. As Lizzie answered, her eyes became fixed upon the screen as her womb became visible in that familiar arching scope. Questions over, they were left with the scan in progress. The operator, a friendly South African physiotherapist, gave a running commentary, most of which Lizzie and Mark were able to take in. The words healthy and normal featured heavily and the moment they heard the 'peeepauu, peeepauu' of the little heartbeat neither could hold back the tears. It would be another eight weeks before they would be able to confidently identify the gender but they left the ward as a member of the yellow plastic folder club once more. Mark waved cheerily as a Harley Davidson motorcycle roared past them as they made their way to the car park, an extra spring in their steps. Just before they got back into the car they embraced again, Lizzie burying her head into his chest and Mark just able to lightly kiss the top of her head without having to go on tiptoes. They were pregnant again, a healthy new life now growing inside her. They would feel even more the complete family with Isaac having a little brother or sister to play with. They drove back wearing sunglasses and Cheshire cat grins; life was good Lizzie thought, praise the Lord, as she held her hand across her stomach, and it just keeps getting better.

Part 2

1

January 2012

Mark 43, Lizzie 34, Isaac nearly 2

A knock at the door

Silence had slowly settled upon the usually noisy household like a dust sheet over antique furniture. At first the sheer absence of noise was deafening. He was supposed to be marking a stack of A-Level Literature mocks, the unseen text, but was distracted by his unseen family, as he always was from the moment they left. Curious, he pondered aloud, as he meandered in and out of every room in the house, lukewarm mug of tea in hand, how someone could crave silence and solitude and yet feel bereft of the very cause of such chaos the moment they were no longer there. Would he ever be truly satisfied? Not that one again as he pushed that thought back amongst the waves of other impulses that crashed against the inside of his forehead, each vying for their own personal tutorial. Instead he focused on being present in the moment, a lifelong challenge for someone used to spending so much of his time either dwelling on the past or attempting to predict how his future would pan out. Procrastination would be his specialist subject if he ever made it on to Mastermind.

Marriage and fatherhood, like many other semblances of the conventional, had caught up with and overtaken him, receiving surprising little resistance. A career bachelor with an acute aversion to the mundane existence the majority seemed resigned to accepting, and a man devoid of any aspiration to work in the conventional way for a living, he now found himself in possession of a wife, child, cat, salary, health plan, pet insurance and even a sensible family car. Recently he'd begun paying into a pension plan. What had become of that melancholic, moody teenager renowned for sulking at parties and parents' evenings, the pasty undergraduate wallowing in existentialism and associated angst, the 'playwright' who'd spent years gazing out of various windows in a multitude of rented cottages and apartments up and down the south coast but still without a published play to his name? Or even a completed one for that matter. A healthy sense of self-depreciation was his saving grace, without which he would be, by his own admission, unbearable to live with.

Leaving the kitchen in a state of semi-tidiness (all used breakfast cups, plates and bowls stacked neatly in the dishwasher, butter and spreads in the fridge and cupboards respectively, stray porridge oats swept from work surface into cupped hand and then into bin) he lingered momentarily at the door to the lounge, leaning on the door frame and taking in the now familiar sight of a play/war-zone left in a state of disarray as the source of such disruption is plucked from his range of brightly coloured tractors and diggers to be replanted into a car seat whilst holding on to the ear of his favourite soft toy (a bunny) and whisked compliantly off to the next destination, in this case a 'play date' with a mum and daughter who were on the same ward as Lizzie when Isaac was born. Despite a new-found orientation towards tidiness (one of the many positive influences Lizzie had brought into his world), he and Lizzie were in agreement that the lounge would be a kiddie friendly environment during the day, with all related paraphernalia being gathered up in a wooden trunk that was then stuffed into the already heaving under-stairs cupboard each evening. Besides, they had a perfectly good dining room to reserve as adults only, free from the Tommee Tippee mug spillages, rice cake mush and regurgitated milk stains that marked Isaac's first year and the scratches and marks to the skirting boards, coffee table and walls that reflected his increasingly inquisitive nature and mobility as he approached two.

Tutting audibly (where once he probably would have salivated) as yet another garish glossy flyer for cholesterol busting pizza deals with free fizzy drinks had been shoved roughly through the letter box he ascended the stripped pine stairs to the first floor landing, unable to resist a peek into Isaac's nursery. A stripy hoody that was borderline wash/wear once more had been draped over the wicker basket that contained duplicate soft toys to those that inhabited his cot (in case of loss or damage and to prevent potential trauma) along with a pair of denim dungarees, a Christmas gift. A cliché I know, he thought, but just how dinky are they? The changing mat was lying at a jaunty angle (as the little fella had taken to struggling every time a nappy change was required) hence the toy elephant and story book lying upside down beside it; a newly discovered distraction technique.

His Winnie-the-Pooh sleeping bag was in a dishevelled pile in the middle of the cot, the faithful fluffy Tigger scrunched up alongside it, his second favourite soft toy to bunny (or buddy as he was known to Isaac) that had accompanied him on his play date, as it did everywhere he went.

All had been left as it had been; a snapshot in time. It had surprised him how he had taken to fatherhood so naturally, especially during the nappy and teething months. He had seen himself being semi-engaged, rising above the 'ga-ga-ga' phase and waiting patiently until his lad was old enough to kick a football before fully immersing himself, as he had done with his nephew Harry. The depth of love he'd felt for Isaac even as a shadow on a 12 week scan had overwhelmed him and had grown steadily ever since. At times he had to check just how tightly he would hold him to his chest, as he would close his eyes and rest his chin on that head of silky golden hair, breathing him in and praying under his breath that the God his wife subscribed to would protect this little miracle they had been blessed with whilst also vowing to do everything he'd ever need to do to nurture his beloved son. His mates from Uni, all experienced dads by now, had, he felt, breathed a collective sigh of relief when (a) he'd announced he had joined their ranks and (b) to hear he'd finally got it; grasped what they'd been banging on about for all those years, stuff that he'd just written off as sentimental cliché, the stuff of shaving product ads and US made for TV dramas.

Ignoring their bedroom and the room that would be Isaac's when he was old enough (and when 'number two' was occupying the nursery) he made his way up a narrower flight of stairs to the rather grand and somewhat pretentiously named third floor guest suite and study. Like many Victorian villas typical of this part of Brighton, the third floor lent itself perfectly to self-contained guest accommodation comprising double bedroom, shower en suite and a small living room that also served as his study. He had always loved his little 'dens' ever since he was a boy; whether bunk bed, wood shed or under one of the many huge shrubs that grew in the garden of that large house in a picturesque village of Dorset, far from the madding crowd indeed. The top floor offered the type of refuge he yearned for, away from the chatter and clatter of visiting mums with their little bundles of joy, from well-meaning neighbours who would far outlive the warm welcome that Lizzie offered to everyone, even at times from Lizzie and Isaac themselves when the long wet Saturday afternoons led to a sense of claustrophobia, dissipated by half an hour on his own on the top floor with the radio murmuring updates on all the day's matches adding to this sense of rejuvenation.

Settling into his favourite battered leather armchair he'd picked up in a vintage furniture shop in the North Laines he lifted the walnut lid to the retro-style turntable that Lizzie had bought him for his birthday a couple of years ago. She'd bought him this partly because he requested it but also in recognition of him trading in his beloved BMW Z3 two-seater sports car for a second-hand silver VW Touran in anticipation of Isaac's imminent arrival; a sacrifice he still harped on about. He shifted uncomfortably, and, reaching into his back pocket found the source of this irritation; a 6-inch green and red cloth very hungry caterpillar soft toy (that had come free with one of the many versions of the book they'd received as gifts for Isaac when he was born) that he must have absent-mindedly stuffed into his pocket as he'd done his earlier rounds of the house. Getting comfortable again he began the ritual that ushered in a morning or afternoon of being home alone. Opening the stained and cracked 7-inch plastic record case he rifled through classics from when he was a youth, starting with The Associates' 'Party Fears Too' followed by 'Blind Vision' by Blancmange, 'Love Song' by Simple Minds and the Tears For Fears hit 'Mad World'. There was a 10 year age gap between him and Lizzie so they each had a different soundtrack to their teens. She had grown up in a small rural village nestled in the South Downs near Chichester so neither could lay claim to being sophisticated urbanites but her anthems were, to his taste, too self-aware and polished, lacking the naïvety and carefree abandon of the early '80s. As was usually the case when he retreated into a nostalgic world of long fringes, long summers, suede pixie boots and cheap cider, he was saturated by a sense of loss, not of the lifestyle, nor even the freedom it afforded him but by the hope that reigned as he and his mates sat up on the cliff tops, swigging from a shared bottle of scrumpy, pretending to smoke and lying about 'how far they'd got' with various girls at the previous night's school disco. Theirs was a shared hope of a life less ordinary, one that lay far beyond the limiting boundaries of Dorset. It wasn't even as if his life had necessarily been an anti-climax, it just hadn't played out as he'd expected it to. This was a difficult emotion to share with Lizzie, who was far more down to earth than he was and possessed neither the time nor inclination for wistful glances over her shoulder to measure reality with life expectation. They were a happily married couple with a beautiful little one and another on the way. They had no financial pressures, a close group of supportive friends and family, either near to hand or within a few hours' drive and a nice house with a sea-ish view (that thing on the horizon between the sky and the land, madam) so what was there to be disappointed about? It was just that back then, lolling on the cliff tops, gazing up at the stars with the whole of their lives stretching before them it really did feel that the sky was the limit.

His New Romantic recollections were disturbed by the sound of the doorbell ringing two storeys below. He ignored it. He always did. Lizzie wasn't due back for hours and he utterly refused to entertain any unannounced visitors so he settled back into his armchair and smiled at the thought of how, having plucked up the courage all night to ask Jenny Ford to dance, he was making his way shakily across the sticky school hall floor to do so only to find that Phil McGladdery had beaten him to it. Conscious of being seen to be a cool customer, even at that young age, he'd pretended that he was heading to the canteen to buy yet another bottle of Panda Pop as Phil and Jenny swayed self-consciously hand in hand to 'Love Action' by the Human League. Bastard! The doorbell rang again, this time with more sustained pressure being applied by whoever was on the front step. Sod it, he thought and made his way clumpily down the two flights of stairs (with the words 'And I find it kind of funny and I find it kind of sad, the dreams I have of dying are the best I ever had' on repeat in his mind). He pulled open the inner glass panelled door with such force that it caused the inset panes to rattle, then the solid green wooden front door to find WPCSO Marshall standing on the second of the three whitewashed steps, her colleague, Sergeant Evans leaning on the side of a Ford Focus patrol car parked outside with one eye on her and one on the cockpit of the car from which emanated the steady static-punctuated stream of murmuring comms. He knew them both as they regularly paid visits to the VI Form College where he taught to talk to the students about the risks of drugs and alcohol, often with Lizzie alongside them in her capacity as a local youth and community worker. "Hi Emma," he said casually, his stomach already beginning to tighten in knots but he quickly convinced himself her unscheduled visit was to do with one of his tutor group being found smoking weed under the pier (again), or to arrange another college visit with Lizzie now the new term had started, "Is everything okay?" Her face looked pale and mouth pinched, "Can we come in Mark?"

*

Lizzie had always preferred quality over quantity when it came to friendships, opting to get to know fewer women in more depth than to attempt at managing a string of acquaintances on surface level. Many of the young women she worked with boasted of the many 'friends' they had on social media and often failed to see the irony in the fact that many of these so-called friends remained unknown to them, many of whom they wouldn't even recognise if they bumped into them on the street. In fact, she hoped that most of the females would never bump into some of their so-called online friends as it was a world laden with danger where a vulnerable young woman could be easily flattered and led down a slippery path resulting in serious emotional and even physical damage. She smiled to herself as she imagined replaying her thoughts to Mark, who always took a lighter route through life than she did. She often wondered what it would be like to view life through his soft focus lens with so many blurred edges but had come to the realisation that she was who she was, someone who had a caring heart (not that Mark didn't) but through her recent professional experience she had fallen in step with the nuances of life for the disadvantaged and, although she had never resented Mark for his polemic experiences, wished sometimes that he would be more sensitive to the needs of others, particularly those born without a spoon in their mouth, never mind a silver one …

Take Mandy, for example. A tough cookie on the outside, she went into labour on the same day as Lizzie with Isaac and gave birth to a little boy she called Cayden (to which Mark had scoffed with exasperation 'it's not even a proper name'). Although eight years her junior, this was Mandy's third baby, all by different fathers, something that fuelled further bitchy and disparaging comments from Mark about her background and chaotic family life, at times sounding like a proper Tory old fart with his references to 'those types of people' and 'a drain on the state' and 'double- barrelled names to advertise how many different fathers the kids have' after he had shared a lift with some of her relatives during visiting hours and overheard their conversations. Lizzie had become exasperated when he had lampooned Mandy, putting on an exaggerated estuary accent "ahhhh look at Talulla, wot a clever little princess, only five and already she can spell her own name in smoke rings." Lizzie had reminded Mark that new life was an equally joyous experience regardless of family history or social stock and that he should check his attitude and develop more of a sense of compassion, particularly towards those who were not as well provided for as they were. He had mumbled something or other and she doubted very much would change but she felt it important to point out his prejudices as he was either unaware that they existed or resistant to a change of view.

Despite Lizzie having a private room in which to recover from her delivery (a cause for relief and embarrassment in equal measures) she would often head out onto the ward to check on Mandy and her little one. She could tell that Mandy was a doting mother to all her brood and felt a wave of compassion towards this young woman who had the odds stacked against her, facing a tough life raising three children on her own (none of the fathers had stuck around once they'd found out she was 'up the duff' she had told Lizzie, without a hint of malice), just a sigh of realisation that the buck stopped with her. This was it, no use looking back or even too far forwards, but just dealing with the here and now.

They had kept in touch since and Lizzie visited at least once a fortnight, often feigning that Isaac had grown out of this outfit or with that toy in order to bless Mandy with gifts without offending her fierce sense of pride, as she had once snarled, cigarette balanced in one corner of her mouth whilst she wiped sick from the corner of Cayden's, 'we don't want no bloody charity sweetheart'. She was always considerate when Lizzie visited, and would only smoke outside the back of their tiny council house on a scrap of mud that was covered in second-hand plastic garden toys that included a slide and a paddling pool, that looked particularly miserable at this time of year (green and grimy, and still full of water that had a scum formed across the top of it) as she could tell that Lizzie wasn't at all comfortable with her cigarette smoke around Isaac, nor around her kids for that matter (although Lizzie would not have stated as much).

On this bright, breezy, sharp Tuesday morning, Lizzie was packing up her portable nappy bag (that was decorated with brightly coloured butterflies) with all that she needed to cope with solid or liquid emissions from any of Isaac's orifices, along with a banana, oat biscuit snack and a drink. Isaac was sitting patiently, cross-legged on the rug in the lounge, pressing the buttons of an interactive book that told the story of 'The Bear Hunt' complete with sound effects. Isaac loved the sound that represented the squelching through the mud and pressed this over and over again, never seeming to get tired of it. Mark, as usual, was hovering, leaning on the door frame, trying desperately not to look like he was trying to get rid of them but she knew he was.

"Got everything then sweetheart."

"I think so, I just need to get Isaac's Buddy."

From behind his back Mark produced the little cuddly that accompanied Isaac wherever he and Lizzie went (Isaac referred to it as 'Buddy' not bunny). "Hard hat, check, bulletproof vest, check, police escort, check."

207

"Very droll, Mark," with a roll of the eyes from Lizzie as she scooped up her little bundle with one arm whilst shouldering the nappy bag with the other. "It's not Mandy's fault where the council has housed her, nor that she is struggling to make ends meet. We can certainly afford to share some of our relative wealth with her can't we, Little Lord Fauntleroy?"

"Say goodbye to Mr Grumpy gills, Isaac," she said in an affected voice imitating Dory from 'Finding Nemo' and grinning as she leaned in towards Mark, allowing him to kiss Isaac on his forehead (avoiding the bruise from where he had run into the edge of the door the previous afternoon) and then hers, making eye contact and exchanging a warm smile. "See you at lunchtime, and have a productive morning." She fixed him with a stare, a slight frown appearing now as she knew full well that the moment the front door clicked behind them he would revert to bachelor mode, mooching about the house before heading up to his den/study to waste an entire morning listening to old vinyl and reminiscing about the good old days rather than getting on with his marking. Consistent or just predictable, she wondered, and when did the former become the latter?

"Bye-bye my little angels," Mark replied, beaming at them both. "You'll get your reward in heaven my love." And with that his beautiful pregnant wife and toddler bustled out into the freezing early morning air and he slowly closed the door behind them.

*

Guy Soames was nursing both a raging hangover and sense of guilt. His wife Polly and the twins were out overseeing the finishing touches to their new place in Corfu, the refurbishments having taken an age, leaving him in Hove to run the business, a string of upmarket seafood restaurants in towns along the south coast. He'd ploughed the majority of his redundancy package from his City trading job into both projects, that along with the mortgage on their three storey Regency town house on Brunswick Square, had left little margin for error but he had plans to expand his property portfolio in Europe and was putting out feelers regarding potential investors; he'd had a reputation in the City for being able to make a silk purse out of a sow's ear and was a living legend when it came to sub-prime debt. He'd been out drinking all the previous afternoon with former clients who'd been in for a long lunch at the restaurant before going on to some of the seafront bars with an old trader mate where he'd picked up a couple of little stunners who he'd ended up taking back to his place for 'champers and charlie'. He'd woken up to find one of them (the curvy black girl) in bed with him but there was no sign of the Baywatch blonde.

Reluctantly he had agreed to drop the tart off near a 24/7 on Dyke Road and was crapping himself that he'd been seen smuggling her out of the house and into the front seat of his XK8. They hadn't exchanged a single word as he'd navigated the rush hour traffic to a pounding headache, his mouth dry and conscience nagging. He had caught her staring vacantly out of the passenger window at the passing traffic, fake fur coat wrapped about her, fiddling absent-mindedly with the ends of her hair in exactly the same way that his girls did. Jeez, she must only be a couple of years older than them he thought. The fallout from this would be seismic if he was caught out and he shuddered visibly at the thought so, once rid of her, he'd head home to clear the evidence before collecting Polly and the girls from Gatwick late that afternoon and insisting on taking them all out for dinner before the girls returned to school the next day after their extended Christmas holiday.

He was sitting in slow moving traffic alone heading back towards Kingsway, having dropped her off without any kind of farewell, and was visualising the various rooms in the house where evidence of his misdemeanours might be found when he was snapped out of it by a call coming in on his hands free. He checked the incoming number, took a deep breath and punched the answer button.

"Johnnie-boy you great poofda!" he shouted enthusiastically, although he felt far from it.

"Guy you old tosspot," came the booming reply. "Didn't expect to catch you up and about so early? Don't tell me, you were on the sauce last night and forgot where you'd parked the Jag?"

"Not quite old boy. Picked up a couple of young slappers and took them back to mine for a line or two. Just dropped one of them off as it happens."

"Bloody hell Soamesy – you old goat! But don't Polly and the girls come back today?"

"Exactly. Which is why I am trying to get back to Chez Soames to clear up the crime scene. Stuck in bloody rush hour traffic though." He yelled an expletive at a white van driver that had pulled out in front of him. On the back double doors of the van (that was covered in thick grime) the driver, presumably, had written in clumsy capital letters, 'I WISH MY WIFE WAS THIS DIRTY' to which some wag had replied in equally shaky capitals, 'SHE ALWAYS IS WITH ME!!'

"Nothing like cutting it fine you randy old swine. Stuck in a spot of traffic myself as it happens, on the way up to the grim north-east to sort out a deal. Anyway, let's cut to the quick. Bank being bally arsey about me paying them back. After decades of practically chucking credit at me they are in it up to their necks so are threatening me with legal action if they can't claim their pound of flesh. The bally cheek of it! Anyway, I could really do with that £100K. Sophie doesn't even know we owe it and this would finish her, especially after having to let Petworth Manor go to that Russian and the Corfu place to you. All we've got left now is the Barnes house and the villa near Malaga that Sophie owns and that's not nearly enough for my little princess, well both of them for that matter."

"Funny you should say that. I have an investors meeting at lunchtime and fully expect them to agree to us releasing the equity from the business so we can settle up. It seems that, despite hard times, the great British public are still eating a lot of fish. Polly also has no idea that we still owe you a few quid on the Corfu pad so let's keep it on the QT eh?"

"Scout's honour! So you really reckon that you could fix it for a transfer by the end of next week?"

"Hand on heart, or rather on wallet, far more reliable eh?" Guy kept his left hand on the polished wooden steering wheel before reaching across with his right to tap his black leather wallet that he always kept on the inside pocket of his sports jacket, only to find his hand go flat against the material. "The bitch!" he screamed.

"Guy?" came Johnnie's concerned voice back over the speaker.

"The little tart has lifted my wallet! It's got all my credit cards in and over five hundred quid in cash!"

Guy had a quick look in his rear-view mirror before swinging the deep blue soft-top round in a full circle across the Old Shoreham Road and powering back up Dyke Road to where he had dropped the girl off just a few minutes earlier. "She's probably spent the lot on fags and vodka by now. I'll wring her bloody neck when I get hold of her."

"Easy tiger," Johnnie tried to calm his friend, who could go from 0-angry in the time his XK8 could do 0-60. "It might be somewhere in the house, sounds like it was quite a night last night, anything could have happened. Why not have a good snoop round back at HQ before jumping to any hasty conclusions eh?"

"She's got it alright. Either her or her bimbo mate. Totally played me the pair of 'em; ah, gotcha!"

Up ahead, about 500 yards from where the V8 engine powered the big cat, was Hope, sitting on a bench, shivering and chatting to a brunette who had a kiddie tugging and twisting to get free from her grasp.

"I have the little cow in my sights now Johnnie." Guy slammed the palm of his hand on the horn as a woman driving a people carrier stopped suddenly in front of him kerbside and he accelerated past her with ease and pulled the Jag in towards the left-hand side of the road once more. Hope looked up, a look of sudden anxiety spreading across her cold but exotic features.

*

Hope was in such a pit of despair she hadn't known where to turn. Her life had become one long cycle of self-destruction. Waking up in a stranger's bed, walking or getting an (awkward) lift back to hers (as they weren't so free flowing with the compliments once the booze had worn off and they'd got what they'd wanted), always getting dropped off at a road nearby, she didn't want any of these blokes knowing where she lived; showering off the grime from the previous night, sleeping through the day, sometimes in front of mindless daytime TV, a deep bath, on with the slap, the lace lingerie and hot-pants only to start it all over again. Numb was how she felt; in fact she seemed incapable of feeling anything at all any more. The anger she harboured towards these bastards that were using her was gradually rising to fever pitch, although she did a good job at concealing it. The majority had girlfriends or were married but didn't think twice about forgetting any vows or commitments in order to get her into bed (or car). The crazy part was that going to bed with them wasn't in her job description. She was paid to make men feel good about themselves, to flirt, to make them laugh, to enhance their experience of whatever club or bar she was working at and to keep the tills ringing as they plied themselves (and her) with over-priced booze but she had lost all sense of herself, of who she really was, and instead had become exactly what these drunken misogynists wanted her to be – willing, available, compliant and discreet.

Her way at getting back at these cheating wankers was quite simply to steal from them. Actually, she saw it more as a balancing of the books as they had all taken just a little piece of her dignity and self-respect with each meaningless night of so-called passion. Passion! Half of them were so wasted by the time they got round to it that they could barely raise a smile but she coaxed and encouraged and pouted and sighed and pretended and put up with their sweaty huffy-puffy all over before it really began, attempts at sex followed quickly by their open mouthed snoring whilst she lay, staring at yet another ceiling, theirs usually smooth and expensively plastered whilst inside her the cracks were widening, spreading into great chasms of self-loathing.

All this acting just so as not to damage their precious egos, so she would wake up before them the following morning and would do some damage to their bank accounts instead. The type of bloke who would pay £80 for an average bottle of champagne in a nightclub or bar would generally have a stack of cash in their wallet as they wouldn't want their wives or girlfriends to be able to trace their payment trail as this might lead to some uncomfortable questioning. She would simply help herself to whatever cash was left in their wallets, sometimes even taking this out the night before when the guy was really wasted and secreting it under a fruit bowl or on top of an en suite bathroom cabinet to retrieve it as daylight penetrated the curtains or blinds behind which she would be lying awake.

It was no use talking to her mum about it. She'd had a tough enough life as it was. A glamour model by profession she was already doing Page 3 at the age of 16 before getting involved in the murky world of minor celebrities and their parties where sexual and chemical excess were the standard. The booze, drugs and late nights quickly aged her mum who, although still a 'busty little stunner', soon lost the youthful glow required for her line of work (ironic that they wanted the girls who got their tits out for the working man to look as if it was the first time they'd ever done this for anyone, all pouting innocence and with no questions asked about how morally healthy it was for a married plumber in his 40s to be slobbering over the picture of a topless teenage girl in a gym slip).

Her mum moved on to the vagaries of 'promotional work' that had, by all accounts, ranged from standing in the city centre at lunchtime in a short skirt and a tight top emblazoned with the logo of the company whose flyers she was handing out to promote a new gym opening or printing service to slinking around a boxing ring in frayed denim shorts, vest and high heels holding the card with the next round on it high above her head to a chorus of wolf whistles whilst the gladiators slumped on stools in each corner. It was after one such event, that a future world champion from London had flashed a smile at her mum and, full of energy after an early knockout had sex with her in the locker room before the post-fight press conference. Hope was the result of this little 'liaison', never officially knowing the identity of her father but being able to have a pretty good guess.

Her mum now wore a worldly weariness that she could feel creeping up on her, despite her young age. You were the sum of your experiences, right? Hers had been, on the whole, damaging. The one person who she could always talk to was Lizzie Wilson (now Woodford). She had met Lizzie at a support group for young women who worked in the sex trade and who had all been in abusive relationships; although Hope didn't qualify on either count, she could trace characteristics of both and was afraid that she was heading on the downward path towards the sex and porn industry that many girls in her high heeled shoes had walked before her. Lizzie had never once made her feel judged about decisions she had taken and the course in which her life had run, always prepared to listen intently and offer gentle words of encouragement and support, taking the time to find out what she wanted to do with her life and then taking practical steps to help this happen. Hope had always loved animals and Lizzie had fixed her up with a work placement at a stable near Rottingdean but she had messed this up by never getting there on time and missing one day altogether due to being hung-over and Lizzie still didn't get the hump but calmly talked her through the agreement she had brokered with the stable's manager and how it was up to Hope as a young adult to take ownership of the arrangement and to make it work for all parties.

Hope had felt so wretched the morning after she and Tia had gone back to the posh house of that arrogant prat with the Jag, Guy, that was his name, (she couldn't remember the name of the fella that had copped off with Tia) that she had called Lizzie in an act of desperation. Lizzie had told her that she was on the way to a play date but typical of Lizzie she said she'd call the other mum to say that she would be running late and drive down to see Hope, telling her not to move from where she was. Lizzie had parked her car on the opposite side of the road, waved, gestured towards the shop then disappeared inside for no more than two minutes before emerging, carrying Isaac and a bunch of flowers (presumably for the mum she was going to be late to visit) to where she sat shivering on a bench outside the 24/7 eating a sausage roll and drinking a can of Red Bull. When

Lizzie crossed over she had begun telling Lizzie a bit about how she was feeling but it had been difficult to finish a sentence as the usually calm Isaac seemed agitated and kept pulling down on Lizzie's sleeve and repeating the word 'Buddy'. The rest happened in slow motion:-

She saw the blue soft-top Jag swerve to avoid a people carrier, with Guy all red faced and angry behind the wheel. He appeared to be talking to someone but there was no one in the car with him. Isaac had managed to struggle free from Lizzie's grasp and in the blink of an eye had made it out onto the busy road. As Lizzie turned to yell at Isaac to stop, whilst sprinting towards him, Hope saw the little cuddly bunny that Isaac knew as 'Buddy' in the middle of the road. He must have dropped it as they crossed the road from the shop to see her moments earlier, which explained why little Isaac was uncharacteristically restless when she had been chatting to Lizzie. He had simply gone to pick up his favourite cuddly toy, unaware of the dangers of a main road full of mums returning from the school/nursery run. Lizzie made it just in time to scoop Isaac up in her arms but not in time to avoid the speeding Jag that, despite braking suddenly, brakes screeching, hit her with such force that her body flew up in the air and came down with a sickening crunch, denting then bouncing off the long curved bonnet and shattering the windscreen before the car veered sharply to the left, mounting the kerb and destroying a litter bin on the passenger's side. There was no sound apart from a voice coming from somewhere within the car that repeated "Guy, Guy," then it stopped and everything fell silent for what seemed like a lifetime.

There was Lizzie, beautiful Lizzie, sprawled motionless in the middle of the road, still clutching Isaac to her, her right leg splayed as if having just crumpled beneath her, blood running from her nose, her body broken. She didn't move. Nor did Isaac. Not a sound. An eerie silence that would haunt Hope for the rest of her life. Then all hell broke loose.

The woman who had been in the parked people carrier had raced across to crouch over Lizzie's prone body, her driver's door still wide open, pushing back her hair and checking Lizzie's pulse whilst gently prizing Lizzie's arm from Isaac to check for signs of life. One of the young assistants came out of the shop, mobile phone glued to his ear, talking rapidly whilst pointing furiously at the carnage before him (as if pointing helps) directing the emergency services to the scene as Hope would later find out. The driver of the Jag leant out of his window, pointed at Hope and with a sneer drew his finger slowly across his throat as per a Gangsta movie, a ridiculous gesture for a whitey to make she'd thought, especially a middle class, middle-aged banker-wanker with a paunch, a wife and two kids. Laughable if it were not for the gravity of the situation. Even more gob-smacking was the fact that he started the car (after half a dozen attempts) and squealed off up Dyke Road, not even staying to check on the two bodies that he had mown down in his haste to get back at her and his wallet.

Hope could hear the sirens approaching and saw the look in the woman's eyes as she raised hers to meet Hope's. She was weeping and shaking her head. Hope moved from the bench to kneel on the ice-cold tarmac beside her, putting her arm around her whilst forcing herself to look down at her friend and her precious little boy. Both had their eyes closed, a trickle of blood also having run from the tiny delicate pixie nose of Isaac who had still managed to cling on to both his mother and Buddy as his little life was so brutally ended before just two years of it had been lived. Hope, who always managed to hold it together, something she prided herself on, felt her eyes begin to mist over and then the tears came, along with sobs that seemed to rise up from her very core and shake the cage of her body from within. This time it was the woman's turn to hold her, and Hope, naturally wary of strangers, allowed herself to be embraced, burying her head into the shoulder of her green woollen winter coat and pouring out her grief for the life that was Lizzie's and Isaac's and that which she was left to live without them.

Before long it was another pair of arms gently lifting her from the hardness of the road; a policewoman who she vaguely recognised; Hope's knees were dimpled through her tights by kneeling on the uneven surface and snot was streaming from her nostrils and sticking to her fake fur collar. As she attempted to control her sobbing her breath seemed to turn the cold air around her into what looked like steam. She was walked slowly towards a luridly marked police car parked near to the bench where she had sat and witnessed this traumatic scene play out. Her half-eaten sausage roll lay on the ground where she had dropped it, the sticky contents of the energy drink encircling the crumbs and trickling towards the cellophane wrapped bouquet that Lizzie had dropped before racing out towards Isaac, the can on its side where she had knocked it over as her leg had jerked instinctively on hearing the crunching impact. A male PC handed Hope's fake designer handbag to the female officer as Hope was helped into the back seat of the marked car not for the first time, but now, despite the stolen wallet contained within it that had triggered this fatal reunion, she put up no resistance.

Straining over her left shoulder to take one last look out of the window at Lizzie and Isaac she could only see the outline of two shapes of contrasting sizes laid out side by side under a single strip of blue plastic sheeting surrounded by yellow plastic markers as ambulance crews talked with one policeman whilst a colleague redirected traffic and two others talked with the driver of the people carrier and the shop assistant, nodding, making scribbled notes and gesturing to the crime scene as the witnesses recalled the grim tableau they had unwittingly found themselves a part of. Hope looked down at her lap and was surprised to find the little rabbit sitting between her hands. She must have prised it from Isaac's fingers without thinking. It felt cold and damp to the touch, speckled with small spots of blood. Comfort for her, for Lizzie's husband? She had heard all about him from Lizzie, who adored him, but had never met the bloke as she and Lizzie had always met at a café or community centre. That poor, poor sod she thought. And pity the poor bugger that has the job of telling him.

*

Mark ushered WPCSO Marshall into the hallway, not used to seeing her wearing her hat that she immediately removed, followed by Sergeant Evans, a tall, wiry clean-shaven man, usually wearing a warm smile but this was not on duty on that particular morning. Mark had often thought that he was not at all what you would expect from a copper, he was neither surly nor burly and very much the bloke next door (albeit armed with a telescopic truncheon, pepper spray and handcuffs), affable and approachable but this morning he was making his way almost reverently through his front door, removing his cap as he entered and wearing a grim expression. Mark gestured for them to follow him through into the lounge, stepping on a Fireman Sam interactive word game that had been left, discarded on the floor, setting off the sound of a siren as they crossed the threshold.

"Sorry folks," Mark smiled nervously, "sounds like some sort of welcome anthem, doesn't it? Tea/coffee anyone?"

"No thanks Mark," WPCSO Marshall began, gradually beginning to assert herself. She sat in an armchair and gestured for Mark to do the same, as if she was welcoming him into her home. Sergeant Evans eased himself onto the corner sofa, sitting upright and on the edge of it. Emma placed her hat neatly on her lap. Mark thought absent-mindedly that it sounded like one of the phonic rhymes he had been trying out on Isaac as they strolled along the seafront on Sunday afternoons; the cap sat on the lap. She took a deep breath and began in a soft, measured tone.

As she talked, he visualised a scene from 24 when CTU had intercepted a message from a would-be bomber and were using voice recognition software to pick out key words or phrases that would enable an ID to be made and a target for Jack Bauer to intercept. He listened to the gentle cadence of Emma's voice, was there a trace of West Country in there? The way her voice elevated in pitch slightly at the end of each sentence, suggesting a question where in fact there was none. Mark also took in key words and phrases as she spoke, such as road traffic collision (not RTA any more then) fatalities, the driver not stopping, witness statements and the need for him to go with them to the hospital to make a formal identification of the bodies as it was their belief that the deceased were Lizzie and Isaac Woodford.

Mark hung on to the fact that they needed him to identify two bodies that they *believed* to be Lizzie and Isaac, so some hope then, as it wouldn't be the first time there would be a case of a mistaken identity and the accident they referred to happened on Dyke Road which he knew for a fact Lizzie avoided like the plague at that time in the morning. They were not at liberty to speculate on details or the outcome of the accident but that Mark's presence was required at the hospital as part of the protocol in these circumstances; their solemn tones and reverential head bowing implied the worst. As he stood he swayed ever so slightly, knowing in the very pit of his stomach that his entire world had shifted to the core, had encountered a fault-line so deep and devastating that he wondered if he would ever emerge from the rubble intact but, before the growling tremor gave way to full-blown catastrophe he had to gather up his keys, his phone, sling on a jacket and follow them out into the cold and into the waiting car.

They drove in silence along the very same route that Mark and Lizzie took when going for scans when pregnant with Isaac and more recently on their unborn child. As he peered out at the familiar rows of shops, the cinema, the pubs, and cafés, doors bolted and shutters down, queues at bus stops, a young mum pushing a buggy at pace, leaning over to make sure the blanket was pulled up to the baby's chin before marching on, a motorised road sweeper crawling up towards London Road, he was struck by how life really does just go on, regardless of how, for some people, families, theirs will never be the same again. He recalled the last scan just four months before in which they'd found out they were going to have a little girl and then the funny verbal dance that parents undertake at this point, for example already having a boy then finding out their second is going to be a girl and expressing their delight at the news whilst simultaneously stressing that they'd be equally happy if it was to be another boy, as there were a multitude of pros and cons for both. Often one parent convinces themselves that they are in fact the happier of the two and then sets about consoling their partner, who might be equally ecstatic to hear the results of the scan but doesn't want to overdo the celebrations just in case *their* partner would actually have preferred to be having one more of the same.

That night, they had stretched out on their huge corner sofa, Lizzie's head on his chest, and run through a list of possible girls' names, in the end settling for Ella, with the 'a' rolling nicely into the Woodford they both agreed. And a middle name? Grace. So, Ella Grace Woodford, with a due date of March 10th 2012, two months to the day. They had agreed to go easy on the buying of brand new clothes, especially vests and Baby-gros as Isaac's hand-me-downs (those that hadn't already been distributed by Lizzie to various families across Moulsecoomb and Whitehawk) would be fine, all pretty generic from 0-3 months after all. Lizzie, however, would routinely return from a walk or play date with Isaac with some distinctly girlie looking additions to the wardrobe, pleading with her wide eyes and disarming smile, that they were charity shop bargains after all so someone would benefit from her purchase further down the line. Soon the nursery began to shift subtly from boy/neutral to pastel/princess, as curtains with large, bright flower prints were hung over the blackout blind and Isaac was promoted to a new room, complete with tiny wooden framed bed with guard for when he outgrew his cot, dinosaur curtains and duvet set, a space station mobile hanging from the ceiling and a bedside lamp in the shape of a toadstool.

He was particularly scathing when encountering cliché in any of its many forms; in films, on TV, in post-match interviews from monotone managers, in literature, language, in life itself, but he now found himself in an extended cliché of his very own. He's had the dreaded 'knock at the door' from the old bill, the hushed tones, the uncomfortable foot staring and shuffling, the drive in the patrol car "it's okay everyone looking in, I'm an innocent man," the dread of reaching its destination and the realisation that his world was about to be turned on its head, whatever he found waiting for him at the hospital but he kept hanging on to the phrase '*it is our understanding that* … He knew that if Lizzie had been involved in an accident that had left her paralysed that he would devote his life to looking after her. They could make alterations to the house, move if needs be, there was nothing he couldn't or wouldn't do to make her life worth living. He would give up work and get Isaac to nursery and back, do the shopping, cleaning (well, maybe get a cleaner, what about that young mum with the excruciatingly named children Lizzie was on her way to seeing earlier that morning? No, her life was far too chaotic and she'd probably be late and/or need lifts and insist on bringing an army of snotty Caydens and Jadens, Tias and Talullas with her and disrupt the calm of their family home. Mrs S maybe? He'd have to make himself scarce to avoid being talked to death. Shopping could be done online and delivered to your doorstop in a matter of clicks. You could get specially adapted cars for wheelchairs also if needs be. Giving birth might prove tricky though. His steady stream of consciousness came to an abrupt halt. Ella, what about little Ella? His stomach lurched and he tightened his grip on the smooth plastic arched handle on the inside of the passenger door). "We're here Mark," Emma said as she touched his right arm lightly. Mark took the proverbial deep breath and, stooping, left through the nearside door held open by Sergeant Evans who remained with the car whilst Emma steered him forwards and into the busy hospital foyer.

What happened next was, actually, a blur. A succession of corridors, a rising sense of nausea, a set of gloss white double doors with what looked like port holes inset, a woman with black hair tied back wearing glasses and a white coat (must be mad to work here then) a clinical room with bare white walls, steel tables with one larger shape under a sheet and another smaller one, also under wraps, on the steel table next to it. The reality of what lay under those sheets had been with him since he had first opened the door to the police that morning if he was to be honest, but he had played out alternate scenarios to retain what little sanity he felt he possessed, filtering away now like sand through a sieve as the realisation that the love of his life and his precious little boy were stretched out in a mortuary before him, like exhibits in a science lab. Tears pricked his eyes and his hands started to tremble before shaking violently as Emma gently led him to the nearest mound, the smallest, the blue sheet that covered it now being partially pulled back by the grim faced bespectacled keeper of this chilled and lifeless cell. Just the sight of the first tufts of bright, almost white blonde hair forced Mark to gasp so sharply that he staggered back a step before leaning a hand on the side of the cold steel surface to steady himself before tentatively peering down into those now familiar features; the button nose, tiny delicate mouth, lips a fraction ajar, not a mark on him, just as angelic and serene as when he slept. But Isaac was now in a deep sleep from which he would never wake, never to call out to his Daddy from in the darkest depths of night, never seek his reassuring hug and gentle whispers that everything was all right as he would rock him gently back into slumber. Mark made a groan that echoed in the sparsely furnished room, a groan that became a strangled wail as his tears flowed freely. "No, no, no, not my little man, my beautiful little angel please no." He sobbed as he stroked the thin soft silky hair of his precious son, numbed by the knowledge that Isaac's life was over barely before he had begun to live it whilst fearing that the worst was yet to come.

He turned to the second table, gesturing with his right hand that he didn't need the sheet to be pulled back and that he would perform this ritual himself. Nothing could have braced him for the sight of his Lizzie, in repose like a pre-Raphaelite heroine, bearing cuts and grazes to the left side of her head, long eyelashes covering those beautiful brown eyes, her full lips closed. He allowed his right hand to trace the outline of her face, pausing to touch her beauty spot with his index finger before turning his hand over and rest it gently on her right cheek, whilst his left hand stroked her hair, feeling matted blood as he did so. He leaned over, closed his eyes, and kissed her lightly on the forehead, the last time his lips would ever touch her skin. "Sleep well my love, and may you find that peace you believe in until we meet again." By this point she was almost a haze before him as the tears were running so thick and fast. "And our baby?" he just about managed to whisper, to be met with a downward gaze and slow shake of the head. He felt all remaining strength and dignity desert him as his body convulsed with the weight of the grief, the impact and the depth of the loss, his legs buckled beneath him and he sank heavily to the floor, howling now, curled in a ball on that cold tiled floor, his face awash with snot and tears as Emma crouched beside him and the attending technician slowly pulled the sheet back up over Lizzie's unflinching face and scribbled scratchily on a clipboard.

Time of death(s) 9.20 am, Tuesday January 10th 2012; the moment this life ended.

*

The tears wouldn't stop flowing, the grief threatening to overwhelm her. She had never experienced loss in her life as she had never held anything or anyone so dearly and not for a moment had she thought it would ever feel like this. What was worse, she turned over and over in her head, the fact that Lizzie Wilson, as she had still called her even though she was married, and her gorgeous little boy and unborn child were dead or the fact that she was responsible? She felt that she was going to erupt as she had no one to really talk to, to pour out her feelings, to make her feel better about it all. But there was a big part of her that didn't want any consolation, that didn't wish to hear soothing words of comfort, as she wanted to go on punishing herself and to harden her heart towards the bastard that had run Lizzie down. The only relief from her pit of despair had been the long list of ways that she was going to make the arrogant wanker pay for what he had done. She would've started on his car, her front door key and a broken brick from the crumbling low wall in her tiny back garden was all she would need, but the car had been pretty smashed up in the accident so that one was out. She had gone back to his house in Brunswick Square against the orders from the police, intending on asking his wife for her knickers back and to hand her his wallet, empty of the cash, just to rub salt into the wounds. But standing in the shadows opposite their grand white painted villa that same day as the dusk seeped silently into that opulent square and witnessing the wife and her two daughters huddled together for strength in an upstairs room before closing the thick curtains on any outside intrusion made her realise that her interference wasn't necessary and that enough damage had been self- inflicted upon the Soames family that fateful morning to last them a lifetime. The one visit she was putting off more than any was to the husband, Mark. How was she ever going to be able to tell him how guilty she felt, and how would he react on hearing in full the part that she had played?

*

An hour or so after having to formally identify the body of his wife and child and accept the death of his unborn daughter, Mark had begun to ask questions. He had been taken back home by Sergeant Evans and WPCSO Marshall, who had made them all tea, that great British response to personal tragedy much utilised by the EastEnders scriptwriters, "Go on, put the kettle on, we'll 'ave a nice cuppa tea." Usually followed by "He/she'll soon come round." Mark had never been any good at small talk, usually defaulting to regrettable flippancy to fill the silence but he felt justified in sitting on his sofa, jacket still on, numb to the core, his head in his hands, eyes sore from where he had been rubbing them when a thought hit him square between those red-rimmed eyes. How on earth had Lizzie been run over on Dyke Road when she always avoided it at that time due to the traffic and headed north on a more circuitous route? And what was she doing crossing a busy road outside a shop that was out of her way? There were plenty of shops she could have stopped at on her usual route. As they blew the steam from the piping hot brews, Sergeant Evans tried as best as he could to answer those questions; apparently, they didn't know why Lizzie had altered direction, that the driver involved in the RTC had not stopped but that eyewitnesses had given enough information in order for the driver to be apprehended, but he had since handed himself in and he was now in police custody awaiting questioning.

It was important that they would be left to get on with their job whilst Mark took the time to rest up after the shocking news he had received that morning. They asked if there was anyone who they could call to come and sit with him. He pictured Mrs Sheridan, whose curtains would be all a twitch with the police car parked outside and decided against her good-natured bustle and twittering, Vaz was an option but he decided that he wanted to be left on his own for now. Lizzie's handbag had been recovered and had been placed in the hallway along with the baby changing bag by WPCSO Marshall and they had placed a 'Police Aware' notice on his car that was still parked in the limited hours parking zone where Lizzie had pulled up to park that morning, he could collect it whenever he felt up to it. They both left their business cards on the coffee table and, promising that they would be in touch as soon as there had been any developments, left as quietly as they had arrived. Mark looked around him, at the familiar scene, Isaac's toys in various states of use on the rug where he liked to sit cross-legged and post brightly coloured shapes through corresponding holes in a solid wooden cube (that more than once threatened to break Mark's big toe as either he careered into it or Isaac dropped it onto his foot), a tractor and trailer upturned with various farm animals scattered across the room, an open children's Bible that he loved, in fact it was rare for him to allow any other stories to be read to him other than the Hungry Caterpillar and Guess How Much I Love You. He said those words out loud, as he often would when bathing Isaac, "I love you all the way to the moon and back," he would say, whilst rinsing the shampoo out, Isaac grinning all the while and slapping his hands on the surface of the bathwater, shrieking with glee whilst Lizzie leaned on the door frame, grinning at this touching interaction between her husband and son. Another wave hit him and threatened to knock him clean off the sofa, he gasped for air and a loud sob left his body. How would he ever begin to live his life again? The void that had been left by their sudden, violent deaths was so vast that he knew it would take all his strength not to be sucked into it, not to drown in his own misery and grief and that he now faced, in a sense, his own fight for survival, for his overwhelming sense was towards flight. He knew that there were people to contact, plans to be made. He knew also that Lizzie would immediately take control of any such situation, drawing up lists and phoning people in the right order and with the right words effortlessly flowing. But he was not Lizzie, he didn't think like her, have her emotional resilience nor have the reserves of time and energy for people that she had, he was Mark Woodford, serial loser, who had placed it all on red and had lost the lot.

The wheels come off

In true Mark style, when the going gets tough, Mark gets going; to the fridge to get a beer. He downed the first ice cold Becks, barely stopping, finishing with a burp whilst wiping the dribbles from his chin and immediately reaching for a second, slumping down on a kitchen chair where just a few hours before, Lizzie and Isaac had enjoyed their breakfast whilst he had been in the shower. The few used bowls and Lizzie's dirty coffee cup still in the kitchen sink waiting to be washed up. An internal struggle was beginning to play out as he sat staring straight ahead at the kitchen wall; on the one hand he knew that he had to inform people of Lizzie's death, family and friends (also college as he had a full day the next day with exam papers to hand back to students and had no idea when he would return to work, if ever). On the other hand, he wanted to get totally wasted, to obliterate his senses and embrace the numbness that had been seeping into his veins since he had returned home. Lizzie and Isaac were everywhere but nowhere, a presence and an absence. He feared that this dichotomy, this tension would finally push him over the edge.

He had just started on the third beer of his path to oblivion when he was snapped out of his morose philosophising by the shrill beep-beep that heralded an incoming text. Mark patted his top left jacket pocket and his phone was still there, but the beep had come from along the hallway. He leaned forwards on his chair and turned to look down towards the inner door and there on the floor at the foot of the stairs was Lizzie's (it had turned out to be fake) Louis Vuitton handbag, open, with gold effect clasps to each side. Of course, he realised, just because her life has ended so suddenly it doesn't mean that calls and messages will stop coming in. A sense of fear gripped him again, "Oh God," he muttered aloud, "how am I going to cope. How? HOW?" He was looking up at the ceiling and yelling through clenched teeth now, tears running down his cheeks and forming droplets on the end of his chin. He sniffed and wiped his hand across his stubbly chin again, awash with salty tears and yeasty lager, coughing and choking uncontrollably until he retched and vomited onto the wood effect kitchen floor, a pool of bile and beer. "She believed in you," he sobbed, "and this is how you repay her?" Again electronic intrusion, this time his mobile ringing, the ringtone, ironically, was the Bitter Sweet Symphony by The Verve that he and Lizzie had danced to on New Year's Eve, just over a week before. Mark removed his phone and saw that it was his brother. He let it go to voicemail. The phone rang again. Persistent as always he thought, but he wasn't ready for Johnnie just yet. Splashing cold water from the kitchen tap over his face and laying a few strips of kitchen roll over his vomit to soak it up he made his way unsteadily along the hallway and fished Lizzie's phone out of her handbag, not wanting to disturb the rest of the contents in case this released yet another torrent of tears, rage and bile. Moving into the lounge, he lay back on their corner sofa, where just the night before they had snuggled in together, and composed a brief text on her phone:

Dear all

Mark here – from Lizzie's phone.

Please excuse the group text, usually reserved for news of a new arrival; tragically this is to let you know of the opposite. This morning my beautiful wife, son and unborn daughter were taken from me in a road accident. By now you may have seen details on the news. Please appreciate my need for privacy right now and understand if I don't reply to individual messages as I'm still in a state of shock. Mark

He had added an x then removed it, added it back then removed it again. He knew how many friends Lizzie had and how quick they would be to respond with good intentions but he couldn't handle any intrusion into his private despair right now, regardless of how well meant. Taking in the screensaver of him and Isaac waving up at her from the beach near the West Pier that blustery New Year's Day, he powered it down. He lay back for a moment, his mouth tasting awful, his throat raw, and closed his eyes, longing for sleep to embrace him, but he forced himself back to wakefulness as he knew he couldn't put off calling his mum and Lizzie's dad any longer.

*

He had been heading up the M1 when he'd made the call from the hands-free on the Range Rover after an early start from London to beat the inevitable choking jams on the M25. He had a crisis with a client based in Newcastle to resolve regarding their hesitation to sign a contract after what should have been a routine trial and sale. The company, backed by American investors, had stalled over some fairly minor application issues so he couldn't help but wonder what really lay beneath the tip of the iceberg. He couldn't afford for this one to go belly up so had decided to handle negotiations himself along with his Head of Development, who would meet him up north. He could have really done without it as he was stressed enough as it was, and was relying on this deal being pushed through before the next Board Meeting as it might represent a 'green shoot' of recovery after an arid few years of trading. He was also relying on the £100K cash injection from Soamesy as he was spread so thinly on the home front, despite selling the country pile in West Sussex and the villa in Corfu. He was still paying the mortgage on their Barnes place, school fees, running his motor and Sophie's latest CLK not to mention her high standards of living, despite her 'belt tightening'.

He had been really disturbed by the abrupt end to the conversation he'd had with Guy, someone he'd known for years after meeting him at a shoot on a country estate near Sophie's folks out in Gloucestershire. He was an ex-army man, officer, that was clear from his bearing and his outlook on life, not to mention how handy he was with a shotgun, but there was something else, something that had made Johnnie uneasy. It was his facial expression as he barked instructions to his loader and then over lunch when he totally overreacted when a waitress spilled no more than a drop or two of red wine on his shirt cuff resulting in tears (hers) and apologies (from Johnnie, notably not Guy). This had worked in his favour as he'd enjoyed a most pleasant half hour with said waitress in the stable block after tea later that afternoon, but it was the way that Guy had set his jaw, the glint in his eye that suggested here was a man not to cross.

They'd kept in loose touch over the years and often met at the same drinks parties, shoots and charity golf events but their business relationship had really cranked up over the past few years or so after Guy had left the City with a pretty hefty pay-off, first with him buying one of their CRM systems for his expanding restaurant business and then their villa in Corfu, for which he still owed the final £100K instalment, of which neither his wife Polly nor Sophie knew anything. It was mildly amusing that all the time that money was not an issue Sophie paid little or no attention to the sums that sloshed in and out like the tide at the foot of his family home in Dorset but with the economic downturn and credit crunch that followed the boom years up to '09 she was now scrutinising every transaction online (other than his business accounts and the little private account he'd kept for any below the radar sorties). They differed on their views of what was essential and what was a 'nice to have' but knew he would always come off second best in any debate regarding her spending habits and his, so chose his battles very carefully. Talking of battles, it would have been more like WW3 if Polly and the girls had returned from Corfu to find empty bottles of champagne and discarded lace thongs in the master bedroom; divorce had been the final nail in the financial coffin for more than one chap he knew and Guy stood to lose it all if he was caught out. His signal had been iffy when he was convinced that he'd heard Guy prang the Jag and he hadn't managed to get through since. What the hell was going on?

When his mother had called with the tragic news of Lizzie and Isaac, he'd had to pull over at the nearest motorway services to gather his thoughts. His mother's voice had cracked on a number of occasions. Theirs was a family that didn't go for all that Middle European wailing or the American daytime chat show therapy-speak but he could tell that, as a doting mother-in-law and grandmother, she was absolutely devastated and was keen to visit Mark right away. Knowing how his brother would have reacted to the sudden deaths of Lizzie and Isaac (and an unborn daughter – bloody hell) he had advised his mother to give Mark a couple of days alone before the family descended, worried about what they would find there to be honest. He also had that sick to the stomach feeling when recalling the conversation with Guy and how that had ended, with a screech, a sickening thud and then silence. Surely not. There must be dozens of accidents in Brighton every day, but the doubt, the niggling feeling wouldn't go away. And why hadn't Guy responded to his messages?

He tried again to get hold of Mark and was surprised when his call was answered, albeit at the fifth attempt. He would be cutting it fine to get to his meeting on time but his instinct told him that there was more going on here, and more at stake than one business deal.

226

"Mark, it's Johnnie. I've heard from Mum. I can't imagine how you must be feeling. I just can't believe what happened to Lizzie and Isaac, Lizzie pregnant and all. I don't know what to say Mark, it was awful, just awful, what the bloody hell happened?"

Mark, still sluggish from his beer and a brief, grief induced sleep had heaved himself up into a sitting position, glancing at the wall mounted clock as he had done so. He'd only been asleep for an hour but it felt as if days had passed.

"The police are still trying to piece it all together to be honest," Mark replied through a yawn and a belch. "It's surreal," he suddenly sobbed, "one minute I'm kissing them both and waving them off and the next I'm visiting them in a mortuary. It doesn't all add up either." He stopped to wipe his nose on his sleeve and then continued, "What I don't get, is where Lizzie was when she was killed."

"How do you mean?" asked Johnnie.

"Well, she was off on a play date in Moulsecoomb and always headed north and up Ditchling Road avoiding Dyke Road due to the traffic. What would make her drive south rather than north?"

"Could have been anything Mark, need to buy nappies, biscuits to take with her, you know Lizzie, she was always so generous and never arrived anywhere empty-handed. Presumably they have the bastard that did it?"

"You could be right but … I dunno. Yeah, they got him in the end, he'd driven away from the scene. Can you believe that, the wanker runs down my entire family in broad daylight and then drives off, as if he's just run over a cat and can't be bothered to stop and find out where the owner lives."

Mark stopped, he could feel another wave of raw emotion swelling up from deep inside him, like the inevitable breaking of the waves once the small white capped foamy arches had been formed 100 metres from shore. "Look Johnnie, I've got to go, let's talk later okay?"

He rushed to the cloakroom and made it just in time, falling to his knees and heaving up the remains of his beer and breakfast. He even managed a joke out loud, speaking as if to Lizzie in the voice of Alan Partridge when the hapless chat show host had been violently sick as a result of a spike going through his foot as he attempted to scale the railings of a country club to host the annual awards ceremony for Dante's Fireplaces; 'it sounds just like the devil' as he groaned and spat the last of the bile out, a string of spit attached to his chin as if a strand from a spider's web latching onto the rim of the toilet bowl. He shuffled down the hallway to the kitchen, stepping over the sick now congealed into the kitchen roll and drained consecutive glasses of water before heading back to the sanctuary of the sitting room, closing the curtains before curling up on the sofa once more, rolling his phone over in his hand, knowing he had more calls to make but hitting another wall of emotional inertia.

The call to his mum had been bad enough, but the one he'd dreaded most was to Lizzie's father. The more he'd got to know Trevor, the more he'd seen through his upright, precise and practical façade and knew that, deep down, he was a broken man who would never stop grieving for the love of his life and would never feel complete again. Mark had an insight into how this might feel already, just a few hours into life as a 'widower' and felt a connection to her father through death that he'd never envisaged they would find in life as they were quite the opposites in character and outlook. How grounding is the death of a loved one, he'd thought, regardless of your wealth or status for whether you wept from a luxury penthouse apartment with uninterrupted views across the Thames or wailed with your face down in the Soweto dirt, the grief was all the same, with the emotional playing field suddenly levelled out. He'd caught Trevor on his work landline as he had returned from his lunch break; he rarely had his mobile phone switched on during weekdays. Mark had pictured his strained expression as he would have attempted to remain as professional as possible in the workplace, refusing to break down, receiving the news of the death of his beloved daughter and grandson with the same nods and "I see" as if handling a complaint from a resident regarding the traffic congestion on the Westhampnet roundabout during rush hour. It was after this call that Mark must have finally succumbed to sleep before Johnnie had woken him up again. He was not blessed with the greatest of energy levels at the best of times, particularly when dealing with an emotional issue, but even he had been taken aback at the sheer weight of exhaustion the trauma had left him with. He didn't want to see anybody nor speak to anybody; he just wanted his family back. He closed his eyes once more, blocking out the world outside.

*

It was the sound of someone singing that woke him this time, a gentle mournful tone coming from the direction of the kitchen. This was accompanied by the dual scent of strong disinfectant and bacon. Mark stretched, turned his head this way and that, as he'd managed to get a crook in his neck, wiped the dribble onto the other sleeve, the one that didn't have sick-saliva on, and made his way towards the source of the sound, knowing immediately who he would find in the kitchen.

Mrs Sheridan had heard the news from Mrs Woodford (she wouldn't have dreamed of calling her June, despite the insistence of Mark's mother) earlier that afternoon, after she had returned from the funeral of one of her friends who had lived nearby. Mrs Woodford had been extremely worried that Mark might do something silly, like drink himself into a coma and/or drive off a cliff, as they all knew just how much he had come to rely on Lizzie, and how lost he would be without her and had asked that Mrs Sheridan look in on him for the family's peace of mind. She had rang the doorbell a couple of times before returning home on each occasion but it was after 6pm now so she had found the spare key that they left under a plant pot out the back and had let herself in, immediately faced by a house in darkness, congealed sick on the kitchen floor and empty beer bottles alongside it. It didn't take her long to get the place shipshape, washing the dishes, mopping the floor, putting the bottles into the recycling bin they kept in the utility room and preparing a strong cup of tea and a bacon buttie for Mark.

When he shuffled into the kitchen, red eyes peering into the light all dishevelled and hunched like an old man, her heart went out to him and she could contain her own grief no longer. "Dear Mary, Mother of God I just can't find the words." But words were not required as each could sense the heaviness that had descended upon that family home, a place now irrevocably changed, likewise the lone dweller in his interior designed mausoleum. They stood for a minute or so in an embrace, with Mrs Sheridan feeling that with each heaving sob that was released from her tiny frame she had become the comforted rather than the comforter. She checked herself, freed herself from Mark and gestured for him to sit at the table, dabbing at her eyes with a crumpled piece of tissue that she had produced from under the cuff of her cardigan before attending to the now well done bacon that was spitting in the frying pan.

They had sat in silence whilst Mark forced himself to part chew, part crunch his way through the bacon sandwich, washed down with a customary flagon of hot tea. No one makes tea quite like Mrs S, he had thought, his spirits momentarily reviving, appreciating her kindness and also her restraint; she usually talked at nineteen to the dozen, rarely pausing for breath, but today her presence was both respectful and soothing and above all welcome as the early evening shadows lengthened, adding to the pervading sense of gloom and emphasising the stillness that had now settled over his once bustling family home. Normally at this time Lizzie would be gently encouraging Isaac to feed himself pasta with 'mini trees' or a homemade fish pie, always patient whenever he threw a food coated spoon over his shoulder to clatter against the wall, or knocked his water beaker off the table and onto the floor. Mark didn't know how she did it. His reaction was more a tetchy "Okay if you don't want it, it goes in the bin and I'm not getting up in the middle of the night if you are hungry." Lizzie would often remind him in that non-threatening way of hers that they always had to remain the adults in the situation and not revert to childish reactions, a tendency of Mark's. He noticed a few crumbs nestled in the hard to reach areas of the plastic tray that clipped onto the front of the high chair and a small mushy piece of 'nana' squashed into the strap that held him safely in it. He had become aware that Mrs Sheridan was watching him take all this in, the enormity of the tragedy so hugely evident in the smallest everyday objects and tasks, some of which would never be repeated as the family dynamic had been altered so dramatically, so violently whilst others would be carried out in solitude from this day onwards. She reached out a thin, vein ridged hand, one worn through decades of honest graft, and rested it gently on Mark's left hand that lay on the table top.

"There's little that an old chatterbox like me could say to ease the pain, and pain like nothing you have ever felt is what you must be feeling now Mark, but please don't give up hope. Hope that they are all in the Kingdom of their Maker, at peace and with one another, and the hope that one day, in the months and years to come you will be able to live a life again. Don't give in Mark, and don't go under, there are too many of us who love you to see you lose your will to carry on."

Mark managed a thin smile and his tears made for blurred vision for the umpteenth time that day.

"But where do I start?" he sobbed, gesturing around the kitchen towards Isaac's hand print painting on the fridge door, one of Lizzie's scarves still hanging over the back of one of the chairs, a framed photo of them on their wedding day hanging on the wall over the door frame. "Where do I start?"

"You start with what is in front of you and you take one step at a time Mark. You'll find strength in the smallest of accomplishments, getting up, eating, getting the washing done, answering the mail, leaving the house. Then one day you stop crying every night when you get into an empty bed, you stop laying the table for two, you don't need to steady yourself for five minutes every time you put on your coat to go to the shops, nor dread any type of social occasion or jump out of your skin if the doorbell rings. Almost as if unnoticed, you feel more capable of functioning once more, still bearing your loss, you're never free from that, but without it becoming such a burden that you can't carry it and move on at the same time. And, what they say about time is true, it is a healer but if someone tells you this when you have just lost your one true love, you just hear empty words that clang like a ship's bell through the fog of grief and despair that threatens to envelop you and cut you off from the world you have known forever."

Mark looked up at that dear little old lady, herself now with tear stained cheeks, knowing that she was speaking from the bitter experience of having her rock, Niall, taken from her a decade earlier just a couple of doors up from where they now sat. He'd always had a soft spot for Mrs S but never had he felt such love for her as now.

"Thanks Mrs S." He managed a whiny response, his voice breaking as he spoke. "I'll try not to give in, but I've already felt like I'm about to sink without trace."

"That's only natural my dear boy," she replied. "The rest of us will have to make sure we're on hand to pull you out next time you look like you're drowning." She withdrew her hand, stood up, and placed the spare backdoor key on the table before giving him a gentle squeeze on the shoulder as she gathered up her obligatory raincoat, something she would appear in whenever arriving on his doorstep despite her living in such close proximity, and left the way she had come in.

*

Not for the first time, nor the last, Mark woke up in a hazy state on the sofa, not knowing how or when he had got there, nor what day, date or time it was. A few empty beer bottles adorned the coffee table but there was no sign of partially eaten takeaway food or of vomit, so a promising start to the first day of the rest of his life he thought. Peering through the gloom, as the curtains were still drawn, he could just make out the time on the French style vintage wall clock; it read a little after 10am. He sat bolt upright as he couldn't remember speaking to anyone at college and he was due in that day with marked exam papers but then sank back into the indented cushion, regretting the sudden movement that made his brain shudder and remembering that Vaz had been round the night before and had things in hand. That was why the empty beer bottles were sitting neatly on coasters.

He'd turned up an hour or so after Mrs Sheridan had left, to find Mark in the kitchen, beer in hand. He'd coaxed as much from Mark as Mark was capable or prepared to offer and sat with him until Mark was too exhausted to speak another word or drink another drop of beer. Being as organised as Mark wasn't, he had gathered up all the work that was owed to students that had been scattered about Mark's study (as Mark had not yet been upstairs, still in the clothes he had been wearing the day before and using the downstairs loo) and stacked them in neat piles according to the year and group that they needed to be handed out to, writing each clearly on a plain piece of A4 paper and paper-clipping them to the top of the corresponding piles. He had then composed an email to the Principal's PA on Mark's laptop that Mark had approved before sending it, along with another to all of his contacts. He had spoken with Lizzie's father and Mark's mother about funeral arrangements and were all in agreement that Lizzie, along with Isaac, would be buried in the family plot in West Sussex with a short service for immediate family and a few close friends at the local church. Lizzie's father was going to liaise with the local vicar over this and the date pencilled in was for the following Wednesday afternoon. There was also likely to be some sort of service of celebration at Lizzie's local church in Brighton so that her friends and colleagues could pay their last respects. Vaz had spoken on his mobile to Lisa, Lizzie's close friend and former flatmate, and arranged for her to visit Mark the following evening with her vicar to discuss this. Vaz had accomplished all of this in his usually calm and efficient manner before he had brought down a spare duvet and blanket for Mark, offering to stay the night also, but Mark had thought this beyond the call of duty. Vaz was to drop Mark's exam assessments into college the following morning whist on his way to school and would drop in on the way back to see how Mark was getting on.

He'd appreciated the thorough, controlled manner in which Vaz had handled his best man duties and how he always seemed to be one step ahead of the game but Mark reflected now on how he had carried that role on, being the best man in his life and not just on his wedding day. He

232

closed his eyes and pictured the moment when Lizzie, having made her way up the aisle with such poise, removed her veil to look up at him and met his gaze with those gorgeous big brown eyes, she had a bashfulness about her that belied her beauty, as she bit slightly on her lower lip, something she did when nervous. This image was then replaced by her with her eyes closed and already cold to the touch as she lay motionless on the hard steel table whilst he leant over to kiss her farewell just the day before. The tears had already begun to forge their way silently down his cheeks to drip off the end of his stubbly chin. He shuddered at the thought of his stunning, radiant wife, someone who had been filled with such warmth now lying on an icy slab, all life having left her. Another picture then popped into his head. It was of Isaac following a cabbage white butterfly around their small garden with those small unsteady first steps of his, all juddery, like a grinning marionette, utterly immersed in the moment whilst he and Lizzie watched proudly from their sun chairs, two doting parents taking their own tentative steps in family life. So this was it then. That life had been ripped from him and he was left to face the rest of it alone.

He knew already that he couldn't continue to live here, that this place would soon become a house haunted by the memories he had shared with his wife and son as they ghosted in and out of his mind and was no longer the home that they had built together that reflected the love and laughter, the vitality and emotion of family life. A quick glance around the lounge, as his eyes slowly became accustomed to the light that seeped in through the gap where the curtains hadn't met reinforced how he had felt whilst in the kitchen the evening before; how could he possibly begin to cope with the constant reminders he would encounter, practical, emotional and sentimental, on a daily basis, let alone when he mounted the stairs to theirs and Isaac's bedrooms and the nursery. God, the nursery he thought. He would have to face sorting all their clothes, how could he give them to a charity shop? Imagine if he bumped into someone in town wearing Lizzie's leather jacket, one of her summer dresses, or a toddler in one of Isaac's stripy hoodies? His reaction may require police intervention as he pictured himself reaching out to touch a piece of fabric attached to a young mum or their child. Burn them? The clothes, not the people. That still seemed a tad dramatic and more the response of a serial killer covering his tracks or some pagan initiating a rite of cleansing than a grieving father in the twenty-first century. What should he do then, where should he start? If their roles had been reversed, and he wished right now that they had, Lizzie would, despite her grief, be writing lists, making calls, managing the situation, following the protocols for such a tragedy, whilst he lay sobbing on the sofa, unshaven, with rank, sweaty armpits and the breath of a greyhound and unable even to make himself breakfast. What hope was there for him?

He jumped as the sound of the doorbell being rung pierced the apathetic air that had descended upon number 83 Waldegrave Road. Thinking it a well-wisher he chose to ignore it, but whoever it was they weren't going away. Mrs S on her way back from church maybe? The sound of the radios gave it away so he swung his legs off the sofa and shuffled his way to the front door. Peering out he noted a bright, fresh winter's morning, and WPCSO Marshall and Sergeant Evans in their usual formation outside, she ringing the doorbell and he a few paces behind, rubbing his hands against the chill. He ushered them in and along the hallway into the kitchen as the lounge was nowhere near as presentable as it had been 24 hours earlier. Mark noticed them exchange a glance, Sergeant Evans' eyes widening, after taking in the state of him and imagined them putting him on some kind of suicide watch as he offered them seats at the kitchen table and made them all a mug of coffee, putting out a plate of digestive biscuits for them to share.

He had once seen a documentary about a bloke who had lost his wife suddenly, in his case she had drowned in a boating accident when they'd been on holiday overseas, and he had said how, in the subsequent weeks after her death, he had see-sawed between utter desperation at the impact of the loss of her life on his and a fear of never being able to feel or function in any cohesive way again, to an ability to do the mundane things instinctively then wondering afterwards how on earth he had managed it. Mark could identify completely with this dichotomy, as moments earlier he had been sobbing at the thought of having to sort through Lizzie and Isaac's personal belongings and now he was hosting an impromptu coffee morning for the local police, albeit in the same crumpled jeans and snot/puke stained top as the day before.

WPCSO Marshall enquired as to how he'd been since yesterday, had he eaten, slept; the basics to which Mark had nodded. She had seemed dubious of his answers, probably due to his dishevelled appearance although he assured her that he was going to shower and shave once they had left. It wasn't meant as a hint. Sergeant Evans then took the lead, quietly explaining how the driver of the RTC had admitted to the charge of driving without due care or attention and of his failure to report the accident before leaving the scene but had denied all charges of manslaughter. He was due to be released on bail later that afternoon pending a court hearing the following week. They wanted Mark to hear it from them directly before seeing or hearing any further details through the various media channels.

"So who was it then?" Mark enquired. "A spotty boy racer in a chavved up Saxo doing over the limit? A Polish home delivery driver texting and not looking where he was going? Maybe a yummy mummy distracted by a child in the back seat. Who took my family from me in the blink of an eye?"

Sergeant Evans took a deep breath and then replied, "It was a local businessman who, he claims, was pursuing a young female he has since accused of stealing cash and personal items from him. It was this young female who was talking with Mrs Woodford when the accident occurred."

"What, so this maniac was chasing some woman and mounted the kerb and ran them all down!" Mark exclaimed, "That's more like murder in my book let alone bloody manslaughter."

"Eyewitness reports claim that your wife had ran out into the road after your son, Mr Woodford, on account of him attempting to retrieve a soft toy that he had dropped whilst crossing the road to speak with the female who was at the scene. There is no evidence that the impact was deliberate."

Mark put up his right hand in a gesture to ask Sergeant Evans to hold it right there, whilst he placed his left hand over his forehead, as if shielding his eyes from a bright summer sun. "So, Lizzie had driven down Dyke Road to speak to this ... mystery female, only to then get knocked over and killed along with Isaac by the bloke who was after the same female she'd been talking to whilst Lizzie tried to stop Isaac running out onto the road after his Buddy?"

"It appears that this is what happened, although we are still corroborating a number of eyewitness statements that were taken immediately after the RTC by the TPT officers in attendance," nodded Sergeant Evans. He paused before continuing, "And there's one more thing. Mobile phone records of the driver show that he received a call shortly before the accident and was in all likelihood still taking this call at the point of impact."

"So you're trying to tell me he wasn't looking where he was going?" Mark was really struggling to keep a lid on his anger. "He was driving with one hand on the steering wheel, is that it, driving recklessly, or what do you call it, without due care and attention?"

"He had a hands- free kit that was fully legal Mr Woodford. It wasn't the fact that he had taken a call that interests us, more the individual who had made the call," Sergeant Evans continued.

"Go on, the suspense is killing me, excuse the pun." Mark was trying to remain on an even keel.

"It was from a Mr Jonathan Woodford."

There followed a pause where all Mark could hear was the ticking of the kitchen clock and the rustling sound that Emma's police issue jacket made as she raised her cup to her lips to drink.

"Johnnie? How the hell did he know this lunatic who killed my family whilst chasing Catwoman?" Mark felt unsteady and his stomach heaved and churned as he gripped the table like a landlubber on a holiday boat trip around the bay.

"Apparently the driver, a Mr Guy Soames, was a business associate of your brother's. Does the name sound familiar?" Sergeant Evans enquired.

"Not ringing any bells just yet – although I'd love to meet him, preferably down a dark alleyway late at night," Mark replied.

WPCSO Marshall interrupted and spoke softly, "Mark, it's understandable that you feel anger towards Mr Soames but please refrain from any language that might be deemed by a court to be threatening as we do have to record any perceived threat of retaliation."

"Okay, okay, I understand," Mark continued, "I'm not the vigilante type, really. But I am just trying to get my head round all this. It's like a scene from The Bill (no offence) so there is this mystery woman linking Lizzie and the killer who had just happened to have been on the blower to my brother when he mowed down my wife, son and unborn child, I mean, you couldn't write this stuff could you? Or if you did no one would believe it. So, who is the 'young female' at the heart of all this and how come she knew the driver *and* my wife?"

Sergeant Evans resumed the lead, "For reasons relating to her own personal safety we can't at this stage, reveal the identity of the female in question. We have offered her police protection, but she has declined. The fear is that, as the key witness, she might be approached by those representing the accused in order to pressurise her to alter her account of the events. When the case goes to court she will be made known to you of course. It appears that she knew your wife through the work she did with vulnerable young females in the area."

Of course, it just had to be, thought Mark. My darling Lizzie killed in the line of duty.

"Has anyone from the hospital been in touch with you regarding protocol relating to the deceased?" Sergeant Evans continued. WPCSO Marshall glanced across at her colleague and Mark detected a slight nod from the Sergeant that effectively signalled the end of his contribution. Marshall continued, "Mark, you will need to speak to the bereavement support team from the hospital."

"Not likely," Mark replied abruptly, "I've done all the talking I need to do and don't need a total stranger butting in with psychobabble and platitudes."

"Not for tears and tissues Mark," she responded, "but to take you through the practical steps. As the deaths didn't occur in the hospital they will need to be registered with the local authorities. They will also need you to sign for the release of the bodies and will be able to give you advice on local undertakers and arrangements for the funeral, if you need any support in these areas." She had placed a printed leaflet on the kitchen table that contained a number on which he could reach the bereavement team at the hospital. "Even though you may still be in shock, and might not have even begun the grieving process there are steps that need to be taken, Mark. Is there anyone who you can call on to help you with these? A close family friend perhaps?"

"Sure, thanks Emma, and I've got people to lean on."

"Just you make sure you do then, Mark. Thanks for the coffee and we'll see ourselves out."

And then they were gone, their waterproof trousers making more rustling sounds as they made their way to the glass panelled inner door that rattled when they pulled it open. Mark was left alone in the kitchen once more with few crumbs of comfort as he had more questions than answers. He knew that there would be much to unravel over the coming hours and days and was left feeling unnerved by the information he'd received from the police and had the urge to call Johnnie straight away but he was also mindful of Mrs Sheridan's advice given whilst he sat in that very same seat the day before about taking things one step at a time. He knew he could no longer put off climbing the stairs.

*

Mrs Sheridan had talked of how accomplishing everyday chores might come to represent some sort of progress on the long road to recovery. Mark was under no illusions, as he knew he had mountains of trauma to climb in the days ahead but he had showered and shaved, put on clean clothes (braving their bedroom for the first time in the process) and put a wash load on, albeit through howls as he could still detect the scent of Lizzie on her 'bed' T-shirt and on Isaac's little pyjamas. But here he was, sitting on his sofa having made a cheese, ham and tomato sandwich and a cup of tea, a marked improvement from the day before. He had drooled at the prospect of a cold beer and had taken one out of the fridge but then returned it, knowing that he needed to keep a clear head for the phone calls he had to make after lunch.

He spoke with the Registrar at the hospital who was really helpful and, after a subsequent chat with a member of the bereavement team he was clear as to the next steps to take regarding the bodies. It chilled him to the extent that he got goosebumps to talk in those terms. He'd had an emotional phone call with his Mum (who was putting on the bravest of faces and was desperate to see him so he had relented to her visiting in a couple of days' time) and with Lizzie's father who had taken a couple of days off to help with arrangements. Mark asked Trevor if he could liaise with the funeral director as well as the vicar and he had seemed to welcome the additional responsibility. Mark had given him all the relevant numbers so he could coordinate with the hospital and had given his assurances that he would complete the paperwork to release the bodies. Goosebumps and nausea again.

After the phone call, Mark had pictured Trevor alone in that little flint cottage, the scene of such a wonderful family visit the previous summer, the grandfather clock ticking loudly in the hallway as he stood, hunched over the Belfast sink in the kitchen, still reeling from the loss of his amazing wife and now eternally bruised by the body blows of his precious Lizzie and little Isaac now being taken from him also. Just how much more could that proud little man take thought Mark. It was all getting too much again and he could feel the black clouds drawing in once more. "F-it!" he exclaimed out loud, apologising immediately in his head to Lizzie who hated to hear him swear. "If this doesn't warrant an afternoon beer what will." Satisfied that he had remained coherent enough to talk to all relevant parties he made his way to the kitchen and opened his fridge to find the last four bottles of ice cold Becks standing on the top shelf. He sighed as he knew that he would have to venture out later that afternoon to stock up, especially as he had Judy Garland and her trendy vicar coming round that evening to discuss yet another send of for his nearest and dearest. Plenty of time to neck a few then snooze off the effects he thought.

The doorbell rang. "Bugger!" Mark exclaimed in that strained angry hissed whisper he reserved for exclamations such as when standing on an upturned plug when Isaac was napping. He froze on the spot. A stupid thing to do really, he conceded, as no one could see him from where he stood, two doors in and partially hidden by the open fridge door. Silence. Footsteps, leaving? Coming round the side path to the back door. Bloody hell! A visit from Mrs S would mean knocking the cold beer idea on the head and he could almost taste it. He remembered now that Mrs Sheridan had agreed to take the family cat in (Mark had forgotten all about having one let alone feeding it). It was much more a Lizzie and Isaac thing as he didn't care much for pets of any variety although Dr Seuss had some redeeming qualities such as an outstanding ability to do keepy-uppy with a ping-pong ball. This had proved both a blessing and a curse as he had chased said ping-pong ball so doggedly, well cattily, down the stairs one Saturday morning that he had smashed into the open inner door, cutting his lip and face on impact. Lizzie had been heavily pregnant with Isaac at the time so Mark had to take control of the situation, cleaning up the blood splattered cat and hallway, booking an emergency appointment at the local vets then chasing the cat round the house before struggling to get him into the carry case and then the car, having received multiple lacerations in the process. It had turned out that, not only were stitches required but there was an issue with fleas that they hadn't clocked (cat not him) that required a course of medication in tablet form. The vet, a tall athletic looking German woman in her early 30s made it look easy but he was sure he'd have problems administering them. He had vocalised his concerns when observing how she had managed to open Dr Seuss' jaw by placing her fingers and thumbs either side of them and pressing on the joint, revealing lethal looking fangs, only to drop the tablet in and hold the mouth closed. "I'll never be able to do that," Mark had muttered. A few minutes later, whilst he was sitting in the (packed) reception area waiting for his prescription to be processed, the vet had poked her head round the door and said,

"I vill phone you at home tonight but if you are having problems getting it in you could always come in and do it viz ze nurse out the back in ze morning." To which Mark had spluttered, grateful that he hadn't been sipping a piping hot coffee from the vending machine. He remembers looking around at his fellow pet owners for a flicker or snigger of recognition for what was clearly a moment from 'Carry on Up Ze Vet'. But nothing. He had then felt like a schoolboy so had thanked her kindly and said he'd try getting it in himself but would do it with the nurse if he encountered any problems (arf, arf). You people, he had thought, as the classic gag had sailed way over their heads.

"Alright, alright I give in," he said loudly striding through the utility room to unlock and opening the back door, letting in the now icy early afternoon air. It took Mark a good few seconds to compute, standing open mouthed and gawping at not a wrinkly little old lady but a stunning young black woman with corkscrew hair piled on top of her head, shivering on his doorstep in a burgundy velour tracksuit that was struggling to contain what his mother might have described as 'a heaving bosom' and clasping an oversized handbag. She seemed out of breath, nervous (she kept fiddling with the elastic cuff of her tracksuit top that she seemed to be using as an old fashioned 'muff' to keep her fingers warm but Mark made an immediate note to self not to use that phrase on someone of the younger generation). After what seemed like an age she spoke, "Can I come in, it's bloody freezing out here?"

Mark stepped back to let this vision in designer casual wear in, noticing, appropriately, the words 'juicy' emblazoned across her shapely backside as she walked through into the kitchen. A bell rang from the not so dim and distant past as he managed to place her. It had to be, even without the hot pants and the make-up it was unmistakable. "Last time I saw you it was on the streets of Faliraki. What are you doing here?" Mark stammered.

"I didn't notice you there," she replied, turning her head and wearing a quizzical expression.

"No, you wouldn't have," Mark countered, "Lizzie was helping you and a mate of yours who seemed worse for wear on Ouzo outside a bar. I was in the background with friends."

The young woman, noticing the fridge door ajar nodded towards the top shelf and asked, "Were you about to crack open one of those? I could really do with a drink."

"Sure," replied Mark, moving across the kitchen, bottle opener already in hand and taking the tops off two bottles, "glass or by the neck?"

"By the neck will be fine," she replied, making eye contact. "Is it okay if I sit down?"

"Of course," Mark replied, "Please." He pulled back a chair and she sat down, back upright and perching on the edge as if ready to make off at the slightest wrong move by either of them. Sensing the unease and confusion surrounding Mark she took the initiative. "I'm Hope," she said, holding out a smooth, soft hand that tapered into talon-like nails, painted in a colour not dissimilar to her tracksuit.

Mark shook her hand limply, still weighing up how to play the situation. "You'll not find much of that here, I'm afraid. You knew Lizzie well didn't you? She told me a bit about you. News spreads fast around here eh?"

Silence.

"It's good of you to come round Hope, but I'm not much company right now and I've a vicar coming round in a bit, deep joy. Hang on, how did you know where we live? I thought Lizzie wasn't allowed to tell people due to confidentiality and all that?" Mark was being cautious, wary, trying to suss her out as he hadn't worked out yet whether Hope had placed him at the seafront on his stag night. Maybe she'd come to blackmail him. God no, that's all he needed!

Hope hadn't said another word. She took a long swig of the ice cold beer, pausing to dab her full lips daintily with the back of her hand, her whole body shuddered. She looked over his shoulder and out towards the utility room before returning her gaze to make eye contact. She really was striking, Mark thought, even without the slap, she had something about her but he couldn't quite work out what. Poise, inner strength, dignity or was it all a front? He looked down at her feet, uncomfortable at maintaining eye contact. She was wearing brown suede fur lined UGG boots with a semi-circle of salt staining the front of each from being worn in cold, wet weather. The air was particularly salty in Brighton.

"Mark, I." He looked up. Again a pause before she continued, this time with a tremor in her voice that was just above a whisper, a single tear ran down each cheek, one just ahead of the other. "I was with Lizzie when she died."

Mark didn't say a word. He remained silent for what seemed like an age. He heard the wall clock make its steady rhythmic clicks and ticks, so time hadn't actually stood still, it just seemed like it. Outside the sudden roar of a motorbike engine made him jump, the backfire from the exhaust had sharply intruded on this quiet, seminal moment in his life and then the sombre silence settled once more.

"So *you're* the mystery woman then?" Mark began slowly, looking up and at her. "The one the bloke in the Jag who killed Lizzie and Isaac was after, the reason why Lizzie was where she wasn't supposed to be in the first place?"

Hope continued, now crying freely, and with a deep intake, "Let me finish your sentence for you 'cos I know exactly what you're thinking, 'the reason why Lizzie and Isaac are dead'." She could barely get the words out through her outpouring of grief and, he expected, guilt. She seemed near hysterical as she sank to the floor, shifting her body weight so that her head rested on his leg just above his knee. "I am so sorry, so, so sorry, please believe me." She was wailing now, her 'in' and 'ex' haling not working in conjunction so she gasped for breath, her sobs causing her chest to rise and sink sharply.

Mark had imagined he'd be furious with her but how could he rant and rail against this poor girl who was so clearly in bits over the part she had to play in this tragedy? Okay, she might have been the catalyst for the heart wrenching final scene that had played out before her very eyes, but she hadn't been the one behind the steering wheel had she? He'd heard that people did some strange things through grief, bereaved husbands throwing themselves into the arms of their late wife's best friend after the funeral and then, before they knew it … He looked down now at Hope. She must have loosened the zip on her tracksuit top to help her breathe and her smooth dark cleavage, dappled with tears, glistened and heaved within a tight white vest. The Mark of old or 'before Lizzie' would have attempted to manipulate this situation to his advantage, he knew that he had been that much of a weasel. But that was then and this was now.

Lizzie had once shown him a wristband she used to wear when she had 'found Christ'. Mark had quipped along the lines of "so where had he been hiding for all these years then?" that Lizzie had ignored. The thick blue rubber band had the initials WWJD on it in white block capitals that stood for 'What Would Jesus Do'. Even Lizzie admitted it was a bit cheesy now, but went on to explain that, when becoming a Christian, Jesus came to represent a moral compass, a rock or solid foundation from which to build your life, so in any given situation, at work or in her personal life, if she was faced with a decision to make she would ask herself the question, what would Jesus do if faced with a similar situation or dilemma? Mark had scoffed at this, and wondered how many times Jesus might have been faced with the problem of teenage pregnancy or substance misuse but Lizzie had shrugged and smiled and told him that he'd get it one day, or at least that was what she had been praying for. He'd preferred the moniker WWLD (although it read like Liverpool's last four results, and that was being generous) and would often imagine how Lizzie would respond to the issue he might have faced when at college, or having been cut up whilst driving and never was this application more critical than now for he had been given the opportunity to help and not condemn this kid, to listen to her story and to reserve his judgement, maybe even go some way to relieving her of the burden she was carrying and was threatening to consume her.

"Hey, hey," Mark said softly, gently lifting Hope up by placing his arms under her elbows and guiding her gently back to her seat. Her head remained lowered, her body still convulsing, snot in abundance so he nudged the box of tissues in her direction. "Listen, why don't you take a few deep breaths, we can have another beer, and you can tell me what happened, in your own time eh?"

And so she did. She talked quickly, pausing occasionally, still not making eye contact. She told him about Soames and how she and Tia had gone back to his for champagne and charlie, feeling sick now at the thought that she'd let him touch her, especially after what he had done, and how she had nicked his wallet as he never stopped boasting about how minted he was, even inviting them out to a villa he had in Corfu later that summer. She described her utter desperation the morning afterwards and how she had been used to calling Lizzie whenever she was that low. Mark hadn't realised how close they were until Hope recalled the many times she and Lizzie had met up for tea and chats in seafront cafés. She said that Lizzie had driven to see her in response to her call and had popped into the shop over the road from the bench where she had been sitting to buy some flowers, somehow Isaac must have dropped his bunny whilst they were crossing over. She'd had to take some deep breaths before continuing. Mark listened to the rest with his eyes closed, the tears now spilling down his cheeks also. He was touched at how respectful and remorseful Hope was being, and felt convicted that she was to carry no blame for this breathtakingly tragic but equally unfortunate set of coincidences that had converged on that nondescript part of town on just one of many busy Tuesday mornings.

"If only I hadn't called her, if only I hadn't been the stupid, weak, filthy slag that I am none of this would have happened." Hope was speaking through tears and clenched teeth, digging the nails of her right hand into the palm of her left. "If I could of changed places with Lizzie I would of, I'll never be able to forgive myself and have a nerve even aksing you to."

Mark really did feel compassion rising towards this strong but fragile young woman who was baring her soul before him and knew this was no time for pedantry (could have, not of and she pronounced 'ask' as 'aks') but for sensitivity, not something he had ever managed with even a modicum of success to date. He reached out and removed her right hand from clawing at her left palm, wincing momentarily at the deep red imprints her nails had made, and held it between his.

"Hope, look at me." Her eyes remained focused on the kitchen floor. "Please." She managed to turn her gaze upwards, her body trembling, eyes red from crying as Mark leaned forwards. "If you know," (pause) "knew Lizzie like you say you did then do you think she would want all this guilt and self-loathing? She was the most generous, positive, non-judgemental, encouraging woman I had ever met, let alone fallen in love with and she would be the first to tell you that it's not your fault. Believe me, you cannot put this onto yourself, you had no idea what was going to happen."

Hope looked down at her feet again before mumbling, "Do you mean that or are you just saying it to shut me up and to get rid of me."

"I mean it. And listen, Lizzie thought the world of you. She told me you were strong and smart and bold and would really make something of your life, but that you needed to believe in yourself first."

"She really said that?" Hope looked quizzically at Mark.

"She did," he said, nodding.

Hope went to move. "Look, I'd better be going. I … You don't need me to tell you how much Lizzie adored you. She wore it. It was in her eyes when she smiled as she talked about you, sticking your fingers together with Superglue or knocking the Christmas tree over, the way you held Isaac after giving him a bath or gazed into her eyes (whenever you could tear them away from her chest she said, in her lovely way)." She managed to smile fleetingly at this point but her face then set. "To say I'm sorry for what has happened sounds pathetic I know, I'll never forget it. I see it and hear it all whenever I close my eyes. That's the curse I've been left with."

Mark was the one looking down at the floor now, biting his lip in the same way Lizzie would as he felt the emotion welling up once more. "Look, Hope, I may not have shared Lizzie's religious beliefs but she was more sure than anything in life that death was just the beginning, a gateway into some sort of paradise, heaven is what it's commonly known as. I know that she wouldn't want you to feel responsible for what happened, nor to keep blaming yourself, Please, try to let those feelings go."

Hope sat back again, folded her hands in her lap and breathed in deeply.

Mark continued, "Listen, there will be a service of remembrance next week. I'd like you to come."

Hope looked taken aback. "What, a church, me? The police would go ape if they knew I was even talking to you let alone going to a church service with you."

"Why not? It's for all those people in this area whose lives Lizzie touched, friends, colleagues and clients. It's been a while since I last darkened the doorstep of a church so it would be good to have your support. Why don't you leave me your number and I'll text you the details when I have them confirmed?"

Hope didn't have any paper or a pen in her handbag so Mark tore an empty page off their magnetic shopping list and gave her a pen. She wrote her name in large, childlike balloon style handwriting synonymous with the lower grades, her scrawled number alongside it then stood up to go. "Thank you," she whispered. "And I wanted you to have this." She opened her bag and produced Isaac's little 'Buddy'. He drew in his breath sharply. "I hope you don't mind but I washed it."

"Thank you," Mark replied, taking the soft toy and holding it to his face. It smelled strange, maybe a different fabric conditioner he guessed, but it was as precious to him now as it had been to his little boy. "For being brave enough to come here and tell me the truth, I'll always be indebted to you for that, and for this," as he looked down at the light brown bunny, now sitting on his left knee. As they reached the back door they embraced spontaneously, cried some more and then she was gone, pulling her hood up over her curls and hunching into the wind on the now dark late afternoon, the street lights already casting soft-glow pools onto the glistening winter pavements.

And so began the most unlikely of acquaintances, two people lost, adrift, with the only thing they could cling on to being the memories each had of a beautiful and remarkable woman that had cast light into both of their worlds.

Mark was still gazing out into the gloom when Vaz appeared along the path that ran around the side of the house. "Don't tell me that was who I think it was?" He nodded his head back to where Hope had walked down Stanford Avenue. "That would be in pretty poor taste even for you, mate."

Mark smiled and put an arm around his old friend, leading him into the warmth. "Come on in me old mucker and Uncle Mark will tell you all about it over a nice cup of tea."

*

The alarm woke him with a jolt. He immediately turned to where Lizzie would usually be curled under the duvet (she suffered from the cold to the same extent he did with the heat and would be curled up in hibernation mode at this time of year, albeit with the ability to get up, something that Mark had always struggled with unless she'd nudged him firmly in the ribs to remind him of their agreement to share the night duties). But her side of the bed remained intact, un-crumpled, save from a small indentation from where he must have instinctively slung his arm out in the night. Grey light leaked in through the blinds that were not fully closed, Mark had suffered from nightmares as a child and to this day panicked when faced with a room in total darkness.

He propped himself up on his stack of pillows and checked the time. 8am. He was due at the hospital to sign the release papers later that morning and then had to register the deaths at the local council offices so needed a bit of time to brace himself for both undertakings, knowing how long it took him to come round any time before 9am. He reckoned that he was doing much better than might have been expected under the circumstances, with one day of beer and bile not bad when he considered how his life had experienced such sudden, violent and permanent upheaval. He had surprised himself at how restrained his rallying against God, the world, circumstances had been and would not at all have been surprised to

246

be waking up in a cheap hostel for the homeless, or even suffering from hypothermia from spending the night under the Grand Pier after day two. The fact that he had made it, sober, albeit with a warm glow from a couple of large brandies still sloshing inside his stomach, into his own bed *and* before midnight was a huge step in the right direction but he was still taking nothing for granted. He glanced across at Lizzie's bedside table to the uneven pile of books she kept to hand. On top of the pile was the one she was halfway through reading, ironically entitled 'Five People You Meet in Heaven'. He could name three right off the bat. If it even existed.

He had felt quite weary when Lisa and the vicar from her and Lizzie's church had come round the evening before, feeling drained from the encounter with Hope but also of having to relay the whole sequence of events to Vaz right afterwards. It was flippin' exhausting having to tell the same story over and over he was realising and longed for a day of peace, free from people and talk. Be careful what you wish for he had immediately countered, for this house was becoming tomb like in its lack of sound, of movement, of life. And talking of quiet, it was strange not to have heard from Johnnie since the revelation that he was present, in a manner of speaking, at the precise moment of impact when his mate's car had hit Lizzie, guilt probably. So much of it flying around these past couple of days, he wondered if the person who should be feeling it more than any other was actually capable of doing so or whether he was a remorseless bastard with an expensive brief who was already on the case, working out a way to wriggle his client off the hook.

His thoughts turned to the night before and the discussions around the service of celebration that was being scheduled for the following Friday week at the big evangelical church downtown that Lizzie had attended. Lisa was her usual self, gentle, kind, considerate, empathetic, moving around almost unnoticed making tea/coffee, bringing in biscuits, the perfect hostess in Mark and Lizzie's home. The vicar was young-ish, maybe mid to late forties with thick dark wavy hair that was greying at the sides and pushed back with the hint of a product. He was relaxed, affable and he insisted on being known on first name terms (Stephen) as is the modern way. He spoke of the impact that Lizzie had made on fellow members of their 'church family', what an inspiration she was to the many young female members of the church and how greatly missed she would be by so many of all ages and backgrounds as she seemed equally at ease with whoever she engaged with. Mark had nodded along but was only tuned in-ish as he was feeling exhausted and it was all pretty much what he'd expected. He was relieved not to hear the service being described as 'not a mourning of a death but a celebration of a life' as he may have gagged audibly at this point, nor did they mention people wearing 'bright colours' as he had cringed whenever this sort of approach had been taken.

Whilst not always conventional in his life choices and views, he had been reared within the solidity of the traditional Church of England and so he still saw funerals as an occasion to wear black and act with dignity and reverence. He had felt ill at ease when this more unconventional service had been mooted as he dreaded walking into some carnival atmosphere with people wearing T-shirts with a photo of Lizzie transferred across them or waving banners or any such outpourings that he shuddered at the thought of. He had expressed these concerns to Lisa and Stephen, albeit not in precisely those terms and images and had received assurances that the service would be managed in a respectful and tasteful manner. The vicar had asked Mark if he had any preference regarding readings, hymns or worship songs and he had passed on this question, along with the request that he stood up and said a few words, only for Lisa to step in to reel off a number of biblical references and song titles that she thought appropriate and the suggestion that she could work with Mark on a tribute to Lizzie that Stephen or her could read on the night (knowing that this wouldn't be the sort of thing he would be up to). All were in agreement, the date and time was set and they exchanged warm farewells all before the News at Ten. Lisa had offered to come back that Saturday to start work on the tribute to which Mark, without hesitation, had agreed. Despite having an inclination to pull up the drawbridge and let down the portcullis, he had been grateful for the support he'd been given so far and surprised at how much it had meant to him. This made him feel resigned not to be quite so dismissive of people's well-intentioned intervention in future. But for the present, time for a shower, a bite to eat and the dreaded drive back to the hospital.

*

He knew that when he ordered Jack Daniel's at lunchtime, or at any time really, he was on a one-way road to self-destruction. He was sitting in a corner of the Tav (full name Preston Park Tavern, his local pub) nursing a JD on ice after downing two pints of Stella in quick succession and having munched his way through an assortment of crisps and peanuts (the tune to 'Two Pints of Lager and a Packet of Crisps, Please' had actually gone through his head as he was ordering). Mark had a weird relationship with food, not eating when he should (breakfast on most weekdays) and often indulging when he wasn't really hungry (crisps, Mars Bars, takeaways late on Friday nights). Right now he seemed hell-bent on doing himself some damage by fuelling his body with crap food and with booze. If he was an ex-smoker or substance addict he'd be fumbling for a fag or setting up a line right now.

The optimism that had framed his start to the day had been eroded by the business that he'd had to take care of, and he wished that he'd taken up the offer of his mum to have someone go with him. It turned out that, despite his best laid plans of getting up early and making an appointment in good time for once in his life he ended up running late and chasing his tail. He'd packed all the relevant documents in his battered briefcase, Lizzie had a portable filing case with everything immaculately labelled and was easy to find, put on his winter coat and headed around the corner to get into the car, even allowing time to scrape ice off the windscreen as it was a bright but bitterly cold morning. He had stood staring up and down Lucerne Road before the penny had dropped; the car was still parked at the scene of the accident. Mark had cursed himself as he'd rushed back inside to call for a cab and failed to get back on an even keel from that point onwards as, once he started to sweat, even on an icy winter's day, he found it hard to stop. The administration was all completed with the minimum of fuss but that word that had become over-used, 'surreal' was how he had felt actually seeing their names in black and white type on documents headed with the words 'next of kin for the deceased' and footed by his signature. The deceased, those that had ceased to live, his deceased family, now fully recognised and authorised with all the relevant parties, it was official, they had gone and he'd even signed their bodies away.

After leaving the Town Hall in St Bart's Square he took the short taxi ride to Dyke Road to pick up the car. This was one obituary he would be quite happy to write, not that he had anything against the vehicle, it was a typically reliable, functional, well-made German automobile that hadn't given them a moment's problem, but he was keen to sell it in favour of something with more character, more 'him' again. As the taxi headed north, leaving him on the pavement behind where the VW was still parked, he noticed the bench on the opposite side of the road and felt a thud in his chest, stopping him in his tracks. This shabby wooden slatted bench set upon greying concrete feet that were sunk into two patches of mud had been transformed into some sort of shrine, covered with cellophane wrapped bunches of brightly coloured flowers accompanied by cards. Half a dozen or so shiny helium balloons danced lightly in the late morning breeze and an array of soft toys sat, nestled amongst the scores of written tributes. Mark had always sneered at these urban shrines, citing the hysterical and irrational outpouring of grief towards Lady Diana Spencer from a public who somehow felt they had a connection with her as the catalyst for countless tacky and tasteless copycat public displays of grief, usually reserved for boy racers who'd taken a bend too quickly late at night, consigning a posse of peers to the grave with them.

Feeling drawn towards this macabre monument of contemporary grief, as one might towards an episode of The Jerry Springer Show, he took a deep breath and over cautiously made his way across to the other side of the road. Picking almost absent-mindedly at the written tributes, as if any lingering contact would somehow contaminate his carefully crafted bubble to protect him from the grubby cliché that the masses represented, Mark huffed and tutted out loud at the poor spelling and lack of correct grammar, almost willing himself to remain unmoved at these hackneyed attempts at conveying an appropriately worded emotional response to the death of his loved ones. *His* loved ones. Just as Princess Di was not owned by the nation, nor were his family's deaths up for grabs in the same way, to be hijacked and used as an excuse for nauseatingly bad poetry or tiresome and tacky references to angels and heaven. However, the closer he looked the more he fought with his default mode of contempt for anyone who confused 'there' with 'their' or who wrote lifes instead of lives. He saw one card containing a message that read:-

We cant describe wot we feel Lizzie. The kids aint stopped crying. You woz an angel and the only one we could turn to. Always loved and never forgotten. All our love forever, Mandy+C+T+J xxxx

Of course, Mark thought, the single mum (or lone parent as Lizzie would remind him, they weren't always single or necessarily mums who reared a family by themselves) who she was going to visit on that fateful morning. How must she have felt on finding out why Lizzie never did make their play date? There were more, too numerous to read, odes to Lizzie's caring nature, her sound advice, her unwavering support, her words of encouragement, her resilience, her strong faith and one that tipped Mark's emotions over the edge:-

My dearest Lizzie

I am one of many who was privileged and blessed to be able to call you friend. You touched the lives of so many, bringing hope where there was none, compassion where there had only been anger and recrimination, love and care to replace hatred, violence and rejection. Vulnerable yet strong, gentle yet determined, you modelled Christ in a way that many of us strive to. You were an inspiration in life and will remain so in death. You and Isaac will always remain in my thoughts and prayers as will Mark, the man you loved completely and who will feel bereft without you, as we all do.

"For I am convinced that neither death nor life, neither angels nor demons, neither the present nor the future, nor any powers, neither height nor depth, nor anything else in all creation, will be able to separate us from the love of God that is in Christ Jesus our Lord." (Romans 8: 38-39).

Your sister in Christ, always.

Lisa xx

He knelt on the cold, damp, hard pavement, one hand steadying himself on the edge of the flower laden slats, the other pushing his sunglasses to sit on top of his head as he allowed the tears to flow freely and the anger, the desolation, the hopelessness to well up and outpour, oblivious to the front page of The Argus from the day before that was still attached to the A-Board outside the 24/7 opposite that read, 'Local community worker, son and unborn child killed in hit and run on Dyke Road, police appealing for witnesses'. Many who had witnessed Lizzie's love of life and for those around her had already been here to give their take on Lizzie, and it was all too much for Mark to bear.

He'd suffered enough without his emotional pressure points being crushed again once he sat in the driver's seat of their family car, at finding Lizzie's sunglasses on the dashboard, glancing back to see Isaac's car seat full of crumbs and then, on turning the ignition, to be blasted by a song called 'Happy Day' by some Christian artist that Isaac and Lizzie loved to listen to as they drove about on their Mum and toddler rounds in and around Brighton, with Isaac always grinning and joining in the chorus with his 'addy day', 'addy day'. He hung his head over the steering wheel as the lyrics boomed out a message of hope, of new life, of sin being washed away. He wished he could feel any one of those but instead felt only despair, darkness, fear at what his life now looked like and an overwhelming desire to block the whole thing out.

An hour later, and he had knocked back his first two pints and, bloated, blowing and belching, was taking a breather before he began his third, with the Jack Daniel's a less gassy bridge on that road to self- destruction. He had taken a look at his phone for the first time in a day or so and had missed a flood of calls and text messages; Johnnie (5) Pete (4) Vaz (3), various colleagues from work, his mum (notably not his dad), Sophie, her sister Tamara (he was even tempted to return this call in his semi-drunken state), Trevor, he really should phone him, and then what about Lizzie's mobile? He'd chucked it back into her handbag on Tuesday afternoon after sending that text to all her contacts letting them know of the accident, there must have been hundreds of replies by now. Tuesday, but it already felt like a lifetime ago. Had only two days passed since his family had been ripped from his life, his precious family now being slid off steel tables and into bags, to be labelled and carted off in wooden boxes. Why them? Why him? He knew he was doing everything he despised, self-pity in public like a cast member of EastEnders in the Vic having just received some bad news but he couldn't face going home and he felt like he couldn't face going on, so he reached for another drink.

*

Not for the first time in his life, nor sadly for the last, Mark had no idea how he had got home. He opened one eye and then the other. He was on the sofa in his lounge (again) with the curtains half drawn. His head pounded and his tongue felt like sandpaper. Despite the drowsiness of having half slept off a lunchtime hangover, he was aware that he was not alone. There was no sound, but that presence you feel when there is someone else in the house, or in this case, the room. He peered across to one of the cream regency style chairs that they had bought as a pair the year before and frowned as he clocked a pair of blue suede moccasin type shoes with gold buckles and the crease of a pair of smart blue trousers. Letting his eyes move upwards, a cream blouse and red cardigan, red chiffon scarf, immaculately set hair and white teeth now showing through painted red lips. "Mum," he muttered, "my mum." June rose from where she sat and came across to perch on the sofa next to him, her familiar scent now filling the room. "My boy," she whispered, "my darling, darling boy," and there they remained, hands held, whilst silent tears marked this poignant reunion and the world he had known replaced the life he had begun to get used to.

A quarter of an hour later, with the curtains fully drawn and each cradling a hot mug of tea, Mark unravelled the mystery of how his mum had come to be sitting opposite him in his Brighton home late that winter's afternoon, wasn't she due down the following day? It was all blurred to Mark, the days, the hours.

"Darling, Mrs Sheridan has been so worried about you. , This morning, when she was on the way back from Mass she witnessed you screaming aloud in the street something about 'where is the 'effin car then you Muppet', whilst bashing your forehead with the palm of your hand and calling yourself a range of X-rated insults. She said you reminded her of a foul-mouthed Basil Fawlty and if she hadn't been so concerned and shocked she might have found it amusing. And we have all been so worried too. You haven't been returning phone calls so I thought, right, I'll just come on down."

"Did dad drive you then?" Mark enquired.

"Your father is rather snowed under with the business at the moment and, by his own admission, is quite hopeless in situations such as this. He did offer to bring me down but I rather fancied the idea of a train journey, so that's what I did, then hailed a taxi from the station and Mrs Sheridan let me in." His mother smiled sweetly, as if on some 'fun' Girl's Brigade adventure or mercy mission.

"But I haven't got round to putting the spare key to the back door in its usual place, so how did she let you in?"

"Oh you know Mrs S. She had a copy cut months ago, just in case of an emergency of course."

They spent the rest of the afternoon catching up and discussing what plans had been made to date. He knew that, with both his parents coming from upper-middle-class backgrounds, there would be a focus on the facts and few emotional outpourings but his mother did have a few of what she termed as her 'silly moments' when she got upset, dabbing at her eyes with a freshly starched hanky and chiding herself as she had not come all this way to make a scene. She tried to avoid talking about Lizzie and Isaac other than sticking to the details for the funeral and to let him know that

253

she would be going with him to the undertakers in Chichester the following morning to finalise all the details regarding flowers and the order of service. It was obvious to her from his blank expression that he hadn't the faintest idea that there had been a meeting scheduled for the following day; so that was why Trevor had called him.

The thorny issue of Johnnie and Guy didn't raise its head until they were halfway through supper. June had 'thrown' a few M&S ready meals into a cool bag before departing from Weymouth earlier and they were tucking into a Spaghetti Carbonara accompanied by garlic bread, washed down with plenty of sparkling water and a single glass of red wine each at the kitchen table. It seemed to Mark that his mother had been skirting around the subject of his brother and his associate, that she knew she would have to broach it at some point but was unsure as to what his reaction would be. "You know your brother's worried sick about you don't you darling?" She dipped her toe into the water.

"No. Haven't spoken to him since, you know, the day," Mark replied, not giving anything away.

"Well, he said he'd been trying to get in touch, and has left several messages, couldn't you have called him back Mark, just to put his mind at rest?"

"To put *his* mind at rest?" Mark stopped eating. "What's he got to be worried about? Last time I checked he still had a wife and two kids, albeit a wife who hates him and two kids who will grow to in time." His mother seemed to flinch at this change of mood and tone from Mark but he continued,

"I don't think any of my mates has recently run his family down in broad daylight whilst on the phone to me mum so I can't see the need to put his mind at rest to be honest."

Despite begrudgingly liking Johnnie, for all his faults, failings and faux pas, it was when his parents seemed to him to be taking Johnnie's side in any matter, regardless of how monumental or trivial, that the old Mark resurfaced, the jealous runt of the litter who felt overlooked and undervalued in favour of blue-eyed son number one, the heir to the family business and, he felt, to his parents' favour.

"Mark," his mum began, speaking softly and placing a hand on his, "your brother feels that he is somehow to blame for what happened, even though we have reassured him that this is simply not the case. He is distraught for you my darling, he and Sophie thought the world of Lizzie, as did the children for that matter and for Johnnie to think that you won't speak to him because you blame him for all this has really troubled him. He might be the elder brother but he still needs to feel that things are okay between the two of you. He really does care for you Mark."

Mark knew that Johnnie's part in the traumatic events of Tuesday morning were just random acts in a macabre set of serpentine events that twisted and writhed through the cosmos and transpired to bring about the brutal and untimely deaths of his little family unit and he couldn't be held to account, unlike his mate Guy, who he would like to do serious damage to. One day, he thought, when the dust has settled, or in this case, the damp earth. "Okay mum," he looked up, "I'll give him a call."

Dust to dust

He was not someone who would have described himself as an emotional man, nor a particularly articulate one. For him life had always been about absolutes; clean straight lines, neatly drawn circles, carefully calculated and meticulously drawn up plans. There was no room in his engineer's mind for superstition or supposition, you just gathered in all the facts and worked thoroughly from point A onwards. He used to marvel at how in awe Rose might be at a sunrise or sunset over the downs, the early morning frost or a waft of woodsmoke in the late afternoon autumn air. Similarly, at how in total rapture she would become as a piece of opera or classical music built up to a climax, her emotions in step with the rising tempo or rousing crescendos that spilled out from that old radio she kept on the kitchen windowsill, tears pouring down her cheeks, flushed at the emotion and the heat of the kitchen, smiling apologetically whilst holding a chopping knife in one hand and wiping her eyes on the sleeve of her other arm, always blaming the onions. He stood now, facing out of that little cottage window, arms stretched out with one hand on either side of that great white sink as she would as she might gather herself to come down from the great height of an aria to serve up their fish pie or chicken casserole.

He never wished for much in life, and never saw the point in wasting emotional or mental energy on anything he had no control over as you simply knuckled down and made the best of the deck you'd been dealt with but, standing on that uneven flagstone floor and gazing out at the teeming rain that mercilessly pounded the bare garden, bereft of flower or bud, of leaf and life, he wished more than anything that he had his girls back; to hear them animatedly sharing views on the morning sermon, colluding over a shopping trip to Chichester or in hysterics as Lizzie tested Rose on her lines for the latest play, affecting the voices of all the other parts, whether a Sergeant Major or a barrow boy. He pictured them when Lizzie was a little girl, holding hands whilst swooshing through the leaves that he had just raked up, and then as adults, these two remarkable women, arms linked, Rose with her head tilted onto Lizzie's shoulder as they headed out, chatting and pointing, to walk the lanes on a bright spring morning, the hedgerows alive with the vibrant colours of primroses, daffodils and wild pansies, the sounds of wood pigeon and thrush, the bustle of sparrows and swifts all full of the joy, the hope of a countryside throwing off the last vestiges of winter and welcoming the soft embrace of spring. But where was the hope now? The house was silent save for the ticking of the grandfather clock in the hallway, outside the rain gushed from a gutter that must have become blocked with leaves and splatted on the patio below, he could picture the join, a perennial problem but, as he made his way carefully up his aluminium ladder every year, he would always hear Rose, one foot on the bottom rung to steady it, maintaining it was a small discomfort in comparison to the welcome shade that the ash tree provided on scorching August afternoons. He snatched at and managed to catch a phrase that she had used one Saturday teatime when at a low point, feeling hemmed in by the grey wet of a late January, spirits hampered by a headache, unable to concentrate on the novel she had been reading, 'pathetic fallacy' as he recalled it, when the elements reflected the mood or dilemma of the character in question. The rain continued to pound the patio outside, the damp chill it carried with it seeping in under the stable door. That's me then, he conceded, with the emphasis on the pathetic.

The steady emission of steam from the kettle on the range snapped him out of this uncharacteristic state of retrospection that was becoming strangely more familiar to him as each slate day passed at a snail's pace. He made himself a large mug of instant coffee: granules then the milk, stirred, then adding the hot water (not boiling) and finally a level teaspoon of sugar, stirred again, always in a clockwise direction and placed it on a coaster on the kitchen table before slumping heavily onto one of the matching wooden chairs, the legs screeching sharply on the cold stone floor disturbing the funereal peace of that once lively family home. He wrapped his fingers around the mug and held it just under his chin, breathing in the caffeine scent; again something he would associate with Rose, taking in the whole experience rather than his usual approach which would be to find an odd job to do whilst the coffee stood, cooling to drinking temperature. Usually it would be nothing more than a household electrical appliance that needed a new fuse, a picture hook that needed straightening or maybe a piece of curling wallpaper that needed to be re-pasted flush to a glossed dado rail. Rose would often tease him when he would return to find his coffee lukewarm as that 'little job' had taken far longer than he had expected and maintained that this routine prompted her to buy a microwave, something he had always resisted.

He picked up the final draft for the order of service that he had run through with the Reverend Poe, Mark and his mother June the day before, meeting at the vicarage that was a short walk from the cottage and a place of hugely mixed emotions for Trevor as it had been the scene for the planning of his wedding to Rose, the baptism of Stuart and Lizzie and the funerals of both the women in his life; 'The Lord giveth and He taketh away', was how the Reverend Poe had put it in his soft, deep, melodious tone. Poor Mark had looked awful, his face ashen with dark bags under his red-rimmed eyes, unshaven and with a shell-shocked vacant look about him. But what had he expected? The dear boy had the knack of looking dishevelled at the best of times so no wonder his appearance reflected the worst of them. Mark said little as he, June and the Reverend agreed on the hymns and the readings, more traditional than Lizzie might have gone for but as 'with it' as they could possibly muster with dear old Mrs Jennings to play the organ, whose definition of a modern hymn was one written post-1850. He flicked absent-mindedly through the slim booklet, past the beaming face of Lizzie that shone up from the cover, through the familiar prayers, readings and hymns and knew that he should read it thoroughly one more time before phoning the vicarage to give the go ahead to get it printed with a cream card cover. He took a long sip of coffee and crunched loudly on a digestive biscuit, his mind wandering again, this time to the funeral of his beloved Rose and how Lizzie had supported him in the emotional and physical sense as the coffin was lowered into the earth and an irrational panic had gripped him, urging him to throw himself onto the lid and scream that it was all a terrible mistake and for the whole thing to stop. It was Lizzie who gripped his arm to stop him from collapsing at the graveside, Lizzie who had stayed with him as the mourners steadily trickled away, always Lizzie, bright, beautiful, confident, caring Lizzie who managed to convey how much she understood, not always with words, sometimes a look or reassuring hug, how deeply she shared his loss. He was tired of hearing from well-meaning colleagues how a parent should never have to bury his child but was now feeling the full weight of having to bury first the love of his life and now his precious only daughter, his sunshine girl, within five years of the other; not to mention his grinning, joyful grandson and the granddaughter that he would never get to hold in his arms. The rain continued its downpour and the kitchen grew a little colder as the gloom thickened around that little corner of West Sussex, where once such radiance dwelt. Outside, the gutter continued to overflow.

*

He didn't find the steady drip-drip in any way annoying, in fact he rather welcomed its repetitive metronome beat as it allowed him to lie back, close his eyes and be released from all the thoughts of darkness and despair that had been crowding his mind. He used to relax in just this way after a thrashing on the tennis court from Vaz followed by a pub lunch at their local, with the loser paying so that was always Mark, bar one occasion when he suspected that Vaz might have been playing with a stomach bug. Mark would dump his sweaty sports kit in the wash basket then ease himself down into the hot foamy tub, just as he had done today (sans the sports gear) with the murmuring from the portable digital radio for company as the football scores and near misses came in from up and down the land. It had been pretty up and down for Man Utd of late, he had reflected, ending the previous year and beginning this with a league defeat (to Blackburn Rovers and Newcastle United respectively, the former 3-2 at home and the latter a 3-0 whitewash up at the Toon) followed by the utterly brilliant and face-saving relief of a 3-2 win away at City in the Cup. Mark expected a routine home win over Bolton that afternoon and, momentarily revelled in the sheer ordinariness of what he was doing.

He had dropped his mother off at Chichester station so that she could return to Dorset after the meeting with Lizzie's father and the family vicar, who Mark had immediately warmed to, despite having a few issues with God at present. His heart had gone out to Trevor once more as, despite the fact that he looked like he had neither eaten nor slept in days, he was the picture of propriety and restraint, willing and sensitive as he nodded reverently at the choice of hymns and readings. It had been agreed that the Reverend Poe (related to Edgar Allen, how cool was that?) would say a few words on behalf of the family as Trevor was, by his own admission not a public speaker, and despite Mark's belief that he could hold an audience in the palm of his hand, this was neither the time nor the place, he knew that he would have crumbled.

He had grown restless during this in-between time, following the raw emotional savagery of the accident, the lead up to the trauma of burying his beloved family and the inevitable desolation that was to subsequently descend. Random flashbacks ran through his head like the constant news-feed that ran in a bright electronic ticker tape across the bottom of Sky Sports News, seeing Lizzie sitting in the staff common room, head down over a folder, and how his heart had skipped a beat, how her hair had slipped over one eye and he almost reached out for it before she instinctively tucked it behind her ear and continued their conversation, blissfully unaware of the effect she was having on this clueless sixth- form tutor; Lizzie skimming stones into the foaming surf on a Sunday afternoon in December, grinning whilst shielding her eyes from the glare, despite the time of year. He had joked at how girly it was how she threw her pebble before completely overdoing it in an attempt at showing off and pulling a muscle in his lower back. Lizzie in the pool whilst on their blissful second week of honeymoon (before his injury), gliding gracefully, hair tied up, ignoring his lewd remarks about joining her for breast stroke but then choking near to death when his final dive to win the gold at the world championships (needing an average 9.5) had emptied half the water from the pool. Lizzie on that fateful Tuesday morning, again enduring his jibes with her usual good nature, this time he had aimed them at the mum she was off to see, and little Isaac, his blonde bed-head waving like a cockatoo in the icy early morning breeze, wide eyed and alert, the last time he had seen them both alive. Music was also a trigger. He had avoided listening to anything that they had shared as a couple, a soundtrack to their lives as it were, but he had the Chill station on in the kitchen and every now and then an intro or a chorus would reduce him to a sobbing mess. It was strangely cathartic to weep it all out, to allow the feelings to sweep over him, overwhelm him, tidal, drowning, cleansing. Despite all the leaflets that had been thrust into his hand at the hospital it was clear to Mark that there was no set course in navigating the unpredictable waters of grief, he just had to keep paddling to keep his head above the water. Just keep his head above the water.

The ringing of the doorbell made him panic; flailing, he grasped the sides of the bath and gulped air in deeply. It didn't take him long to assess the scene; 'idiot' he thought, the last place you should fall asleep is in the bloody bath. He heaved himself out, ungainly, sloshing luke-warm bathwater all over the tiled bathroom floor whilst grabbing a towel and quickly securing it around his waist as he made his way to the top of the stairs. Usually he would have ignored the doorbell, especially when relaxing in the tub but he was expecting Lisa and needed her help, hence the undignified rush. "Coming," he yelled as he tumbled down the stairs, yanking at the inner door whilst reaching out for the handle to the front door, the movement causing the towel to loosen and fall. He would never forget Lisa's face as her warm smile was replaced by a shriek, her hands covering her eyes as he stood, stark naked on the mat that read WELCOME in block capitals, icy drafts wafting in from the winter afternoon.

Lisa had offered to make a pot of tea whilst Mark had gone upstairs to dry off and throw on some clean clothes. Before long he had bounded back down in jeans and hooded top, hair still damp, to find Lisa sitting at the kitchen table nursing a steaming cuppa.

"Hope you don't mind," she said, "I've poured myself a mug and helped myself to the biccies."

"Of course," Mark replied, "I said make yourself at home." He paused, "Lisa, about earlier."

"It's alright Mark," she looked nervous once more, "no need to dwell on it eh?"

"It's just, well, a bit delicate really," he blundered, "I'd been in the bath for ages and fallen asleep so the water had gone cold, also, it's bloody freezing outside so you didn't exactly see me in my, well, full glory so to speak."

Silence, as Lisa poured Mark a mug of tea. "Sugar?" she enquired.

"One please," he answered sheepishly.

"Let's move on can we Mark," Lisa said gently, her face looking slightly pained.

"Sure, Lisa," Mark responded, glad that he had put his point across but equally relieved to be changing the subject.

They discussed the visit from her church pastor ('a la vista' he had chimed in to which Lisa had forced a smile). It turned out that Lisa was employed by the church in an 'outreach role' and that she was visiting him in a professional as well as personal capacity. He hadn't known that she had actually worked for the church, in fact he knew very little about her at all as she was always such an in the background person. Lizzie was really fond of Lisa and this had clearly been reciprocated in the card that she had left at the 'shrine'. Mark had embarrassed her enough by opening the door to her 'tackle out' so had decided not to make reference to her touching testimony and to focus on the matter in hand. Mark had told her that he had really appreciated the visit earlier in the week from her and her vicar, that he was happy for her to make decisions over the order of service as she had a better idea about the songs and readings that Lizzie liked and how happy he would be for them to work together on the tribute to Lizzie. He had expressed mixed feelings about the minister in that he was not used to a vicar who wore jeans, referred to them as 'guys' and littered his conversation with 'kinda' and so would probably not be 'walking a journey' with him/them as was offered as he didn't really feel comfortable with their faith or how he 'wore' it. "No offence." Lisa had nodded along and smiled in a 'none taken' way at this response and had reassured Mark that, as one of Lizzie's closest friends, she wanted to offer whatever support she could, regardless of her role within the church ministry team. Basically, she was going nowhere, and he respected her for this, especially as he kept picturing her face when he had opened the door less than an hour earlier; many women with less resilience would have run a mile at that point, especially a saint in the making such as Lisa.

Lisa had flipped open her laptop and run through a gallery of photos that they were planning on projecting on a timed loop on the big screens at her church as people came into the service. He was amazed at the range of images that Lisa had collated, from Lizzie's childhood through teenage years right up to her wrapped in her trademark puffa coat and scarf pushing Isaac in a swing taken less than a month ago. Modest to the core, she said that she'd been in touch with friends and family members and hadn't wanted to bother Mark as he might have found the whole process too painful. How resourceful, Mark remembered thinking, and just how bloody thoughtful was she? Lisa had also 'thrown together' some ideas for a tribute that read in much the same vein as the one that Mark had read when at the scene of the accident. It was beautiful, perfect, he was blown away by how she had managed to combine Lizzie's passion for her work, her faith and her family in a non-cheesy, amusing, warm, touching and heart wrenching way. He couldn't hold back his emotion any longer as she described key moments in their relationship; Lizzie meeting him, how they had fallen in love, how he proposed (over a bacon buttie whilst overlooking the Thames), how he had nearly knocked over their wedding cake as they prepared to cut it by pretending he was a Jedi, how he had managed to fall off the balcony having locked them out of their villa whilst on honeymoon and broken a collarbone and had practically fainted when in the delivery suite as Lizzie brought Isaac into the world (he was actually in the loo when Isaac had finally arrived but had come close to passing out during the labour). She had described them as like two rose bushes, who held their ground, maintaining their own identities, but whose roots had become entwined under the earth so they were completely united in their love for the other, always bringing out the best in each other. She spoke of the depth of that love and how it culminated in the little miracle that was Isaac.

She went on to explain sensitively and articulately just how tough it would be for those who were close to them to let them go, as it was always harder for those who had been left behind, reminding all who would be listening at how certain Lizzie was in her belief that one day she would be called home to Paradise and that she never feared when that day might come. Mark laughed and sobbed freely throughout, allowing Lisa to hug him when she had finished in that restrained and respectful way that friends of a deceased wife would. When he finally managed to control his breathing and finished apologising for the tears, snot and dribble, a feature of the past week he had joked, he took a deep breath and commented on her piece.

"Wow. Lisa, that is just amazing, spot-on, all of it, thank you so much, I'm quite overwhelmed by it all to be honest. I had no idea that you were so gifted," Mark began.

"I can't take any credit for it," Lisa replied modestly, "I just opened a blank page, prayed for the right words, and out they came."

"Seriously?" Mark frowned, "so how does that work?"

"Simple really, I asked God for help and got it."

"But …" Mark stammered, "Are you trying to tell me that God just ''appened to be pissing by' (in his mock 'Allo, 'Allo accent) and helped you to write this?' I mean wouldn't God be a bit too busy mending this broken world he has made to just drop into central Brighton to help you write Lizzie's tribute?" Mark added, now with a hint of sarcasm.

"We believe that God works outside of our limited perceptions of time and space Mark, I called on His Spirit to inspire me to write the words He felt best captured the essence of your beautiful wife, my precious friend and His beloved daughter and this is what He came up with," Lisa concluded.

"Divine intervention? It all seems a bit far-fetched to me," Mark sighed, shaking his head wearily.

"Mark, we believe that God can be in all places and all things at once, that he is infinitely awesome and equally approachable, as well as His power and influence spanning the cosmos that He is here with us in this room right now," Lisa responded.

"So he must know how hacked off I am with him right now then eh?" Mark flared up, looking around the kitchen. "So, where was this so-called Divine Intervention when that car was careering towards my family? Why did he allow Lizzie, Isaac and Ella Grace to be ripped so violently from the world and let the bastard of a driver survive?" Mark was getting quite angry now.

"I don't know Mark and it's not for me to answer on His behalf," Lisa replied with a lightness that didn't reflect the bitterness that she now had to deflect, "have you tried asking Him yourself?"

Mark immediately calmed down, apologising for his outburst, stressing that it wasn't aimed at her, and that he was so grateful for her help, her kindness and concern. He had one more favour to ask of her though and that was, if she could spare a bit more time, to go through Lizzie's mobile phone that he had on charge and respond to any text messages or calls made to her since her passing as he just couldn't face doing it. Lisa told him that of course she would so he led her into the lounge and left her perched on the corner sofa, head down over Lizzie's phone whilst he headed back to the kitchen to make a fresh pot of tea. So, like the Wet, Wet, Wet classic about Love, God was all around them, he mused, in that case they would be, in the modern parlance, 'having words'.

*

As expected, United recorded that routine win over Bolton (3-0) to keep pace with Man City. Mark would usually have been more excited by this but could feel the walls closing in a bit after Lisa had left and was nursing mixed emotions. He was genuinely touched by her warmth, generosity of spirit and her calm resourcefulness. He was also impressed by her quiet determination and, like Lizzie, a complete belief in her

263

Christian faith. However, despite all this, he still had serious questions to put at the feet of the Almighty but was not ready to do battle just yet, needing to nurse his anger and allow it to grow to fever pitch before unleashing the full force of his fury at heaven's gate. He knew that, once again, he was enjoying the calm before the storm and that he would have to endure a tsunami of grief over the next week that would threaten to drown him without trace but by this time next week it will all be over. Again a dichotomy as he was reaching out with one hand to the tunnel light that the following weekend represented whilst clinging on desperately to the pain and loss that had en-cloaked him since the previous Tuesday as this was now all he knew, he had grown into it and wondered how he would feel if, when, he ever threw it off? Doing so would mean that he had survived, that he had made it through the worst possible chapter of his life. Survival meant carrying on, but carrying on with what and what was the point anyway? Lizzie and then Isaac had been such an integral part of his very being that doing something, anything, without them seemed hollow, somehow, shallow. He knew that he couldn't face going back to work, probably ever, and that he certainly wouldn't be able to stay in their family home but again the thought of organising a move threatened to overwhelm him. It was Lizzie who had driven the project to refurbish home and garden, husband and wardrobe, Lizzie who had chosen all the fixtures and fittings and drawn up schedules for the contractors, having sourced them and negotiated on the price and deadlines in the first place. He had watched on, again the guppy fish, floundering in awe of her skill in decision making, project management and logistics; the cheery way in which she managed to haggle over the plastering or wiring, the staying power she had displayed in spending hours each evening deliberating over colours of paint and fabric whilst he was slumped in front of the TV. He could picture the frown, the chewing of the lip, the pencil behind her ear, a tape measure and notepad to hand. It was all a weird alchemy to Mark, who now wished that he had taken more notice as he hadn't the first clue how it all worked, having previously only ever rented before inheriting from his godparents.

His pride would prevent him from seeking advice from Johnnie over the process of buying and selling, despite his experience in both (sadly for Sophie it was particularly the selling in recent years) and he was too out of touch with his father to seek his input. He still hadn't heard from his father, imagining him reaching out for the outdated handset that sat in the hall on a small wooden table next to the settle in their family home but replacing it before calling him up, knowing that he would be utterly lacking in the language of comfort, despite clearly adoring Lizzie, along with all the

Woodfords and de Montfords. The shadows lengthened on the walls of the lounge and in the halls of his mind as the night drew in, 'pathetic fallacy' he grimaced and reached for his mobile phone.

*

She had been putting the finishing touches to her war paint, re-applying her lipgloss, when the call had come through. She had been surprised to hear from him and was a bit wary at first, her default mode as her mother called it, but she soon relaxed, perching her bum on the edge of her single bed warming to this likeable character whose loss was something she carried with her everywhere she went. It felt nice to be chatting to a bloke who didn't want anything from her for a change, he asked her what she had been doing and how she had been feeling and, as promised had invited her to the service of celebration at Lizzie's church for the following Friday evening. She had received a text about the service from a friend of Lizzie's earlier that day as it happened but she appreciated him taking the time to call. She was so used to men letting her down, telling her they would call her and never doing so that she felt a warm glow from this phone call. Here was a decent bloke who had just had his family ripped from him finding the time to call her to see how *she* was! He had restored a fraction of her faith in men that had previously lay like a shattered mirror before her; harsh, jagged shards of memories carved deep into her subconscious. Once the short chat had ended she lay back on her bed and sent a quick text to Tia letting her know that she was running late. So much going on, so much to think through.

Since her first visit to the station on John Street she had been called back, for the rozzers to go through her statement again and again, the duty solicitor wanted it to be watertight she had told her as they knew that the defence counsel would be looking to tear holes in both her statement and in her character. It seemed odd to her that someone might look to discredit (her word not hers) her account of events based purely on her class, colour or occupation when the whitey in the other corner had cheated on his wife whilst taking class A drugs and then tried to cover his tracks, even resorting to sending a shady looking bloke down to wait for her after a shift at The Zap a couple of nights back to offer her £20K in cash to change her version of events. Yet she was the one who was going to be branded unreliable and dishonest. Tia had tried to talk her into accepting the cash, getting excited over a couple of Bacardi and Cokes about how they could fly out to Ibiza and work the clubs there, maybe put down a deposit on a bar of their own on the beach, away from all the shit they had to face in Brighton. After a few drinks, Hope had to admit to herself the thought had been tempting, even though her mum would have been pretty gutted to have been left on her own, but she could never do that to Lizzie, or to Mark. Lizzie had been so good to her and stood by her whatever she had done so she owed it to her memory to stand up to these arrogant, rich arseholes who seemed to have no concern for the pain of the lower classes, thinking they could just be bought off, well she was going to stick her two fingers up at the lot of 'em and make sure the dick that did it got put behind bars for what he had done. Tia sort of got it but Hope could tell that she was still gagging for her to take the money and run but she didn't know Lizzie like she did so lacked the emotional connection, now made even stronger by meeting her husband. No, she would be strong on this one, and they would soon find out that she was someone not to be messed with; a fighting spirit, something she had inherited from her dad who, apparently, was not one to ever throw in the towel.

*

Johnnie had been relieved to hear from Mark, concerned that his brother had somehow held him responsible for the accident. Bloody spooky though he had thought, that he was on the phone to Soames just as he had run down Lizzie and co; what were the chances of that? Sophie and the kids were distraught at the news, Sophie in particular, he had never seen her so emotional since they had been forced to sell their houses in Sussex and Corfu. He had found it extremely difficult to focus on the meeting and was relieved to have Dave Burnett in with him, as it turned out, the client's issues were around the compatibility with the system used by their US based mother company and not with the actual product or price point itself, so he was able to take more of a back seat than he had expected and let the boffins battle it out. He actually found IT mind crushingly boring but knew it was a case of either be on-board or get left behind, so he had launched his company Global-Tech Solutions at the turn of the century along with scores of others, surfing the wave of new innovation and application in the world of e-commerce. The truth was, he preferred the solidity and familiarity of their family shipping business, with its rich heritage and reputation, the oak panelled board room with crystal decanter and whisky glasses, family portraits on the walls, but he couldn't see how he could grow this already established operation at the same way he could with the right backers and a new enterprise in emerging markets with huge and rapid growth predicted. He'd certainly reaped the benefits from his investments, year-on-year growth for over 8 years followed by a double dip recession and now a few green shoots of recovery after a barren few years. Sure, the big old place in West Sussex had had to go, along with the villa in Corfu but they still had the mews house in Barnes and Sophie owned a place just north-east of Malaga so they weren't exactly on the breadline, as Sophie would have him believe. The school fees were over £35K a year, nearer £40K with extra-curricular clubs but that was covered by his directorship with the family company and he had a few bits tucked away here and there for a rainy day·so it certainly wasn't all doom and gloom. He had driven back down south with a greater sense of optimism than when on his way up. In fact, he always felt a lightness descend upon him whenever he saw signs to London and the south, not having anything against the north but always relieved to be leaving it behind him. He had always felt depressed by the huge industrial landscapes, particularly around Sheffield with its huge towers belching out great grey spumes of smoke around the clock but this was tempered by the smell of coal tar, a reassuring scent reminiscent of home, of washing your hands before afternoon tea after having thrown a rugby ball around in the garden until it was beginning to get dark. Funny how smells can have that effect he had reflected, creating such instant, vivid and nostalgic flashbacks. He recalled the many fruitless attempts made by him and their father at getting Mark interested in rugby or cricket. He would, it would seem, deliberately drop either shaped ball, leaving him and their father visibly frustrated as, with a shrug Mark would retreat indoors to his world of comics and superheroes, long after most chaps had grown out of that sort of thing and had become interested in a different type of magazine *all together,* excuse the pun he thought ruefully.

Poor Mark. Always the butt of family jokes, never quite making it, until he finally found some sense of purpose having met Lizzie. What a cracker that girl was, fit as a butcher's dog and lively with it, not like that sulking sliver of ice that he was hitched to. He'd tried it on, of course, in a subtle way, but she was having none of it and he'd respected her for that, begrudgingly. Quite what she saw in Mark was beyond him though as, despite his dry sense of humour and well-meaning nature, he was a bit of a bloody disaster area to be honest, unshaven and dishevelled most of the time, with no real drive or direction, not knowing his arse from his elbow. He would laze about in that inherited house playing at being a teacher and a playwright but achieving no great success in either. What a change Lizzie had made to the picture. Her influence had made him appear much smarter, more confident and organised and at last with some sort of grasp on what it was like to inhabit the real world, taking responsibility for maintaining a home and supporting a family. The Woodfords would always thank her for the impact she had made on his, their lives, as she was just such a joy to be around; always so positive and without a bad word to say about anyone, cheery, helpful about the place, taking an interest in others, particularly Tiggy and Harry, what a loss, what a tragic loss, and what a fix he now found himself in as he was having to walk a bit of a tightrope between family loyalty and self- preservation.

He had been contacted on the phone by a 'third party' representing Mr Guy Soames, essentially a fixer with a fee (who had casually thrown in the fact that he knew Johnnie was owed the £100K by Soamesy who might not be in a position to pay if he went down for a stretch). The bloke went on to ask him all manner of questions about Mark's history and home life, whether or not he had vices such as heavy drinking, gambling or anything of a sexual nature (maybe a fling with a student or a colleague). They had pushed him on Mark's marriage and Lizzie, and whether or not the late stages of her pregnancy may have left her weary or not in full control of her faculties. He knew exactly what they were doing, despite the pseudo-friendly tone, digging for dirt, looking for even the tiniest scrap of evidence that might have implied that there were problems at home, debt for example, that maybe they had rowed on the morning of the accident, or that she had been so tired that she may not have looked where she was going when she stepped out onto the road in front of Soamsey's Jag, anything to exonerate him and get him off the hook.

He knew that Soames used Granville, Bingham & Brown, a top-end firm of barristers based in town that could have got Saddam Hussein an acquittal on the grounds of diminished responsibility if he could have afforded their fees. Part of him wanted to warn Mark as he knew he would be so far out of his depth when called for cross-examination from this lot that they'd have to launch a lifeboat to rescue him, but similarly he had become quite used to the comforting weight of his testicles nestled inside his chinos and knew that, if he put one foot wrong, he could either lose them to some black leather glove and balaclava wearing thug in an alleyway late one night or, equally terrifyingly, to a bobbed, Boden and Bvlgari wearing wife on finding out that his blunder had just cost them £100K. Decisions, decisions. With a deep intake of breath he polished off the last of the Scotch and left the warmth and security of his gentleman's club, where he'd come to find a quiet corner to reflect on his current dilemma, and headed for the more chilly and potentially choppier waters of home.

*

There was something about a train journey that he'd always loved; the sense of stepping out into the unknown perhaps; despite the fact that you knew your destination, anything could happen on the way to it, anyone could cross your path en route. Today, however, was not one of those days. This was probably due to his travelling time of four o'clock on a Tuesday afternoon, and his sombre state of mind. The carriage was fairly empty as he settled into a window seat looking grimly in the direction in which he would be travelling. Chichester; Lizzie's home patch.

The days had dragged beyond belief since the weekend, Sunday in particular, when he had found himself back in The Cricketers by lunchtime, morbidly nursing a pint and a packet of peanuts at the same table where he had met Lizzie on their first date, sinking deeper into morose retroflection, the melancholy gripping his gut and twisting more fiercely every time a couple eased themselves into a seat and nestled into each other, side by side and exchanged so much as a smile. By 2pm he had sent texts to his small select band of friends appealing for company, the majority of whom, including Pete, were up to their necks with the grease and gravy of their family Sunday roasts so couldn't get away. It was the faithful Vaz who had answered his friend's desperate plea, shaking off Mark's grateful hugs (whilst probably lying in telling him that his fiancée had a stack of marking to wade through so it was no bother for him to be there). They had sunk a few more beers, shed a few tears, well he had, Vaz was being his usual sensible self and limited himself to just a half of lager and the occasional, sympathetic pat on the shoulder. They then wandered aimlessly along Hove esplanade, the backdrop to so much of the narrative that was Mark and Lizzie, before winging their way back towards Preston Park as dusk began to fall to where Vaz had left his Mini in its usual place. Is this it? Mark had contemplated after Vaz had left and the silence settled in once more. Struggling to get through the long days yet at the same time dreading the onset of evening? He then spent most of it dozing on the sofa in front of Antiques Roadshow and Countryfile until the familiar and reassuring music of Match of the Day 2 boomed out to put him out of his misery, conceding that this was just about as depressing as it could get.

He had slept pretty much all of Monday. The churning anxiety that was slowly building up in the pit of his stomach rose every time he opened his eyes so he had simply closed them and pulled the duvet back over his head. His mum had changed the bed linen for him and washed the set that had been on the bed before she had left, so Mark hadn't had to get a waft of Lizzie each time he went to bed. He resisted this at first, clinging to every shred of her existence, but knew that this was all part of the grieving process, remembering the person but relinquishing the physical reminders bit by bit. It was still so early on in that process, however, that Mark had no idea as to what a sensible course of action looked like; what might be considered morbid and weird (trying to squeeze into one of her bed T-shirts or brushing his teeth with her electric toothbrush fitting for example), and what may be deemed too clinical (piling all of her clothes, toiletries and trinkets into bin bags and taking them to the local tip); again it was the lack of a Beginners Guide to Managing Grief and Bereavement that had left him floundering. Flounder, he wondered if this was a word that Miranda Hart might have liked, along with thrust, cusp, plinth and plunge?

One of the strangest things about his current state was what little influence or control he retained over his thought process. He had always been something of a dreamer, happy to occupy his time in an alternate existence when he was growing up, losing himself in comic books or mooching in the few underused rooms upstairs in that big house whilst his father and Johnnie played out an Ashes demolition of the Aussies with bat and ball on the lawn, crying out for him to be a wicket keeper. He knew that, over the years, they had both grown increasingly frustrated at his lack of interest in what they viewed as character building activities; proper outdoor pursuits such as cricket, rugby, grouse shooting, fly fishing, anything that involved chasing, hunting, rutting, rucking and mauling and were left exasperated as he developed instead a love of the great indoors. His affiliation first with fictional superheroes and then wrestlers of the WWE bemused them, as did his inclination to remain cooped up in his room on a sunny day.

As a mop haired Echo and the Bunnymen and Psychedelic Furs loving sixth-form student he had staggered them all the more with the experiments in his appearance, his slender frame emphasised by skinny black jeans and vests, his pale complexion complemented by eyeliner and a touch of his mother's mascara, in direct contrast to Johnnie's ruddy complexion and penchant for England rugby tops with the collar turned up and an inclination to refer to anyone who didn't conform to his preppy style as 'shirtlifters'. It was his mother who always remained neutral whereas his father might sigh as Mark came down for dinner wearing a black jumper with holes in, or headed off into the village in one of his grandfather's old winter coats and army surplus boots. He seemed far more concerned as to what people might think than what was actually going on in Mark's head, how the increasing bond between father and number one son seemed to push him further into his shell, to rebel, to seek attention through a nonconformist route. His mother, however, would always make sure that he was okay, raising her eyebrows subtly, conspiratorially in his direction as his father might have commented on his appearance for the umpteenth time, pulling him in for a hug, laughing, as he struggled to free himself even though what he really wanted was to remain in her comforting embrace to breathe in that familiar scent, knowing that she truly loved him no matter what.

He was a late developer when it came to an interest in sport, well, full stop if he was to be honest. His first real kiss didn't come until he was 15 and that only really came about because he and his friends had plied the French students (who had been on an exchange trip with families in the village) with cider at a barn dance given in honour of the links between their home town and Weymouth. His memory was vivid, despite forgetting the name of the girl in question, she had mousy, wavy shoulder length hair, freckles, and was yet to develop much of a figure, but she allowed him a full on snog that seemed to go on forever round the back of the village hall before she broke it off in a fit of embarrassed giggles and shared something in her native tongue with her girlfriends who were all either fighting off other local lads half-heartedly or engaging in equally prolific bouts of Anglo/French relations whilst the taste of her remained on his tongue, still tingling after their epic jaw-lock. Within half an hour she had got off with his mate Jaz Downs of course, who claimed the next day that he managed more than just a French kiss, requiring a French letter to complete his Norma conquest, so he had felt deflated at the end result but relieved to at least have been in the game in the first place. That was all part-and-parcel of their teenage years, trial, error, rejection and ritual humiliation.

It was when he was in the year below (in modern money year 9) that he'd noticed how many of the lads who played in the school football team managed to get really fit girlfriends, regardless of how ugly the boys were. There was, it seemed, something about their testosterone fuelled encounters with local rivals on the sports field that stirred the most physically attractive, well developed lasses in the year. Sadly, the more academic girls that he would naturally be around for most of the day, being in the top sets for arts and humanities, left a lot to be desired in the looks department so he began to assimilate information on top teams and formations and soon became fluent in a language that he hoped would be the gateway to broadening his sexual horizons. Useless at any sport, he purchased a Figurine Panini football sticker album and began channelling his pocket money into the purchase of said stickers, building up such a formidable collection that he became known as the 'swopsy' king, or in modern parlance the 'go to guy' at break and lunchtimes. Sadly, such a foray failed to gain him any physical access to the bra wearing cheerleaders from the lower sets but an occasional acknowledgement in the canteen queue represented progress of sorts. Liverpool were the top dogs at the time but it was the majestic Becky Foster who influenced his choice of team.

Becky Foster. Sigh. She would cause a mass weakening of the knees (and other mass activities most evenings as he was sure he wasn't the only one who fantasised about her in the privacy of his own bedroom) as she strode purposefully out onto the netball court, slender legs seeming to go on forever beneath that small pleated navy blue skirt, white Aertex shirt taught across her developing breasts; hair tied up in a ponytail and wearing a Manchester United sweatband on each wrist. That was it then. Mesmerised by her beauty, athleticism and determination, it was clear to Mark that, just as she would always be the only girl for him, United would be the only team.

He was watching her at netball practice one lunchtime, his nose and fingers protruding through the mesh fence when Becky and the almost as lovely Claire Pates thundered towards the goal at 'his end'. The ensuing attack resulted in the ball looping over the fence and rolling to a stop in the long grass just ten or fifteen feet from where he stood ogling. This is my chance to impress her, he had thought, jogging casually towards the hard white ball with such intense focus on putting one foot in front of the other without falling over that he almost went cross-eyed. The ball had become slightly damp from the uncut grass so he struggled to get a good grip before turning to be faced with a line of bright coloured bib wearing teenage girls with letters such as GA or GD emblazoned across their chests, all with hands on hips waiting for the return of their netball. Mark smiled, making clear eye contact with Becky (GS) without a hint of a response as she wore a look of frustration at having her momentum interrupted. Mark had energetically lobbed the ball two handed up towards the top of the mesh fence but his hands had slipped on the greasy circumference and it crashed just halfway up the fence before spiralling back in his direction. Cue groans from the other side of the fence. He now rued the missed opportunities to improve his coordination and catching skills with his father and Johnnie as the rebounding ball hit his outstretched fingers, jarring them in the process, before squirming out of his grasp and back into the damp grass to a chorus of huffs and tuts from the assembled Amazons.

Now more nervous than ever, Mark scrambled for the slippery sphere and, with all the strength he could muster from his skinny arms, turned to hurl it skywards and back over onto the tarmac court but instead, almost as soon as he had unleashed it, the ball had clattered into one of the shiny metal struts that held the flexible fence up and cannoned straight back into his face. The pain was excruciating as he felt the full force smash into his nose, crimson blood immediately spurting forth and splattering over the offending object. Mark had instinctively sunk down onto one knee, his hands covering his face, eyes watering from the intense pain and the sheer embarrassment of it all, of how that tiny shred of credibility and recognition that he'd fought so hard to muster over the past year was evaporating right before his eyes. He could have cried and did everything he could not to.

He remembered the jeers that had followed, the howls of laughter, the wolf whistles and collective slaps on backs of the most popular, pretty and influential group of girls in his year then the piercing screech of the court gate being unlocked and opened and the soft athletic footfall as someone made their way towards him. He felt an arm gently stretch across his shoulder and a casual, "You alright there mate?" Looking up, there she was, the Goddess that was Becky Foster kneeling in the grass next to him, frowning, grey-blue eyes showing real concern, the skin on her legs so smooth, so soft. She leaned in to get a look at his nose, her body smelling faintly of sweat and deodorant, an intoxicating mix. He went giddy as he felt her firm right breast brush against his left arm as she reached back to produce a handkerchief from a pocket at the back of her skirt, on the inside of it, and he thought he'd faint with desire, furthered by the skirt falling open for the briefest, headiest moment, revealing her Daz white pants before she quickly drew it back in. Handing him a white cotton handkerchief, she took possession of the netball, wiping his blood from it on the damp grass where he still knelt, glanced back with a half- smile and a nod, then strode back towards the court, pointing and barking instructions to which the girls all obeyed, scattering back into their positions ready to resume their game. He wasn't demoralised that Becky hadn't known his name, nor that she ever spoke to him again, not even to ask for her hanky back, but he would never forget that magical moment as he crouched, crestfallen in the damp grass, that unexpected and deeply sensual act of kindness that had erased his sense of embarrassment at a stroke, determined his choice of football team for life and stoked his fascination in the fairer sex that had remained with him ever since.

Interestingly enough, by the time he had reached VI Form College most of the swotty girls seemed to have blossomed with many growing confidently into their late teenage figures, whilst the Becky Fosters and Claire Pates' of the world had all found boyfriends with cars that had projected them into a league even further from that within which he operated. So Mark had re-set his aspirations, grown his fringe and accepted his lot, and there just so happened to be a fellow literature student called Rachel McGovern who, for six long months, gave him the most wonderful backstage tour of that mysterious world that the fairer sex inhabits.

He allowed his forehead to loll forward and to one side, resting gently on the cool of the window as he reflected on just how exhausting doing nothing but grieving over lost loved ones was, despite practically an entire day either in bed or on the sofa he felt knackered beyond. Mrs Sheridan had warned him of this and the importance of keeping up some sort of a routine, advice he had taken until the previous 48 hours when his entire being seemed to go into some sort of shut down. He still didn't feel fully booted up. The station stops came and went, Portslade with its working docks, all angular and industrial, Lancing with its delicate spires rising towards the low hanging sludge grey clouds, all the Worthings (East and West), Angmering then Ford with the twin marvels of Arundel's castle and cathedral dominating the gloomy skyline and on they rattled towards Barnham and then Chichester (or Chi as Lizzie had always called it) where he would be picked up by her father who insisted he would take him on to the hotel he'd checked into rather than letting Mark walk or get a cab. Mark couldn't face the prospect of spending a night in Lizzie's family home without her. Trevor had offered him a room of course, but hadn't persisted when Mark said he'd already made a reservation at a hotel in the town. The website had described it as 'A Georgian hotel with marble hall, bar and restaurant'; always the pedant, he was very much looking forward to grabbing a beer in the marble bar before eating in the marble restaurant.

On the seat next to him sat his travel bag, containing the dreaded but obligatory white shirt, black tie and jacket, uniform of the bereaved. He had opted to travel in his black jeans, overcoat and shoes to minimise the amount of luggage he'd need to take with him. Despite plenty of seats still being available, each time a passenger got on the train he reached across and took hold of the handles of the leather holdall, as if to say, "I'll move it if you want the seat." One of his pet hates (of which there were too many to name) was of people hogging seats with their luggage, particularly on trains full of passengers. He had once fumed at the huffy response he had received from a woman when on a train to London a couple of years before, when he had asked her politely to remove her laptop bag and a pile of paperwork from the seat next to her so that he could sit down. She had glared at him and, for a moment, he had thought she was going to refuse his request so he had attempted to expedite the process as there was a queue of irritated passengers forming behind him, all hunting out potential seats in that predatory way of the seasoned commuter.

"Sorry madam, I should have asked, but did you also pay for a seat for your luggage?" to which she had winced ever so slightly so he'd continued, "in which case might I ask you to please stop being so unreasonable and let me have the seat that I have also paid good money for. If you do require more space, I believe you can see the guard and pay for an upgrade to First Class; it's how I usually travel."

He could feel the anger rising just thinking about it. Another character flaw, allowing experiences long since buried or those yet to happen to colour his existing mood. He would fritter away hours whilst in the bath or pottering about in the garden having imaginary conversations with students or colleagues regarding performance or photocopying that never came to fruition thus representing a total waste of mental energy. Lizzie had often encouraged him to 'just enjoy being in the moment', particularly when one of his 'distant looks' descended, usually when Isaac was refusing to eat his spaghetti soup and instead had spread half the contents of his bowl over his head and the rest all over the kitchen table whilst screaming for ice cream. How he longed for such a messy challenge now. The guard announced that they would shortly be stopping at Chichester so he gathered up his coat and bag and made his way towards the door. As the train rattled into the station he clocked Trevor waiting on the platform, in beige raincoat, brolly in hand. So this is it, he thought, taking in a deep breath, the countdown to the funeral really begins here. The train slowed almost to a halt, jolting slightly before finally stopping. Mark opened the door and strode towards his dead wife's ashen-faced father, both greeting the other with a nod and a firm handshake, quickly exiting the station without a word, out into the drizzle that had seeped up from the coast.

275

If this had been the funeral of anyone else but his beloved wife and son then he would have had a completely different set of recollections. His remain shaky, blurred, as if seen through the lens of a drunken cameraman. Right from his waking moment his attitude was set; let's just get through this. He showered, shaved and dressed mechanically, heading down to the breakfast room with a small piece of white bathroom tissue applied to the right side of his neck where he had absent-mindedly cut himself whilst shaving. He had forced two glasses of chilled orange juice down whilst still at the dispenser, wondering why grapefruit juice was still an option (did anyone other than Margot and Jerry drink the stuff), before helping himself to a meagre plate of scrambled eggs on toast with two rashers of bacon, most of which was left on his plate as he accepted the advancing young waiter's offer, nodding towards the taller white jug in his left hand that contained the fresh coffee.

He had gone back up to his room to brush his teeth and collect his overcoat, noticing how grey he looked in the harsh light of the en suite bathroom, how puffy under the eyes. He steadied himself before putting his coat on over his black jacket and heading back down to the reception area for the dreaded wait for the hearse. He sat on an upright occasional chair with a pale blue striped pattern, a matching piece was positioned on the other side of a dark wooden table upon which were fanned piles of leaflets advertising local attractions, mainly featuring the theatre season and art exhibitions. In another life I think we would have been happy here, he thought. Directly opposite and above his seated head height, a huge, ornate gilt framed mirror dominated the cream painted wall, with tall potted plants arranged on either side. He jumped when hearing the swish of the hotel door being opened and nearly crumbled on seeing Trevor, in matching attire, jaw set, eyes slightly downward raise his eyes to his and gesture to the small fleet of cars that waited outside. Oh God, he thought, this really is it.

He had left all the arrangements to Trevor and his mother so hadn't really known what or who to expect. As it happened he was led outside into the bright, chilly morning air to see a row of sleek polished black cars parked on the wide cobbled street outside the elegant hotel, the green-spired cathedral directly opposite. The main mourners' car door was opened for him by a short, broad, clean shaven, grey haired gentleman bedecked in full mourning suit, who managed a welcoming but grim expression all at once, honed from years of experience Mark had thought. He glanced towards the car behind and could just about make out Johnnie and then Sophie, she resembling the widow of a mafia don or maybe a Hollywood legend, with wide rimmed black hat complete with veil and dark glasses; probably from the Prada range 'Mortis Chic'. The children would be with them he had thought, what a day for them. His gaze returned to his car, inside which sat his brother-in-law, Trevor and his father, and from which his mother was emerging, red eyed, a crumpled tissue in her right hand, arms outstretched, probably in anticipation of his reaction at seeing the two pale coffins sitting side by side in the back of the hearse that was parked in front of their car. One was so small that he actually staggered on first setting eyes on it as if he'd been punched in the stomach and he allowed himself to be steadied by a combination of his trembling mother and the strong left arm of the burly undertaker, the name of whom escaped him. He ducked his head and entered the shiny limousine with such plush interior and settled into his seat between his parents. No one said a word but he could see that they felt a part of his pain. His father reached out and placed a large but smooth-skinned hand across the top of his for a full five seconds before withdrawing it, his eyes conveying what his words never could, a gentle sense of care and affection that Mark rarely experienced but sent more gentle shock waves through his emotional fault line on this, the most desperate of days.

He remembers little of the drive to the neat historic flint built church at the heart of the picturesque village where Lizzie grew up other than how flat it all was, the fields consisting of ploughed earth and pale leafless, lifeless trees, shrouded in mist, reminding him of the Paul Nash paintings that were currently on display at the art gallery in Chichester, Pallant House, as he recalled from one of the glossy pamphlets he had seen back at the hotel. They could have been in northern France. He noticed the driver of the car, upright, neck still red from a close shave against a starchy collar, his burly colleague in the passenger seat and how those drivers of oncoming cars changed their expressions as they passed, setting their faces respectfully on seeing the hearse and reducing their speed, apart from one group of rowdy teenagers who continued to shriek with laughter above the boom of the bass (Prodigy?) that emanated from their crowded hatchback as all cars slowed on opposite sides of the road due to a home delivery van, the driver of which was attempting a U-turn. The noise had seemed so intrusive, so disrespectful that Mark had strained to get a better look, maybe to vent his anger, hadn't they seen the convoy, the coffins? But then both cars moved on and the moment passed. Within less than a quarter of an hour they were outside the church of St Mary's and could hear the ominous strains of the organ music piercing the still, chill surround.

Mark had remembered how Lizzie had described this church and its surroundings and how, as a little girl, it had become a playground of awe and wonderment, so he felt a familiarity settle as first he noticed the frost glistening on the sloped slated roof, the sparkling edges gradually fading as the morning sun encroached inch by inch, like an image on a children's drawing board being erased as the artist wiped the slate clean before starting over. As he was gently ushered through the heavy studded oak door and across the threshold into that sacred place that had provided the backdrop to so much in Lizzie's life, and would do so now again in her death, he relished the mustiness and closed his eyes to inhale the air that Lizzie had once breathed but would never do so again. He had made the conscious decision not to visit (strange term) Lizzie and Isaac in the chapel of rest as he had heard too many stories of how loved ones had been 'changed' not beyond all recognition but enough to leave the mourning family members traumatised by the experience. He had so many pictures in his mind (and on Lizzie's laptop) of exactly how he wanted to remember them and was not prepared to have these superseded by ghoulish apparitions wearing too much blusher. He had helped to choose outfits for both. Lizzie was still carrying pregnancy weight, and carrying little Ella Grace who was to be carried to her grave still inside her mother's womb, never to even have gulped in a breath of fresh air before being lowered into the darkness, what would she have looked like, Mark had wondered? So strange to only have ever seen her on a scan; hopefully her mother's skin tone, deep brown eyes, thick dark hair, her beautiful smile. Isaac had been dressed in jeans and a Thomas the Tank Engine hoody that he insisted on wearing everywhere whilst announcing in his prominent lisp 'twouble on the twacth' to whoever he met.

As he was led towards the ancient pews at the front of the church he was aware of the rows of pale faced mourners who had already been seated, some looking down at their feet, others nodding in his direction, but failed to pick out any recognisable faces, which remained the case until the wake afterwards in the village hall as he was in a daze and everyone appeared indistinct from the other.

He was placed on the end of the pew, his mother to his left, Johnnie and his father to hers with Sophie and the children, her parents and sister behind him with further rows containing various aunts, uncles and cousins who didn't hold a significant place in his life but were there all the same. On the other side were Trevor, Stu and his girlfriend, who hadn't been with the funeral cortege and appeared to be in black leather and an assortment of Lizzie's relatives, some of whom he vaguely recognised from their wedding day. The cast was all assembled. Mark yawned nervously then belched into his hands, tasting coffee and scrambled egg, and feared for the worst, but the sudden and rising panic soon subsided and his breakfast slid back down once more.

The Reverend Poe emerged from a small door set into a boat-bow shaped concrete arch to the right of the altar area wearing bright green robes embroidered with gold stitching and clutching a dark blue portfolio, within which would be his copy of the order of service. He made his way across to where they were sitting to shake their hands in a solemn manner and check that they were all ready to proceed. The deepest of breaths, the shakiest of hands, the briefest exchange of glances between those on the front row and the approval was given. The organ, played by the sprightly Mrs Jennings heralded in the pall bearers who made their way with military precision to place those two wooden boxes upon the trestles that had been set out in readiness; one set about four feet apart, the other barely two. He had been bracing himself for this moment, gripping the edge of his pew until his knuckles went white, aware of his mother's right arm resting on his left, but the reality of what was being played out before him was simply overwhelming. He was not aware of any words ever leaving his now dry lips, and hadn't envisaged such an outward show of inner turmoil, but the simplest of words, just a 'NO' reverberated throughout that ancient place of worship as Mark sank to his knees, too distraught to consider putting the thick cushioned brightly embroidered kneeler in place, his bones jarring on the bare stone floor, his hands covering his eyes, shoulders shaking uncontrollably as the grief, raw and unrefined, made its presence felt once more. After a few gasps from the congregation and even a slight pause from Mrs Jennings who missed a beat, the service continued, with Mark being present in body alone. Reverend Poe spoke warmly and eloquently of that 'little ray of sunshine' that was so much like her mother, of how she used to play hide and seek with her brother in the empty church on long wet Sunday afternoons before evensong, of the Easter egg hunts in the churchyard, the Christmas Crib services, the choir recitals, harvest festivals and summer fetes.

Mark did his best to tune in as the Reverend reflected on the deep sorrow felt by so many in the area at the passing of Rose, how close mother and daughter had been, of the inexplicable tragedy that had just passed, of how challenging it can be to discern God's will, how firm Lizzie's belief was and how important it was to support those who were grieving. The readings, one of which was read by Lisa, who it turned out had come with the same set of friends that had shared Lizzie's hen night, talked of a loving God, and a faith full of hope, of rooms being made ready in Paradise, but he was still left feeling so absolutely wretched, numbed by it all that he was unable to see even the slightest ray of hope through the dense, swirling fog on his horizon. The final hymn however, coupled with the removal of the coffins, threatened to tip him into the abyss once more, as the words of 'How Great Thou Art' poured forth, revealing the joy that a believer would feel to be 'called home'.

When Christ shall come with shout of acclamation

And take me home – what joy shall fill my heart!

Then I shall bow in humble adoration

And there proclaim, my God, how great thou art!

It hit him, not for the first time, how a funeral isn't just for grieving for the ones you have lost but for everything you have ever lost and the loss still to come. It is the one place in life where it is quite acceptable to sob uncontrollably without anyone asking you if you are all right. Of course you're not. He felt torn between accepting the concept of the supreme peace that Lizzie, Isaac and Ella Grace must, according to the Christian faith, have experienced at being 'called home' alongside the reality of the ragged, jagged despair that he was experiencing as the one who had been left behind. There was a tension between the deep love that he felt for his precious little family unit and the simmering rage he felt towards God, who has a hand in all things, so both a creator and a destroyer then, as in one of the modern songs that Lizzie so loved and accepted, 'he gives and takes away'. How could anyone want to celebrate that? How could anyone put so much trust in such a malevolent being?

Sobs and sniffs accompanied the congregation as they shuffled out into the mid-morning, the icy air still cold enough to leave little clouds where it collided with warm breath. Around the corner of the church they snaked to the graveyard dominated by an ancient yew tree and dotted with assorted tomb stones, mostly flint grey-hewn slabs sculpted into crosses or angels, many now conceding to the steady spread of moss and relentless assault of sun or sleet, to where the freshly dug mound sat, the damp earth in a neat pile not far from the headstone of Lizzie's mum a couple of rows back near the perimeter wall. Lizzie, Isaac and Ella were to be buried together, both children leaving the world as they would have entered it, with their doting mother in attendance. His brother and father had positioned themselves strategically, both in flanking positions, anticipating further hysterics from Mark at the graveside but both wore looks of compassion and concern and not the usual frowns of disapproval so often reserved for his, to them, abstract behaviour.

Lizzie usually visited her mother's grave alone when they had returned to visit her father so Mark only had her description to go on. She had drawn an accurate picture in his mind, the gentle slopes, grassy knolls, wooden benches with bronze memorial plaques, huge foreboding yew (apparently with a thick hollow trunk that lent itself to hide and seek and all manner of imaginative games that Lizzie, her brother and generations of village children growing up in that corner of West Sussex had enjoyed over the centuries). The low flint wall that bordered the rectangular garden of rest, allowing views across the farmland for miles save for a small copse that sat right in the middle of the nearest field thus obstructing a chunk of the rural idyll. The surrounding farmland, held in the freezing grip of winter, nothing moved save the occasional flutter of the St George's flag on a pole high above the mourner's huddle. Mark was suddenly reminded of a Christmas Carol called 'In the Deep Midwinter' that always made him want to cry ever since he was a boy but he could never remember why. Two raucous rooks suddenly flapped and cawed in a nearby tree before wheeling away towards the west adding to the sense of the Gothic macabre; rooks, a freezing churchyard shrouded with mist, a funeral presided over by a Poe; on another day he would have warmed to this literary connection, the type he would have shared with his students, but on this day he wondered if he would ever feel anything but ice in his veins again.

The words spoken by a priest at the graveside are so familiar, more so from the movies or TV dramas than through personal experience that they usually passed him by, today they were barely audible. It was as if a screen had been set up allowing him to see everything that was happening all around him but unable to take in what was being said or engage with any of it. He also felt a step or two off the pace, light headed, distant, vacant. Were those words really for them, for him? Had his beautiful wife, son and unborn daughter really been packed into little wooden boxes to be lowered into a hole in the ground, to be covered in damp earth and left to rot, ultimately becoming food for the worms, their dry bones one day being bulldozed to make way for fresh corpses? This seemed too barbaric, too final, too primeval, was he the only one who could see this? Fortunately for Mark his brother was alert enough to notice him close his eyes and sway before murmuring something under his breath and lunge towards the ropes as the larger of the two coffins was being lowered into the freshly dug grave. It took all his strength, assisted by his father and, he found out later, Vaz and Stu to pull him away as Mark was now beyond reasoning with, his eyes wild, body shaking with the cold and the trauma of seeing his family now so emphatically out of his reach. The undertakers resumed this grim descent as the four men calmed Mark down, allowing his breathing to return to something resembling normality before letting him go once more. The respite was brief as Mark then hurled himself onto the mound at the graveside letting out a scream that was so piercing, so raw that the remaining rooks in the vicinity scattered into the wind and the mourners began to disperse, shaking their heads in sympathy, rubbing their hands together against the cold, leaving Mark on his knees, wailing into the breeze, his fingers clawing at the earth whilst his tears ran down his face and dropped off his chin to mingle with the mud and remaining morning dew.

*

He had never been one bound by convention, social or otherwise, so couldn't wait to get out of the village hall where tea, coffee and sandwiches were being served. The atmosphere was suffocating. For a start there were too many people and the noise of their conversations, restored to full volume after the hushed tones of church and graveyard, made his head swim. Add the extreme heat as the radiators must have been on full blast and he had come out in a sweat. Then there was the small talk and well meaning comments such as "what a loss" (you don't say) "you have our sincerest condolences" (what does that really mean anyway) "they had their whole lives ahead of them" (thanks for reminding me) and "at least it wasn't raining, that always seems to make it even worse somehow, a funeral in the rain." (How could it possibly get any worse, do you think I would have cared, I would have welcomed the rain, come on, do your worst!) He desperately needed a drink.

Lisa and co were at least a meaningful link to Lizzie and they managed the right balance of not gushing with platitudes nor drowning him in a flood of mundane comments. He spoke briefly with Vicky, Lizzie's old friend from Chichester who seemed almost translucent she was so pale, with Janice and Sue from Lizzie's team, with Sophie's sister Tamara who had also managed to look sombre and chic and with Sophie who was the warmest and most sincere that Mark had ever had the privilege of witnessing. It turned out that Sophie had been keeping a watchful eye on Mark from a distance, even booking into the same hotel with Johnnie and the children so that he wouldn't be left on his own that evening; he was definitely beginning to see a different side to his sister-in-law. Both his parents were doing their very best to appear sociable and grateful for the attendance of all and sundry, his father looking extremely strained by the whole process whereas his mother always excelled in situations such as these, shaking hands warmly and immediately putting people at ease by remembering a face or a family connection. Trevor looked as stunned and as lost as Mark felt, as he stood on the fringes, still wearing his raincoat and clutching a green china cup and saucer as if his life depended on it. Mark detached himself from the group of Lizzie's close friends that he was half listening to and made his way over to stand side by side with his father-in-law, neither of them speaking, but simply acknowledging the presence of the other and the loss they had shared. It was Trevor who broke the silence, with a small cough to clear his throat whilst leaning across to place his cup and saucer back on the service counter, thanking sincerely the ladies who had provided it.

"I'm not one for speeches Mark, I think you know that. Nor am I one for great shows of emotion. But I am one to give credit where credit's due. You really grew into it, your role as husband and father, despite some reservations that I might have had, and it was clear to all who ever saw you together how much you adored Lizzie and Isaac, and how this was reciprocated. I just want to say thank you Mark, for loving my girl the way you did, and for bringing her so much happiness. I will treasure the memories I have of her, always, of course, but also of my grandson, whose new life did so much to help me to come to terms with the loss of Rose who, of course, would have spoiled him rotten. You are a good man Mark and I hope that one day you will be able to build a new life for yourself. You know that you will always be welcome if ever you want to visit. I am just so sorry for you, for us all that we now have this huge loss to deal with. Keep going though son, don't give up will you and remember just how much Lizzie loved you and believed in you."

Mark was so surprised at the tenderness in the tone of this little man he had thought was made of granite, so touched at his sentiment that tears pushed forth and stained his cheeks once more. He opened his mouth to respond in kind but no words would come forth. Trevor simply put out his hand as if to say 'no need' and the two exchanged a firm handshake, Trevor placing one hand on Mark's shoulder then turned on his heel and went, back to his little cottage, where new layers of sorrow had settled and must be dealt with over time. Mark blew out through his cheeks and then found a hand on his elbow, it was Sophie, perfumed and poised as she scanned her surroundings like a hawk at a roadside cutting.

"How are you bearing up?" she enquired, continuing before he had a chance to answer, "A far cry from Harvey Nicks this, isn't it? I think my fur is the only one that (a) is real and (b) doesn't reek of urine and mothballs." She was attempting humour, and he appreciated her efforts as it had never seemed to come naturally to her. "If you're looking for an excuse to leave, Tiggy and Harry are getting a bit restless so Johnnie has promised them a trip to some local Roman ruin or other. All sounds dreadfully dull to me but at least it would let us all off the hook? We could get you back to Chichester, get a decent drink and something to eat that isn't a potted ham sandwich then you could get some rest. No offence but you look bloody awful, even more so than usual."

"Don't pull any punches, will you? We'll all think you were going soft," Mark replied with a smile so Sophie knew that he was recognising her way of being supportive, even if it had to contain caustic comments. "What are mum and dad doing?"

"They're heading straight back to Dorset on our advice and we said we'll look after you. I think they have visions of you getting blind drunk and drowning yourself in a river, or even worse, getting yourself arrested. The first scenario would be manageable but the shame of the latter would be unthinkable."

Again, humour, he thought. Maybe she wasn't such an evil bitch after all. They were joined by a red-faced Johnnie, who shook his head in Mark's direction as if to say 'words fail me old boy' and the children who were trying to hide their boredom by hugging Mark and telling him how sorry they were about Aunty Lizzie whilst tugging on their father's jacket sleeve and asking when they could go. Within minutes they had extracted themselves from the lingering groups of mourners, having first sought out Vaz, his colleagues and Lizzie's close friends to bid farewell, and made their way out into the now milder early afternoon, a weak sun at last having made its presence felt. Stu and his girlfriend were leaning against a tree chatting and smoking so Mark and he exchanged a nod and a 'right' before Mark received a hug from his mum, a handshake and pat on the shoulder from his dad (it must be a generational thing with him and Trevor he thought, they probably think it some form of homosexual act for two grown men to hug regardless of them being family) before he and Johnnie's lot piled into a silver people carrier taxi (ordered by Sophie of course) and away from that quaint picture postcard scene that would forever represent the extremes of joy and loss that would accompany Mark wherever he went from that point onwards.

*

"I know that there really isn't anything at all that one can say at a time like this, but please don't interpret a lack of words as a lack of care. The whole family has felt this, Mark, right to its core. Your father has by all accounts hardly slept a wink, your mother has been at her wits' end worrying about you, your brother feels so guilty that he can hardly bear to look at you and as for the children, well they have been distraught, Tiggy in particular. Lizzie made such a huge impact on us all."

Sophie was picking her way through a Caesar salad back at the hotel, they had made it just in time to grab a bite in the (granite) restaurant. She had practically forced Mark to order a burger and fries to soak up the lager he was consuming at, in her view, an alarming rate. After a change of clothes, Johnnie had taken Tiggy and Harry to the old Roman Palace at Fishbourne. Sophie and Mark were still wearing their mourning attire, her hat removed and hair teased into its usual perfect position, sunglasses as ever perched atop her head. There was just one other couple in the restaurant and they were ordering coffee after desserts. Mark was sure he heard one of them mention Keats but couldn't be sure. He began to recite Ode on Melancholy in his head before remembering he had company.

"But what about you Sophie?" Mark asked, half-heartedly dipping a chip into a small white ramekin containing barbecue sauce.

"What about me?" she replied, taking a small sip from a cold glass of Chardonnay.

"How do *you* feel?" Mark continued. "In all the time I've known you there are a few things that have become pretty clear to me, one, that you think I am a total loser and a complete waste of space, two, that you wouldn't be seen dead having lunch with me if circumstances hadn't forced this upon us, please excuse the pun, three, that you took to Lizzie despite wondering what on earth she might see in me, probably because you thought she might drag me up from the gutter where you imagined I spent half my life, and four how you always manage to convey a view but seem to hold something back, always a barrier, unless you're bollocking Johnnie for ogling the backside of a waitress that is, never quite revealing your hand. I wonder how you're actually *feeling* in all of this, Sophie, after all I believe that you are capable of feeling and death can be a catalyst to reflecting on how we live, right?"

Sophie placed her wine glass very deliberately on the white tablecloth and looked across at Mark, fixing him with a new expression, not one of disdain nor of pity so it threw him momentarily as it was bordering on respect. "You have made some pretty astute observations there Mark so maybe too much beer doesn't always have a negative effect on you. True, I never have quite understood you, why you didn't seem to want to make anything of your life, choosing to live like a student decades after ceasing to become one and even after teaching them, circumstances have thrown us together in a way that neither would have chosen, but here we are all the same." She paused to take a sip from a glass of San Pellegrino before continuing, "I agree, I took to Lizzie right from the word go and no I couldn't work out what she saw in you at first but then the more I saw of you together the more I got it."

"Got what?" Mark was draining his third pint of lager and gesturing to the barman for another.

"Why it worked." Sophie half smiled, "Your relationship was not based on some matrix of what makes a good match, of what would be mutually acceptable to the respective families, it was not a trade, a deal; it was based on something far more basic than that, the fact that you clicked. Anyone could see that. Sure, at a glance you might think how on earth did he manage to catch her, she was after all an absolute stunner, but she looked past your scruffy appearance, and dare I say, laissez-faire approach to life and clearly saw more than the rest of us, probably because she was prepared to invest the time in getting to know you rather than writing you off because you didn't tick the boxes that most of us insist on being ticked."

"Money, job, status, prospects and all that," Mark drawled, drawing on his fresh pint.

"All that," Sophie said with a resigned tone. It was quiet for a few moments as Mark pushed the last of his fries around his plate and Sophie took another small sip from her wine glass before going on, "Of course it came as a relief to all of us to see you so happy and settled and not shirking from the responsibilities of marriage and family life but it wasn't all about what Lizzie did for you. Look what you gave her in turn, you adored her, you made her feel good about herself, you supported her in her career, and I doubt you ever tried to make her change, to conform to your views of how a wife should look, act, speak? You simply loved her for who she was and that was clearly reciprocated. You brought out the best in each other Mark, it wasn't all one way traffic."

"Wow," Mark responded, beginning to slur his words a little now, "so the Ice Maiden really does have a heart after all."

"Careful, I can freeze back over pretty quickly." Sophie raised her eyebrows as if to warn Mark not to push it despite the circumstances.

"Sorry Soph, but you have always seemed such a closed book, there has to be a reason for that just as there are reasons why I became such a dosser."

"Sorry, was that with a 't' or a 'd' as you're beginning to slur your words? Can't blame you though. I'd probably be knocking back a few if I'd just buried Johnnie, more in celebration though. Sorry, that was in poor taste. But as you're asking, and this has become like some frightful heart to heart from a US made for TV drama, I'll continue, knowing full well that you'll be too pissed to remember a word of it by teatime let alone in the morning. Imagine, if you will, the life of the eldest daughter of a high-ranking army officer who then went into the diplomatic corps, always on the move, always having to start afresh, always under scrutiny and protection. Consider the precision, the protocol, the practicalities and you end up becoming a product of the environment, of the system, one that favours a cool head over a hot heart. So your 'ice maiden' was not birthed but created, evolving over the years, conforming to the regimentation, the regime, the rigours of overseas empirical existence and meeting all expectations along the way so as not to have let the side down. So, there you have it."

Through the slight beery haze that always descends after a few pints at lunchtime, Mark saw quite a different sister-in-law. Slightly out of focus, admittedly, but opening up more in the past hour than in all the years that he had known her. In his fuzzy mind he had just managed to form an adequate and eloquent response to her description of her upbringing and how clearly that had shaped her character and how he shouldn't have been so judgemental as we are all the sum of our influences, memories and experiences but could only manage, instead, a huge, echoing burp, that caused the barman and the couple drinking their coffee to stop what they were doing and glare disapprovingly in his direction.

"Quite the philosopher, then," Sophie quipped.

"Must have a pee before I wet myself," he commented before pushing back his chair abruptly, causing it to screech on the wooden floor. He turned unsteadily bashing into the table behind them that had been set for the pre-theatre dinner set, causing the glasses to shake and clink loudly and the by now bored barman to look across angrily once more.

When he returned, swaying and bleary eyed, Sophie was standing in her most upright position, like a Norland Nanny, jacket back on and hat in hand. "Bed," she commanded.

"My, this heart to heart has taken a most unexpected turn," Mark announced, through a spluttering laugh that turned into a hearty cough.

"We'll put that down to the booze and the grief shall we?" Sophie clipped, whilst ushering Mark out of the restaurant, apologising to any who could hear, that it had been a most trying day so far.

*

He knew that he was going to broach the subject sooner or later and equally knew that he was putting it off. He should have had a perfectly clear conscience, after all it was nothing to do with him that Soames got himself caught up with that little tart, but it was irritating that she had known Lizzie, that narrowed the boundaries somewhat. It was beyond macabre that he had been on the phone to Soames at the precise moment that he had run down and killed Lizzie, somehow Mark would find him culpable despite him not being in any way involved, let alone responsible. He had been left to sweat over the release of the £100K that Guy owed him as all Soames' assets had been frozen and his passport confiscated whilst he was out on bail pending the court case. Of course it would be in his best interests if Soames did get off with a slap on the wrist and a hefty fine, if he was sent down then how would he explain to Sophie that he had allowed Soames to pay for Chez Corfu in instalments due to cash flow and the expansion of his restaurant business that Johnnie was also a stakeholder in and that they might not see the money for some time, if at all. Didn't bear thinking about. Whichever way he cut it, he was in it up to his what-sits. Bloody business called for a Bloody Mary he thought so he headed down to the hotel bar, fresh from a shower, to wait for his errant brother who would, no doubt, be late.

*

Mark had fallen into a sleep typical of one induced by too much lunchtime booze; fitful, light and vivid. He had dreamed that he and Lizzie were strolling along the cliff tops back home in Dorset, hand in hand, with Isaac just a few steps ahead of them. It was a hazy afternoon in late summer and a heavily pregnant Lizzie looked radiant in floral dress and wide brimmed straw summer hat as she let go of his hand to catch up with Isaac, turning to laugh at something he had said as she did so. He closed his eyes and raised his head towards the sun, pushing his sunglasses up to feel its full power and warmth. Suddenly, a scream of warning from Lizzie as Isaac started to stagger too close to the cliff edge. She lifted the hem of her dress and ran after him, just making it in time to grab his right arm with hers as he disappeared over the tufts of long grass that swayed in a gentle breeze. Turning to face Mark she placed her left hand protectively over her tummy and mouthed, 'I love you' before being jerked backwards and out of sight, now hurtling down towards the crashing waves and jagged rocks below with Isaac. "Lizzieeee," Mark howled, waking suddenly and jerking into an upright position. He panted frantically before dropping his head back onto the thick foamy pillow that he had plumped up behind his head before dozing off, a light sheen of sweat across his lip and forehead, his mouth as dry as sandpaper. He glanced at the time on his phone that still lay in his left hand, 18:02. Just enough time for a shower and change of clothes ahead of drinks with Johnnie at the bar; a prospect that neither of them appeared to be relishing.

*

Most of the now familiar journey along the A27 had been conducted in silence; not the edgy silence that is palpable after an argument or a heated

289

exchange of harsh words but that which descends when thoughts need to be reflected upon, ordered, re-ordered when there is a need to make sense of it all, once *it* has been identified to start with. Mark had allowed his body to sink into the plush leather armchair of a passenger seat in the Range Rover, tilting his head to stare vacantly out of the window whilst Johnnie, fingers only lightly touching the mahogany steering wheel acted more as a pilot than driver, as there were so many instruments in the cockpit that it felt as if the car was on autopilot; Johnnie seemed as if he was in a similar mode, not his usual chatty, vulgar self by any stretch. Mark took his brother's more thoughtful demeanour as something bordering on a sense of occasion and respect but even that didn't ring true, he seemed more preoccupied than anything and Mark was attempting to figure out why. He was nurturing a hunch that, not for the first time, he was missing something. Sophie had driven back up to town in her CLK the previous night with the children leaving the 'boys' to it. They'd had a couple of drinks in the hotel bar before heading into Chichester for a few more, eventually settling for a curry. After their first couple of drinks in a wine bar Johnnie had taken a deep breath and addressed the link with Guy Soames, that murdering bastard (Mark) unfortunate driver in that most tragic accident (Johnnie). He reminded Mark of a visit he, Sophie and the kids had made one Sunday afternoon a few years back when Harry had puked all over Mark on his doorstep to which Mark had managed to raise a smile. It had turned out that Johnnie had taken Soames and his family out for lunch that day to butter him up in advance of a business proposition. Not only had Guy taken the bait, as it were, but had ended up buying the seafood restaurant along with half a dozen others, of which Johnnie was now a partner. On the fateful day of the accident Johnnie had made a routine call to Guy about share prices ahead of a board meeting when Soames had told him that he'd been the victim of an awful scam in which two tarts had got him pissed, probably drugged him, had blagged their way into his home and fleeced him of his wallet containing credit cards and hundreds of quid in cash. He had been in such a state due to the booze (he'd been on the sauce since the previous lunchtime and had no idea what those toms had put in the champagne that evening) that he couldn't remember much about the night at all and was terrified that these low-lives may have taken photos of him in a compromising position that they might then use to blackmail him with. His wife and daughters were due back from abroad later that day so he wanted to resolve the issue before picking them up at the airport. I bet he did Mark had thought.

It was whilst he was in the process of tracking down one of the tarts involved in the scam that he had swerved to avoid Lizzie and Isaac who had been in the middle of the road. It was a gruesome twist of fate that he had just happened to be on speakerphone when that appalling accident had occurred. He had asked Mark how Lizzie had been that morning, was she overtired due to her pregnancy, distracted maybe by her change of plans and had she ever let Isaac out of her reach before so near to a busy road. It may have been that the girl guilty of scamming Guy was going to 'fess up' to Lizzie which was why she had called her – did that girl have a history of fraud perhaps, a criminal record? His line of enquiry had rankled with Mark, despite the almost too deliberate softness to his brother's questioning tone. There was also the fact that, unbeknown to Johnnie, Mark had heard Hope's side of the story and it certainly didn't tally with the account of events that Johnnie had shared. Was his brother being played by this Soames? If so, what a piece of work, but if not, was Mark being gently manipulated, manoeuvred into place for an endgame he couldn't see coming? He had laid awake in his hotel room the night before, conscious that the pieces just didn't fit even through a beery haze, but equally aware of the rising heartburn due to the Chicken Jalfrezi and an overwhelming desire to sleep despite these nagging thoughts and that the room seemed to be on a gentle spinning cycle.

*

His home had returned to precisely what it had been before he'd married Lizzie, a house, albeit with a better taste in interior design and soft furnishings. They had embarked upon their modernisation programme with such gusto; well, mostly Lizzie, but had shared the experience, the excitement of creating a home, *their* home where they would embrace the early months of married life, to make plans to have a family, to dream, to bask in the newness of it all and the limitless opportunities that lay within and beyond their freshly painted walls.

Mark had reflected before on how the absence of Lizzie and Isaac had become a presence, not in a spooky way, but more a heaviness, a melancholy that had seeped into the cavity walls and now insulated their former family home, a deep sense of sorrow that would reside in that place for as long as he did. He knew that he couldn't live there any longer and yet couldn't bear to be apart from the backdrop to so many precious scenes that formed the narrative to the most unexpected, breathtaking and memorable chapters of his entire life. It was as if he had been shuffling along in an emotional daze until he had met her, before she had unlocked a range of feelings he had only read about or scoffed at in the movies. He could remember every detail of that crappy seminar in that drab building, the way she colluded with her colleagues without ever seeming harsh towards him, bumping into her in the pub that evening, then again at college in the senior common room; heart-poundingly stunning, her hair, her eyes, her smile, her figure!

What on earth did she ever see in me he thought, shaking his head, holding her winter scarf in one hand, still with the scent of her and a small metal Thomas the Tank Engine that he had just found rammed down the back of one of the cushions of the armchair upon which he was slumped. The gloom of the lounge, curtains still closed, was almost suffocating, likewise the sheer size of the task ahead, not just how to deal with the overwhelming sense of grief and loss but the practicalities, the sorting, the shifting, the throwing, the keeping, the recycling, the charity shop giving. It was all too much. He now dreaded returning to the life he had convinced himself he had wanted all along, with loneliness and isolation revealing themselves from behind the pillars of solitude and freedom that he had mistaken them for all his life. He knew that it was better to have loved and lost then never to have loved before but the splintering cracks that he felt shattering his heart and his mind frightened him. He knew that he was slipping, that he was losing the battle for sanity and serenity and that he would be forever lost unless he had help. He felt like a child again, retreating into a world of comic books and superheroes as mortality and reality were just too harsh to face. He had to decide for himself whether to let go and sink beyond trace into the swirling depths or find a reason to haul himself up onto the rocks and re-establish a foothold, no matter how slight. Sitting in the dark and cold alone in the limbo between the funeral and the service of remembrance he was afraid that the former option felt increasingly inevitable.

He had seen a documentary a few months before about functioning alcoholics (he was watching more and more informative TV since being married to Lizzie as she had proved to be a positive influence on him, simply giving jack about the world around them and the people in it, a previously alien concept to the insular peninsular that was Mark Woodford) after which Lizzie had raised an eyebrow and patted him on the knee before heading into the kitchen to make them both a coffee. He had asked her about this gesture as they sipped their Gold Blend de-caff and shared a bar of Fruit & Nut. Lizzie had noticed that Mark couldn't go a single evening without a cold beer or two before supper, a large glass of wine if he was on cooking duty and at least two maybe three with their supper to her one/one and a half. She was keen not to come across as being judgemental but in her Lizzie way challenged him on this, whether or not he craved the beer and wine or just drank out of habit? Did every meal need practically a full bottle of wine or would a glass do? Mark had been typically defensive but she had hit a nerve as his default mode since his teens had been to hide behind something; Marvel characters followed by a long fringe followed by a long binge – he had needed these props, these crutches as he had always felt socially inadequate, inept, happier when being apart from rather than a part of the seething mass of shallowness and hypocrisy that society represented to him.

He hated it when the likes of Lisa and Lizzie's other church friends came round for dinner as all they wanted to do was talk about 'what God was doing in their lives' and would often go the entire evening drinking half a glass of dry white wine that made his constant topping up of his own glass all the more conspicuous despite his jokes about Jesus turning water into wine and then how they had all probably got pissed on it, as it was the good stuff. On one such evening he launched into a (he thought hilarious) tipsy soliloquy about what a laugh it would be to be at a wedding and witness Jesus getting pissed and turning people who hated him into frogs or statues. It later dawned on him why Lizzie had got back into the habit of going to Lisa's for their midweek catch up, maybe it wasn't just for a change of scene but through embarrassment at Mark's offensive drink-fuelled humour and a non-appreciative audience. She had been right – his drinking had become an issue.

When Johnnie, Vaz or Pete formed their company he felt he could up the ante as they all enjoyed a few glasses. Lizzie had raised an important question; did he feel that he may be drink-dependant (to which he had answered an honest yes). The second part of that question was harder to deal with as it explored reasons why and possible steps to be taken to resolve the situation. He had remembered suddenly being overcome by tiredness, yawning theatrically and pointing to an early start in the morning (10am but still early for him) in what Lizzie had later classified as 'classic avoidance techniques'. He adored Lizzie beyond imagination but wished sometimes that she wasn't quite so insightful, nor gently persistent as he felt uncomfortable when digging around for reasons why he hit the booze so hard and so regularly, despite toning it all down since getting married, and even more so when Isaac had come along. The truth was he knew that

293

he had it in him to be an alcoholic and the doors to that potential pathway loomed larger now than ever before. He had to get a grip but he was struggling to find something to cling on to.

*

"Get off me you sodding fascist!" Mark screamed, as he was led out of the bar by two bouncers dressed in regulation black shirts and jackets, one of whom had the fingers of Mark's right hand bent back and up with one huge meaty hand whilst his other hand was placed flat to his elbow as if the slightest pressure up or down would lead to a sickening sound of bone splintering. Mark was on his tiptoes as he was marched out and the pain was excruciating but the bruiser hardly seemed to be making any effort, he hadn't even broken sweat. His colleague, grim faced and gum chewing, opened the door and he was hit by a blast of freezing cold air that made his eyes water. Hope was tottering alongside him due to her high heels, not a restraint and control technique, and spoke with the bouncers who she was on first-name terms with in rapid tone, pointing back into the bar area. They both nodded and let Mark go with a gentle shove in the back as she told them she'd 'sort it' whilst wrapping a handful of loo roll into a ball to stop the flow of blood that was streaming down Mark's forehead. What on earth (or in heaven) would Lizzie be thinking of all this he had thought as he glanced up at the cloudy night sky, the moon partially blocked by an ominous looking grey mass, "what have I become without you my love," he sobbed loudly as he retched against a wall, leaning his forehead against it and wincing as the rough, gritty mortar from between the brickwork stabbed into the cut, opening it up once more.

The evening had started shakily, with Mark downing three brandies at home before Johnnie had arrived to pick him up for the church service. Mrs S had been round earlier that afternoon to pay her respects, to see how he had been coping and to explain that she wouldn't be attending that evening on account of the service being in one of those loud, trendy modern Protestant churches but "God rest Lizzie's immortal soul all the same," she had added whilst putting a homemade cottage pie in the oven for when he got back in later. "Just put it on gas mark 5 for 30 minutes dear." She half sang as she let herself out the way he had let herself in. Sophie, Harry and Tiggy were in the back of the Range Rover, with Sophie struggling to maintain her Falcon's Crest aura with a lack of leg room compared to that in the front, with Mark riding shotgun. Harry was full of observations on the church they were heading to, the fact that it actually played rock music and that there was even a picture of a woman curate on their website whilst Tiggy hushed him up; Sophie seemed happy with this abdication of her iron rule, patting Mark on the right shoulder and asking if he was okay before settling back the best she could between her two bickering little darlings.

The service was everything that Mark had expected, packed, loud in places, reflective in others; maybe not as gut wrenchingly raw as the actual burial but respectful and fitting in its own way, as after all, this was Lizzie's spiritual home. The tribute from Lisa was as powerful and poignant as if Mark was hearing and seeing it for the first time and the songs were surprisingly moving, the lyrics of which were projected onto a huge screen at the front of the church and smaller screens attached to the walls down each side. His mother and father had chosen to remain in Dorset and he thought this a good idea as his mother in particular would be so busy making comments on the modern way things were done that she would be at risk of letting the meaningfulness pass her by. Bless her.

Just as at the funeral, when the words of 'How Great Thou Art' had brought him to his knees this time it was a song that, apparently, was another of Lizzie's favourites, called 'In Christ Alone'. He was frozen in his spot as he read the lyrics, even finding himself miming along in that way a foreign manager of the England national team does on TV when hearing the national anthem of the team he coaches being played, knowing millions of viewers at home expect him to know the words off by heart, despite him being a Swede or an Italian. He felt a bit of a fraud but was drawn somehow to joining in.

In Christ alone my hope is found,
He is my light, my strength, my song;
this Cornerstone, this solid Ground,
firm through the fiercest drought and storm.
What heights of love, what depths of peace,
when fears are stilled, when strivings cease!
My Comforter, my All in All,
here in the love of Christ I stand.

In Christ alone! who took on flesh
Fullness of God in helpless babe!
This gift of love and righteousness
Scorned by the ones he came to save:
Till on that cross as Jesus died,
The wrath of God was satisfied -
For every sin on Him was laid;
Here in the death of Christ I live.

There in the ground His body lay
Light of the world by darkness slain:
Then bursting forth in glorious Day
Up from the grave he rose again!
And as He stands in victory
Sin's curse has lost its grip on me,
For I am His and He is mine -
Bought with the precious blood of Christ.

No guilt in life, no fear in death,
This is the power of Christ in me;
From life's first cry to final breath.
Jesus commands my destiny.
No power of hell, no scheme of man,
Can ever pluck me from His hand;
Till He returns or calls me home,
Here in the power of Christ I'll stand.

It was when they sang 'There in the ground his body lay' that the floodgates opened once more as he pictured that freezing corner of West Sussex with the freshly dug grave, the flint walls, the frost, the rooks, the feeling of utter desolation as the bodies of those he loved so deeply were lowered into the ground and he was left on his knees clawing at the earth as he was separated from them for ever. But in this song, death was not the end as they erupted into 'then bursting forth in glorious day' with a section of the congregation actually cheering at this point, leaping up and down, tears of joy in their eyes, their arms raised, looks of total ecstasy on their faces. 'From life's first cry to final breath' prompted a flashback to when he first held Isaac in that regulation green blanket to when he last kissed his warm soft head as he was about to head out into the perishing cold of that final morning, and then again this idea of being 'called home', were they really at that 'better place' that everyone deep down hoped there would be without all having that unshakeable belief that it exists?

Mark bowed his head, trying to gather his spinning thoughts, angry with himself that he had even considered that there might be anything in this religious tripe that had been used to brainwash the great unwashed for centuries. It was the emotion of the occasion he had concluded, the pictures of Lizzie and Isaac, the loud music, the euphoria from some sections of the congregation that can prove to be intoxicating, infectious, can't it? Just think of the Nuremberg rally; that was electric. He was out of control again, internally, and knew he needed air. As calmly as he could manage he took a step to his right into the aisle, turned and walked with his head facing the floor towards the back of the church. Johnnie had instinctively gone to follow but Sophie had placed an arm across his as if she knew that Mark needed to be left alone and that he wouldn't be coming back to join the fruit punch brigade for the refreshments afterwards.

The music still pounded from within the building as he leaned back on the wall outside, breathing heavily. He noticed a small glow of orange followed by a jet of smoke to his left accompanied by a slight sniffle. As his eyes became accustomed to the gloom of the winter's evening he realised that it was Hope, having a cigarette and perhaps even shedding a tear or two.

"Thanks for coming Hope, are you okay?" he said quietly, moving in her direction.

"Oh hi Mark," she replied, as if snapped out of her thoughts, "I'm fine, but how are you bearing up?" she added whilst exhaling a stream of smoke once more. "I mean that was pretty heavy going in places for me so heaven knows how you were feeling."

"Heaven knows indeed. That's if it ever existed," Mark sighed. "Lizzie believed without a shred of doubt that it did, so according to her belief and that of the church, she'll be up there now bouncing Isaac on her knee whilst sharing a hot chocolate with Jesus. But what about Ella Grace? She was never born so how can she be dead and resurrected into eternal glory? Bursting forth on glorious day and all that bollocks?"

"I don't know Mark," Hope frowned, "I've never really given it any thought, until now that is."

"I don't know about you," he said, "but I could murder a drink and we're not in any danger of getting one here, not the type that I need anyway."

Hope had questioned Mark on whether he should stay and chat to those who had attended the service and thank everyone who had put it together but he felt that he had done quite enough talking this week and not enough drinking. It turned out that Hope had booked a few hours off before she had to work later that evening so they headed down past the Pavilion and towards the more familiar environment to both of them, the pubs and bars of Hove seafront. They had been in the Funky Buddha when Mark was returning, unsteadily, from the loo that he saw a bloke having a go at Hope whilst another looked on, turning his head from side to side to take in his surroundings. Despite wearing his binge drinking goggles this didn't look right at all. The one doing the talking looked totally out of place; he was clean-shaven with gelled wavy hair and a ruddy complexion in pink shirt, jeans, brown suede loafers and long brown coat with velvet collar, the sort favoured by city bankers and hedge fund managers. The bloke with him wasn't that tall but had a definite air of menace about him, shaven headed with a trim goatee, black crew- necked top and leather jacket, dark trousers and shoes. Like a designer hit man Mark had thought. The beers, tequila and Jack Daniel's had reduced his capacity for clear, coherent, cogent thought but this was obviously not a good situation he concluded as he stumbled his way over towards the corner where they had led Hope. Just for a moment he thought that he recognised the toff, but couldn't place him. Was it from real life, the TV, the papers, or was he one of Johnnie's friends or business associates perhaps? Then the penny dropped and it dawned on him; it was all of the above. The one pointing his finger at Hope's chest was Guy Soames, the man who had murdered his family. He knew he only had one shot at this because if he was identified by the minder he wouldn't stand a chance so he returned to where their drinks still stood on the bar and tried to think of a plan. Slowly one begun to form.

Minutes later, having left his jumper and jacket on his bar stool, now just in black T-shirt and jeans, he did everything he could to walk in a straight line as he cleared empty glasses from the low tables and returned them to the bar. It was loud, busy and cramped so he knew no one would question him. He just needed a few more seconds to edge near to where Hope stood, gesticulating, fighting her corner but with a look of fear that he hadn't ever associated with her. As he reached them he smiled at each of the group in turn and said to Hope, "Excuse me, madam, whilst I just punch the man who murdered my family." There was a moment's pause whilst his words sunk in, confusion reigned as the pounding bass hindered an assimilation of what was going on and before anyone could react he threw an absolute haymaker in the direction of Soames, his fist connecting with the pasty flesh around Soames' mouth at precisely the same time as he found himself being hurled sideways and onto a table by goatee, a table that, unfortunately, he hadn't yet cleared of glasses. Within seconds the bouncers had arrived and, he felt, dealt with the situation heavy-handedly. The minder of Soames had got him up onto his feet and was in the process of getting him out of the bar as the two black shirts descended on Mark and manhandled him in some sort of ju-jitsu hold whilst Hope tottered along behind, with the presence of mind to pick up his jumper and jacket and prevent him from taking a kicking for causing such pandemonium. Not for the first time in recent history he had no recollection of how he had got home but he later found out that Hope had taken him up to Preston Park in a taxi and had made sure he was okay before hopping back into it and back down to the seafront clubs to do a night's work. He could remember a rage rising up from deep inside him and the realisation that he was now so totally alone in the world; words could not express his sense of isolation. He can remember wanting to express his anger, his feelings of utter futility but that was all. Then, darkness.

*

"OH. MY. GOD. You, upstairs NOW!"

Everything was so bleary that he thought he might still be dreaming. He could only open his eyes a fraction as the light hurt them so much that he moaned audibly and the hammer and anvil on loan from Tom and Jerry was still pounding inside his head. He remembered seeing some weird stuff like the huge TV that had sprouted legs and chairs that were somehow upside down and a figure surrounded by bright light so had come to the conclusion that he was definitely still asleep, that or dead. It was only when he found himself moving, as if doing an exaggerated spacewalk, up the stairs, arms around a blonde who smelled of expensive perfume but who kept huffing and wincing at the smell of his breath that he wondered if maybe he *had* actually died and was on his way up to meet with Lizzie, Isaac and Ella Grace. Could angels be huffy, did they smell like that? People always talked of a white light and a floating sensation. Was he on his way to meet his Maker? Nothing more, sliding again, trying to speak, no good, sinking, sinking, darkness once more.

*

"What am I doing up here? What are you doing here? What time is it?" groaned Mark, propping himself up on his right elbow whilst rubbing his eyes with his left hand and looking around the guest room.

"In order, I put you up here this morning owing to the fact that you totally trashed your living room. I am still here as I have spent the day sorting out your mess and it is a little after 6pm." Sophie took a deep breath, screwing up her nose and frowning before reaching over to plump up his pillows then gestured with her head for him to sit up before handing him the steaming cup of tea that she had placed on the bedside table. "And you smell like a Viking by the way."

"Six o'clock?" Bloody hell, I must have been totally wasted last night. But then Vikings do like a drink or two, don't they? Especially when mourning the loss of loved ones. What time did you come in?" Mark winced as he sipped the tea, scalding the roof of his mouth in the process, a habit he really must give up.

"Just before nine. Mrs Sheridan had put her head round the door first thing to see how you were and decided that she needed to call for the cavalry, so here I am, fortunately we had decided to stay overnight so I wasn't far away. Listen, there's a hot bath ready for you and some clean clothes on the chair there and then when you're done come down and have some supper." Sophie rose from the side of the bed and headed for the door.

"Sophie," Mark called after her. "Thank you." She shrugged and half smiled. He continued, with a grin, "That's twice in a week that you've ordered me into a bedroom, is there something you're trying to tell me?"

Sophie rolled her eyes. "Nothing that you didn't know already Mark, that you are a total pain in the arse, so please make yourself presentable and report to the kitchen in half an hour." And with that she turned on her (expensive) heels and headed off down the stairs.

*

300

Mark discovered, over an M&S chicken breast wrapped in Parma ham with new potatoes and asparagus washed down with fizzy water (for once he didn't complain at a lack of booze), that Sophie had been more than busy whilst he had slept the effects of his overindulgences off all day. She had sorted all of Lizzie's clothes and had them sent to various charity shops, along with the majority of Isaac's clothes and toys, ordered and had installed a new plasma screen (as he had hurled one of the nest of tables through the existing one) and hired some cleaners to scour the place from top to bottom; basically a one woman army armed with nothing more than a mobile phone and iron-clad determination. She had kept back a few of Isaac's soft toys and a couple of his favourite books but had his bed and the cot dismantled and removed from the bedroom and nursery respectively. Mark was speechless with gratitude and equally staggered at the amount she had managed to organise in one day and was so grateful for how sensitively she had handled things, to which Sophie had merely shrugged.

"When you're used to moving at the drop of a hat you don't have time to dwell, you just get on with it. Knowing that logistics isn't a natural strength of yours Mark, I thought I'd get a handle on things, I'm naturally resourceful and believe in getting the experts in to do what they do best. It was just a few phone calls really and a bit of people management, nothing more. I have spoken with the chap who decorated the place for you first time round and he's on standby to repaint Isaac's room and the nursery, just let him know when you're ready."

Mark exhaled heavily, sending a small piece of potato back out and onto his plate. "It was a lot more than nothing Soph. I had no idea where to start on all this. I knew it had to be tackled but equally I felt that I was somehow betraying Lizzie and Isaac and even Ella by removing their stuff from the house, somehow eliminating them so soon after their deaths. I reckon if you hadn't done it for me it would have all sat there for weeks, months even. I really don't know how to thank you, not just for today but for how you've been with me since, well, you know."

Sophie put her hand on his arm and smiled whilst getting up to remove her plate and put it in the washing-up bowl, the cutlery clattering noisily as she did it as the plates were just that bit too big in circumference to sit flush on the bottom of the bowl. Returning to sit at the table she topped up her glass with fizzy water, her facial expression moving to the more familiar searching frown. "I thought you might go AWOL after the service last night and by the look of you, you had quite a night." As she gestured with her eyebrow towards the cut above his, "As we're now such good chums, care to enlighten me?"

"I felt claustrophobic towards the end of the service, my emotions were all over the shop and I just needed some air and when I went outside I bumped into Hope so we went off for a beer," Mark said casually.

"Hope?" Sophie queried.

"Yes Hope, Lizzie knew her as a client and then a friend. It was Hope who was with Lizzie when she died."

"Christ, Mark," Sophie looked serious, "you mean that you went on a bender with the key prosecution witness?"

"We've had a drink before, here actually," Mark continued, absent-mindedly pushing a piece of asparagus around his plate.

"Bloody hell Mark!" Sophie looked concerned, tucking her hair behind each ear to make her look even more businesslike. "You're blurring some lines here. She was the brass that fleeced Guy wasn't she? Please God don't tell me that you two …?"

Mark tutted, "Of course not, do you take me for a total loser Soph. No, don't answer that. Hope has been going through a really tough time since Lizzie's death, what with the guilt of being involved in the run up, actually being there to witness Lizzie getting murdered, then the bribes and now the threats, it's a lot for one still so young, streetwise or not."

"Bribes and threats?" Sophie looked really concerned now.

"What, didn't my dear brother tell you? Someone acting on behalf of Soames offered her a substantial sum of money to change her version of events and as that didn't work they're threatening to 'do her over' along with her mother."

"But … Hold on a second here, Mark. First you tell me that Soames' lot are breaking every rule in the bloody book by intimidating a witness and now that somehow Johnnie is involved?"

"He must be. Something just doesn't ring true here. I would have asked Soames last night but (a) the music in the bar was too loud (b) his minder looked like a complete psycho and (c) I felt that giving him a good right hook would do me more good."

"Whoooa!" Sophie exclaimed, getting up and pacing up and down the kitchen before turning to lean her back against the sink and continue, "Let me get this straight, you were out drinking with the girl who drugged and robbed Soames that led to him running down Lizzie whilst in pursuit of her and you punched Soames? What were you thinking, Mark? How is this going to look in court? It was an accident Mark, a terrible, terrible accident and as angry as you have every right to be, you can't go around punching Guy Soames if ever you bump into him."

"Well that's just it Sophie. I didn't bump into Soames, he and a heavy had come looking for Hope and were having a right go when I stepped in. And I tell you what, their stories don't half contradict each other."

"Well of course they would, Mark" Sophie sighed, "a young tart, even if she does have a heart, is hardly going to come clean about drugging and stealing from a wealthy businessman, is she?"

"According to Hope, she and her friend Tia were invited back to Soames' place to snort some lines of coke, drink champagne and have sex. Apparently, his wife and girls were away abroad at his holiday home in Corfu so the house was empty. Ring any bells?"

"Yes, Polly and the twins were out there but this does little to change the facts."

"It does if he was a consenting adult Sophie. Hope is adamant that neither she nor her friend *touched* his drink and that he was equally adamant that they came back to his to 'party'. She did admit to nicking his wallet as he was boasting about a property deal and how he was going to be 'Ks' in whilst she performed, well, a service. She reckoned he must be so loaded that he wouldn't miss a few hundred quid. Apparently, the next morning he was bricking it about being found out by his wife and couldn't get rid of her quickly enough, her friend had long gone by then. If they didn't drug him, as they insist they didn't, and his wife found out exactly what the mouse got up to while the cats were away and then divorces him, wouldn't he have a lot to lose?"

"Mmmm. I guess I wouldn't put it past him. He's tried it on with me on more than one occasion. Poor Polly and the girls, the embarrassment of it all, so grubby, so, well, belittling. And I know what you're thinking but at least your brother has the decency not to crap on his own doorstep and bring shame on the whole family. But how does he fit into all this? Sure, he was on the phone to Guy when the accident happened but they were just talking business, it's a cruel, cruel, twist of fate Mark but nothing more." Sophie seemed calmer now as her rational mind kicked in once more.

"I agree on one hand but Johnnie hasn't been the same with me since it all happened. Can hardly look me in the eye." Mark drained his glass.

"We've been through this Mark. It's because he somehow feels guilty, because he was on the phone at the point of impact with darling Lizzie, he feels that he might have been a distraction, that maybe if he hadn't been talking to Soames then none of this would have happened."

"That makes sense Sophie, it does," Mark continued, "but something is niggling me and it won't go away. When we were out in Chichester, the evening after the funeral, when you'd gone back up to London, Johnnie was really on edge, not his usual jocular, boorish self. At first I put it down to him actually attempting to be sensitive to the fact that I'd just buried my family, but there was something else, the way he kept questioning me, that left me feeling, well, narked, unsettled."

"What type of questions, Mark?"

Mark shook his head slightly as if sifting through his memory, ordering his thoughts. "Like whether or not Lizzie and I had argued on the morning of the accident, or if she was overtired due to the pregnancy or distracted in any way and if she had ever let Isaac wander out onto a main road before. Also about Hope and if she had a criminal record, and was that why Lizzie had worked with her in the first place, the sort of questions I would be expecting the police to ask actually, not my brother. It was almost as if he was looking for a way to take the heat off Soames. Why would he want to do that Sophie, over getting justice for his dead sister-in-law?"

"I don't know Mark, I really don't. Johnnie's done some pretty shameful things in the past but trying to leverage your emotional state with a view to getting his business partner off the hook for running over your wife and family in a fit of rage at a trollop who'd nicked his wallet?" She exhaled, "That would beat the lot. But why Mark? What would he have to gain by Soames getting off lightly?"

Mark met her quizzical look with one of complete calm and clarity, "That, is for you to find out Sophie. I think you'll agree that it might alter the picture somewhat."

Sophie's phone, sitting on the kitchen table, simultaneously bleeped and glowed. She checked it, "Talk of the devil, he's outside with the kids, we're heading straight back up to town." Sophie sent a quick reply, put her phone into her designer handbag, clicked the clasp shut and took her jacket off the back of the chair. "Goodbye Mark and take care. I'll call you in the week to see how you are doing. I'm sure it will all come out in the wash, you know, all this with Johnnie and Soames, and I'm sure your brother has a perfectly good explanation for the way he's acting." She paused for a second, gathering her thoughts, "If not, his life will not be worth living."

There was such steel in her gaze, her voice that it made Mark shudder so he quickly changed the subject. "Thanks again Soph, for everything. Oh and how much do I owe you for the cleaners not to mention the new TV?"

Sophie smiled. "That's on me Mark. Maybe Match of the Day will help to take your mind off things for a bit, eh?" Sophie was already making her way down the hallway and Mark trotted behind in an attempt at catching up. "We'll get to the bottom of all this."

Mark shivered, watching from the front step, wearing just a T-shirt and his jeans and waved in the general direction of the Range Rover as Sophie, releasing light from the cabin as she opened the door, climbed up elegantly into the warmth and comfort of the plush interior that he had sunk into just a couple of days before, the day after the funeral. That still felt weird to say or think, as if it had happened to someone else, was this really happening to him? How many times had he done this before he had met Lizzie, hovering on his doorstep like the little lost boy as the grown- ups took their children home? Now he was at it again, but feeling more lost than ever, as he had tasted that life, and the love that was at its core only to have it ripped from him in a second, all gone, now just graves and grief and a more pronounced loneliness as he had something so beautiful to compare it with. Harry had his head buried in some console or other but Tiggy waved a restrained wave whilst Johnnie sort of grimaced as he indicated and accelerated up the hill. Mark stood for a minute or two, long after the rear lights had faded from his view, numbed by the cold, the tiredness, the emotion and the knowledge that life would never be the same again.

2
February 2012

Darkness falls

Silence, along with her sisters, darkness and melancholy had slowly settled upon the previously noisy household like dust sheets over antique furniture in a house vacated by its owners. At first the sheer absence of noise and presence was deafening but after a few weeks it became familiar, the norm. There were of course exceptions to this new normality, when personal items previously forgotten about were discovered by chance, a home-made birthday card in a drawer in his office, a family photo wrapped in cobwebs that had fallen behind the fridge, dates brightly circled and planned activities written on a calendar in Lizzie's hand, moments that would never come to pass, as they now had. Mark had become the keeper of the mausoleum, himself a ghost padding about with neither place nor purpose, aimlessly alighting on a step, a sofa, a bed, before moving on to fill his days with nothingness. Despite the lack of personal effects, he could still close his eyes and hear their voices, picture their smiles, feel their touch. It occurred to him on many occasions that he may be losing his sanity but this function was something he'd always felt was overrated so wasn't overly concerned at the thought of being without it. The flame of his anger had diminished to more of a soft glow, always present and easily fanned but more often replaced by a questioning, a searching, an eagerness to understand why his life had peaked then lurched so emphatically, so irrevocably in such a few short years. Solitude had always been a welcome companion but it now felt like a firm friend from his past that was looking to reassert itself into his life after a period of absence, but his was a life much changed from when they first bonded, their relationship now uneasy as they had become out of tune, out of step. Likewise, the cloak of isolation that he had once worn with such distinction was no longer the perfect fit but he allowed these familiar elements in as they echoed a former frame of mind that had become gilt- edged but was now much in need of restoration.

Of course, the apathy that had seeped in under his doorways like a dawn sea mist had not gone undetected by those around him; Mrs Sheridan was a regular visitor, depositing a home cooked meal in his oven at least twice a week, Vaz dragged him out whenever Mark could face it, Pete had dropped round and had started talking about getting back to work on the script, Lisa called weekly but he drew the line at meeting up as her energy always drained him of what little he had left. His parents had visited and his mother had fussed and Sophie, the arch organiser, had managed all Lizzie's mobile phone and broadband provider accounts after Mark had gone ballistic at being told by a call centre operator that the account holder must verify the details in order to cancel the account. "What, from beyond the f*****g grave!" he had exploded, "what part of MY WIFE IS DEAD don't you understand, you moron? Unless you provide a medium service you'll have to talk to me!" The tearful customer care assistant had passed Mark onto her supervisor and that hadn't gone any better so he had allowed Sophie to intervene and tie up all the loose ends in a calmer and more controlled manner. He'd exchanged texts a few times with Hope but, once the hearing had concluded, felt it was best for them to both move on, or at least have a bit of space. Not surprisingly, Hope had been cautioned over stealing Soames' wallet but could not be found guilty of drugging him as he had insisted, (funny, she had said, to be in the dock, accused, when she was the witness to a nasty arsehole who'd run a family, and not just any family mind, over in broad daylight having just cheated on his wife). The picture painted by Soames' barrister was of a diligent and committed family man, who fully supported the local economy by employing staff from the town to work in his restaurant, having been out celebrating a commercial success with an investor when he had been callously targeted by two well-known and disreputable young women with reputations gained through dubious work in local clubs and late night licensed establishments. He had gone on to describe how his client had been duped into letting them into his home (a move he had conceded as ill-advised, considering the reputation of the young women in his company that evening) and had at no point had nor implied any intention of embarking on sexual relations but was simply enjoying the release of pressure after a difficult few years of trading by letting his hair down and enjoying a few bottles of champagne. His friend Toby (of course, Mark had thought, it was going to be either this, Giles or Rupert, cut from the same expensive cloth) testified to having taken a sudden turn for the worse when consuming the alcohol served by

307

the young females when at Soames' place and put his dizziness and light-headedness down to a substance that must have been secreted into his drink as he can remember little of what occurred afterwards. Mark had commented afterwards to Vaz that this was just a lengthy, flowery upper-middle-class way of saying they were both as pissed as newts; how often had he passed out after a heavy session and would struggle to piece the events of the previous night together the morning after? Drugged indeed! Anyway, surely if Soames had been breathalysed at the scene of the accident any illegal substance would have been detected. But of course, he had driven off.

Bingham, the senior partner and Savile Row clad assassin, short, stocky, suave, winter tanned, well fed and with a low, bassy voice as smooth and rich as honey went on to describe how his client had simply sought to reclaim what was rightfully and legally his, when (despite being deceived and drugged by her the previous night he had gallantly driven the young woman to a place of her choice the following morning), he realised that his wallet containing a considerable amount of cash and his credit cards had been stolen; it hadn't taken him long to work out who the culprit was. Returning to the place where he had kindly dropped her off just a few minutes earlier, he had been forced to swerve around an illegally parked vehicle and was then horrified to witness a woman struggling with her young child in the middle of the road before him. Despite him braking hard, the collision was, tragically, unavoidable (at this point he had paused to look down for dramatic effect, as if composing himself, revealing his smooth, brown head and his talent for the theatrical). No wonder he didn't come cheap, Mark remembered thinking, a part of me is beginning to feel sorry for the scumbag. Bingham had then continued, painting his client to be more a saint than a sinner.

"In attempting to avoid the inevitable and with no regard for his own safety he did what he believed any father would do, as his paternal instincts kicked in, steering the car away from the mother and child thus sliding sideways and colliding with a concrete bin at the side of the road. Suffering from trauma, whiplash and concussion he drove from this awful scene to realise immediately this error of judgement and so reported into the police station in Hove to give a witness statement. Such had been the emotional stress experienced by his client as a result of the collision that he had been receiving post-traumatic stress counselling and had not been able to return to his various business ventures."

The picture that had been painted was of a dedicated family man, a hard-working pillar of the local business community who had been the victim of a callous scam whilst innocently celebrating a turnaround in his fortunes after a tough few years. Such was his decency of character that, despite the deceit that he had fallen foul of, he was still prepared to drive the perpetrator of this crime to a place of her choice, an act that displayed remarkable powers of forgiveness and generosity. Only when it had become clear that, on top of spiking his drinks and ordering bottles of champagne on his behalf that he was left to pay for, she had stolen a considerable sum of cash and his credit cards from him had his patience finally, and understandably, become strained; therefore, he had set out to right this wrong as any law-abiding citizen would have done.

The bit that had made Mark's blood really boil (and led to him being escorted from the courtroom) was how Lizzie's part in the accident had been portrayed. Bingham had started by describing her as a much loved and valued local community worker who had supported many disadvantaged and vulnerable young women *but* (and there lay the crux of the issue) was someone who had formed such emotional attachments to her clients that she found it difficult to maintain a cut-off point, to draw a line between the professional and the personal. On the morning in question she had, he explained, been preparing to head out on a 'mission of mercy' to deliver food and second-hand clothing to a lone mother with three children all by different fathers, (a comment that had received an abrupt objection from the prosecution upheld by the judge), living in social housing on a local estate but had then changed her plans whilst en route having received a phone call from the perpetrator of the scam, (another objection upheld along the lines of being innocent until proven guilty). Such was her (Lizzie's) erratic state of mind, exacerbated by the extreme tiredness caused by the late stages of her pregnancy that her decision making had to be called into question.

It was, he argued, *the deceased's state of mind*, the result of such devotion to lost causes (that extended to her family as her husband had spent most of his adult life out of work and running up debt and was on a final disciplinary warning at a local college where he worked part-time adding to the stress and burden of responsibility felt by the deceased) combined with the hormonal onslaught that pregnancy represents that, sadly, was at the heart of this most tragic incident and not the state of mind of his client, a calm and measured former City trader, used to making critical decisions under pressure and clearly immune from the biological time bombs that the fairer sex must endure, particularly during pregnancy.

He concluded, "This must clearly explain why an innocent child, not yet two years old, was allowed to wander unchallenged onto a busy main road during the morning rush hour whilst the mother, and primary carer, was talking to the nightclub hostess accused of drugging and then stealing from my client. If that was not enough, he was then forced to endure the type of trauma that can scar a man for life, the innocent taking of the lives in question through a most tragic accident that, to make the tragedy even greater could so easily have been avoided if the mother had done what any mother of sane mind surely should have done and prioritised the safety of her child and unborn child over the emotional welfare of a young woman of dubious character."

This had been enough for Mark who could not contain himself any longer, "You lying tosser!" he had screamed, "He ran down my family in cold blood and you have the nerve to blame Lizzie. You ask that murdering scumbag, if he was so drugged up how come he managed to get it ..." This was as far as he got, coherently anyway, as he continued to spew obscenities as he was led away by the police officers stationed in the courtroom. So this is how it works then he thought, as he blew the steam away from the watery looking black coffee that had been served to him in a plastic cup by a prison guard. This is the law that this proud nation stands on, the bedrock, cornerstone, a pillar of its democratic society and constitution, the scales of justice 'equally stacked', where in reality the guilty party with the most cash can buy their way out of a manslaughter charge because the victim was portrayed as an incompetent pregnant woman whose emotions were all over the place and the key witness, in the eyes of the privileged and influential, was nothing more than a common thieving little tart. To say that the law was an ass seemed a gross understatement.

His pride had also been dented and he was smarting from how he had been painted as some sort of irresponsible loser. Sure, that may have been the case before he'd met Lizzie but the turnaround in his fortunes and self-discipline that Lizzie had been the catalyst for had been totally overlooked. His former image had been manipulated, exaggerated to fit the picture being so cleverly composed by the great master himself. And where had they got all this from, he mused? Lizzie was as strong, focused, organised, determined and clear-headed a woman as you were ever likely to meet yet here she was being described as a stressed, emotionally and hormonally charged do-gooder, incapable of making up her mind or looking after their boy, of which she had been amazing, the most devoted, caring and nurturing mother any child could ever wish for.

As good as Bingham had been and as equally incompetent as the prosecution counsel, the judge had not been totally taken in by the defence and had found Guy Soames to be guilty of death by misadventure but not of manslaughter. He had, however, been charged with leaving the scene of the RTC, failing to stop and report his part in the collision that, on top of the points he had on his licence added to a hefty fine and a one year stretch in that Alcatraz of incarceration otherwise known as Ford Open Prison, with a minimum of 6 months to be served of his one year sentence. Wow! That sure was more than just a rap across the knuckles for ruining his entire life in a matter of seconds Mark had thought. Good old justice system!

In the taxi home he composed and sent a text message to Hope thanking her for her honesty and loyalty to Lizzie during what had been a really trying time for her and her family and he hoped that she would be able to move on from this now, free from either threat or insinuation. He also sent a text to Johnnie.

Dear spineless former brother of mine

I imagine you are delighted that the smug piece of crap that you associate with got off so lightly and congratulations for putting your own self-interest so highly above any sense of loyalty, decency and compassion that you may have had towards your own family and for deciding to sell out so callously for, presumably, your very own thirty pieces of silver.

At least now we all know where we stand and the bravado that you have displayed throughout our lives has been proved to be just a cheap mask that has slipped irrevocably, smashing into shards of deceit and betrayal that has punctured our relationship and probably others in the family beyond repair.

I hope you think it's worth it JUDAS.

PS Don't contact me ever again.

PPS Didn't he hang himself out of a sense of shame, unable to live with such an act of betrayal?

He had been pleased with the imagery, metaphor and dramatic tone that he had crammed into that short but fully loaded message but felt a great sense of sorrow upon sending it. He knew, beyond any doubt, that Johnnie had been probing him for scraps of information as to Lizzie's state of mind on the morning of the accident to feed to the shark of a barrister, as some of the insights Bingham had shared with such conviction during the trial could only have come from within family circles, likewise his damning character portrait of Mark. He wondered if his parents would see this or whether they would be taken in by Johnnie's bluff and bluster. He was pretty sure that Sophie wouldn't. In six months Soames would be out and trading again. They wouldn't even have had the headstones for Lizzie, Isaac and Ella in place by then. Mark very much doubted whether Soames' or Johnnie's marriages would survive the scandal but he and Johnnie were the stuff of 'bounce-back-ability', a phrase coined by the somewhat eccentric former player and now manager Ian Holloway and would soon be back in the black. So the final line had been drawn Mark had thought. This really is the full stop.

But that was the weird and intriguing way of life, how a full stop could turn out to be a comma or a semicolon, flowing from one sentence to the next, re-defining the sense or meaning of the passage to come. And, as with so much of life, his life in particular, there was no telling from how far left of field this shift in direction was to come.

*

He had been filling his days, in survival mode. Getting up late, not bothering to shave, sometimes not even showering; mooching about the house in his tracksuit bottoms and an old T-shirt, dozing in front of daytime TV or through Blackadder or The Office DVDs, almost as if he had travelled back in time to the pre-Lizzie years. There was a little voice somewhere that told him not to give in to the apathy that had coiled itself around him, suffocating whatever zest for life he had discovered and embraced over the past few years. It was strange, he knew that at some point he would have to kick-start his life but he wasn't ready to do so just yet.

Shopping online was a new skill he had acquired purely as he couldn't bear the thought of going out and bumping into anyone he knew. He could look for anything at the click of a button (succumbing to temptation at times in the restless midnight hour) and had even dipped his toe into the water regarding cars and properties but had quickly withdrawn it as he wasn't quite ready for such significant action, not just yet. "Not yet," he would say aloud in the voice of the African warrior from Gladiator who fought alongside Maximus in the Coliseum, over punctuating the t's. He talked aloud to himself often, sometimes shrieking, or cackling for little or no reason, giving even himself a cause for concern. A Robinson Crusoe bereft of his girl Friday marooned on an island of melancholy. He had sensibly brought into force a self-imposed ban on alcohol before 5pm during the week but it was a case of anything goes at the weekends, especially if there was a big game on the telly. United, not lions.

He had gone crazy, leaping and whooping loudly when a Rooney brace had seen United beat Liverpool 2-1 in the League with Suarez once more the villain of the piece during a highly-charged lunchtime kick-off in which a lot did kick off apparently with players having to be restrained in the tunnel at half-time and after the match. He enjoyed a good few beers during that game and others to follow. Sometimes Vaz would come round to watch a game with him and as Mark suspected, keep an eye on him. He was now canny enough to make sure he had showered and shaved and had a bit of a tidy up before anyone came round, to give the impression of coping, and that he was taking the time to work through his grief and related issues when the reality was he had shoved them into the under-stairs cupboard and had needed to put his shoulder against the door and lean on it with his full weight in order to get it shut.

One bright but chilly midweek morning Mrs Sheridan popped round as she usually did after morning Mass on a Wednesday, knocking on the glass panel of the back door before letting herself in but this time she had company. Mark had been thrown by this and it rankled that she felt that she could invade his home in this way without forewarning him (forearmed and all that) and being caught on the hoof left Mark feeling sullen, irritable and inhospitable. Mrs S had ignored his teenage-like show of petulance and proceeded to make them all a pot of tea whilst chattering away in her usual sing-song way. With her was a priest who looked like he would be in his late 50s or early 60s, round faced, with pale skin and ruddy cheeks, receding sandy hair and neatly trimmed goatee sitting at the kitchen table, legs crossed and hands clasped in his lap. His eyes were a watery pale blue and he smiled with them whilst nodding to himself as he took in his surroundings but said nothing until he was introduced by Mrs Sheridan, who immediately scolded herself for such an appalling lack of manners.

Over tea and biscuits she explained that he, Father Robin, was a visiting priest from a church in Johannesburg, staying at the priest's house nearby for a few months and she was showing him the ropes and introducing him to members of the local community. I bet she is, Mark thought, the little busybody that she was. Father Robin shook Mark's hand firmly, sincerely and smiled, apologising for arriving unannounced and opened his hands, as Mrs S refilled the pot, shrugged as if to say 'you know what she's like' a gesture that immediately allowed Mark to remove a layer of hostility, as this situation, this atmosphere was not of the priest's doing and so Mark warmed a little to him and reassured him that it was fine, and to ignore him as he was going through a cranky patch. This was a cue for Father Robin to reveal how he knew all the details of Lizzie, Isaac and Ella's deaths and how Jesus would right now be giving his family unicorn rides around heaven and that Jesus loved him and that Mass was at 10am the next day but he did none of this, he simply made eye contact with Mark and said, "I hear that it has been a time of intense loss and pain for you Mark and I am so sorry to hear that. The last thing I want to do as a stranger is to intrude in something as personal and painful as an individual's grief but rest assured that there are people in this community praying for their souls and for your healing. We won't keep you any longer. Thanks for welcoming me into your home and I hope to see you again sometime." Mark was so surprised by this sensitive and restrained approach that he found himself inviting them both round again the following Wednesday morning, an invitation he was staggered he had offered long after he closed the back door behind them.

The following week the visit took pretty much the same format as the first visit, tea, biscuits and polite conversation whilst all sat at the kitchen table. Father Robin talked a little about growing up in South Africa and some of the tensions he had witnessed, and still did in communities he knew and ministered to. Mark offered a highly edited and précised back story whilst Mrs Sheridan just smiled and nodded and kept the tea coming. It was during their third visit that Mark, having had a tidy up beforehand, invited them into the lounge where they settled into comfy seats and where the conversation took a more inevitable turn. They had been discussing a member of the local church congregation whose daughter had found out her husband had been having an affair and how it had torn two families apart when Mark had asked how could it be expected of the woman to forgive her husband, someone she had trusted and who had betrayed her in such a public and humiliating way.

Father Robin, rather than getting on his high horse, admitted that it was a tough one, and that we all had the right to express our anger if we genuinely felt wronged (after all didn't Jesus go a bit crazy when he found that the temple had been turned into a market place). The key, he explained, is not to let our anger control us; we need to own it and not the other way around. If it remains internalised to such an extent that it is allowed to fester, to become fortified and set into deep-rooted resentment it can lead to mental and emotional scars that can take a lifetime to heal. He referred to a man out in the outback who had been bitten by a poisonous snake and, when being attended to by medics had asked, "Doc, will this bite kill me?" To which the Doctor replied, "The bite won't but the poison might unless we get it out if your system." Mark found himself, to his absolute disbelief, nodding as Father Robin spoke, liking the way he put things across and the fact that he was talking to Mark as an equal, and neither from pedestal nor pulpit. Not knowing whether it was the South African accent or Mark's desire to find some peace, Mark felt comfortable with this man of God but then reminded himself that he had some pretty serious issues to raise in the aftermath of Lizzie's accident and he inwardly kicked himself for being taken in by the priest's charm and mesmerising tones.

"So, we have to forgive those who hurt us otherwise we'll end up doing ourselves in, basically," he asked, that familiar edge creeping into his gut, his bones, his voice.

"In a nutshell, yes," Father Robin replied gently, "but I'm trying to make the point that, for us mere mortals, it can be easier said than done. Anger, hurt, resentment, pain are all fruits from the same tree really, that of loss. Whether the loss of face in an argument, of good health, a job, or even a loved one, these emotions are all rooted in a sense of loss and with that can also come a feeling of being hard done by, of being dealt a bad hand. Like most of us who have ever gambled and lost, we will automatically look to blame the person who dealt us those cards and not necessarily reflect on how we played them. Of course," (he paused at this point and then spread his hands in an open gesture towards Mark), "there will be times when factors beyond our control impact an outcome that proves so monumental, so devastating that we wonder how we'll ever be able to find our way back from it. I just feel that harbouring anger, bitterness, resentment or even thoughts of retaliation and revenge will prove barriers to overcoming personal tragedy, the poison if you like, that comes after the bite."

Mark took a second to take this all in. His head was spinning slightly again as Father Robin made perfect sense and this unsettled him, it was as if he had reached the point in his teens when he finally understood why he should have his jeans washed and not leave dirty cereal bowls under his

315

bed for a week but to admit this would be to accept defeat and there was still a fire burning in his belly that stoked his desire for a fight.

"Isn't that a bit rich though Father?" Mark went on the offensive, "I mean hasn't God been punishing the world since we crucified his Son, how is that the model for forgiveness?"

Despite Mark's scathing tone, Father Robin refused to be goaded into a confrontation; instead he tilted his head slightly to one side and responded calmly, "I can see why you might think that Mark but I can't agree. You see, even as Jesus was dying on the cross, having been brutalised beyond our imagination, he was raising his voice to the skies to ask his Father to forgive those who had put him through that torture and onto that cross. Surely this is the ultimate act of forgiveness just as allowing his Son to suffer and die in that way was the ultimate act of sacrifice from God, this is the model that I refer to, Mark."

"But what was the point?" Mark replied, "I mean what has it changed? I thought the whole point of Jesus dying on the cross was to alleviate or eradicate pain and suffering. Well, that went well."

Father Robin smiled, glanced across at Mrs Sheridan and turned to Mark once more. "Mark, you are clearly a clever fellow, and one who, quite rightly, is angry about what happened to your family. I don't claim to have all the answers, and certainly won't attempt to preach you into forgiveness; I will however, highly recommend it. I would also be humbly willing to attempt to answer as many of your questions as I could if you would be happy to allow me to try."

Mark allowed himself to smile back at this genial man of the cloth who had somehow managed to stand his corner without seeming to have even donned his gloves. Mark nodded, "Same time, same place next week?" And the little group broke up once more with genuine farewells and best wishes as they put on their coats and scarves and headed off into the pale early winter afternoon.

Over a chicken cup-a-soup with crispy croutons (burned roof of mouth) and toasted cheese and onion sandwich (ditto) Mark reflected on their conversation and on the 'poison that came after the bite' that was coursing through his veins. Strangely he couldn't work out for whom he had reserved the majority of his venom, was it Soames or Johnnie? Soames was an obvious target, an arrogant, devious, divisive little prick with scant regard for anyone but himself and someone whose show of remorse was akin to something on a US daytime TV show, as genuine as if it was 'from the heart of his bottom'. His brother on the other hand, well, he had severed any bond they might have enjoyed at a stroke once he had decided to do a deal with the devil and help the other side and so deserved everything he had coming to him, but the idea of forgiveness? Phew. It had never even entered his head, unlike all the other thoughts that had snuck under the cover of darkness as he lay under his duvet, partially awake in the early hours, fantasies 'but not as we know them Jim'. Images of him, lean and trim, gym trained and toned, wearing black shorts, boots, boxing gloves and gum-shield, standing in the centre of a boxing ring and moving his weight from foot to foot as he waited to face a pasty, podgy Soames, standing in the opposite corner, his red trunks hitched up to cover his soft flabby belly, the result of one lunch too many, looking unsure of himself, slightly knock-kneed. The bloated killer of his family turning to his corner to see Johnnie, red faced and sweating, white towel over his shoulder, massaging Soames' shoulders and giving last minute instructions. Round after round would pass (the numbers of which were held high in the air by a beaming Hope) in which Mark gave Soames an absolute battering but every time he went down he would find a way to use the ropes to haul himself up again, as if relishing the mauling. Johnnie's towel was becoming so stained with the blood mopped from Soames' face after each round that it was hard to believe that it started the evening as crisp fabric conditioned white. The prison crowd roared Mark on until the last round slow motion knockout blow that saw Soames' gum shield shoot up into the air in a shower of sweat and the brutalised inmate fall, arms at his sides, heavily onto the canvas, his head hitting it hard and bouncing up before coming to rest. It was always at this point that Mark would sit bolt upright in bed, his T-shirt soaked in sweat, feeling as if he had actually been through those 10 rounds, but had in truth been on the receiving end. He'd spent so many idle hours allowing his furnace of rage to burn with thoughts of vengeance he hadn't even considered the possibility of forgiveness ...

*

It was one bright and breezy morning in early March when Sophie descended, looking magnificent in black polo-necked jumper, skinny jeans tucked into knee-length suede boots, three-quarter length overcoat and regulation dark glasses clutching two takeout lattes and a bag of almond croissants, not a hair out of place and every inch the yummy mummy from Barnes. Mark smiled affectionately as he watched her shimmy her way through the open gate and click-click her way up the tiled pathway to the front door. He had seen so many different sides to his sister-in-law since Lizzie had died that the old sense of dread, awe and a humiliation-in-waiting prior to an audience with her had subsided, to be replaced with a newfound warmth and respect allied to an understanding as to how she was the way she was; shaped by her experiences as we all are to a greater extent. She was killing two birds with the same stone effectively, always one to maximise her time, as she had been to see Polly Soames, the estranged wife of Guy, who was looking after Tiggy and Harry whilst Sophie looked in on Mark.

"So how is she bearing up?" Mark enquired whilst sipping the latte through the small slit in the top of the plastic lid (burning the roof of his mouth *again*).

Sophie shrugged as she pulled another small soft, still warm piece of almond croissant and sparrow pecked at it as if eating in Mark's company, or at all was somehow beneath her, that old aloofness, the air of disdain briefly returning to roost. "Not bad, considering what she's going through," she replied, seeming distracted for a moment.

"How does she feel towards Guy? Has she been to visit him?" Mark pressed.

"Hardly!" That familiar steely focus returning, that little flash in her eyes, "It turns out that he *was* in it up to his knackers the night before Lizzie died and all this crap about being drugged by those two tarts, well she just doesn't buy it and nor do I quite frankly. Fancy doing that in your own house?" She noticed Mark raise an eyebrow. "Polly and I are not naïve, Mark, we know how easily men of a certain age with fat wallets and expanding midriffs can be flattered by pretty young girls, it's been happening for millennia, but *in his family home*, that's unforgivable! If you ask me, either of us, we think he got off bloody lightly; 12 months in Ford Open Prison, probably out after 6, what a joke."

Mark considered for a moment the morals, the ethics of the scenario painted for him by Sophie, the status driven social climber, that somehow, in the world that her and Polly inhabited, it was verging on the acceptable for their husbands to chase some young totty whilst the boys were 'on tour' but it was an absolute no-no to get caught with your pants down on your own patch. "And what of that brother of mine?" Mark couldn't even form the name on his lips that were now coated in the fine icing sugar that coated the delicious pastry he was devouring with as much gusto as Sophie had shown reserve.

"Currently skulking around at his club in London with a bloodied nose and his tail between his legs whining to anyone who will give him the time of day by all accounts." Her eyes had briefly narrowed.

Still flippin' scary thought Mark as he reminded himself not to get complacent as many a lion tamer had ended up being the lunch of a big cat whose claws they'd thought were permanently sheathed.

"Not at home with you and the kids then, Sophie?" Mark continued tentatively as if handling high explosives.

"No," she said emphatically. "You weren't the only one who smelled a rat, especially with all that insider stuff that Bingham knew about you and Lizzie so I asked Daddy to do some digging, he still has friends in high places, and it turned out that you were right after all. Johnnie was acting purely in his own selfish best interest and not that of you, the family or the memory of Lizzie."

"Go on," Mark urged her, hooked by this semi-revelation.

"Turns out that they were embroiled in some property tax avoidance scam, don't know the details, but Soames was paying for the Corfu place in instalments and still owed us around £100K. Polly knew nothing about this, neither did I, of course. With his assets frozen and Johnnie with creditors baying at the door your brother was going to be screwed unless somehow Soames could get off lightly and resume trading ASAP. Hence that spineless husband of mine assisting the other side."

Mark exhaled, this time managing not to spray his food over the table. "Quite a piece of work then eh, my big brother. I mean, I always knew he was prone to lapses in good judgement but cold-blooded betrayal, I thought more of him than that Sophie. I'm really sorry, it must be awful having to pick up the pieces after such a stab in the back."

"*You're* sorry?" Sophie reached out and put her hand on Mark's arm before retracting it instinctively as if jolted by an electric shock of revulsion at such a display of warmth and affection. She had never been the most tactile of creatures. "My husband has been scheming with the killer of your family just so he can protect a hundred grand and you are apologising to me?"

"Well, the thing is Sophie, I have always been the runt of the litter just grateful for any of the bigger pups to even wag their tails vaguely in my direction. You on the other hand are a social thoroughbred so you will feel this all much more acutely than me as the negative publicity will be like water off a duck's back to me but ..."

"Mark please," Sophie actually laughed out loud, "enough of your mixed metaphors, no more dogs, horses or ducks, but I take your point, my reputation is, in some circles, in tatters, not quite at leper status, but you really do know who your friends are at moments like this, when even the invitations to children's birthday parties, or 'gatherings', dry up. But this whole awful experience has given me so much more perspective, Mark. Forget how you and I used to view each other, the fact is that you have lost the woman you adored, your wife and mother to your children and my husband and his business partner both carry the blame. My loss of social stock is small fry in comparison. So, how are *you* doing Mark, TV still looks to be in one piece and I didn't have to step around any little piles of vomit on the way in so are things slowly heading in the right direction?"

"It's weird," Mark began, 'I hadn't expected to be feeling so calm so soon. I mean I still weep like a baby at almost every song that comes on the radio, avoid playing the majority of our CDs and don't think I'll ever be up to watching Cold Mountain again, but that burning furnace of rage that I was willingly stoking every day has now become more of a glow. It hasn't gone out, and I reckon it wouldn't take much to fan the flames to scorching point once more but I don't feel the anger, the despair, the hatred, the injustice quite as sharply as I did a few weeks back. Sure, I get overcome with waves of inadequacy when I think of how will I ever carry on in life without Lizzie by my side but am just taking one step at a time, like a drunk in recovery I guess."

"Mmm," Sophie responded, "I know a few of them. You wouldn't believe how many yummy mummies are on the Chardonnay by 11am. How is the drinking at the moment?"

"Just about under control," Mark replied honestly. "It'll always be a weakness but I am aware of it so I know when to steer clear of the fridge."

"And what do you put this new sense of calm down to Mark, I mean have any of your mates been any use? I know that Vaz can talk some sense, despite that ridiculous nose piercing and ponytail at his age; is that who you've been spending time with?" Sophie seemed genuinely intrigued.

"You're not going to believe it actually." Mark seemed bashful.

"Oh please, not that Lisa with her permanent halo and happy-clappy friends surely?"

"Close but no cigar. It's someone who Mrs S had been bringing round, a priest actually."

"A priest!" If Sophie's latte had still been hot enough to drink she would probably have choked on it. "But you can't stand priests."

"I know," Mark admitted. "But there is something about this bloke that has got to me. He's not in any way pompous; he doesn't make me feel like I'm stupid or, I dunno, some worthless sinner or something. I can't put my finger on it but he has definitely got me thinking about so much that Lizzie believed in, how I might somehow come to terms with what has happened and the part that Johnnie and Guy Soames had to play in it. If I can't deal with it I won't ever be able to move on."

"Christ Mark, will you listen to yourself." A touch of exasperation creeping into her tone, "There is no great spiritual reason for what has happened, no machinations deigned by the deity, just two greedy middle-aged men caught out for who they are and what they place their faith and value in; their very own God, money. After all, doesn't it say in the Bible that money is the root of all evil?"

"I thought it said just that Soph, until Lizzie had pointed out that this was possibly *the* most mis-quoted line from the entire Bible along with the notion that an eye-for-an-eye is still a valid reason for taking vengeance. What it says in the Bible is that it's *the love of money* that is the root of all evil. So money per se is not the issue but it's more to do with your relationship with it – has money replaced God in your life, that sort of thing."

"Well, John the Baptist, serve me up a plate of locusts and tell me more," Sophie said, with all the cynicism that Mark usually reserved for all things Christian.

"Please, don't take the piss Sophie, Lizzie's faith meant so much to her and I know that she didn't fear death no matter when it came or what form it came in as she was so sure in the promise of salvation, of eternal life. It must be quite something to have such certainty, such clarity and to face life without fear surely?"

"Look Mark, I respected Lizzie, I really did, and everything that she stood for, and I guess I can't knock anything that is helping you through all this but you're not telling me that you believe in all that superstitious guff about sin, redemption and a place in heaven? It was really designed in the dark ages to keep the power with the church and the people in their place."

"I'm not sure what I believe any more Sophie, I'm really not but I'm definitely not as cynical as I was and am more open to the idea of there somehow being more to this. I mean come on Sophie, look around you. Look at your life and mine, if this is it was there really any point to it in the first place?"

"To be honest Mark, I simply can't allow myself to think that way. I understand how you might do, especially in the light of all that you've recently been through but now it's my turn to take one step at a time as I attempt to rebuild my family life from the rubble of Johnnie's betrayal."

"Do you think you'll ever have him back?" Mark sensed that it was the right time for a shift in their conversation, to something less ethereal than the afterlife and to the here and now of everyday life.

"They say never say never but right now I can't see it. The kids have to see their father and I would never stand in the way of that but as for Johnnie and me, well I fear that the rift has now run too deep to bridge, the cracks that I was prepared to paper over for years have become more a chasm and now I feel I'm on the brink of defeat."

"I wouldn't look on it as a defeat Soph, because that means there is a winner and a loser. I think we've all lost something over the past few months but there are some things that are retrievable."

"Well, well, Dalai Lama," Sophie smiled, "such wise words. Maybe this priest isn't such a dead loss after all. But sometimes the religious folk smell an easy target, especially those who are struggling with grief, so try to keep some perspective, Mark. On the other hand, I suppose that if listening to an old priest friend of Mrs Sheridan's can keep you off the booze and give some sense of hope, of a future, then you're right, why knock it?" And with that Sophie gathered up her props, pecked him lightly on the cheek, promised to keep in touch and was gone, leaving only an empty coffee carton rimmed with ruby lipstick, a plate full of crumbled croissant and a waft of expensive perfume that lingered in the kitchen for the rest of the day.

3
April 2012

The cruellest month

"April is the cruellest month, breeding lilacs out of the dead land, mixing memory and desire, stirring dull roots with spring rain."

(T.S Eliot, 'The Wasteland')

He always knew that his next big hurdle in his 'recovery' was going to be the wedding of Vaz to Nicki as it would force him to confront so many of his 'demons' head on; interacting with people (he had been borderline hermit since Lizzie's death), alcohol (still his Achilles heel) and celebrating the love of two friends knowing that he had lost the love of his life just a few short months earlier. As always Vaz was amazing, proving yet again what a patient and loyal friend he was, keeping Mark as his best man whilst discreetly allocating most of the tasks associated with the role to his team of ushers thus removing the weight of responsibility from Mark whilst retaining his sense of belonging. They had met up as a group a few times for planning meetings in local pubs that had passed Mark by in a blur (the sheer number of pints he'd downed due to his nerves hadn't helped) but Vaz kept faith in him despite the raised eyebrows of a couple of his colleagues and fears of his fiancée Nicki who'd made her feelings known to Vaz that she saw Mark as a liability, a loose cannon, and cringed at the prospect of what his best man's speech might contain. Mark had often joked that Vaz should have a haircut, remove his nose piercing, don a pale blue beret and set out to resolve the world's conflicts, so good as he was at keeping the peace – a trait he had loved in Lizzie.

Although Nicki (with an i) lived with Vaz just north of Brighton, she had grown up in Godalming (the Beverley Hills of Surrey as she described it) so she was to be married in the picturesque parish church there with the reception to be at a stunning country house just a short drive away (of course, what else for Daddy's little princess). Although Vaz embraced his Sri Lankan heritage he felt fully anglicised so was happy to bow to the wishes of the bride's father, a former airline pilot, who had favoured a traditional wedding complete with vintage Rolls Royce and all the trimmings. Her hen night was the typical fare; girlies off to a health spa for a weekend binge on champagne, beauty treatments and massage whilst he, Vaz and the boys were off to Prague for, as he'd joked with Vaz on the short flight over, much of the same re. the massage with six packs replacing the face packs.

He had experienced such a lurching mix of emotions as the weekend for the stag do approached. Normally he'd be in his element at the prospect of a boozy weekend away in one of Europe's top cities but he was wracked with a sense of nerves and anxiety on this occasion, at times wondering if he should and could go through with it at all. Somehow drinking himself into a sofa-stupor in his own home didn't seem to be in any way being disrespectful to Lizzie's memory, he was simply dealing with her loss in the way he knew best, but to be 'out there' in one of Europe's party capitals where there would inevitably be the bars and booze and sexy eastern European women, well he just wasn't sure he was ready for that. He had found himself reduced to a sobbing mess on finding the flight tags to and from Rhodes still on the overnight bag, still stuck to the handles in memory of their honeymoon four short years before. Four years! During which time they'd brought Isaac into the world and were preparing to welcome Ella Grace into their lives. He had knelt on the floor with his head resting on their bed, the duvet cover now wearing a large damp stain from his tears upon which sat the overnight bag, unable to even contemplate what to take with him as what was the point? He'd be putting his favourite shirt, bought for him by Lizzie, on for whom? He'd shower and wear the aftershave (Paul Smith bought by Lizzie) get drunk and even more morose as even his clothes and scent would remind him of her and bring the whole mood down and then return, a few pounds heavier and a few hundred euros lighter, to what? Weeks, months, years yawned before him, how was he going to fill them all? By staring at the TV all day and eating ready meals at night? Not by returning to lecturing that was clear. He had informed the college that he would be resigning and, despite being offered a further term on compassionate leave, he knew that they would hardly put up a fight so, wifeless, jobless, clueless and lifeless, not that he would ever contemplate online dating but he thought this was a profile that would get lips licking and fingers clicking. He really had such a downer on himself he wondered when things might ever look up, just tunnel, no light.

How he saw himself and his anxieties ahead of the trip came across during his weekly meeting with Father Robin. Mrs Sheridan had excused herself on this occasion and Mark wondered if she was on the errand she had told him she'd be on or whether or not she felt satisfied that she'd made the introduction and could now let the men get on with it. Robin, as he insisted on being called (another brownie point in Mark's eyes, informal but without the 'guys' and over familiarity of Lisa's vicar) had asked Mark what he remembered of the stories of some of the well-known characters from the Old Testament, Moses, David and Gideon. Mark remained pretty clued up by the first two but less so about the third (wasn't he the bloke that put those little Bibles in the drawers of bedside tables in hotel and hospital rooms)?

He'd explained how each man was ordinary and flawed like the rest of us but that God had a plan for them and so by trusting in Him and with His blessing these three ordinary men achieved extraordinary things in their lives. Moses was hugely nervous of public speaking and lacked leadership experience but was sent to negotiate the release of his slave people from Pharaoh, one of the most powerful men in the known world, and then lead them on an epic quest. David was a shepherd boy who became a great warrior and king who made some serious mistakes along the way but crucially, he acknowledged and atoned for these and the lesser known Gideon was a nervy farmer who led a small army against a mighty invading force and came out on top. The point was that we can only achieve so much, journey so far in our own strength. If we feel that we are falling then we can cry out to God and He will pick us up and carry us through the dark times, with His Son shouldering the burden of our wrongdoing. Just as those biblical men didn't believe they were up to the task, he pointed out, maybe Mark felt that he lacked the emotional resilience and practical tools to pick up life again and live it without Lizzie by his side? It's in moments like this when we most need God so it pays to think carefully before turning your back on Him altogether as God lives in our pain and sorrow as much as in our laughter and joy. He told Mark that God loves him just the way he is, before pausing to add, "but He loves you that much that He's not prepared to leave you that way." His words conveyed such warmth and sincerity, the tone rich, soothing and whilst Mark knew that he was nowhere near being ready to call out to a God he still doubted even existed, he took some sense of comfort from these discussions with this quiet, earthy priest and never once doubted the strength of conviction that sat behind his softly spoken words.

*

"So, everything comes down to this; all our hopes, dreams, aspirations, pride, self-worth, all on the line now," (pause for effect), "my last card and only hope of clawing my way back into the game, the Flying Fortress maximum ceiling 31,850 feet. There's only one card in the pack that can trump it."

Mark paused. Bit his bottom lip in the way that Lizzie used to do, shook his head, feigned a look of resignation, then broke into a wide smile, "And it just so happens to be top of my pile, Soviet TU-95 also known as The Bear, ceiling altitude 40,010 ft. Game set and match, and it's not often I get to say that to you, Vaz." With this he revealed the card that he had switched for a Lightning jet whilst Vaz wasn't looking to ensure his victory, a victory that tasted as sweet as the Budweiser they had been consuming en route, warming up for the inevitable buckets of the Czech brewed Budvar they would be consuming over the weekend ahead.

Vaz looked shocked, deflated, but this immediately turned to indignant suspicion. "Lads, check his sleeves, his socks, his pants, everywhere! I know this man and as incompetent as he is in life, he is wily as a fox at Top Trumps. He once won a game round mine with Iron Man only for me to find The Black Widow down the back of my sofa weeks later."

Aidy, a PE teacher mate of Vaz' who Mark found to be a bit of a prat grinned luridly, "Blimey, what would I give to find her down the back of my sofa, that would be Christmas and birthdays all rolled into one!" Accompanied by him bending his right arm at the elbow and placing his left hand into the v-shaped crease as he moved his right forearm up and down, white van man for, well, 'Phooaaarr'.

"*You'd* be rolled into one mate," Vaz replied. "She'd eat you up for breakfast, clue's in the name."

Mark smiled along with the banter as he had all journey. It had been easier than he'd expected, once he'd got over the anxiety of going through the security checks at Gatwick. He'd sweated furiously, as he did when under pressure, thus drawing attention to himself for no reason. The sweating made him feel really self-conscious and irritable and he'd fumbled his keys and coins, spilling the latter on the floor as he was about to place his hand luggage through the scanner. He was too flustered even to make a joke to the burly security guard who had the job of 'patting him down', remembering how Vaz had been at pains to point out to the group of six that any joke with an airport official or flight attendant in this day and age would be likely to cause a security alert.

Mark had, of course, cheated to win the game of Top Trumps but this hadn't diminished his sense of pride as he had weaselled his way to the top of the podium. "Victor Ludorum," he announced in a plummy accent, remembering a school sports day when he was young. Chris Wallis had won every event by a country mile and, when the Town Mayor had presented him with his trophy and boomed his endorsement of this 'winner of all' (in Latin) the lad had simply replied, "No sir, Chris Wallis." The beers and jokes (but not about bombs) had flowed pretty much since take-off as they'd chatted, had a few games of cards and ribbed Vaz about what they had in store for him in Prague. The reality was, not a lot. They'd booked a budget city centre hotel, a table at a medieval banqueting bonanza for that evening and at another classier looking restaurant for the Saturday night but no surprises, no strippers, no plans to chain Vaz naked outside the castle walls dressed only in a sign reading 'Free entry after 9pm', but that hadn't prevented them from filling Vaz' head with such images.

Mark imagined creating Top Trump cards out of the group currently wearing their 'Vaz on Tour T-shirts (white with a headshot transfer of Vaz on the front wearing a cowboy hat and 'Last Chance Saloon' across the back). Of the six heading out on the stag weekend, four of the group, including him and Vaz, had been on his stag do; Rob lectured in politics and Steve in English at the same college as Mark and they'd hit it off so well with Vaz over the lead up to and his wedding day itself that they were now considered mates of Vaz as well. Ben was a colleague of Vaz' who taught science and then there was Aidy, the sort of bloke who once swam across the Manchester canal at 1am, drunk, for a bet; his prize being a large doner kebab. There were two notable absentees, Pete, whose wife was about to drop with their second, ("heaven help me if she went into labour whilst I was on the lash in Prague" seemed a reasonable enough explanation for him having to miss the trip), and Vaz' elder brother Manura who hadn't integrated into western culture to the same extent as Vaz and remained back in Leicester running the family grocery business, frowning on the vulgarity of a group of men travelling to such a beautiful city just to get drunk and ogle pretty eastern European women. "Just jealous," was Vaz' typically incisive appraisal. He wasn't far wrong, Mark had seen pictures of Vaz' sister-in-law and suggested to Vaz that he'd have thought his brother would welcome a few days away.

Mark looked out of the tiny porthole window at the banks of cloud dispersing below the flashing lights on the right (port or starboard?) wing and reflected upon his state of mind during the lead up to the stag weekend. The 'normal' Mark would have organised the T-shirts, albeit at the last minute, to have their heads Photoshopped onto the bodies of Marvel characters; Vaz would have been Dr Octopus with Ben the Green Goblin (that was maths and science dealt with), Aidy was clearly The Thing from Fantastic 4, Steve maybe Thor, less down to his physique but more down to his love of Nordic literature. Rob would be the Silver Surfer, enigma personified, leaving him, Mark Stark, the embodiment of Tony, charismatic millionaire, playboy, flawed but faithful hero of the human race.

He was brought back from these dizzy heights by a striking if over made-up blonde air stewardess who swayed gracefully from aisle to aisle ensuring everyone was clicked in ready for the descent. Into what, exactly, Mark wondered, into what.

*

Vaz had suggested that they muted their boisterousness whilst in line for passport checks so they suppressed the childish instincts and antics that seem to overwhelm a group of men given free rein, particularly abroad and shuffled steadily towards the sullen uniformed staff in their indistinct booths.

Mark became aware of a group in the line parallel to theirs that hadn't applied the same restraint so glanced rather than glared across so as not to be perceived as being condemning, just curious. He took in a similar number as theirs, but two girls and four blokes, all looking as if they were heading on a sales convention; the men with those awful cropped mullets that had somehow found their way into contemporary culture and the two girls (late 20s to early 30s) positively glowing and sparkling with foundation and lip gloss, somehow predatory in skinny jeans tucked into knee-high boots with spiky heels. One, the taller of the two had long black hair, part in a ponytail and the rest under an oversized cream woollen hat with a few strands of hair covering her ears whilst the other had dyed blonde hair in a sort of soft spiky bobbed style, not sleek like Sophie's but stylish all the same. The striking girl with the black hair, chirped, "Can we help you sweetheart?" in a south London accent.

Mark immediately flushed from cheek to ear and back as it must have looked as if he was slyly eyeing them up. Before he could stammer a response the blonde, whose back had been to him turned to check out the object of her friend's amusement and there was a moment when it seemed as if time stood still.

"Mark?" she questioned, a frown on her immaculately shimmering forehead.

"Jo!" Mark exclaimed, pausing before taking a step towards her and moving in for a 'French kiss' as his mum would have put it. This was a bit awkward for as Jo went for a classic air kiss, he stepped onto the pointed toe of her black leather booted foot and stumbled off course kissing the top of her right ear as a result then pointing this out to make it all the more embarrassing.

"You haven't changed a bit," she laughed as Mark pulled a face at getting some of her hair product on his tongue. If only you knew he had thought. "So what are you doing here in darkest Prague?"

"Totally not a cliché in any way, we're on an ironic stag do – just mineral water, art galleries and as many other cultural sights as we can take in along with a bit of clothes shopping, what about you?"

"An equally non-cliché sales team jolly," Jo replied, "We've had a few tough years, particularly on the paper-based products but the online trends have been positive with year-on year growth and so we're out to celebrate some solid year end results."

It was veering on Johnnie speak but with breasts and Mark was momentarily lost for words, he felt uncomfortable at the ungainly nature of their meeting and also at the fact that he considered her not unattractive. "Couldn't you have just gone to an All Bar One in Croydon?" was all he could muster. Her party laughed at this but he wasn't sure whether this was with or at his witty retort.

"Oh Mark, you are funny," Jo smiled. "Listen, here's my card, give us a call sometime over the weekend and if we're in a bar, or museum near you we'll come and join you, would be great to catch up." Before he had time to blink she had pressed a small white card into his hand, pecked him on the cheek then returned to an obvious grilling from her team, two of which, mullet senior and mullet junior kept looking over their shoulders in his direction and smirking gleefully.

"Plaaayer," cried Aidy, practically dribbling over the pale grey polished arrivals hall floor as his eyes bulged whilst staring at Jo and her female colleague's behinds before grabbing Mark in a vice-like headlock that he wriggled unsuccessfully to free himself from. Aidy let up before asking, "Go on then spill the beans … before I do!" He cackled furiously, breaking out into a coughing fit (the irony of being a 'fitness' instructor who smoked), before Vaz nudged him in the ribs and jerked his head in the direction of two stern looking security officers, peaked caps down, each with a hand on a black leather holster and probably not relishing yet another group of Brits intent on puking over their olde worldly cobbled streets and urinating in their medieval fountains. Aidy immediately calmed himself and they continued through to the exit without incident picking up two white Mercedes cabs and heading to their hotel to check in.

*

As it turned out, Mark needn't have been so anxious. The weekend passed without great incident and was, overall a resounding success. There were a few hairy moments as he'd expect from any such occasion but no one was imprisoned, no one got left behind but no one could remember the full extent of photos taken on their disposable cameras so agreed to symbolically dispose of them as a group before their return. Mark, of course, disposed of an unused camera and kept the one loaded with pictures, just in cases, as the Portuguese waitress would say in 'Love Actually' one of Lizzie's all-time favourite movies.

The medieval banquet on their first night had set the tone. The venue was amazing; a whitewashed crypt deep below the quiet city streets, the noise within hitting them after they'd jostled their way down the wide, spiral stone staircase lit with mock flaming torches and into a cavernous historic dining space. The walls were adorned with medieval arms and heraldry with some full sized suits of armour standing 'on guard' at either end of their reserved dining area, one of a number of vaults that ran off the central open hall, all formerly storage places for ale or mead in a bygone age that were now perfect for a private party experience that enabled diners to still remain connected to the noisy whole, creating a buzzing environment that allowed conversation to be heard easily above the background din.

The food was spot-on for half a dozen ravenous blokes; a meat feast with stodgy suet and huge portions of red cabbage and mash, the lager was excellent, cheap and didn't stop flowing from start to finish and the waitresses were all exquisite, in long flowing skirts and tight-fitting corset style tops that would have the temperature rising of even the most sober of clergymen. Despite the season, huge open log fires roared at each end of the hall, completing the increasingly soporific medieval atmosphere. If Pete had made it he would have no doubt told them the significance of the heraldry and various imitation weapons that lined the walls but Aidy simply wanted a photo of himself either striking a Rocky type pose in front of one of the suits of armour or mock (thank the Lord) 'mooning' Braveheart-style shot before a huge wall mounted pewter broadsword. Mark exchanged a complicit 'eyes rolled' with one of the glamorous waitresses, who added a beaming smile thus adding to an all-round glow that is traditionally associated with a hearty bowl of Ready Brek.

Any glow that was generated by that most memorable experience was soon extinguished as they stepped out into the night air. An unseasonal sleet shower had descended, giving the roads and pavements a slickness that was exacerbated by their alcohol induced unsteadiness. A chill wind licked the narrow lamp-lit streets nullifying conversation as the bunched, bloated, belching princes of Prague plodded methodically back to their hotel, oblivious to the elegant architecture that rose all around them as they had just one collective thought; hotel, bed, sleep.

*

"I know you always say 'alright' but you're talking to me now, so how are you doing really, mate?"

"I'm surviving, that's the only way I know how to put it, but my head is still just above the water."

They were having an early beer in the bar before their big Saturday night out and so far it was just Mark and Vaz nursing their oversized glasses in the hotel bar. The day had been fine, a typically touristy affair, with a walk across the Charles Bridge, a mooch around the castle, (cue more prattery from Aidy), lunch in an understated restaurant near the castle

331

followed by an open-topped carriage ride around the old town that Aidy had objected to on the grounds that it was insanely effeminate. The truth was, Mark had let it all wash over him, operating on autopilot, laughing in all the right places but failing to instigate or be at the heart of the banter, a place he usually occupied. Vaz was doing his intense best friend bit; despite the fact he was on his stag do it was important for him that Mark was doing okay. Mark had often expressed his opinions but had never been the best when asked to articulate how he felt emotionally, the words never quite managed to do his feelings justice, whether attempting to encapsulate the intense joy of being with Lizzie or the utter despair at losing her, mere words always seemed inadequate.

He shared this with Vaz. "I know that I am usually associated with drunken acts of stupidity or of acerbic swipes at the general public and not with emotional outpourings or insight but I have been learning the language of self-expression since Lizzie died, I mean of how you feel not just who is the fittest Charlie's Angel or who will win the Golden Boot award. After a really shaky start, I mean, I was in the pits, I thought I was beginning to pick up the pieces but, and this is obviously not unique to my experience, the first year is one anniversary after another so there's a relapse around every corner. You remember last month when I drove across to visit the graves on what would have been Ella's due date?"

"Of course," Vaz replied, nodding slowly, "I offered to come with you but you said it was something you should do alone."

"Not even the new Z4 could give me a sense of being alive," (he had exchanged the VW family car for a gunmetal grey BMW two-seat-sister to his former love the black Z3 at the beginning of March), "but I was numb from start to finish. I sat in the car outside the church for over 25 minutes before plucking up the courage to walk around and place the flowers at the graveside. As I entered the cemetery I saw a figure standing motionless, just gazing down at that mound of earth, now covered in turf, beneath where the three of them had been laid to rest. It was Trevor. I don't know how long he'd been there but I hadn't seen him walk past as I sat in the car so he must have been in there for over half an hour at the very least. I imagined him becoming a permanent sentinel at that graveside, with their deaths becoming the focus for his life, his feet somehow taking root and his energy being steadily drained as he fed their dry bones with his silent tears. Who could blame him after all? He'd lost his wife, now daughter, grandson and granddaughter before he had even had the chance to hold her. My legs almost gave way when I considered the depths of his grief. It somehow deflected mine. Does that sound weird?"

"Bloody hell mate, I can't imagine what you've both been through, both of you." Vaz looked down at his beer glass and shook his head, lost for words, as Mark usually was at moments like this.

Mark drifted off for a moment and pictured the scene. Trevor had turned slightly as he'd crunched along the gravel path towards him. They hadn't made an arrangement to meet but both sort of knew that the other would be there. Trevor had stood more upright as Mark got closer and Mark could see that he'd been weeping. They had stood there shoulder to shoulder in silence, just the wind rustling through that great old yew tree and the occasional cooing of a wood pigeon as Mark had leant forward and added his flowers to Trevor's. He had told Mark that this is exactly how he and Lizzie used to pay their respects to Rose, together in silence, and he turned his head to where a fresh bunch of carnations had been carefully arranged in a metal pot before the headstone of his beloved wife. He added that each death had taken something from him, a part of him that would always be lost, dead to the world. He had patted Mark on the shoulder, unable to add anything else (there was nothing left to say) and trudged off towards the little lane along which he had picked his way so many times before. He seemed oblivious to the hedgerows that were alive with early spring; the flowers, the chatter of the chaffinches, the breeze full of scent and the late morning sun that was gradually beginning to make its presence felt as they clearly offered no sense of joy or hope to him.

Mark looked up to where Vaz sat, thoughtfully and continued, "I saw a shell of a man Vaz, as I'd imagined an officer returning to rural tranquillity after serving on the Western Front, retreating into himself, at odds with his surroundings and convinced that no one could fully comprehend what he'd been through. Forever traumatised, forever alone. And my fear was that I saw myself in him. Do you remember that chilling moment when a young Anakin says a tearful farewell to his mother on Tatooine and his rucksack casts a shadow on a small whitewashed building that at once looks like the outline of Vader? Well in that moment I saw myself as a washed-up husk, unable to live or die, forever doomed to forego the living in memory of the dead. It chilled me to the bone Vaz."

Vaz swirled the dregs of his lager in the glass and breathed out a long sigh. He was struggling to formulate a response that came anywhere close to the enormity of what Mark had just shared when they were interrupted by Aidy, bursting into the bar wearing a huge grin and equally large comedy breasts that he fondled crudely as he chanted a lewd song of conquest that certainly wouldn't do anything to endear himself to the locals as it ended in a line that implied violating the local women and drinking all the beer that rendered Vaz' response redundant. Mark and Vaz smiled at each other as if to acknowledge the relief that this interruption afforded them before Mark reached across to pat him on the arm and announce, "Once more into the breach dear friend," and they both flicked internal switches and moved seamlessly from emotionally moving and morose to imbecilic and moronic as the evening unravelled in its own predictable way.

*

He remembered reflecting upon the emotional impact on his drive back to the family home when he first took Lizzie to meet his parents and Johnnie's lot almost a lifetime ago. He had been dreading his looming 40th birthday celebrations until he had met Lizzie and beyond all belief she had agreed to accompany him to Dorset to share the occasion. That drive down had been on a crisp, bright late November morning and she had dozed in the weak sunlight like a contented kitten, wrapped in her puffa coat as he struggled to concentrate on the road ahead such were her magnetising looks; he really couldn't take his eyes off her. His mood had been buoyant, expectant and he was energised by this sleeping beauty and the impact that he knew she would have on his long-suffering kin. This drive couldn't have been conducted in greater contrast. An angry shower pounded the windscreen, the late afternoon skies slate grey, tetchy and restless, reflecting his mood as he prepared himself mentally for an overnight stay with his parents. He had only agreed to visit on the condition that his brother wouldn't be there at which his mother had sighed and allayed his fears. He knew he was going to face the third- degree over his fallout with Johnnie and was already preparing his defence as familiar landmarks came and went, gently nudging his memory as an old friend might dig his ribs over an historic joke, prompting his signals and manoeuvres as he powered ever closer to home. He was used to a cloud of foreboding descending to wrap itself around him like the sea mist when the turning to Charlestown off the A354 came into view but his brief and overwhelming time spent with Lizzie at his side had burned off that mist and shone so radiantly into every experience since that he had almost forgotten what the dread felt like. It concerned him how easily he had allowed it to infiltrate once more, like that familiar old wax jacket that hung on the back door of the boot room, still a good fit despite the months that might have passed in between visits.

The private lane that led to Charlestown Manor was pocked with pot-holes and puddles so he took his foot off the accelerator aware of how easily an expensive alloy could be dented beyond repair by what lay beneath a seemingly innocuous-looking shallow pool of muddy water; besides he'd had the car hand washed by an enthusiastic group of Polish lads the day before that did a cracking job for a fiver (even the sills inside each door). The entrance was impressive, even he had to admit to that. The rhododendron bushes were in early bloom and the shrubs that jostled with them, forming the hedges on either side of the gravel driveway were neatly trimmed as always. The front door seemed more dark green and glossy than ever (just a fresh lick of paint as his father told him over drinks) and even the metal benches appeared to have enjoyed something of a facelift. Reassuring to see the terracotta pots that housed the bay trees on either side of the red tiled porch still wearing the cracks and chips that added to the character of the place, Mark thought. Lived in was what a well-bred family was content with his mother often used to say, clearly finding the regular upgrading of some of the local 'new money' properties to be extremely gauche.

His mother's blue Suzuki Swift was parked in the same place as always, the Aston would still be garaged but there was no sign of his father's Range Rover, what day was it? They all seemed to merge and had done since Lizzie's death. His father would either be in the boardroom or on the golf course, two environments that led to certainty and conclusion, unlike the less tangible territory of family discord. His mother would have been left to smooth the way, unwittingly of course, as she didn't operate to an agenda, she would just be her usual warm and adorable self, with his father probably skulking back for pre-supper drinks having stayed away for the greatest length of time that could be explained without appearing rude; how he loved his family's slavish devotion to social etiquette and their avoidance of tackling the issues that really mattered.

Like the shopkeeper in Mr Benn, she appeared, as always on the doorstep, gently wringing her hands, as Mark grabbed a rucksack containing a few essentials and a bunch of flowers from the boot. As he turned towards the house she stepped out towards him and he had a flashback to when she had scrunched her way across the gravel, all beaming smiles and arms wide open, to welcome Lizzie on her first visit that November afternoon less than five years earlier as he had unloaded the luggage and grabbed the flowers on that occasion and a huge lump formed in his throat. As she embraced him he took in her familiar scent, the softness of her woollen cardigan, the significance of him being here a single man again and he broke down, uncontrollably, inconsolably, clinging onto his mother (and the flowers) in a way he wouldn't have allowed himself to do if his father had been lurking uncomfortably in the hallway staring down at his brogues.

He had howled like a banshee for a full two or three minutes before allowing his mother to gently lead him into the house to be met with the smell of wood polish and wax jackets, eternal reminders of where he was and a catalyst for so much nostalgia; there was almost too much welling up for him to bear. June fussed about in the kitchen making a 'nice pot of tea', setting out the paraphernalia for a cream tea with the precision of someone who had done this so many times before. Mark lacked the energy to make his usual joke that an average pot of tea would suffice and sat at the pine table, elbows propping up his chin as he struggled to regain a sense of equilibrium. His eyes were drawn to a familiar knot in the wood that, with the smutty imagination of two teenage boys, more than faintly resembled a pair of breasts, something that he and his brother would snigger at over their cornflakes whilst their mother made their toast, oblivious to their puerile obsession. Mark requested that they stayed in the kitchen that caused a brief frown and raised eyebrow from his mother who was busy loading up the trolley with china cups, saucers and plates. He preferred the warmth and informality of the kitchen, finding the family drawing room oppressive and somewhat ridiculous in a dated, bourgeois Downton Abbey way. The library was different, equally upper class and outmoded but he loved to meander in and out of the shelves, trailing his finger along the spines, taking in the smell and the touch of those old books, allowing his imagination to roam also whilst ignoring the shelves of 'fake' collections added by his father to give the place a feeling of well stocked academic grandeur. What a love/hate relationship he had with this place and all that it had come to represent.

His mother's breeding prevented her from starting their conversation about how he was coping in the wake of losing his family, there were strict guidelines and protocols that must be followed lest we all become like Americans or those families from south London who bare all on trashy daytime TV shows just for their 15 minutes of fame, all so shameless, so vulgar. Instead, as he chomped (and she nibbled daintily) through their scones (butter, jam and then cream of course) she updated him on village life, the ructions at the golf club now ties were no longer required in the clubhouse and women were allowed on the greens; she had smiled as if in collusion at this point. How well attended the Easter services were and how lovely it would be if some of the families attended church more regularly than just Easter and Christmas as they do tend to clog the lanes with their huge 4x4s making it difficult for the regular congregations. (Mark refrained to point out that they are immune from such criticism only because they leave their V8 monster on the driveway and walk to church, not everyone lives within walking distance); how the youngest Villiars-Sprott lad (Charlie) had to be taken to A&E as he was far too competitive during the Easter egg hunt and had tripped and hit his head on Major Dunston's headstone. Ironic, his mother had pondered, that the Major, a personal friend of Monty, had himself died of a head wound inflicted at the battle of El Alamein.

The steady warmth of the Aga and the rich contents of the cream tea settling in his stomach had left Mark feeling decidedly drowsy and so, before matters could shift from the trivial to the meaningful he excused himself, thanked his mum, planted a kiss on her forehead and said he was going to get his overnight bag unpacked and take a shower before his father got home. "The red room is made up for you sweetheart," his mother chirped as he heaved himself up then plodded back along the hallway and up the two flights of stairs, dragging his rucksack behind him. There was such a spring in his step when he first showed Lizzie to the yellow room and without thinking he dropped his bag outside his room and made his way along the landing to the room where she used to lay her head.

He took a deep breath and pushed open the wooden door. The room had that static feel that rooms have when not in regular use. How is that, Mark thought? How can an empty room tell us so much about its inhabitants, the regularity of their comings and goings when not even a curtain tie is out of place? Somehow, a room can contain not only a tone or fragrance but the memory of a movement, the presence of a loved one, a footprint so light, so transient, barely heavier than the motes of dust that had danced in the winter light that afternoon when Lizzie first explored this room. He could see her vividly, curled into one of the armchairs or taking in the view across the lawn and out across the bay. He knew how she would have struggled to have contained her excitement at the little lounge that intersected the bedroom with the bathroom and oh how she would have squealed with delight on seeing that roll top bath. How Lizzie loved to soak in a hot, deep bath. In a playful way she was quick to banish him to his room that first afternoon as he could tell that she wanted to lose herself in her new surroundings, almost taking on the role of a pantomime

Cinderella with a 'is this really all for me' look in her huge brown eyes. The faded rug that would probably have slowed her down and prevented her from skidding had one of its corners turned up slightly, something that Lizzie would have noticed immediately so Mark crossed the threshold and straightened it with her in mind. He eased himself down into one of the yellow and white striped armchairs, closing his eyes, picturing Lizzie as she was on that momentous afternoon, urging her to reappear, a glowing vision to light up the April twilight and reassure him that she was at peace so that he could be. The house remained still, just the faint sound of the waves in retreat from the cliffs below, a lone herring gull letting out its piercing, solitary cry and the sweeping strings of Debussy from the drawing room two floors below.

Mark rose slowly from the armchair and moved with leaden legs through into the small lounge. The fireplace contained old twisted newspaper and a tepee of kindling ready for a lighted match and on the small writer's bureau sat the slim pale blue copy of 'Chesil Beach' that Lizzie had read the night of his 40th. He picked up the slender copy, the cover silky smooth to the touch and flicked through the pages, stopping to breathe in the now faintly musty scent of a book that hadn't been picked up in a long while. She had held this very copy, had immersed herself in the tragic narrative as he was now drowning in theirs. He suddenly felt overcome, light-headed and, replacing the book, had to steady himself, one hand on either end of that small desk, positioned to take in the breathtaking roll of cliffs stretching west towards Bridport and Lyme Regis now shrouded in mist once more, damp, dismal, depressing; my life he thought, shrouded in grief, clouded with uncertainty. Oh Lizzie, why did you have to leave me, my love? He was jolted out of his melancholy by the sound of the front door opening and closing, shoes being wiped on the inside doormat and his father's voice calling out to his mother. Blimey, time must have flown thought Mark as he tiptoed out of 'Lizzie's room' and back down the hallway to his own. He wasn't quite ready to face both parents so decided to remove his shoes and to stretch out on that black wrought-iron bed to gaze at the reassuring solidity offered by those red walls and white ceiling (a family home can simultaneously prove reassuring and haunting) as he settled himself before the 'dance of manners' that was surely to evolve as the evening wore on. At least, in that great family tradition, it would remain civil he conceded.

*

"I think the point I am trying to make is this; how could I ever trust that POMPOUS BLOODY HYPOCRITE *ever again*? He lied to ME, lied to SOPHIE and to YOU TWO, actually going behind *all of our backs* to do all he could to save the skin of that bastard who KILLED MY FAMILY? How could you possibly think there is any way back from betrayal on such a monumental scale? How could you even suggest it in the first place?" (Mark was practically shouting the roof of the drawing room down by this point, red faced and furious.) "And why did he do it? Oh, do tell?" (His parents remained tight-lipped, his mother looking tearful as she perched on the edge of an occasional chair, twisting her coffee cup round on its saucer whilst his father stood behind her with his jaw set, teeth grinding in silent fury at yet another drunken outburst from son number two.)

"To protect him and that slimy piece of crap Soames in a tax avoidance scam that would leave them both quid's in! For money, my dear parents, the love and pursuit of which was instilled in him from a very early age. HE LIED IN COURT UNDER OATH PEOPLE but hey, why change the habit of a lifetime, why blame the blue-eyed boy when we can put the boot into the black sheep eh?"

"That's enough now Mark," his father said slowly and sternly, with a hint of menace in his voice, "you are clearly drunk and you are upsetting your mother."

"Oh deary me, has the big disappointment in your lives gone and overstepped the mark of the socially acceptable, *again*? So maybe you could tell me, why is it okay for Johnnie to get pissed and chase every piece of skirt he can get his grubby little mitts on thus committing ADULTERY to go with the FRAUD, BRIBERY and PERJURY on his charge sheet but you object to me having a few brandies and letting off some steam as to the role MY BROTHER, YOUR SON had to play in the BRUTAL DEATH of your (so-called) *beloved* daughter-in-law and grandson, not to mention a granddaughter you never got to meet! Why is it he always gets let off the hook, whatever have I done to you to be treated as the lesser of the two, we both have your blood running through our veins so why do I always feel like THE ODD ONE OUT!"

At this Mark turned his back on them, after slamming his glass down on the small table next to the armchair from which moments earlier he had leaped up angrily, finally releasing the tension that had simmered all evening; over drinks before dinner, the fish pie, apple crumble and custard then finally coffee and liqueurs, small talk, chit-chat, one inconsequential event after another. He knew the bloody great elephant dominating each room they entered was Johnnie and became infuriated at how his parents edged around it, looking pale and pinched as they ate, barely touching a drop of the Sancerre that Mark was more than happy to polish off, exchanging (what they thought) were secretive glances as if to say, "now might be a good time, dear." He just wanted to have it out, and had now got his wish.

"Oh Mark!" his mother exclaimed, "this is threatening to tear the whole family apart."

"Tear THIS family apart," Mark replied sharply, turning to face them once more, "what about MINE 'cos your darling son sure has played his part in destroying *my* family let alone his own, yet still you keep him on that bloody pedestal where he's always been in your eyes."

At this, his father actually took a step forward, to do what Mark had no idea, but he was stopped in his tracks by his mother who simply put out an arm into the space that he would have strode into if he had continued any further.

She then placed her coffee cup and saucer purposefully on the table to her left, rubbed her eyes before looking at Mark and sighing. "I am afraid we seem to be talking ourselves around in circles and getting nowhere. I can't keep telling you how desperately sorry we are at the tragic loss of Lizzie, Isaac and little Ella Grace, sweetheart, it has been felt profoundly by your father and me, but you drinking, shouting and swearing at us is hardly going to help any of us to pick up the pieces. Your brother has made some serious errors of judgement and has been left in no uncertain terms as to what your father and I think of these. But this grudge, this bitterness, this *hatred*, if allowed to take hold, could damage what relationships we all have left beyond repair. Is that what Lizzie would have wanted do you think, Mark? We're not asking you to become best of chums with Johnnie, we're not naïve enough to expect that, but urge you to start thinking about some form of forgiveness, for all our sakes." She paused and the silence in the room was deafening. "I'm going to retire and maybe we can talk again in the morning when you've a clear head and we've all had a good night's sleep behind us. Goodnight Mark, darling." She moved across to Mark and kissed him on the cheek and then she nodded in the direction of his father who was now standing next to the grand piano, hands clasped behind his back and eyes still narrowed, as if to say 'your turn'.

There followed more uneasy silence as his mother left the room, accompanied by the faint tinkle of fine china as it rattled on the tray, as if both he and his father realised that one wrong word or even intonation could prove explosive. It was his father who spoke first, shaking his head slightly,

"Mark, your mother is right. We can spend the rest of our lives pointing fingers and laying blame but none of it will allow you, or any of us to move on with our lives. I can't even imagine what you have gone through, none of us can, but we don't want this tragic event to cause some sort of emotional chain reaction from which we may never recover as a family, and yes Mark, a family is what we are, come hell or high water. You probably think we are being selfish in the extreme wanting some sort of peace to be brokered between you and your brother, and in a way you'd be right to think so, but even if things can never return to how they once were and civility is the most we can expect then at least please consider how reconciliation might come to replace resentment."

His fury had subsided and his voice had softened as he bade goodnight and, with head down and hands still behind his back, like the minor royal he seemed to imitate, made his way out into the hallway to begin turning off lights and locking and bolting doors for the night.

Mark slumped into his chair once more, allowing everything to settle, the angry words that had been spoken, the accusations made, the desire for the path to reconciliation that his father urged him to pursue; was this from heart or head though he wondered. Was it more important from his parents' perspective that peace prevailed to keep face or that deep emotional and psychological scars were examined and healed and not just covered up for the sake of perceived harmony. He drained the dregs of brandy from his fine cut crystal glass and decided that enough was enough for now and that bed was the only thing his head could cope with.

*

Despite the wine, brandy and emotional outbursts he had slept surprisingly well. He always did when in his 'own' bed. It was strange that, when in Brighton he would almost keep one ear open at night, ready for the shattering of glass that heralded a burglary but here, in a much bigger house that was a far likelier target for a break-in he felt totally safe and able to sleep more deeply than anywhere else. This sense of security clearly extended to his formative years where he knew that any intruder would be met by his stern-faced father in dressing gown and slippers, brandishing shotgun or fire poker. Though he knew the harsh reality of a homeowner tackling an intruder in today's society differed dramatically from those old black and white movies when said intruder would mutter 'it's a fair cop chummy' and allow themselves to be escorted out of the premises on tiptoe by the red-faced victim who'd be twisting the criminal by the ear. He still trusted in the fact that his parents would protect him, regardless of the potentially fatal outcome of such a physical confrontation, he just felt safe and secure in his own bed.

He gradually eased himself up and out of bed to pull back those heavy curtains that did such a good job of blocking out the daylight that he never had so much of a hint as to what lay behind them until he drew them back. Hopeful of a bright spring morning he was met with a continuation of the previous night with the damp, dreary mist lingering, seemingly without point or purpose other than to put him in a bad mood. He struggled to remember the definitive answer his father had given him when he was a kid as to when, technically, mist became fog; it was something to do with density and visibility but the exact definition evaded him. Lost in the swirling mists of time, oh you are a wag he thought as he made his way to the en suite bathroom.

Feeling refreshed if not a little bashful after a hot shower and ready for the day ahead he trotted down the stairs, pausing on the bottom step and cocking his ear like a spaniel to ascertain who was where and doing what before proceeding. He could hear the murmur of Radio 4 coming from the kitchen and so made his way along the hallway in that direction. His mother, in a stripy pinafore, and trimming the stems off a huge bunch of colourful flowers turned to greet him warmly, wiping her hands and extending them to him, he took her hands and she led him to a seat at the table, placing a hand on each of his shoulders and giving them a gentle squeeze. Not surprisingly his father had departed for the office sometime earlier so he felt he could relax even more in his absence. With absolutely no reference to the previous night she asked him what he wanted for breakfast and began preparing the scrambled eggs with toast and coffee as if there had been no scene at all. Mark asked her who her secret admirer was to which she had visually scolded him; that look that all mothers possess that is equally effective whether the recipient is 4 or 40 years old. The flowers had, she explained, come from the leader of the Sunday school to thank her for stepping into the breach to manage the Easter egg hunt when the leader had taken little Charlie over to the A&E at Weymouth when he had hit his head on Major Dunston's tombstone.

"Would you believe they call it Junior Church now," she had tutted "whatever next, church light or church-to-go? Aren't they beautiful though," she had gasped before adding "and better late than never."

As he devoured his breakfast and slurped his coffee his mother sipped a cup also. She wasn't as gushing as she usually was but neither did she look at him reproachfully as she chatted about her plans for the rest of the week and asked him about his. He had to get his best man's speech written for Vaz' wedding and a few other bits and pieces, waiting for the change in tone from her as he did so, but it never came. He disappeared upstairs again for a few minutes to gather up his things and brush his teeth and as he was doing so a thought popped into his head. Once back downstairs he sought out his mother again, this time she was fussing about in the drawing room trying to decide where was the best place to display the flowers she had just housed in a heavy clear crystal vase. Mark requested some paper and a pen and, once he had these, he took himself off to the library, stilled himself, breathed in that musty air, shuddered as it was chilly in that huge space and then wrote a note to his father as he figured this was the safest form of communication between them.

Dear dad

Look no comma after dad – how thoroughly modern I am! Dad I am sorry for my outburst last night. I can't apologise for everything I said but I can for how I said it. I could see the disappointment in your face, a look that has become sadly all too familiar to me over my life, and want to attempt to make amends. The truth is, I know what a disappointment I have been to you since day one and what a jerk I was in my teens, twenties, oh and let's add thirties and early forties to the mix whilst we're at it. But why do you think that was/is? How could two sons raised in the same way by the same parents who have the same opportunities turn out so differently?

Somehow, and this is difficult to explain, I have never felt as loved by you as Johnnie has. With mum it's different, but you, well there has always been a hesitation, a tendency to always step away from me rather than towards me, to offer a half-hearted pat on the back rather than a full-blooded hug or ruffle of the hair from way back to when we were kids; a lack of warmth at best and almost a sense of repulsion at worst, and this is something I have wrestled with all my life. If Johnnie fell over and cut his knee you would pick him up, dust him down and carry on playing with him, offering him encouragement with a gentle tone to your voice that I never remember hearing. If that was me you would call me a clumsy oaf and send me inside to seek out mum; identical scenario, two different responses. Remember when he crashed his remote control plane into the rocks on the beach that Sunday afternoon not long after his 11th birthday? He was in as many emotional bits as the sea-plane and you praised him for such a good attempt before asking Bill to fix the plane up before trying again the next day. I wonder if you can recall your reaction when you came home from work to find out that Johnnie had let me have a go and not only had I crashed the bloody thing but most of it got washed out into the bay. You actually slapped my legs and sent me up to my room, calling me a 'hopeless case' how empowering is that!!

I am not going to list all my experiences that mirror that, as I don't think we have enough paper or time to do so, but hopefully you get the point. The further you withdrew from me the more I craved your attention, your approval, classic and clichéd I know but in the end I would do whatever I could to get recognised by you in some way, even if it was for being a complete prat. In the same way some of my students self-harm in order to feel <u>something</u> over an emotional numbness or as a cry for help, I would do stupid or dramatic things just to get noticed by you reckoning that a bollocking from you in your study at least enabled me to be in the same room as you even if it was for a few brief moments before being grounded for a week. And I guess that's been the pattern ever since (although the accident with the Mini was neither me trying to get noticed or was a cry for help but me genuinely being a complete eejit as Mary would put it).

Lizzie somehow changed all that. I could see the impact that she had on all the family, even Sophie came out of her ice palace and was partially melted by the warmth and light that positively radiated from my beautiful wife. I could see your expression change dad, you didn't seem to view me as such an abject loser any more as how could I be if Lizzie had agreed to date and then marry me! Surely I must have some redeeming qualities to manage such a catch (and before your mind races I am hardly a 21st century Errol Flynn) but Lizzie just decided to dig a bit deeper than the rest of you to see what lay beneath my acerbic and sarcastic veneer – why does anyone create a veneer I wonder? And now she has gone, along with my own number one son and the daughter I never got to hold, let alone watch grow up. The loser has lost it all. And Johnnie's scheming is at the heart of it – instrumental in the circumstances leading to that fateful *morning and then stooping to a point lower than I thought imaginable to ensure his partner in crime got off almost scot-free, betraying me, the memory of Lizzie and all that you worked so hard to instil in him from day one; honesty, integrity and family loyalty and yet he remains at your bosom; number one son in all ways. So indulge me a little here dad and allow me to rant and rage as for some time it was all that kept me going as I stumbled blindly through the dark pit of grief that I found myself in, and still do, in the wake of all that I loved and held so dearly being ripped so brutally and suddenly from my grasp.*

I would like to find and make peace, I can't tell you just how much, but this has to be at my own pace and not to fit a social agenda. A wise man (not from the east, from South Africa actually) has taught me a lot about forgiveness. If you rush to forgive someone because you feel pressurised by social convention to do so you are potentially (a) being hypocritical as you are not genuinely 'feeling it' and (b) being unkind to yourself as your process to reach the point of forgiveness might take a wee bit longer than those around you might like or expect. What I'm saying is, 'never say never'. I have not ruled out moving towards forgiving God for not intervening and saving them, to Johnnie for deceiving and general treachery and even Guy for attempting to influence the verdict by threatening a witness and then feigning remorse in order to get a reduced sentence. If it is humanly possible to reach this point then it is a peak I will endeavour to scale but not to please or appease you but to be able to live some sort of life without the woman I adored and children that I treasured. Imagine that dad, to truly treasure your offspring and mourn their demise.

Maybe one day, standing side by side in the garden and whilst gazing out across that vast ocean with you pointing out the ships in the distance the way you used to with Johnnie, you might reveal a little as to why you have always viewed me the way you have, why the coldness, the harsh looks and tone, the criticism and contempt. I tell you what, in the meantime, I won't write you off as a father if you promise not to write me off as a son. Deal?

Always your son,

Mark

A huge fat tear plopped onto the sheet of writing paper, like a watery seal replacing the wax of old as he folded the letter neatly and placed it into the crisp white envelope supplied by his mother and addressed it simply to

'Dad'. Standing it in the letter rack on the hall table he turned to embrace his mother and set off for the drive back along the coast once more, at which halfway point, the New Forest firmly behind him and signs for Chichester and Brighton coming into view, a switch always flicked in his mind and his thoughts turned from what he had left behind him and returned to what lay in front.

4

June 2012

Green shoots

Music had the most remarkable knack of transporting the listener back to a time and a place in a matter of chords, to invoke emotion, shift a mood, in a heartbeat. That was why Mark had been so careful as to what he had listened to over the past five months. At times he had avoided tracks he and Lizzie had a shared love of, ('One Day Like This' by Elbow or 'Paradise' by Coldplay to name just two). At other times he'd played them loudly at home (never in the car for fear of losing control and crashing, although the thought had crossed his mind on more than one occasion that this wouldn't necessarily be a bad thing).Closing his eyes and picturing an embrace with Lizzie in the lounge, her head resting on his chest to Coldplay, the soft touch and wonderful smell of her hair, or lifting and swaying Isaac in the kitchen to Elbow, inviting the emotion to come in powerful waves, bracing himself and then submitting as they pounded his emotional defences, overwhelming him, only to emerge a few exhausting minutes later a bedraggled wreck, choking and spluttering and gasping for air. This self-imposed emotional water-boarding was his way of gauging if he was making any progress at all in working through his grief. Was he managing to gain even the slightest of footholds after having the sand shift beneath his feet so radically, so violently? As he accelerated smoothly, leaving Portslade behind him and heading out towards Shoreham on the A27 with the hood down and 'If I survive' booming out of the speakers (the dance track by 'hybrid' without the *will* that might suggest Gloria Gaynor, an altogether different proposition) he had come to the conclusion that he had done just that, survived. Small steps, green shoots, the pain was not quite so raw so much of the time. Sure, wounds would easily open when scratched, but the healing process was showing signs of beginning at least and for that he was thankful.

He had returned to making lists in recent weeks, something he had done mentally for as long as he could remember, for example: 'top 5 fittest women of all time', 'top 5 Man Utd players of all time', and 'top 5 Marvel superheroes of all time', (he wasn't so keen on the DC characters, Batman aside). Lizzie was a writer of lists that were of a more practical nature; what food shopping was required, what jobs needed doing around the house, (Mark was always sure to give this one a wide berth, particularly on a Saturday morning as he made a brew and bacon buttie and tiptoed into the lounge to watch Soccer AM on Sky), which friends and family members' birthdays were due and gift ideas, that sort of thing. The previous night over a glass or two of red wine, Mark had finally opened the faux Dickensian style notebook that Lizzie had given him as one of his Christmas presents as a way of recording ideas for his plays but which had become more of a journal. He had, on the advice of Father Robin, been recording his emotional journey and charting the highs and lows along the way. He'd scoffed at this suggestion at first, thinking it a bit Bridget Jones (did men keep a diary of emotions? Not any he knew), but soon began to embrace and value the process. Some of the pages contained more underlined capital letter angst than a schoolgirl on learning that Take That had split up (again) but on the whole it had proved helpful and somehow cathartic.

His most recent list recorded some of the positive steps that he had taken recently that had proved significant, as they either went some way to addressing his bitterness, isolation, anger, fear and sorrow, and/or involved interacting with people, something he had avoided at almost all costs in the months after the accident (this was progress in itself as he had stopped calling it murder). There were one or two glitches on the list also, but as Mark reflected, 80%+ of it recorded steps being taken in the right direction. The list read:-

1)   Managing incahol antake (deliberate gag there) and not smashing the place up like a petulant rock star (sticking to the not drinking before 5pm on a weekday rule and not drinking just to get smashed, well not always – see note on Vaz' wedding day).

2)   Meeting with Lisa for a coffee and actually enjoying her company (albeit in a small dose – she kept persisting and said she wouldn't take no for an answer. At first I thought she was being a right royal pain in the arse but now I realise that she was being a faithful friend to Lizzie in looking

out for me – she was careful not to keep telling me that Jesus loves me though!)

3) Meeting Hope for a cuppa on the seafront, in a café she used to meet Lizzie in (this was so tough at first, seeing Hope and all that brought back and gazing out across the restless ocean where both me and Hope had sat doing the same thing with Lizzie on separate occasions) but it was okay after we got over the initial awkwardness, back to old Hope though, barriers up and giving little away. Managed to cop an eyeful of her cleavage just the once, but in a respectful way.

4) Visiting Mandy in Moulsecoomb ((that was so depressing but Lizzie would have approved). Felt guilty for not staying for a cup of tea and tried so hard to smile rather than grimace at her grubby looking brood, still half-dressed and all standing in her tiny lounge hypnotised by The Tweenies on full blast. She refused the Sainsbury's bags full of groceries (including some exotic items such as carrots and apples) at first but I insisted, telling her it was what Lizzie would have wanted and she relented; so her pride remained intact.

5) Visited Polly Soames (albeit with Sophie) for afternoon tea at their villa off the seafront. She was a lovely woman and so apologetic on behalf of her husband. I found myself reassuring her as she broke down in tears, not for the first time (cue American movie voice-over man), *"In a world when bereaved becomes the counsellor, the comforted becomes the comforter ... "*

6) Totally screwed up my Best Man's speech at Vaz' wedding having downed about a bottle of champagne beforehand, kept drinking and made a half-hearted drunken pass at the maid of honour (a cringe inducing cliché) before being carried to my room by the ushers. Vicki has just lifted the embargo on me, and Vaz, bless him, still maintains that he saw the funny side.

7) Returned to Charlestown to see the 'rents and actually enjoyed a pleasant weekend stay (I could see dad still floundering on the rocks of emotional expression and still feel disappointed that we didn't have the watershed father/son talk I'd expected) but he did make reference to my letter and mumbled some sort of an apology – at least a start point for a more positive relationship?

8) An appendage (ooh-er-missus) to No 7. Actually went to church with mum and dad on the Sunday morning (found it at the same time nostalgic and quite peaceful, familiar prayers and hymns followed by a

stroll back for a Sunday roast, surprisingly enjoyable). Still not on 'besty' terms with God but at least have stopped railing him with expletives like a pagan with Tourette's!

9)   Another addition to the Charlestown Herald, and breaking news of sorts, have agreed to attend family barbecue over August bank holiday and not set fire to Johnnie. Sophie and the children also to attend so the UN Peacekeeping Force on standby.

10)   Called Jo Martin! Twice actually, but on each occasion I quickly rang off before she picked up.

Had managed to work out how to withhold number so she'd be none the wiser; felt guilty at even thinking of her at all, so clearly not ready for this yet!!

There had been some other advancements made, he'd had a beer with Pete who had forged ahead and finished the first draft of their play 'Over the Top' and given a copy to Mark to read, Mark was so touched by this and it felt like such an accomplishment to have the sheaves of typed script, *their script* in his hands, albeit in draft form. The decorator friend of Keith's had been booked for later in the month to repaint Isaac's room and the nursery and he was currently on the way to Ford Open Prison to visit Guy Soames. Yes, *the* Guy Soames.

He'd continued spending his Wednesday mornings with Father Robin and over the weeks and months after Lizzie and the family's passing they had gone deeper into the whole area of how burdensome hatred is to carry and how liberating forgiveness can be. Mark knew that there were no cast-iron guarantees that he would be able to forgive Guy Soames, or Johnnie for that matter, but he had taken a deep breath and decided that it was about time he gave it a go. He had signed up for a restorative justice programme through the local probation service and had attended a couple of preparatory briefings to ensure that (a) he was ready to undertake the process and (b) so they could gauge on a level of 1-10 what was the likelihood of him attempting to murder Soames when sitting opposite him. (Mark was guessing the second point but it made good sense to be on the safe side.) The truth was he had no idea how he would react on meeting Soames, to a large extent this would depend on how arrogant or remorseful his brother's business partner appeared.

He had driven this stretch of road countless times before but on this afternoon his anxiety had kicked in over an hour earlier than it usually did as he left Worthing in his wake and exited the A27 at Arundel. He had mixed feelings towards Arundel, loving the castle and the lake, the cafés and antique shops but all this was marred by the one experience he'd had of living with a girlfriend. In the end even the waterside views from the balcony of their rented apartment failed to compensate for the sinking feeling he'd experienced in his stomach that he had made a terrible decision and one he'd be stuck with until humanely acceptable to break the tie, something he had done with some relief. He was beginning to enjoy driving the Z4 auto, another sign that he was emerging from the ice age he'd endured those past five months where he'd remained numb to almost everything that had previously given him pleasure. Okay he had gone through the mangle on the last day of the season when Paddy Kenny had made a complete hash of an injury time Agüero strike to gift City the title with practically the last kick of the season (in injury time and on goal difference from Utd – groan) but he had generally existed in a state of indifference, even to this stunning 5 year old gunmetal grey convertible with tan leather interior that he had bought in part exchange for the VW people carrier three months earlier ("aren't all cars people carriers" he had said to the sales assistant in the showroom to which he'd smiled but still looked bemused).

But today was a different story as he flicked through some of his favourite 'in-car-hood-down' tunes and unleashed the 2.5 litre engine on that familiar route between Hove and Chichester. He'd eased off the gas as he wound his way down towards Ford, past the railway station on one side and the pub on the other (landmarks he'd scribbled on the back of an envelope before he'd set off that morning) to where he found the prison on the route to Climping. The road carved the facility in two, with the residential area on one side and the workshops on the other. It looked less like a prison and more like an industrial unit or aerodrome maybe, with row upon row of neat little white brick built huts that housed the inmates. He was expecting razor wire, corner turrets manned by armed guards and German Shepherd dogs snarling ferociously on the end of short leashes controlled by burly, expressionless tattooed warders, especially since the previous year's high profile New Year's Day riots and countless subsequent newspaper exposés since on how easy it was to get in and out of the facility. But instead he was stopped at a barrier manned by a single officer, who checked his ID before waving him through, with no more security than at the entrance to his local Waitrose car park. He followed the signs to the parking area and then the visitors' reception, all very civilised he thought, where he presented his ID, signed in and was asked to wait. Nothing out of the ordinary, like a doctor's waiting room with easy chairs set out around low round tables but with a different theme of poster on the grey walls and not a National Geographic in sight. Within 5 minutes he was asked to follow a uniformed warder who was no taller or broader than him, with crisply ironed short sleeve light blue shirt, dark blue trousers and cap and the regulation chain of keys. They went through a mini airport security set-up where he was asked to hand in money, wallet, keys and phone (his passport and driver's licence had been checked at reception). Mark had been online to check out the routine in advance and so, on depositing his personal belongings in a plastic tray said casually, "Just the rub down with passive drugs dogs option please." Amazingly not one of the four wardens even hinted at a smile at this witticism although as he turned towards the officer holding a friendly looking spaniel who was rather comically wearing a high-visibility harness (dog not handler) he thought he saw one of the group mouth a word that seemed to end in 'anchor'?

Cleared for drugs, concealed weapons and iron files secreted into a hollowed out bible, he was led through a set of locked doors with steel grey bars, through a narrow grey painted corridor and then through another set of identical locked doors with bars. Mark had again attempted to punctuate the silence with his wit, "Bit of a bugger to go through all this rigmarole only to realise you've left your phone in reception eh?" Again, silence. He was led out into a small canteen style area where other visitors were sitting, heads bowed across the table, conferring with the inmates they were visiting. Mark was shown to a table with a plastic chair positioned on either side and was asked to sit and wait. He looked around him, taking in the scene and the low hum of conversation, his mouth dry and head spinning a little. He wished he'd drank more water but hadn't as he knew he'd need the loo at the least opportune moment. He glanced up again in the direction of a dishevelled looking fella with untamed red curly hair and stubble who was having a lively conversation with a young peroxide blonde woman whose complexion was on the Satsuma skin colour scale and who seemed dressed more for a night out than a prison visit; maybe that was the source of his ire, Mark thought, as he certainly didn't look to be 'a happy bunny'. Mark did a raised eyebrow as if to endear himself with the inmate in a 'women eh?' gesture but this obviously got lost in translation, possibly owing to the nervous grin that Mark wore at seminal moments. "What the feck are you looking at shirt- lifter," was the somewhat aggressive response

352

he received. A sort of Irish rogue-brogue come Johnnie comment. Mark spread his hands out as if to say "you've read me all wrong guv", but the inmate had already resumed his finger pointing at his visitor who, on closer inspection, was pregnant; not great if her fella had been banged up in here for over 9 months whilst she was getting banged up out there Mark thought, but decided, wisely, to keep this clever observation to himself.

He turned back to look towards the door from which inmates were being led in and out and his heart started hammering as a vaguely familiar figure was being shown in and directed to where he was sitting. Guy Soames looked different to when he'd last seen him, well-groomed and ruddy in court, he'd lost weight not only physically but his gravitas was also diminished, reduced to a level playing field in a grey T-shirt and tracksuit bottoms with yellow sash representing an inmate with visiting rights. He had run this scene so many times before, his body language, acid one-liners, the spitting recriminations and spewed threats, even throwing another punch had crossed his mind. As he stood weakly he froze on the spot, all anger seemed to drain from his body and out through his Converse trainers. As Soames got closer Mark swayed a little, a trickle of sweat running down his back and sticking to his T-shirt and thought how camp he'd look if he'd swooned, especially in front of the bare knuckle fighter and his Mrs to his right who'd probably assumed that Mark had become over emotional at visiting his boyfriend. So they stood, on opposite sides of the table, both looking extremely uncomfortable in the other's presence, neither knowing how to greet, how to start.

"It's one round apiece you know." Mark broke the silence whilst pulling back his chair to sit and gesturing for Soames to do likewise.

"Sorry?" Soames replied, seeming nervous and not surprisingly confused by Mark's opening line as he took his seat.

"I've pictured your face countless times these past few long months," Mark continued, "like Marvin Hagler did with images of Tony Sibson back in the '80s before he knocked seven bells out of him in the ring. I've had a similar inclination by the way, even dreaming about softening you up round after round before delivering the knockout blow. Not a reoccurring nightmare, no, more a burning desire. But then, just last month, totally out of the blue, it came to me, you haven't actually got a bad right hook on you yourself."

"Forgive me," Soames responded, frowning and shaking his head, "I just don't follow."

"We've had a little tête-à-tête before you know; February 2008 to be precise, in the bar at the Number One Aldwych. I'd taken Lizzie up to town to the theatre and then was planning to propose to her over dinner in Axis downstairs, but she had gone down with chronic period pains and was curled up in our room whilst I got steadily pissed at the main bar. You were there getting rowdy with some friends and you kept bumping into me, so we exchanged a few words and you punched me. Pretty good shot too and I certainly didn't see it coming. So me chinning you in the Funky Buddha makes it all square."

Soames exhaled loudly and looked down at his hands that were clasped in front of him on the table.

"I do recall an incident, vaguely," he shook his head again, "was that really you? My, what a small world."

"Indeed it is," continued Mark, "I mean what were the odds of my brother being on speaker-phone at the precise moment you ran down my family, leaving them for dead, oh, of course, they were, before driving off, I mean what were the odds on that?"

Mark hadn't meant to get to this point so quickly, nor so angrily. He had intended on asking a few mundane questions about prison life and hoping that Soames would have offered an apology but the tension of the atmosphere in the room, the realisation that he was finally face-to-face with the perpetrator had obviously proved too much for him to handle.

Soames winced, but before he'd had a chance to respond Mark opened his hands in a gesture of apology and continued, "Sorry, that wasn't meant to come out that way."

"Bloody hell Woodford, you've got nothing to apologise for, if our roles were reversed I'd have probably started round 3 by now!"

Mark was reminded of how ex public school boys retained the habit of referring to each other by their surnames, something he hadn't experienced in the past as his parents had decided against sending him to public school with Johnnie, opting for the local state secondary option instead. At first he had resented this decision as yet another example of Johnnie's preferential treatment, but had, on observing his brother's outmoded hooray Henry approach to life, appreciated the decision and, for once, was in agreement with his parents that he'd be better suited to a secondary modern.

"Look," Soames continued, staring at his once manicured hands, that now carried a few nicks due to the work he had been doing on a local farm, as Mark found out later in the conversation, "there is no way on God's earth that I can apologise nearly enough to you for what I have done, for the pain I've inflicted on you and your family, whatever I say will sound pathetic, derisible, insincere. I know this is hardly death row in here but you do spend a lot of time by yourself, when the other inmates leave you alone, to do some serious soul searching and I honestly cannot comprehend what you have been through, no, what I have put you through. It would be far easier if you had come in here shouting the odds and making the sort of threats I would probably want to make if I were in your shoes, it's harder that you're not. Hardest of all is that you are here and I have to face you like this."

"I didn't come here to make you feel anything in particular," responded Mark, "to be honest I've spent more time wondering how this would affect me rather than you. Up until recently it would have seemed absurd to have even considered it, and it still feels totally surreal to be here having a conversation with you without exploding, but after much reflection and since visiting your lovely wife and daughters …"

"Oh God no," Soames pleaded, "please, not Polly and the girls, I'd understand you wanting some sort of justice but please take it out on me and not them for the love of …"

"Soames, you complete Muppet," Mark cut in, "I'm a former part- time college lecturer and would-be playwright, not one of the bloody Sopranos. I didn't mean I visited them to leave a horse's head on your pillow you fool, but I went for tea with Sophie to see how they were recovering from it all. Blimey, you've only been in here 5 minutes and you've gone all Mafioso on me!"

This little exchange was the one that helped to break the ice and they carried on talking about how their lives had changed irrevocably since that fateful day back in January, conversing increasingly as new found acquaintances rather than bitter foes until a stern looking warder standing on a small raised wooden platform called out that there was just five minutes left of visiting time. Mark was staggered first at how quickly two hours had passed but also how he had been moved by Soames' expression of remorse that was so heartfelt, the man so completely different from the arrogant prick who had angered him so intensely prior to and throughout the court proceedings. And Soames in turn had wept silently after Mark had produced a few photos and lovingly described his relationship with Lizzie, Isaac and the joy they had shared at discovering they had a daughter on the way; not with the intention of making Guy feel so desperate but to share his/their story and go some way to conveying the full impact of their lives colliding in such a violent and lasting way. Neither seemed to care less about the glances they were receiving from some of the more hardened cons who were more than likely completing a longer sentence here rather than just dropping by as was the case with Soames, as the conversation rocked gently back and forth and tears were spilled on both sides.

As Mark got up to go he gathered his thoughts, extended his hand to Guy Soames and said, "I'd like to thank you for seeing me Guy, it was brave of you. With your permission I'd like to visit your family again, with Sophie of course, to tell them about this visit and reassure them how you will be a changed man as a result of your time in here. I can't salvage my family life but am prepared to help you to rebuild yours, as at least you might have a chance to start again." Soames, who was standing, having shaken Mark's hand, started to weep silently once more, his head bowed. "And Guy," Mark whispered, his tears now falling freely that his vision was blurred, "I forgive you."

Now it was Soames' turn to be overwhelmed, he let out a wail that caused the last few visitors and inmates to jerk their heads sharply in his direction as he was led gently away by a warder. Mark stood and watched this once proud man shuffling off in tracksuit bottoms that sagged as they were too baggy for him, his shoulders hunched and still shaking from the sobs. Mark breathed in and out, holding the exhaled breath as Lizzie had once taught him when instructing him on how to remain or regain a sense of composure and then followed the same warder out who had led him in. He knew he wouldn't be returning, he wouldn't have to, for he had uttered the few words he'd never thought he would hear himself say, and in doing so had gone some way to release them both from what seemed an irreconcilable burden; that of a life that would for ever stand still on January 10th 2012.

Driving back to Brighton, the hood down, the late afternoon sun still strong, the warm air full of impending summer and blue skies, of possibility accompanied by the sound of Faithless booming from the speakers, Mark found himself breaking into a smile. Okay, he thought, small steps, green shoots, but Father Robin was right, oh how he was right. Mark has suffered the bite but would not allow the poison to spread. What was it he had said that reminded him of a quote that Lizzie once shared with him? That was it, 'My yoke is easy and my burden is light'. You clever man, he thought, you clever, clever man.

5

September 2012

A glimpse of sunlight

A huge part of reclaiming his life was to revisit familiar places that still haunted him due to their, or rather his, association with Lizzie and/or Isaac. Growing up in Dorset with those vast, stunning sea expanses that stretched without limit before him from his family home had instilled in him a great affinity with the ocean that he had carried with him since, never veering too far away from the south coast, and if so, always looking for a way back. Part of the draw of Brighton was Hove seafront; the long, wide promenade leading to the bars, cafés, gift shops and street traders in and around the worn arches, a part Shoreditch-by-sea but without fear of ever being over-gentrified. There seemed a collective consciousness amongst those who lived and worked in Brighton and Hove, embodied in a strong sense of character, of individualism, of creativity and independence; big ideas without the big brands. Mark loved this, and although he was someone who shuddered at the thought of being part of a group, club or movement, he still felt that energy on a day such as this in early September when he sat on a bench, feet up on the railings, eyes closed, as he faced the late morning sun and breathed in the scent of the coffee he'd bought from a kiosk near the row of brightly coloured beach huts at West Hove. He listened to the gentle rhythm of the breakers, probing the shoreline followed by their whooshed retreat over the shingle and surrendered his senses to all that surrounded him. This was a little slice of heaven, as Lizzie would have called it. As the sun's gentle rays cradled his face and the waves continued to rise and fall he allowed his mind to meander, to have free rein of its own corridors, to roam and reflect, pause and persist, Mark the willing recipient of snippets or scraps as his thoughts followed the ocean's pull, gently this way, then that.

Shortly after his seminal visit to Guy Soames he had once more been received into his family home by Polly, accompanied by Sophie his ever-watchful guardian angel. Guy had written to Polly in the light of his conversation with Mark and had vowed to put everything straight and start over, if only she and the girls would be prepared to give him another chance. Listening to Polly and Sophie discuss the relative failings of their spouses, he doubted that this would ever happen so decided to surprise them both by sharing some of what Father Robin had taught him about working towards being relieved of the burden of resentment in order to be free to look ahead and not constantly over your shoulder; not to allow the past to define the present to such an extent that it prevented some sort of a future. Sophie, who knew Mark better than Polly, was still cynical of this approach, and seemed to prefer the option that simply required a pair of bolt cutters and their husbands' privates, but when this philosophy was extended towards Johnnie at the family barbecue over the August bank holiday she realised that Mark meant business, and that she must either get with it or get left behind.

He had been extremely sad to finally say goodbye to Father Robin, whose time in the UK was up and so had flown back to whatever awaited him in Johannesburg. What a coincidence, (Lisa, whom he still met up with from time to time to discuss matters of life and faith, called it God-incidence, an expression that still made him feel nauseous, bless her, with all her little 'isms'), that Father Robin had been staying just around the corner from him at the time he most needed him. Mark wasn't so sure about God putting Robin in his path 'for a reason' but this gentle friar certainly proved to be the perfect foil, someone who could absorb his anger at the Creator yet respond with such a depth of wisdom and compassion that he'd only ever encountered in Yoda. He knew that Mrs S was quietly patting herself on the back for making the introduction in the first place and had high hopes of inducting Mark into her local church community, so had been taken aback when Mark had refused to accompany her to 'holy Mass' to give thanks for Robin's safe return to South Africa. Nice try, he had thought, but he was still at the toddler stage in his understanding and acceptance of the 'broad church' that Christianity represented and was still unsure as to whether he'd ever want to progress to the walking stage let alone running, or even the flying as Lizzie had done.

He had taken another huge step on his path of personal redemption just a fortnight or so before, when the tombstone had replaced the small wooden cross that marked the spot where Lizzie (beautiful Lizzie), Isaac and Ella Grace had been laid to rest. He met with Trevor (faithful, broken

Trevor) and dear old Reverend Poe, who said a few short words as they laid flowers and consoled one another again. The headstone was in a rustic grey to fit in with the flint of the church and so many of the other headstones in that old graveyard. The inscription had been inspired by the note that Lisa had left at the site of the accident and had remained scribbled down in the little notebook that Lizzie had bought him the previous Christmas, but paraphrased due to the limited number of digits to fit:-

"For I am convinced that neither death nor life, nor anything else in all creation will be able to separate us from the love of God that is in Christ Jesus our Lord." (Romans 8).

Here lies Lizzie, Isaac and Ella Woodford, taken in 2012, all before their time.

Loved and missed, cherished and remembered always by all who knew them.

Trevor had been his usual upright and dignified self, raincoat over his right arm as always, despite the heat of the mid-morning August sun but he looked increasingly drawn, large purple bags gave him a bruised appearance contrasted by his grey complexion and Mark had noticed a few patches of white stubble under his chin where once his face would have been shaved with military precision. As Mark departed that poignant scene, Trevor still rooted to the spot, he feared for his father-in-law's future as he knew he would never be the same man again. Mark conceded to himself that, although he had changed almost beyond recognition over the previous 5 years and had almost sunk without trace since the beginning of that year, he had rekindled a little flicker of something that seemed to have been distinguished conclusively in Trevor seven months earlier; that of hope.

He also had faith, faith in his ability to emerge from this car crash intact, to click all his bones back into place and to limp purposefully towards his future without the feelings of futility and dread that had first left him physically and emotionally incapacitated. He had made some alterations to the interior at Waldegrave Road and had put it on the market, to receive an offer within days from a pleasant couple, he a lawyer and she a doctor, on their first viewing, both recently qualified and married and looking to start a family. It certainly is a fabulous family home, he had told them, and had accepted their offer with *just a shred* of jealousy at the thought of them dreaming their dreams, of starting a life for themselves and their would-be family in the same way, same place that he and Lizzie had. But these feelings soon subsided and gave way to a genuine hope that they would be happy and healthy in his and Lizzie's home and that the walls would resound once more with howls of laughter and disagreements, with shouts of joy and frustration (and tears of both), remembering instances from the full range of experiences that had reverberated off the olive, cappuccino and raspberry walls that he and Lizzie had so lovingly installed and then chipped and scuffed once family life had begun in earnest.

To his back, across the green and Kingsway sat the fine row of regency buildings that comprised Brunswick Terrace, one of which, a 'stunning top floor two-bed apartment with bags of character and uninterrupted sea views', was soon to become his, having had an offer accepted earlier that week. Again, all part of the catharsis, the reclamation, being able to live and breathe this air that he'd once shared so memorably with Lizzie, so tenderly with Isaac, and, ironically, just around the corner from the Soames' villa. He would be just about strong enough now to be able to gaze from his new lounge or balcony out across the promenade to view other parents shepherding their kids on scooters or bikes, removing the stabilisers as a new phase of childhood was reached, reflecting the point he was at on his emotional recovery; taking the stabilisers off and taking his first short and unsteady strides towards his new life alone.

He opened his eyes and sipped his coffee, the takeaway cup retaining its warmth. On the beach to his right a couple sat back-to-back on the pebbles reading, occasionally stopping to take in the vast expanse of blue/grey swell that maintained its steady progress towards the sea wall. A woman who was probably in her late 50s was to his left, sitting on the next bench with her bare feet tucked up and her chin on her knees, also taking in the serenity of the scene before her. This was a place where he had sat and gazed for hours whilst with a napping Isaac on many a Sunday afternoon or had walked hand in hand with Lizzie, all loved up and carefree, before they were in the family way and when it seemed that they had it all in front of them, this world at their feet. The sun had been momentarily obscured by the clouds but now reappeared. This sudden burst of sunlight coupled with a soft, salty breeze brought his skin out in goose bumps. It was as if they could read his thoughts, he shivered, that they knew he was thinking of them and missing them so, so much. He closed his eyes once more, whispered their names, shed a tear, wiped it and whispered once more, aloud, 'I know you are all safe, in that place you always talked of, Lizzie. Thank you for reassuring me my darling girl – you will always be my one and only true love whatever happens from now on. How I love you. How I miss you, all of you. But I'll be okay now, sweetheart. I'll be okay. You be at peace now my beautiful girl. You go now and be at peace.'

A lone jogger stopped at the railings near to where he sat and gasped for breath before slurping noisily from a water bottle. A sprightly looking older woman tugged at the lead of her Scottie dog that had taken an avid interest in the leg of said jogger. A sun-kissed young couple laughed at an unheard joke as they crunched their way unsteadily across the pebbles below. And Mark Woodford decided to live the rest of his life.

ACKNOWLEDGMENTS

Where to begin ... The most FAQ to most authors, other than, 'did they pay you an advance?' tends to be 'where did you get the idea for your book from?' Here is the long answer to that question, if you are interested in hearing it.

In 2009 I took Jessi on honeymoon to the charming hamlet of Lusignac in south west France, having rented a gite from some (now) friends, Issy and Jeremy Lafferty who I had met a couple of years before through another mutual friend. Issy and Jeremy had bought a number of properties some years before as a lot, done them up, sold the majority and kept a property in the hamlet for themselves, moving from Gloucestershire to set up and manage a gite rental business. When asked by Jolyn Tricky, my line manager at the time, what would constitute my ideal week off, my answer was immediate and emphatic; to go to France to write! He then put me in touch with Jeremy and Issy who, over subsequent years, were extremely generous in allowing me use of vacant properties off peak at discounted rates, picking me up and dropping me off at Angouleme station, and generally welcoming me into their home and life in Lusignac. I soon fell in love with the hamlet (knowing the area, having holidayed at Chalais, west of Lusignac some years before) with its ancient church, its chateau and fabulous little bar/restaurant run by Joel and her family. The properties were bordered by acres of farmland, including huge swathes of sunflower fields and was the perfect setting for the aspiring writer. I had majored in creative writing as part of a related arts degree (at what was then Bishop Otter College, Chichester but is now Chichester University). When seeking the sage advice from my brilliant and equally droll creative writing tutor John Saunders as to how I could progress to becoming a full-time writer he offered me the following words of wisdom that are as relevant today as when I first posed the question in 1989: 1) write something and 2) show someone. In modern parlance, 'what a legend.'

By the mid 2000's I had no major work to my name, a stack of ideas, a slim vanity-published poetry anthology, a portfolio full of corporate communications material and ad campaigns but no novel. I did, however, possess a letter from a then editor (Penguin) who had encouraged me to set down some short stories or the synopsis for a novel so I just needed to carve out the time to do one or the other.

My frequent trips to Lusignac had stirred my imagination, not just to write, but to re-locate to that little corner of the Charente region. I imagined earning my baguette, cheese and wine by doing odd jobs for UK based gite owners during the mornings (possessing DIY skills in the same league as Frank Spencer would not deter me from this romantic idea). After a gloriously long siesta, I would write late into the evening on the balcony until the bats swooped in from the nearby church tower; my cue to descend on Joel's bar for a black coffee and a cognac, notebook in hand. She and the locals had already dubbed me 'the English writer' so I really had to start living up to the billing.

When on our honeymoon and sitting outside Chez Kelly, gazing out across the sunflower fields one bright mid-morning as we shared coffee and pain au chocolate, I revealed this master-plan to Jessi who went incredibly quiet. It was all too much. Being Surrey born and bred and having never lived outside its borders and now married at the tender age of 22 to a man of the world a few years her senior, life had suddenly become full of expectations but also complications. Jessi was and is far more practical in her thinking than me in mine and immediately began to explore my motives for this proposed upheaval. I can recall rather theatrically gesturing in a sweeping movement with my right arm (hang-on; that would have knocked Jessi's coffee cup over, maybe my left then) to all the beauty that surrounded us (the fields, the architecture, the glimmering swimming pool) as if to say, just what else could one need? Well, Jessi responded with a list that included such humdrum concerns as our accommodation, income, language barrier, employment prospects (for both of us) it really did burst my bubble. The nub of the issue was that I didn't feel inspired to write when at home when all around me were the reminders of chores that needed doing, work assignments that needed completing; I needed a complete change of scene in order to compose and couldn't imagine one being any better than that which stretched out before us. Jessi though, had another idea. When her late grandfather had left her parents a small sum of money they had purchased a modest plot of land that sat at the bottom of their property in the little village of Grayswood, situated between Godalming and Haslemere. Jessi loves the village, having grown up there, attended the village school that was opposite the salon her parents ran (both her parents were hairdressers) and was in no rush to move too far away. On said plot of land sat a small brick build former slaughter house, complete with iron rings that had been used to tie up the doomed livestock. Over the years this building had been re-roofed, re-pointed, whitewashed and decked out with a smart wooden table and chairs, various lanterns and décor suited to its new use as a summer house. Jessi suggested that I spoke with the trustees of the charity I was running to negotiate a day off each week to write and she would square it with my father-in-law Geoff for me to have use of the summer house. And so it was that Friday was the agreed day off and, on 6th November 2009 I embarked upon the diary of a first time novelist, essentially my memoirs, to prove to myself that not only did I possess the talent required to write a book but also the discipline to complete it. I gave myself a target of a day a week for a year but it took until the 6th November 2011 to finish 'Tales from the Slaughterhouse.'

Whilst conceiving my memoirs, we also conceived and delivered Noah into the world. By 2012 Jessi was pregnant with Aaron. Faced with our increasing brood and all that comes with having little ones (the general chaos, mess, visits from other mums with babies/toddlers), we decided that I would need to move out of the spare bedroom that I was using as an office to make space for Aaron and to create a space for me to think, work and write. We took out some fruit trees and demolished a huge, rickety old shed that was swamped by foliage at the bottom of the garden and had installed a patio and small summer house; my new office and writing den that has served me so well ever since, and from where I am typing this.

Early in 2012 I was flicking through one of my faux-Romantic notebooks and musing over ideas for my next work, but was unable to settle on developing any of the ideas I had recorded over the years. I had still retained Friday as my writing day and Jessi would visit Geoff, her father (who had retired early) with Noah for the day each week. One chilly Friday morning I was practically pushing Jessi (early into her second pregnancy) and little Noah out of the front door and into the car so I could have the house to myself but missed them as soon as the car had left our little gravel driveway. Restless, I mooched about the place a bit, picking up one or two of Noah's toys and smelling one of his discarded hoodies when the thought hit me square between the eyes; what if I never saw them again? What if they were involved in a road accident and I was visited by one of the police officers I knew through my work with young people in the area to inform me of their deaths. How would I respond, how would I cope? How would I ever move on from such personal tragedy? And so the seed for *To Have And To Hold* was planted. It took another 4 years of nurturing, nudging, tilling and toiling to finally see it bear fruit.

Location, location, location.

I loved my time at college in Chichester and, after I graduated, remained in the area, getting involved in the setting up and running of a small theatre company that focused on youth and fringe theatre until I entered the world of secondary school education second time round, this time as a teacher of English, Drama and Media Studies. I spent a fabulous year living in Preston Park, Brighton and attending Sussex University in order to achieve my PGCE and returned to Brighton and Hove annually when writing *To Have and To Hold*. The house that Mark inherited is based on the lodgings that I took with an amazing Polish lady called Mrs Jaknik. I created the Park Tavern based on the Preston Park Tavern that has changed a bit since I used to pop in occasionally. I have never been inside the Funky Buddha Bar or the Fortune of War pub but have frequented the OhSo bar and, once or twice, the Zap Club. Thanks to Claire at the Inn on the Lake in Godalming for filling in some of the gaps in Brighton's night life for me. Not being familiar with the hospitals in Hove, I picked one from a map to suit the narrative. Any factual inaccuracies relating to hospital visits can be explained away simply as the locations featured in Brighton and Hove are part based on reality and the rest from my imagination. For the record, I haven't ever been inside Ford Open Prison.

There are many beautiful villages in and around Chichester, with Funtington being one of them. I can picture the type of flint cottages typical of that part of the world but Lizzie's family home is not based on a house that I recognise. I know that there is a church in the village called St Mary's but I have never visited it (and have taken liberties with the saints featured on stained glassed windows to fit Lizzie's character) and added a Rectory that may or may not even exist. The churchyard in the book is remarkably similar to that of St Peter's in Hambledon, the church where I worshiped with Jessi and the boys for nearly a decade, so again a mix of what stands and what might. As for the Dorset locations; mostly from my imagination. I wanted Mark's family to live somewhere where I haven't (as a personal challenge) and settled on that stretch of coastline that seemed fitting as the home to a family who had made their money in the shipping industry. A map shows Charlestown and Chesil Beach (title of a most poignant short novel by Ian McEwan) and the roads in and out but as for Charleston Manor is concerned – purely fictitious.

Further afield now and I haven't ever stayed at a hotel near Gatwick airport but I have stayed on the island of Rhodes, although the villa that features in Mark and Lizzie's honeymoon was one I invented. I did have a night out in Faliraki as an experiment in the deprivation of the human race but mine was less eventful than theirs, with no medical treatment being required. Back in my media days (I was a copywriter before I ran an ad agency) I used to lunch at the Axis restaurant fairly regularly and have enjoyed drinks in the bar of Number One Aldwych, somewhere I look forward to becoming reacquainted with in time.

Thanks to:-

My wonderful parents deserve a huge nod of recognition. My dad passed in 1999 after a long and dignified battle with MS but my amazing mum is still going strong in the corner of Devon where I grew up. They endured my pretty extreme appearances when I was a teenager, from self-styled 'Numanoid' to arch Goth but always supported my creative aspirations, regardless of how outlandish I may have looked! I am indebted to the Trustees of the Trinity Trust Team (namely Jolyn Tricky and Alan Lion) for being so supportive of my desire to carve out time and space in order to focus on my writing, to Issy and Jeremy for those weeks in Lusignac that proved to be such a catalyst and to Di and Geoff, who defy all in-law jokes, for allowing me exclusive access to their summer house in order for me to start (and crucially finish) my first ever book and for their ongoing encouragement and involvement in the lives of me, Jessi and the boys.

I am clearly indebted to the team at Austin Macauley for publishing this book. I am grateful to the medical advice given to me by Helen Billinghurst and the legal facts from PC Jim Lavery, Waverley Youth Intervention Officer. Any inaccuracies are simply due to me shaping the facts they gave me to suit the characters and plot. Not only did a pregnant Jessi and a toddling Noah form the catalyst for the novel but they have walked the entire journey with me, Jessi scribbling her thoughts in the margin and Noah taking an interest from the moment he could grasp the concept of daddy being a writer. Aaron's favourite cuddly toy happens to be a rabbit given to him by Noah that goes by the name of 'Buddy.' I would like to thank God, for blessing me with the opportunity and the people around me (too many to mention who have taken a genuine interest in the progress of this book) to enable this writer's long time aspirations to be met in these pages. I hope you have enjoyed it. If you have, I certainly don't envisage this to be the end of the road for Mark Woodford ...